D0019473

THE GODFORSAKEN DAUGHTER

CHRISTINA McKENNA

THE GODFORSAKEN DAUGHTER

LAKE UNION

PUBLISHING

Text copyright © 2015 Christina McKenna
All rights reserved.

Published by Lake Union Publishing, Seattle

www.apub.com

Amazon, the Amazon logo, and Lake Union Publishing are trademarks of Amazon. com, Inc., or its affiliates.

ISBN-13: 9781477827451
ISBN-10: 1477827455
Cover design by David M. Kiely
Cover photograph by Michael McKenna

Library of Congress Control Number: 2014952404

Printed in the United States of America

For my sisters:
Marie
Ann
Sarah
Rosaleen

And brothers:
William
John
Michael

God is a concept by which we measure our pain.

—John Lennon

Chapter one

Ruby Clare sat in a velour recliner in the kitchen of Oaktree Farmhouse, knitting a tea cozy. A cupcake tea cozy.

Knitting steadied her. It was her therapy. Her meditation. Although Ruby didn't know those labels, she knew the feeling. And she needed to hang onto that feeling more than ever these days; these grief-stricken days with her dear father gone. At his eternal rest these seven months, under a plaster angel and globe of plastic tulips in St. Timothy's churchyard on the outskirts of Tailorstown. A mere twenty-minute walk from where his daughter sat.

His now fatherless daughter, Ruby Vivian Clare—thirty-three years of hope and dreams and fear and woe packed into a size 16 frock, sunk deep in the old chair—was only vaguely aware of the June sun steady at the window, open just a crack. Of the alder leaves kissing the glass, of the hens' clucking, a cow mooing, and birds twittering in the big ash.

Ruby had knitted more tea cozies than were teapots to cover in these past months of mourning. But no matter; she'd a lot of time on her hands and needed to use it fruitfully. For, like milk left standing too long, idle moments could surely mass together, curdle, and grow sour. Stagnation could haul you down depression's road, with only indolence and self-pity for company along the way. And such a situation must be avoided at all costs. No, moping and feeling sorry for yourself were to be kept well at bay in Mrs. Clare's home. Emotions were dangerous. They pointed to a sensitive nature, or "a weakness" in mother-speak. Weeping could only mean you were "bad with your nerves."

The knitting, filling the hours and filling the house, stood as testimony to Ruby's stoppered grief; tears of purl-one-plain-one for her departed father, stitched out in tea cozies, cushion covers, throws, and chair backs, were safer than displays of dramatic despair.

She glanced at her watch. Two minutes past two. Maybe she'd have the tea cozy completed before her mother awoke from her nap with the chiming of the big grandfather clock in the hallway.

That was about an hour away—a whole hour of calm.

So she sat there, the tea cozy taking shape as her fingers flew, enjoying the quiet of that lazy afternoon. An afternoon as yet unsullied by the mother's demands.

She'd been driven indoors by her father's death. Those hands, so toughened from years of labor—milking cows, hauling buckets, shaking fodder free from bales, pulling calves from grateful wombs— were now softening against their natural bent, under a frivolity of household chores her mother deemed necessary to keep her from a breakdown.

"I don't want you getting bad with your nerves 'cos your father's not here no more. You'll stay in the house and keep yourself occupied. There's plenty for you to do. Knitting and baking got me through my mother's death. Got me through many a death, truth be told. And it'll get you through, too. And if you don't stop that blubbering you'll have to go to Derry . . . like . . . like your uncle Cecil and your aunt Marjorie and . . ."

Mention of "Derry" had struck fear into the hearts of all three Clare children when they were growing up. For they knew that by

"Derry" the mother didn't mean a shopping trip under the bright lights of that metropolis. No, for Mrs. Clare the name was code for a formidable mental institution: St. Ita's, on the outskirts of the city. And, no, Ruby had no wish to pass through its somber doors like Uncle Cecil, Aunt Marjorie, or the succession of relatives on her mother's side who, whether for good or ill, had all done stretches there.

Ruby's childhood was pockmarked by visiting hours within its soulless, sick-green walls. She carried memories of a hollow-eyed Marjorie sitting wordless in a tub chair, staring forlornly at the floor. And the alcoholic Cecil shaking and chain-smoking his way through the trauma of yet another bout of post-Christmas blues, which, with relentless regularity, would bring each year of his to a close.

As a teenager, Ruby herself had come close to being incarcerated.

Barely out of high school, with two C passes in Religious Knowledge and Cookery, career choices narrowed to the convent or the kitchen, and Mrs. Clare had promptly packed her off to a waitressing job in Donegal to "take her out of herself."

The convent could wait. She needed "to mix more." First time away from home, and sharing a dorm with six young women—slim, quick girls, flitting about like finches in brightly colored clothes and dainty shoes—had made Ruby all too painfully aware of her shortcomings. Ruby, the country bumpkin, in her bulky gray pinafore, self-made using a *Woman's Realm* pattern, feet jammed into a pair of low-heeled castoffs from a maiden aunt. An outfit certainly appropriate for that first, pietistic career choice, if the grounding in hospitality didn't work out.

She was a figure of fun to those giddy roommates. She knew that. Could sense it in their smirking faces, the eyes that slid away guiltily from her hopeful smiles when she tried to connect. Slow Ruby, last at everything: in the classroom, on the sports field, on the dancehall floor. Not that her roommates ever gave her the chance to accompany them to dances . . .

They'd stay out late and alight in the small hours, perching on the edge of their bunk beds, giggling behind painted fingernails and discussing boys till dawn broke.

Sleep-deprived Ruby, out of her depth completely, stumbling into work, forgetting orders, dropping plates, tripping over a toddler and going headlong into the dessert trolley. And the last straw: scalding a woman's bosom when handing over a cup of tea. "I'll have you up for this, you clumsy lump!" The woman jumping up, screeching at the sight of her crimson cleavage and saturated top.

She lasted a week. Mr. Ryan, the manager, calling her mother. Ruby in tears in his office. "Come here, Mrs. Clare, and take yer daughtur home. She's a bloody liability, so she is."

Mr. Ryan.

Ruby's grip tightened on the needles. The frantic *click-clacking* slowed. Mr. Ryan's red face. Fist flexed for combat. She shut her eyes tight. When she opened them again, she was riding home in her father's Hillman Imp. The memory of that journey: painful, but safer. Yes, a whole lot safer than Mr. Ryan's office.

Her mother's berating voice reaching down the years: "What are you *like*? Couldn't stick at a good job for a week. Mr. Ryan moved mountains to get you into The Talk of the Town. So many young ones queuing up for that job, but he was doing me a favor, being a third cousin of your father's half brother, Jamesy, on his daddy's side. Now look what you've done. What am I going to tell the neighbors? I told everybody you were going away for the summer."

Her daddy's big hands gripping the steering wheel. Capless, in his Sunday suit and it not even Sunday. Hair Brylcreemed into a shiny skullcap. Fixing it a bother to him on a weekday, but needing to look respectable for this unexpected trip. Having to leave the hayfield in midafternoon to make the two-hour journey to Donegal.

Oh, the trouble she'd caused! But he never blamed Ruby for that.

"Och, leave Ruby alone," he protested. "She doesn't need to be goin' out tae a job. She can help me on the farm. She's good with the animals, so she is. Aren't you, daughtur?"

Ruby nodding through her tears, affirming his kindly look in the rearview mirror.

What would she have done without him? What would she do *now* without him?

"I'd try her in the convent, but she's too fat." The mother, not listening, rattling on like a Gatling gun. Never listening. No thought ever left unspoken. No insult ever left unaired. Her wrath filling the car like mustard gas. "Gluttony, the second deadly sin. Father Cardy said as much. Nuns lead lives of fasting and abstinence. That's why they're so thin. They live on Christ's wafer and the Holy Ghost." She turned back to the sobbing Ruby. Powdered face rigid with scorn. Discount earrings shivering in the coppery light. "So, if you want Father Cardy to consider you for the Oblate Missions of Mary, you'll have to go on a diet first."

Now the fatherless Ruby, sitting in the old chair in Oaktree Farmhouse, allowed tears to blur the last few rows of the tea cozy.

She left off knitting and fumbled a tissue from her apron pocket. Dabbed her eyes. Checked the clock. A quarter to three. She got up quickly and went into the pantry. The mirror above the sink threw back a comely reflection, even though the eyes were puffy. She splashed some water on her face, released the band that held her ponytail in place, letting her amber hair—her best feature—fall loosely about her shoulders; all the better to hide behind.

Fearing the convent, and to thwart her mother, the teenage Ruby had remained plump. Father kept his promise and Ruby joined him on the farm. For fourteen years she'd worked the land, but his sudden death had changed everything. The dairy farm with her beloved herd of Friesians had died along with him. Mother was having none of it. No amount of pleading would turn her.

"I'll carry it on, Mammy. It's what Daddy would of wanted. Please, Mammy. I know nothing else but the farm. I know nothing else but milking the cows and feeding them and helping with the calving. Please, Mammy."

"No, you will *not*. It's my farm now and I'll do what I want. And no daughter of mine's going to stand on a Fair Day in Tailorstown, haggling over the price of a heifer. That's men's work. You'd be a laughing stock."

"But, Mammy, *please* . . ." Ruby in tears. "I'll—I'll—"

"I said *no*. The herd's going and let that be the end of it. There's plenty for you to do around the house. I need peace in my life, now that your father's gone. God knows how long I've left myself. My heart's not good. Dr. Brewster said so. Even going up them stairs has me puffed. What if I dropped dead like your father? What then?"

So the herd was sold off, the land rented out, Ruby's muddy Wellington boots retired behind the pantry door. Ruby the house-maid still dragged herself from the old divan at 7:00 a.m., though. But now, in place of a boiler suit and boots, she pulled on a shapeless dress, stuck her feet into size 8 slippers, before galumphing down the stairs.

Apron on, fire on, kettle on. All in that order. Her mother's needs always coming first. Everybody else's needs always coming first.

Ruby returned to the old chair, calmer now, and took up the knitting once more.

But, within seconds, she was stuffing the unfinished tea cozy into her sewing bag. The pearl-button decorations would keep for next time. A stirring overhead meant that Mother was already on her way. A whole five minutes before the chiming of the clock at 3:00 p.m.

Ruby got up hurriedly and shoved the kettle back on the stove.

Time to make the tea.

Time to set her troubled thoughts aside and set the table instead.

Chapter two

Henry Shevlin was cursed with a listener's face. It was the reason he'd gravitated toward the mental health branch of medicine. Psychiatry sat well with the silent, attentive Henry. He was the perfect fit. The key in the lock that could unbolt so many secrets, and have them freely tumble from the darkest recesses of the closeted self. The many fractured souls who sat before him, day in, day out, trusted him completely.

He heard as much as the cleric in the confessional. And who knows, perhaps at one stage he could have donned the collar and strode purposely through life like a ministering angel. His mother had wished it for him.

But not Henry. Strong-willed as he was, with an inquiring mind, religion was not for him. Like his father, he was a pragmatist—a leader not a follower. With his kindly eyes and detached manner, he'd been special from the start.

Little girls in the school playground ran weeping to him when they fell over or got teased. Teachers circled him like planets, wary of his aloofness. Bullyboys wilted when he stared them down. Those eyes, warm and watchful as a feted saint's one minute, could turn as cold as storm-washed pebbles when angry. In childhood, he rarely threw a tantrum; that look of displeasure when he didn't get his way was enough to have others caving in. His needs met without having uttered a word or expending an ounce of energy.

Histrionics were not his way. He'd witnessed firsthand how they destroyed his mother, a quick-tempered woman who'd lived largely at the mercy of her feelings. She externalized everything. Blamed everyone else for her unhappiness.

His father—the magistrate, stoical, reflective—could not afford to get involved in what he termed "those fearful displays." A clear head was needed for his judgments on the bench. His career, a much-needed escape route from an unhappy marriage, meant more to him than his wife.

Where Ava Shevlin saw coldness and detachment in the husband she once loved, the young Henry saw patience and forbearance. Admirable qualities, which served him well as a doctor. The great gusts of pique and wrath he often observed in his patients—"those fearful displays"—were the result of having ceded control to that most invidious of emotions: fear. "Fear, Henry, is what makes the world a terrible place. Your mother isn't upset with you and me; she's merely afraid of life."

Having become a therapist, Henry understood all too well what his father meant. He couldn't take away the fears that each of his patients presented, but he could stand with them at the cliff edge, on the riverbank, the lip of a high-rise building, and gently pull them back from the metaphorical brink. He offered hope and medication, and he listened to them with a finely tuned ear and a brotherly heart.

He was forty-two and starting an unexpected new phase in his life. The city of Belfast, where he'd spent his career, could no longer keep him bound. He'd requested a transfer from the Mater Infirmorum Hospital, his employer of fifteen years. Had spotted an ad for a temporary consultant at an outpatient clinic in the town of

Killoran. The clinic was run by the community health center, and referred its serious cases to St. Ita's mental institution in the city of Derry.

Henry secured the position with ease. Killoran, with its catchment area of a few thousand souls, as opposed to Belfast's half a million, seemed the ideal place. Fewer patients meant a less hectic schedule, a narrower focus, and fewer demands. Just what he needed.

This dramatic shift in circumstances was not of his making. Sadly, the decision had been forced upon him. Constance, his wife of nine years, had vanished. Weeks of feverish searching had proved futile. The weeks had ripened into months, to become a year of waiting. He'd finally faced up to reality: Constance wasn't coming back. It was time to draw a line under the tragedy, to move on.

He could no longer remain in the home they'd shared for so long. Because it was no longer a home. Her absence had regressed it to the mere house it had once been. There were too many memories. Too many lonely nights of waiting for the phone to ring. Too many days of waiting for her to come through the front door. Yes, it was time to move on.

The memory of the evening she went missing would never let him go. He'd gone over it and analyzed it so many times. He'd found a note on the kitchen table when he'd arrived home from work at his usual time of 5:30. It was May 25, 1983.

"*Going for a walk, darling. Love you. Always.*" That was what the note said.

He'd thought nothing of it . . . to begin with. Had grown used to such notes, especially at that time of year. Constance, a born walker, had always looked forward to the finer weather. May was her favorite month. The pre-summer days meant saying good-bye to heavy clothing, and dispensing with the gloves she loathed, yet was forced to wear against her Raynaud's syndrome.

But with darkness falling and still no sign, Henry poured himself a brandy—an uncustomary indulgence. He wasn't much of a drinker and prided himself on his imperturbable nature. Psychological crutches were for his patients. She's dropped in with Betty, he told himself, after finishing the drink in two gulps. Yes, that's it. She's chatting with her sister over a coffee and has simply lost track of time. Betty would be back from her weekend with the mother-in-law in Bangor. There would be much to discuss.

He had to remain calm. This unexpected warp in his routine was a challenge in ways he couldn't have anticipated. He subscribed to the psychotherapeutic model of Émile Coué. Had been using it very successfully in his practice for years. Émile Coué, the man who coined the famous maxim, "Every day, in every way, I'm getting better and better."

Now Henry Shevlin called on the great master's precepts to steady himself. The conscious will was what you focused on. To feed and strengthen your conscious will, it was imperative to bring the unconscious will—the imagination—under control, by feeding it only positive thoughts and images. What you think about exclusively turns into reality. Therefore Henry immediately began picturing the best possible outcome, his eidetic memory coming to his aid when he most needed it to. The pictures were coming. Clear and detailed pictures.

He was picturing Connie in Betty's pristine parlor, chatting over coffee. What was she wearing? He went further back: to the breakfast table. Yes, her white dress with the forget-me-not pattern. How extraordinary! Forget-me-not. Over the dress: a white cardigan, the final two buttons done up at the waist. Shoes? He hadn't noticed those, but it was a fair assumption they were the beige slip-ons she favored for walking.

He saw her check her watch. Betty halting in midflow, scowling at the interruption.

"God, is that the time? Really must be going. Henry's long home and I didn't mention I'd be dropping in with you."

Call Betty! Wouldn't that be the most sensible thing to do? Henry's eyes locked on the phone. No, he decided. Calling Betty would mean giving voice to his anxieties. Endorsing his doubt. No, Connie would come through the door any minute. Plant a kiss on his cheek. Apologize. Settle opposite him in the armchair with a glass of her favorite Sancerre, and ask him about his day. That's the way it had always been. And that's how it would be now.

However, sitting there in the armchair made him feel unproductive. Action! He needed to take action.

Her handbag. Maybe she decided to do some late shopping after the walk. The city-center shops were open late on a Thursday. He looked in all the usual places for the handbag and was relieved when he couldn't find it. She *had* gone shopping then.

And so the minutes ticked away. The clock striking down the hours till the shops shut at 9:00 p.m. A taxi back home would take twenty minutes at most.

At 10:00 p.m. he was forced to phone Betty.

"No, she never came here. Is something wrong?"

"She went for a walk this afternoon and didn't come home."

"Oh my God! Have you called the police?"

No, he hadn't called the police. Betty was a catastrophist. A black-and-white thinker with few wanderings into that much more yielding zone of gray.

He waited until midnight. Half an hour later, he found himself at his local Royal Ulster Constabulary station, filling out a missing-person's report.

A bulky constable, yawning his way through a list of questions.

"Five foot four, you say?"

"Yes."

"Hair?"

Henry reached into his pocket and took out his wallet. "Here, I have a snapshot."

The RUC constable studied the portrait.

"Blonde," he said aloud, while scribbling the word down. "Recent pitcher, this?"

"Yes, a couple of months back. It was taken for a gallery brochure."

The constable looked up. "Right."

"And how does she wear it?"

"Wear what?"

"Her hair, sir. Always tied back like that?"

"Yes, usually . . . in a ponytail." Henry made an explanatory gesture at the back of his head. "Worn . . . worn high."

The constable studied the shot again. "Eyes . . . blue?"

"Blue, yes."

"Any distinguishing features?"

"No . . ."

"What was she—?"

"Sorry, sorry, yes, she has . . ."

"Has what?"

"A distinguishing feature." He pulled back the cuff of his shirt. Pointed to a spot just above the wrist on his right arm. "A small tattoo, *here*. A butterfly . . . blue. A blue one."

"Right. Wouldn't be seen by anyone, unless she'd be in the short sleeves," the constable said, stating the obvious. "And clothes. What had she got on, sir?"

"A white dress with a blue pattern . . . small flowers. Forget-me-nots, I think. Knee-length and . . . and a cardigan . . . white as well."

"Just plain white?"

"Yes . . . no, no. At the back it has a sunflower . . . embroidered into it. She . . . she did it herself."

"What color? This sunflower?"

"Eh . . ." Henry thought it an odd question. "Yellow. Yellow, of course . . . yes, yellow with a brown center."

"How big?"

"Size twelve."

"No, sir, not the cardigan, the flower. Did it cover the whole back or—"

"Yes, yes, of course . . . sorry, Constable. Yes, it covered the entire back."

"That's good."

"Sorry, why's it good? I don't follow."

"The cardigan's distinctive. You say she embroidered it herself, therefore there wouldn't be another one like it."

Henry shook his head. "I never thought of that."

"Shoes?"

"Sorry, can't remember. But she did have her handbag. Brown leather . . . a shoulder bag. I know that for sure, because it's not in the house."

"You're positive?"

"Yes."

"And you say she usually walked in Lady Dickson Park?" The constable sat back in his chair and relaxed his viselike grip on the pen. "Would she usually take her handbag on a walk, sir?"

"No, not usually. But if she intended to do some shopping afterwards, she might."

"There are no shops in Lady Dixon Park."

"I'm quite aware of that, Constable. But there's late-night shopping on a Thursday."

"This is Wednesday."

Damn! How could he have mistaken the date? A calendar on the police officer's desk was showing *Wednesday, May 25*.

"Marital problems?"

"No. Why are you asking that?"

"Procedure, sir. Could she have been seeing someone else?"

"No." Henry looked the man straight in the eye. He dropped his gaze to the form again. "If you're looking for a chief complaint, Constable, I can assure you that you won't find it in that area."

"Chief complaint? I don't think I follow . . ."

"I'm sorry. That's professional jargon. I doubt if it's relevant here." How remiss! What would a simple policeman know about psychiatry and diagnostic procedure?

"A suitcase missing?" the officer pressed on.

"I didn't check. Why would I check such a thing? I love my wife. She loves me. I've absolutely no reason to doubt her. I'm missing her already and you're painting her as some kind of harlot."

"We need a full pitcher, if we're to find her. These questions might be hard, but *we* must have facts, and *you* must *face* facts."

Henry relented. He knew he'd get nowhere by being awkward. "I'm sorry," he said, letting his gaze fall on the constable's pen, poised again over the report form. Bitten nails. A slight tremor in the left hand shielding his note taking from view. Conscious of his spelling, despite the uniform. *Be patient, Henry*—he heard his father's voice—*everybody is afraid of something; everybody has lost someone.* "You have to do your job. It's just that . . . well, it's just that I never expected to be sitting here at this hour of the night answering questions about . . ."

Out in the corridor a pair of duty boots marched past: heavy, assertive. In their wake a scuffling sound. A slurred voice raised in song. "And I'm off tae join the IRA and I'm off tae-morrer morn—"

"Aye, you wouldn't be much bloody good to the IRA in your state. Get in there!"

A door slamming. Keys jangling.

Silence.

"It's good that she took the handbag," the constable said into the pause. "More for us to go on. We can check for bank withdrawals."

"I see."

He slid the statement across the desk for a signature. "Go home, sir. Try to get some sleep, but not in the marital bed."

Henry was nonplussed. "Why not?"

"We'll need to see the bedroom. Look at her effects. It's important you don't tidy anything up. Stay by the phone. Keep it free, in case she calls."

The constable got up. "We'll check phone records, of course." He opened the door. "Don't worry, Doctor. Ninety percent of people show up within forty-eight hours. Perhaps she just wanted to be on her own for a bit. Women are hard to fathom at times." He smiled. "But you don't need me to tell you that—you being a psychiatrist and all."

Henry managed to reciprocate the smile, grateful for the man's reassurance. But he knew, as he walked away, that in the troubled city of Belfast, with its relentless succession of shootings and bombings, a woman missing for a few hours would figure low on the RUC's list of priorities.

He returned home in the early hours, finding the house eerily quiet without her. All the warmth and comfort he'd taken so much for granted: gone like a puff of breath in winter. He went immediately up to the attic to check on the suitcases.

No, they were still there, gathering dust from the last vacation. Relief swept over him like a blessing. So she hadn't left him.

He sat down on a beanbag and stared at the cases. Connie's: the biggest of the set. She loved clothes, and always insisted on taking most of her wardrobe with her. So many happy holidays had been packed into that blue Samsonite. Their most recent, on the island of Crete the previous August.

He saw them on the terrace of Hotel Hyperion, sipping Metaxa as the sun sank over the Mediterranean. Connie's blonde hair burnished bronze in the evening light; her easy smile, eyes bright with happiness. Her pale fingers clasping the glass, savoring each tiny sip of the Greek brandy. His butterfly. She loved butterflies. Loved seeing them in summer. That delight in them mirrored so keenly in her own life. So hungry for adventure. Trying out new things: jobs, hobbies, hairstyles. Flitting from one experience to another, eager to soak up the thrill of it all.

"Why don't we move here, darling? Wouldn't it be heaven?"

Henry, the realist. Always the realist: "Yes, it would be lovely, but not practical, as you—"

"Oh, stop spoiling the moment. Just say 'yes' and let me dream. I'm tired of Belfast. The shootings, the bombing. We've no ties, really. We're as free as birds. We could live anywhere in this big, bright, beautiful, scintillating world."

"Hmmm . . . You see the world as bright and beautiful because you're on holiday. Unfortunately, I'm under contract. My patients need me."

"You're not indispensible! I expect there are mentally ill people in every country. You'd always find work." She'd taken a larger sip of the brandy. "Only trees stay in the one place all their lives. And we're not trees."

"I'm sorry."

"'Why can't I try on different lives, like dresses, to see which one fits me and is most becoming?'"

"Oh, stop quoting that morose poet! *Now* look who's spoiling the moment."

"Sylvia Plath was *not* morose. She was a realist, trapped by others' expectations. A bit like *me*."

She'd gotten up then and slammed down the glass.

"Connie, I'm sorry. I didn't mean—"

"I'm going for a stroll."

"On your own."

"Yes, on my own. I'm not a toddler. And I wish you'd stop treating me like one."

Is that why she'd done this? Just to show him? Had he been too restricting?

The doctor put his head in his hands. *Maybe I should have listened more. Maybe I should have given her the same ear I give my patients.*

He got up and went downstairs. Clear, almost palpable in his mind, the image of her rising from that table at Hotel Hyperion and stalking off.

He went immediately to the writing bureau. Opened the locked drawer and dug down through their shared collection of personal papers: birth, marriage, graduation certificates, bank statements, until he found the object of his search.

He drew out the passport and leafed through its pages, hopeful. But, alas, it was his own face that stared back at him.

He reached back into the drawer, a feeling of dread taking hold. His fingers made contact with bare board. He pulled the drawer out as far as it would go, and hunkered down to get a closer look.

But the back of the drawer was empty. Connie's passport: gone.

Chapter three

In the time it took Martha Clare to rise and dress, Ruby had the tea made, the table laid, the mother's favored cup and saucer in position, and her chair cushion plumped, ready to receive her.

On the table: a cream sponge Ruby had made that morning, perfectly risen and finger-light springy, due to the care she'd taken in beating sufficient air into the mixture. Baking came as naturally to her as breathing. As a child she'd watched her mother, and as a girl had helped her aunt Rita, who used to own a cake shop. The farm work had taken her away from all those domestic pursuits, but now she was rediscovering, as with her knitting, the joy of those long-neglected skills. And it pleased her that her foray into farming hadn't diminished her talent in the kitchen.

Martha Clare, a brittle-boned sexagenarian, frail as a festive meringue, sharp as a hacksaw when her blood was up, sighed her way down the stairs and proceeded unsteadily to the table.

She waited for her daughter to pull out the chair—"*Might put my elbow out. Them chairs are too heavy for me these days. Have to watch my bones. Dr. Brewster said so.*" Ruby knew the mantra well and was on guard like a lady's maid, obeying a set of unspoken commands just to keep the peace. Being indoors with the mother day after day was a fresh trial to be gotten through, a burden to be borne.

Martha gathered her cardigan about her and settled herself. The garment seemed much too big for her, but Mrs. Clare, always on the slight side, had lost even more weight following her husband's death. Vincent Clare had taken care of everything outside the home. The farm business was his world, the domestic sphere hers. But with his passing, Martha was forced out of her comfort zone and into a world of lawyers and paperwork pertaining to his affairs and their sixty-plus acres of land. The stress of it all had taken its toll, robbing her of sleep and the desire to eat.

Lately, however, all that grief and despair had turned to anger—anger at the injustice of it all. She was angry with Vincent—barely a month into his sixty-eighth year and rarely ill in his life—for causing her such grief by exiting so early. She was angry at Ruby, for she'd been his favorite. She knew that Vincent would have wanted Ruby to carry on the farm. He'd said it often enough. But his death was a betrayal too far.

So she took her revenge on both, by selling off the dairy herd and renting out the land. Not only dishonoring her dead husband's wishes but depriving the daughter of the only world she knew.

"Did you have a good sleep, Mammy?" asked Ruby, pouring the tea, stewed to the color of oxblood, just the way her mother liked it.

"Enough sleep? I never get enough sleep. Why d'you think I have to lie down during the day?" Martha, her usual cantankerous self, held out her plate for the slice of cake. "That looks like one of your auntie Rita's?"

"No, Mammy, I baked it this morning."

"Is that so? Looks very like one of Rita's to me . . . always great at the sponges, Rita. She learned it from me, of course. Not that she'd ever give *me* any credit. She wouldn't have had that bakery business if it wasn't for me."

Ruby said nothing. She was getting tired of defending herself. A lull was better than a row.

Mrs. Clare sliced the cake into tiny pieces, as was her way. "Well, what have you been doing with yourself?"

"Finishing off the tea cozy. The cupcake one I started on Monday. It's very nice. But I won't show it to you till it's ready."

"You're still at that, then?"

"Mammy, there's something I want to ask you."

"What's that?"

"You know the way when Daddy was alive he always . . . he always give me twenty pound a week for me work on the farm."

Ruby waited for the mother to fill in the blanks so she wouldn't have to spell it out, but Martha just sat there, staring into the middle distance.

"Well, you haven't give me any since . . ."

"You're not working on the farm no more, so why would I give you money? Besides, don't you get my pension money every Monday?"

"But that's for groceries. I've nothing left over for meself. For things . . ."

"And what things would you need, Ruby? You don't go out. You've no responsibilities. You've got your bed and board here—which is more than a lot of people have."

"Did Daddy leave me anything in his will?"

The mother looked askance. "What kind of question's that? Your poor father hardly cold in his grave and all you're concerned about is how much money he left behind him."

Ruby wished she hadn't broached the subject. The atmosphere of calm she strove always to maintain around her mother was ruffled now.

An uneasy silence fell.

Ruby was seated in the carver chair at the head of the table. The one her father used to occupy. The chair that had forgotten how to hold her father now held his beloved daughter instead. She felt closest to him when she sat in that chair.

It looked out on the field where he died. The field her mother now decreed was cursed. Back in 1926, it had taken the life of Arthur Clare, Ruby's grandfather. Killed in a tractor accident at only forty-two, when Vincent was ten. Ruby had sown a patch of flowers on the spot where her father fell. A memorial to both men.

So, as the mother nibbled on the cake and took tiny sips of tea, sitting in her own isolation, Ruby reran the images from that fateful day. As if putting herself through the misery of it time and time again would somehow heal the pain and bring her father back.

She recalled peeling potatoes at a basin on the table. Head bent over the task, stripping the skin from a King Edward with an old knife.

Something had made her look up.

That's when she saw her father, just standing there out in the field, stooped like a question mark, studying the ground, a hank of baler twine in his left hand.

His cap had fallen off. It lay in front of him. A November wind was lifting his hair. *What's he looking at? Why doesn't he pick up his cap?*

Suddenly, he toppled forward. As if pushed by a sharp gust. He didn't use his arms to break his fall.

Something was wrong.

Ruby dropped the knife. She ran, crashing down on her knees beside him. But in the seconds between the knife falling and her knees touching the ground, he was gone. His ear pressed against the soil, staring into eternity, peaceful.

She screamed.

"Daddy! Daddy! Wake up!"

She'd heaved him over onto his back. Grasped his shoulders, leaned close. Shook him hard. "Daddy, Daddy, wake up!" The left sleeve of his jacket was caked in mud. The smell of it filled her nostrils. Tears fell from her face onto his. She gripped him more tightly through the rough tweed. But it was useless. He was dead. Father no more. Her protector: gone.

"Oh God! Oh dear God, bring him back! Please bring him back!" The words breaking from her throat got lost on the wind, carried away over the bleak hills and dales of Oaktree Farm.

A raven alighted beside her, transfixed.

But too late. Too late. God had already shut the book on Vincent Clare's life.

"You're not crying again, are you?" Her mother's voice. A knife tearing into the sacredness of Ruby's memories. "'Cos if you are, I'll—"

"I wasn't, Mammy. I think I have a cold coming on." Ruby brought a hankie to her nose and feigned a sneeze.

"I was going to say: May and June are coming home this weekend. May rang this morning when you were out."

May and June: the twins. Five years younger than Ruby.

May born one minute to midnight on May 31. Three minutes later, on June 1: her sister. The pair of them away in Belfast, working for Boots department store on Royal Avenue. May in the pharmacy department, doling out drugs. June on the Rimmel counter, doling out cosmetics. Yes, away in the city, but not far enough away for Ruby's liking. The weekends they came home were torture.

She hated the pair of them, and flinched as she thought of them now. Petite, rail-thin, and snooty in their stretch-stirrup pants and pointy high heels, clopping in off a late bus, clutching vanity cases and buckling the air with their censure.

"I hope our beds are made up fresh, Ruby." May marching in first and up the stairs.

"Yes, I hope they are, Ruby." June, echoing behind her, forever in her shadow: indebted to her sister for having braved it out of the birth canal first. "We know the smell of mildew, you know." Heads bent over the twin beds, sniffing pillows. "Mrs. Hipple is very thorough. Changes our bedding twice a week. Doesn't she, May?"

Mrs. Hipple, their landlady on the Antrim Road, was held up as a paragon of good housekeeping.

"Yes indeed, June. City people know about cleanliness."

"I washed the sheets this morning." Ruby, breathless from the stair climb, filling the doorway. "They've been drying on the hedge since morning."

"Hmm . . . if you say so." May, holding fast to her disappointed face. "God, have you put on even more weight?"

"What's it to you?"

"Well, she hasn't got any thinner, that's for sure." June chipping in, always siding with her twin, but never with Ruby.

"So you'll have to change their beds," Martha was saying now, eyeing her daughter, knowing the request would upset her. "And I'll have another cup of that tea."

"I changed them last weekend." Ruby got up to refill the teapot. "And they only sleep in them for two nights."

"Well, I don't want no rows in this house. I want peace. So change them again and be done with it. They like fresh beds when they come home."

Ruby sighed. Replenished the teapot and took it to the table.

"And there's another thing I want you to do before I forget. In the attic. Been meaning to tell you, but it keeps going out of my head. And is it any wonder, given what I've had to suffer these past months? So I don't need you complaining about your sisters or asking about a will."

Ruby wouldn't hear the end of "the Will Question" now. She wished her mother would just shut up and leave her alone. She longed to be free of Oaktree House, now that her dear father was gone. Yes, free of the house, her whining mother, and her grudge-bearing sisters. But there wasn't much chance of that, with no money and two O levels.

Life behind the walls of a convent might be better after all.

"What *about* the attic?" she asked, exasperated.

"Did you say a decade of the rosary for your father this morning?"

"I always do. First thing when I wake up."

"Good. He needs all the prayers we can say, to get himself out of purgatory."

"I think Daddy went straight to heaven. He never did anything wrong in his life."

"Nobody's that good. Only saints go straight to heaven. Did you learn nothing from your catechism? Your father's mother wasn't a good one. I can say that now 'cos your father's gone. So he'll be in purgatory a good while, on account of her."

Ruby had never known the woman; Grandma Edna had died when she was a baby. She was rarely talked about, and then only in hushed tones. To add to the mystery, there were no photos of her in the house.

"Why was she not a good one, then?"

Martha, still imagining her husband having the dross of his earthly transgressions cleansed in the purgatorial fires, looked at Ruby, distracted.

"Up in the attic there's a case your father kept, belonging to her. A filthy thing, with a naked woman on the front of it. I wanted to pitch it out years ago, but he wouldn't let me. So, I want you to go up there. Take it out the back and burn it, d'you hear me?"

"Why d'you want it burned?"

"You don't need to know why. She wasn't a good one: Edna Clare. Came from bad stock. One of them Romany soothsayers, who claimed she could see into the future and talk to the dead. She did the Divil's work, in other words. Aye, I married beneath myself when I married your father. But he was . . . he was—"

Had the daughter been looking her way she would have registered the sudden pall of fear tensing the mother's features.

But Ruby was staring past her, out the window. She set her mug down hard on the table.

"Who the hell is that? And what the hell is he doing in Daddy's field?"

A tractor was driving into the field Vincent Clare had died in. The field her mother had promised Ruby she would never rent out.

"I forget his name. He rang the other day and asked about it and—"

Ruby pushed back the chair, her ire rising.

"You promised me, Mammy! You *promised*." She jumped up and bore down on her mother, close to tears. "I told you: any field but that one. I *told* you."

"Well, we need the money, and I own the land, and—"

Mrs. Clare didn't get to finish because Ruby had taken off. Out the door, belting down the yard, scattering the chickens, raising dust. She arrived, panting, at the mouth of the field, shouting at the stranger to leave.

But the man tearing over the grass on the tractor, his cutting machine in tow, heard nothing. She caught up with him, swung round in front of him, and stood waving her arms.

The shocked stranger braked suddenly, the grille guard of the tractor a mere foot away from Ruby's bibbed bosom.

"What the hell are you doing in this field?" She demanded, arms akimbo, face pink with anger. "Get outta my field this minute!"

The man killed the engine. "Jezsis!"

Ruby stared hard at him as he clambered down from the tractor seat. On the short side, shabby, wearing old trousers with the knees gone, held up with a set of frayed braces. His shirt could have done with a wash and he wore a cap pulled low over his eyes against the strong sun.

"Jezsis, I could'a kilt you there!" was all he said, shoving the cap peak off his eyes to get a better look at her.

"Get outta my field this minute!"

"You're not Mrs. Clare?"

"I'm Ruby Clare, her daughter, and my father died in this field." She pointed to the flower patch. "Right there! So it's *not* for renting. Who are *you?*"

The man studied the flowers. "Jamie . . . Jamie McCloone. Well, I'm James Kevin Barry Michael, but I get Jamie for short." He took a step toward her and held out his hand, shyly. "I'm . . . I'm sorry for yer loss."

Ruby was taken by surprise. She hadn't expected the farmer to be so respectful. Hesitantly, she put her hand into his. It felt as rough and callused as her own.

"Thank you. Daddy's only dead these seven months."

"Yer . . . yer mother didn't say. I saw the ad in the *Vindicator* and thought I'd give it a ring." Mr. McCloone pulled on his earlobe and stared at the flowers again. "I wondered why them flowers were there. Naw, it wouldn't be right to cut a field where yer daddy died. Not right atall." He looked back at the road. "I'll get ground off somebody else. There's plenty rentin' these days. Just needed a bitta . . . a bitta hay for the cows and the like." He touched his cap and climbed back into the tractor seat.

Ruby watched him go. As he turned onto the main road he looked back and raised a hand. Part of her wanted to hurry after him and tell him it was okay; he could cut the grass if he wanted.

She stood, watching his tractor until it disappeared from sight, wondering how her attitude toward the field could change so quickly. Then wandered back the way she'd come, turning over the name "James Kevin Barry Michael McCloone," as she bolted the gate and retethered it tight.

What an odd long name!

As she walked slowly back to the house, something told her it wouldn't be the last she'd be seeing of the strange man in the shabby clothes. The strange man in the shabby clothes with the very long name who'd accorded her such respect.

But first there was the attic—and that thing that needed throwing out.

What was it? Oh yes: Grandma Edna's old case.

Well, Ruby knew one thing for sure: she wouldn't be burning it. If the case meant so much to her father, she'd be having a look inside and hiding it in a safe place.

If Grandma Edna had secrets, Ruby was determined she'd unlock them. And her mother would never know a thing.

Whatever she learned would remain with her, and with her alone.

Chapter four

In the grounds of Killoran's community center sat Rosewood Clinic. A five-roomed, ashlar-faced building on an acre of closely shaved lawns dotted with rose bushes, it formed part of the town's health-care facilities. One accessed it through a revolving door into a waiting room and reception area, where the soft tones of the rose garden were carried through in the pale moss carpet, cream walls, pine furniture, and cushioned seating.

Not for the first time, Henry marveled at the fine timing that had brought him here. He'd spotted the ad early in the middle of May, and put it to one side, having given it no more than a half-hearted appraisal. It wasn't exactly tailor-made for him. He was a city boy, had never considered a career far from Belfast. Moreover, the position was for a period of three months; the ideal candidate would be prepared to function as a locum, a stand-in, really—for the man who ran the clinic. He'd understood that Dr. Sylvester Balby, the psychiatrist in question, was working on an important paper, and his research was taking him to Massachusetts.

Henry had diligently logged the number of days since his wife's disappearance. He had not given up hope. Not even with the approach of a second May. But finally, as May 25 loomed, his will broke. He told himself it was hopeless. His lovely Connie was never coming back.

On Monday morning, he slipped quietly into his office and retrieved the advert from his desk drawer. He arranged an interview over the telephone, was hired immediately, and began work in Killoran at the beginning of June.

Senior psychiatrist Dr. Sylvester Balby and newly appointed Dr. Henry Shevlin were to share the building for the time being, prior to Balby's departure for the United States. Each had separate offices and consulting rooms either side of the corridor. They also shared a secretary, Miss Edith King, who was stationed at a reception desk in the foyer and supervised patients in the waiting room.

Miss King, a brisk lady in her midfifties, was, to Henry's trained eye, the epitome of the dedicated, no-nonsense secretary.

Just a week into his new job, in rare idle moments, he'd find himself glancing at her through the venetian blinds of his office and wondering about her home life. She had the posture of a ballet dancer, her ringless fingers striking the typewriter keys with exacting diligence. He'd never had the luxury of a personal secretary. At the Mater, there was a pool of secretaries—mostly young women—who kept the wheels of administration turning in a large office on the ground floor. The Rosewood Clinic was different; being smaller, it had more of a community atmosphere, which was a welcome change.

The cases that came his way were no different, however; the vagaries of the human condition presented themselves in a litany of all-too-common disorders. Broken individuals, some more fractured than others, all wishing to be returned to their true selves under the attentive gaze and ready ear of the therapist.

Those outpatients who couldn't be helped at Rosewood would be referred for committal to St. Ita's, the sprawling mental institution outside Derry City. It was Henry's task to assess referrals from GPs in the Killoran area.

The patients within the walls of St. Ita's, in common with the Mater Infirmorum, were mainly women. Women sought help more readily than men. Women attempted suicide more often than men; but, sadly, too many males would rather die at their own hand than seek help. In Henry's experience, those trends had remained unchanged.

"The political situation has added significantly to our workload," Dr. Balby informed him on their first meeting, tapping the bowl of his briar-wood pipe. "But I suppose that isn't news to you, having practiced in Belfast for so long."

Balby, tall and stooped with a craggy face, and assertive hair more suited to an American news anchor than a workaday doctor, should by rights have retired long ago. The more Henry listened to him, the more the older man reinforced this view. But, as with so many members of his profession, work was his lifeblood. It was hard to let go. Balby had assured him that his planned paper would "revolutionize the whole damned business" of psychiatry, and would "make people sit up and take notice." Henry had to admire his confidence and zeal.

"Victims of the Troubles?" he said now. "Yes, I've seen my fair share."

He was sitting in Balby's office, on the opposite side of a commodious desk. Its top surface, a gleaming plane of varnished walnut, was remarkable for its lack of paperwork. A Newton's Cradle sat at one side. He found himself staring at it while wondering whether Balby didn't believe in taking notes or was simply fastidious.

"Edie does all that for me. Shorthand skills second to none."

"I beg your pardon?"

"My secretary out there," Balby said, nodding at the door. "Yours, too, now that you're here for the next few months." He struck a match and rekindled the pipe. "You were wondering about the lack of paperwork on my desk? Can't stand paperwork. It's all in *here*," he said, tapping his right temple.

Two perfect puffs of smoke escaped the pipe bowl and rose toward the ceiling. Henry decoded the message in the Apache smoke-signal language of his beloved boyhood Westerns. One puff for attention. Two puffs: all fine. Three: something wrong.

"Isn't that a bit intrusive for the patient?" Henry said, not minding if he sounded presumptive.

"Not a bit of it. Edie might as well be a piece of furniture as far as most of them are concerned. She has access to every case file, so she knows them all already. Why wouldn't she? It's her job."

"I take your point." But he could not really hold with his colleague's view. It was difficult enough for a patient to confide his innermost secrets to one stranger without having another in the room at the same time.

"That damn Janov and his primal-scream nonsense. There's a glut of them now, coming our way to join the bombers. A pack decamped to Burtonport, across the border there in Donegal, ten years ago. The townspeople had enough and hunted them. So, what attracted you to our little neck of the woods?"

"I needed a change. Hunted them where?" He had no intention of telling Balby about his private life.

"The Isle of Innisfree, no less. An island's the best place for them. They can scream their silly heads off without annoying others. I blame that Lennon fellow and his deluded wife. What's her name . . . Sounds like an egg?"

"Yoko."

"That's the one. Where do you stand on *him*?"

"Lennon or Janov?" Henry smiled. "Sorry . . . well, interesting theory, Janov's. But I don't believe reexperiencing early trauma actually benefits the patient much. Helping the patient understand why it happened and how they don't have to keep recycling it is a more worthy approach."

"Hmm . . . You're a 'talking' man, then. Medicating not much on your radar?" He lifted a steel ball on the Newton's Cradle and released it, thereby setting its tick-tock mechanism in motion.

"It has its place, but not at the exclusion of listening."

"Good luck to that! Cathartic discharge is all very well, but give me imipramine any day. Cutbacks, Henry, cutbacks."

"Sorry, I don't follow."

"We're here to keep them out of St. Ita's, if at all possible. The place is at bursting point. Alcoholics and battered women, as usual. Here at this clinic we hold back the tide. Bottom line: If they don't actually try and kill you, they can be managed in the community."

His temporary replacement was flabbergasted, but said nothing. He resolved to do things *his* way, cutbacks or not.

"Now, there's one fellow you might find a strain. He refuses all medication—so he's right up your street. Thinks he's John Lennon. Has got the hair, glasses, and Liverpudlian accent all down to a T. It's D.I.D. without a doubt. Spent ten months in Burtonport with Janov's lot."

"Interesting."

"Well, I never usually give up on a patient but this one takes the biscuit." He puffed sharply on the pipe, thrice in succession. "Were you born in Belfast? Any family there?"

"As good as. Lisburn. Not far from it. My father still lives there. And you?"

"Born and raised here in Londonderry—or Derry, depending on your persuasion. Know the psyche well. That's a bonus in this line of work. Doesn't do to shift about." He gripped the pipe stem between bared teeth; his cadaverous face, dappled in the light reflected from the Newton's Cradle, reminded Henry of a Mexican sugar skull. "Been about a bit yourself, have you?"

"Here and there."

"A married man, are you?"

"Yes . . . yes, indeed."

"How many times?"

"What?" Henry was taken aback. "Why, once . . . of course, and I hope, my first and last." He allowed himself to think of Connie for one brief moment.

Balby let out a laugh. "Good luck to *that*. Give it time. I'm on my third. The first couple of times, I married accidently, you could say."

Henry grinned.

"We psychiatrists . . . hard bunch to live with, apparently."

From the waiting area came the clamor of raised voices. Miss King was declaiming loudly.

"Please sit down, Mr. Flannagan! Dr. Balby is not ready to see you yet."

Seconds later, two curt raps on the door and the secretary put her head in.

"Excuse me, Dr. Balby, but Finbar Flannagan is here and is being abusive, as usual."

"AKA John Lennon to you, Henry. Show him into Dr. Shevlin's room, Miss King. He's Henry's problem now."

"I wish you courage and forbearance," Miss King said, addressing Henry over her spectacles, before withdrawing promptly and shutting the door.

"Well, he's all yours." Balby got up. "I'll be interested to know how you fare. Treat him as a test case. You must come to dinner on our return from Massachusetts. Beatrice would like to meet you."

"Yes, I'd love to."

"Right, that's settled. You'll be needing that." He handed over a file of case notes with *F. Flannagan* printed on the front. "And so to work."

"Thanks. Yes, indeed. To work."

———

Dr. Shevlin entered his consulting room to find "John Lennon" sprawled in one of the armchairs, trying to roll a cigarette. Difficult, since his hands were shaking so much. The masquerade was perfect. Long dark hair, parted in the middle and held in place with a beaded headband worn low on the forehead. Wire glasses perched on a beaky nose. He was wearing a black T-shirt two sizes too big and bearing the epigraph *Give Peace a Chance*, a pair of baggy trousers with a hole in the left knee, and bright green flip-flops.

Henry held out a hand. "Hello, Finbar. I'm Dr. Shevlin. How are you?"

Finbar looked up, briefly. "Who the feck is Finbar? I'm John Lennon. And who the feck are *you*? Where's Balby? You're not Balby. I want Dr. Balby."

He'd spoken, Henry decided, with a near-perfect Liverpool accent. He'd ended his little rant as abruptly as he'd begun it. Now his full concentration was on the cigarette.

The consulting room had five easy chairs placed about a sturdy coffee table. In keeping with the theme of the garden, the tones were muted: cream walls with watercolor prints of roses, pale green carpet, two waist-high plants in pots by the window. A room that, of necessity, had to be minimalist and functional with nothing in it that could be used as a projectile. The plant pots were of immovable granite. The pictures nailed to the walls. The coffee table bolted to the floor. The ashtrays were of disposable foil.

Henry drew up an armchair opposite Finbar.

"Dr. Balby thought you could do with a change of scene," he said, careful not to use the name "Finbar." He placed his notes on the coffee table. "I like your hair. How long did it take you to grow it?"

Finbar took a lighter from his pocket and sucked the roll-up into life. He sat up abruptly in an effort to stop shaking, crossed his legs, uncrossed them again, sighed deeply, gazed about the room.

"D'you want a bifter?"

"Sorry?"

"A bifter. A *ciggy*, you divvy."

"No, thanks. I don't smoke."

The patient's eyes locked on the foil ashtray. In a low voice he said, "I never held with wonders. I never held with gods . . . I never held with Jesus . . . I never held with rishis. . . I never held with yoga . . . I never held with cosmic truths . . . I never held with the bleedin' Beatles. I only hold with *me*."

"That's good. So tell me about the 'you,' the real you, Finbar."

"You're like me auld fella, you are. Left me mam when I was four."

"Oh . . . ?"

"Oh, aye, up and left her. He was a fecking sailor, so what would he know? Brainless gobshite."

Henry, no expert on John Lennon's life story, found himself having to ask a leading question. "And where were you living then?"

"Merseyside. Why you asking that? The whole bleeding world knows that. John Winston Lennon, born October ninth, nineteen forty, in Liverpool Maternity Hospital, to Julia Lennon née Stanley and Alfred fecking Lennon. I got John after me grandda, John 'Jack,' and Winston for Winston fecking Churchill, prime minister of Britain at the time. I—"

"Sorry, John, would you mind if I had a word with Finbar?"

"Why you asking that? Eh? Eh? You winding me up, you divvy, 'cos if you are, I'll clock you one. I will."

"No, I'm not winding you up. John Lennon died four years ago. So, you are *not* John Lennon."

Henry was sitting within easy reach of the alarm buzzer. He hoped he wouldn't have to use it. Balby had been correct in his diagnosis: D.I.D. Dissociative Identity Disorder. A rare condition seen more often in females than males—and all the more unpredictable for that.

"I know I died four years ago, you divvy. Shot four times in the back with a point thirty-eight revolver, 'cos I said the Beatles were more popular than Jesus. That gobshite Chapman . . . that's why he did it: 'cos I spoke me bleeding mind and told the bleeding truth. Me spirit lives on in Finbar Flannagan."

"May I speak to Finbar?"

"No way, 'cos I left him on Innisfree, didn't I?"

"What's he doing on Innisfree?"

"You wha'?"

"Why is Finbar on Innisfree?"

"Screaming his brains out with the other woollybacks. He went there 'cos of me. I thought I could scream me pain away. But singing's easier than screaming. And writing songs is easier than talking bollocks to some bleeding therapist like *you*."

Without warning, he stubbed out the cigarette, shot to his feet, and launched into song, playing air guitar as he circled the room.

Father, you left me, but I didn't leave you.
I looked for you, but you'd gone away to sea.
So I just gotta ask you: oh why, oh why?

Just as abruptly, he stopped, and meekly returned to his chair.

"You sing very well," Henry said.

"Of course I sing very well. I'm John Lennon, ain't I?"

"Where's Finbar's father?"

"Don't know. Me mam was killed in a car accident when I was eighteen. Left me with me aunt Mimi when I was six. Me dad didn't want me neither. That's why I wrote that song. Left me when I was five." Finbar's voice began to break.

Henry pushed the box of Kleenex across the table. Finbar removed his spectacles and dried his eyes.

"Tell me about Finbar's parents."

The patient said nothing. Pushed the tissue into his trouser pocket and put the glasses back on, taking care to loop the legs round each ear one at a time—inadvertently showing Henry the needle marks on his inner forearms. He laced his fingers in front of him, an elbow on each knee, and stared at the ashtray, left leg going like a piston.

"Finbar . . . ?"

"They didn't fecking want me," he said in a broad Ulster accent. The air in the room tightened. "He took off when I was seven and she . . . She took up . . . with . . . with *him*."

"Your stepfather?"

"Yes."

"And he didn't treat you well?"

"No."

"What did he do to make you unhappy?"

"He beat me 'cos I wasn't his. And he . . . he . . ."

The pause said it all. It was rare for a victim to give voice to the sexual abuse he'd suffered in childhood. The shame was too great. Better keep it in the dark and suffer. The wound that couldn't heal because it would never be exposed to the light of day.

"He had power over you once, Finbar, but not anymore."

"She didn't fecking keep me, me mam."

With that comment he'd lost him, as Henry knew he would. Lennon was back. It was safer to be someone else than face the truth about his young self.

For the rest of the session, Henry listened to John Lennon's ramblings. But he'd met Finbar, for a few moments. That was a start.

He could build on that.

Chapter five

Monday morning, and Ruby was pinning sheets on the line. The weekend had been a disaster and she was still recovering from the fallout. May and June had come and gone but the memory of the upset they'd caused her still lingered. Getting their bedding laundered and done with was one way of dealing with the hurt. It was a household task she hated. Having to steep them in the bath, then scrub with a bar of Sunlight soap before putting them in the washing machine, meant an aching back and ragged cuticles for the rest of the day. But better now than have the chore hanging there in the future like a rain-fat cloud, ready to drench her every time she passed their bedroom door.

On Friday, they'd arrived at their usual time: the twins. Performed their customary inspection of the twin beds, then retired to the mother's bedroom and shut the door.

It had become commonplace, since her husband's death, for Mrs. Clare to retreat to bed an hour prior to their arrival and prepare her martyr act. Box of Kleenex at the ready, rosary and novena leaflets to hand.

On this occasion, however, Ruby had made the mistake of tiptoeing up the stairs to eavesdrop. She knew for certain she was being talked about and decided to take the chance. But May had pulled the door open at the precise moment she'd gained the landing.

"What are you like? D'you think you couldn't be heard creaking up them stairs? If you want to be a sneak, lose some weight, then you can tiptoe about all you like."

"Some chance of that." June's face at her sister's shoulder, giving the illusion of a two-headed fiend. "We weren't talking about you anyway, Ruby."

"Dinner's ready," Ruby said, wrong-footing the pair. Dinner wasn't really ready, but she thought she'd risk it.

"Well, why didn't you say so? We'll be down in a minute when we help Mummy up."

When they were growing up, Mrs. Clare had been simply referred to as "Mammy," but Belfast had turned the twins snobby. So "Mammy" got swapped for the more pretentious-sounding "Mummy."

At the dinner table they discussed their week at Boots department store, May holding forth as usual.

"Mr. Ross praised my work this morning." She scooped a tiny portion of Ruby's shepherd's pie onto her plate and inspected it, fork poised. "I hope there's no fat in this, Ruby. June and me are watching our figures, you know." She raised an eyebrow, the unspoken "unlike you" implicit in the gesture. "Yes, he's so impressed, Mr. Ross, with how I deal with customers. He took me into his office and said, 'May, you're a wonder, you are. I saw how you dealt with that lady.'"

"What lady was that?" asked the mother, mashing her dinner up, as if preparing it for a baby.

"Oh, she was hardly a lady, Mummy. A crude old bag from the Shankill, by the sound of her. She was returning a packet of laxatives."

"That's a Protestant area, isn't it," remarked Ruby.

June rolled her eyes. "Well, of *course* it's a Prod area, Ruby. What a silly question!"

Ruby shrugged. "Just wondered how you knew she was Protestant just by lookin' at her . . . That's all."

May left down her knife and fork with a resigned expression. "God, Ruby, you know nothing, do you? June and me know what part of Belfast they're from by the way they speak. Don't we, June?"

"Dear me." Martha sighed.

"Anyway, where was I before I was so rudely interrupted?" She looked pointedly at Ruby.

"Just askin'," Ruby said.

"She was returning a packet of laxatives," June put in.

"Thank you, June . . . Yes, she was returning a packet of laxatives with half of them gone, *and* she wanted her money back. Can you believe it? So I said, 'What was wrong with them? You've used fifteen.' And she said, 'They're good for bloody nathin', so they're nat. My husband hasn't been to the toilet for a week and he's been takin' them every night and nat a dickey bird.'"

"And what did you say?" asked June, prompting like an understudy. She'd heard the story already on the bus home, knew what was expected of her.

"'Well,' I said. 'They're the strongest constipation pills we have, madam.'" She scoped the table. "Mr. Ross says we must all address customers as 'madam'—even oul' slappers like her—or 'sir,' to give a good impression. So I said: 'In that case you'd best take him to the doctor. It could be serious. He might have a blockage.' And d'you know what she said, right out in front of everybody? 'Cos there was quite a queue forming, with her keeping everybody back. She says, 'Blockage, me arse, missus! Gimme me effin' money back.'"

"Not much breeding in that one. God, there are some very crude people in Belfast. Is it any wonder they're all killing each other?"

"Oh, Mummy, you don't know the half of it. What I have to put up with!" She looked down at her plate. "This dinner's cold."

"Ruby, put that in the microwave for your sister."

Any wonder it's cold? You've been gabbing so much. But Ruby did as she was told.

"You know, next Sunday is the blessing of the graves," continued the mother. "Could you get another one of those angels for your father's plinth?"

Ruby replaced May's plate and took her seat again. She saw the twins exchange furtive looks.

"Oh, we'll not be coming home next weekend, Mummy," May said, avoiding her mother's eye. "We're going to—"

"Manchester," June blurted out, and winced at once. Ruby knew by May's peeved face that she'd just kicked her sister under the table.

Martha stared at the pair of them. "Manchester! And what's in Manchester that could be more important than the blessing of your poor father's grave?"

Ruby saw May hesitate. "Well, it's . . . Alistair in work. He's . . . a—"

"He's a cousin of George Best's," said June, coming to the rescue. "And George will be playing at Old Trafford next Saturday, so he got us tickets for the match."

The mother set her cutlery down and glared at them. "So a hairy-faced, womanizing Protestant who kicks a ball about a field is more important to you pair than Cemetery Sunday. I must say I'm very disappointed in you, May."

"Och, Mummy, don't be like that. The tickets were really expensive and it might be the only chance we'll ever get to—"

"I thought George Best retired last year," Ruby cut in, risking May's wrath again.

May glared at her then busied herself with the food plate. "He did. But this is one of those . . . What's it called, June?"

"A friendly," June said, but she was looking daggers at Ruby, too.

"That's the one: a friendly."

"Could you get me his autograph?" George was a heartthrob for the entire female population of Northern Ireland, and Ruby was immediately envious that her sisters were going to actually see him at such close quarters.

May said nothing.

"Well, we'll see, Ruby," June said, finally. "But we can't promise."

"We'll bring you home the angel the following weekend," May added, covertly eyeing her sister. "Now, tell Mummy about that new nail polish you were telling me about."

Martha took up her cutlery again. She shook her head. "I don't know what your poor father would say."

"Yes, Mummy, we launched a new color—Spice Romance—last Tuesday," June began. She splayed a hand of perfectly painted nails. The twins were blessed with slim, tapered hands. Fingers made for rings, nails made for painting. "Isn't it lovely? What do you think, Ruby?"

Ruby put down her knife and fork, and dropped her hands into her lap, conscious of her bitten nails.

May smirked. "What a daft question! How could *she* wear nail polish? She's got no nails. They're all chewed off her."

"They're not chewed off me, May!" Ruby had had enough. The twin had been itching for a fight from the moment she'd stepped over the threshold. Well, now she was going to get one. "I can't keep them long like youse two, 'cos I wash and cook and clean here every day. It's easy for youse, standing behind counters, doin' next to—"

"How dare you speak to us like that!" May jumped up.

Mrs. Clare whacked the table with the serving spoon, staining the white tablecloth Ruby had so painstakingly starched that morning.

"Stop bickering this minute!" The room filled up with a stunned silence. But not for long. "Your sisters work hard all week. They need peace when they come home."

Ruby, close to tears, but using her anger to buttress herself, took aim at the mother. "Oh, and *I* don't work hard all week, too. Why do you always take *their* side?"

When her father was alive, he'd kept the peace at the dinner table, always supporting Ruby. Since his death, it was as if all three of them were taking their revenge. Pent-up vitriol held in check for years, erupting like a Yellowstone geyser.

"Oh my good God! What have I reared at all?" Mrs. Clare's beseeching whine heralded the onset of one of her "turns," a devotional spectacle of theatrical proportions, guaranteed to make Lady Macbeth look like Bo Peep. She slid to her knees, clutching her heart, directing her entreaty to a picture of Dymphna, patron saint of the mentally afflicted, which hung above the kitchen door.

May caught her wrist, trying to placate. "Mummy, Mummy, get up! Get up. Don't listen to her. Don't upset yourself."

But, too late, Mrs. Clare was already in character, gripping the table edge, face twisted in a show of agonized supplication. "Oh Holy Mother of God. And your poor father gone. Oh, my heart . . . my heart, my—"

May turned on Ruby. "Now look what you've started! You couldn't leave it alone, could you?"

"*I* didn't start anything. *You* did. You said I chewed me nails."

"And you *do* chew your bloody nails. I was only stating a fact!"

"Oh God. Why can't I have peace at this time of my life?" Mrs. Clare hung her head and beat her breast. She was working herself up to a grand finale, a set piece that would see her helped up the stairs like Jesus climbing Calvary, followed by the rosary, a cup of Horlicks, a Mogadon, and finally, mercifully: sleep.

But no, this time the set piece was to have a very different ending.

Suddenly, she shot to her feet and flew at Ruby, slapping her hard across the face. Ruby stumbled, shocked.

"Get up them stairs to your room!" the mother wailed. "And if I see your face down here again I'll—"

"Do as she says, Ruby," June frightened, pulling her mother back. "Go on, Ruby. Go on. If Mummy has a heart attack it'll be your fault."

Ruby held her smarting cheek, staring down at the table. In a heartbeat she'd been returned to childhood: a childhood of beatings and insults at the hands of her mother. Why did she hate Ruby so much? Ruby the punching bag.

Silently she turned away from them, straining to yell, to scream, to rend the air with all the injustice she felt. But she kept her mouth shut, kept the tears at bay until she reached the safety of her bedroom.

Once inside, she collapsed on the bed and surrendered to the luxury of weeping, using her pillow to stifle the sobs.

"Daddy, Daddy, why did you leave me? Why, oh why did you leave me with *them*?"

Exhausted, she fell into a deep sleep, and dreamed.

A lucid dream, full of mystery and foreboding.

Ruby, a little girl again.

It was her First Communion, and she was standing in front of the mirror in her parents' bedroom in her white frock. Her mother was tying a ribbon in her hair, pulling the ribbon so tight it was hurting the sides of her head. But little Ruby didn't complain. She felt so special in her "bride's" frock, her stiff patent shoes and frilled socks.

Task completed. The mother straightened. She was wearing a blue two-piece in shiny satin. A white pillbox with spotted net that came down to her eyebrows and matching gloves up to her elbows.

"That's you," she said, looking down at Ruby. "Now I'm Father Cardy." She mimed, holding a chalice and extracting the host. "Body of Christ."

Ruby obediently shut her eyes and stuck out her tongue—only to be rewarded with her ear being twisted so tightly that she cried.

"How many times do you have to be told? Say 'Amen' before you put out your tongue."

"A-A-Amen," Ruby repeated, tearful.

"Stop that this minute or I'll pull the other one."

Ruby dried her eyes with the back of her hand.

"Now, when you're coming down from the altar, what must you remember?"

"Not tae . . . Not tae chew."

"Why not?"

"'Cos . . . 'Cos it's . . . it's the, the b-b-body of C-C-Christ, so it is."

Next she was being pushed into a candlelit room, still in her white frock. There were elderly people huddled on chairs around the walls, murmuring the rosary. The smell of candle wax, heavy on the air.

At the back of the room sat a coffin on a bier.

Her mother was behind her.

"Go and say a prayer there, for your granny."

Ruby was terrified. She wanted to run away, but her mother was behind her. She didn't want to look in the coffin. She wanted to scream.

"Her first death, the wee critter," she heard a woman say.

"Aye, and the sooner she gets used to it, the better."

Seven-year-old Ruby shut her eyes tight. Her mother's hand was on the nape of her neck, forcing her to look at the corpse.

"*Look,* for heaven's sake!" The mother's grip grew tighter. "*Look!*"

Ruby opened her eyes. But the corpse was no old lady. It was the present-day Ruby, lying there in her old gingham dress, arms stiff by her sides. A pendant gleamed on her chest. A flat circle of red flanked by two half-moons: one white, one black.

"A NEW BEGINNING, RUBY. A NEW BEGINNING."

She woke with a start.

The voice—a woman's—low and soft, had been right there in the room.

Ruby's heart was pounding. She sat up, fearful, saw that the window, with drapes undrawn, was murky with night. The dressing table, the closet, the old armchair with her stuffed toys shouldering out of the gloom, all reassured her. The clock read 11:00 p.m. She'd slept a whole three hours.

The house was silent.

They must all be asleep.

The events of the evening came back to her. She put her hand to her cheek. It still stung. No, she hadn't dreamed that part. Her mother *had* slapped her. May and June *had* been nasty to her. But instead of feeling vengeful toward them, she felt unusually calm. Forgiving, almost.

These charitable feelings, which in the past would have seemed so alien, seemed right somehow. She felt fortified by them. Was this the birth of that new beginning the voice in the dream had promised? Could it be so?

She got up, and stood foursquare by the bed, as if testing the fact that she could stand up for herself.

Her head felt light, but at the same time she felt strangely energized. She crossed to the door, aware for the first time that she was putting one foot down solidly after the other. She found herself counting the paces. Only four from the bed to the door. She'd lived for the best part of twenty years in that room and had never before been conscious of the distance.

This detail surprised her, and it was accompanied by thoughts that were equally surprising. This was her territory. She, Ruby Clare, would take her place. No one would steal her peace away from her because she—Ruby—would not be giving it away. Not any longer.

She left the room and tiptoed onto the landing.

In the darkness of the corridor she saw a seam of light coming from under May and June's bedroom door.

Unusual, at that hour.

Sometimes, however, they fell asleep reading. She'd just slip her hand around the door and switch the light off.

As she drew nearer she heard their voices. They were still up. Her sisters were arguing.

Intrigued, she put an ear to the door.

June's voice: "What else could I say? I . . . was . . . trying to save you from—"

May: ". . . bloody Manchester. You eejit. Of all places. Dublin. Cork, maybe. But Manchester!"

Ruby heard footsteps, a closet door opening.

It was too risky to linger. She tiptoed down the stairs.

The table was just as she'd left it. The discarded dishes scattered about, awaiting her attentions. The remainder of the pie left uncovered. The chairs in disorder.

Ruby took in the scene. She would clear it up in the morning, as she always did. She would keep the peace for the remainder of the weekend.

She went to the fridge and helped herself to a generous portion of sherry trifle. A reward of sorts.

She carried the bowl back up the stairs. Saw that the light in the twins' bedroom was now off.

What was going on? Why had they been arguing over Manchester?

They rarely fought about anything. There was something mysterious going on. And Ruby knew that, whatever it was, *she'd* be the last to know.

Chapter six

Belfast, 1983

They'd come within forty-eight hours, as promised: two police
officers. A female sergeant named Hanson, together with her
assistant, Constable Lyle. Lyle did not inspire confidence: tall and
lanky with the diffidence of a schoolboy. But Hanson, who could
easily have passed for the young man's mother, made up for the lack.
Unprepossessing, with dark hair and plain features, she exuded a
solemn air of grim professionalism. The only clue to a life beyond
the uniform: a discreet wedding band.

At their request, Henry led them up to the bedroom.

"What exactly are you looking for?" he asked, standing in
the doorway, peeved at their aloofness and the nonchalant way in
which they were invading this most private of spaces. Hanson had
opened Connie's underwear drawer and was casually rummaging
through it.

"We'll know when we find it," Lyle said, hunkered down at one
of the bedside lockers. "Like this, for example." He was holding up
Connie's diary.

"You can't have that!" Henry said, annoyed that he hadn't done
a more thorough search of the locker himself. "It's private."

"Yes, and for that very reason we'll be needing it," Hanson said, not bothering to look his way. She pushed home the lingerie drawer and turned. "Nothing is considered private when a person goes missing, sir. It's the personal items that often hold the key." He didn't much care for the way she was sizing him up. "You *do* want us to find her, don't you?"

"Of course I do. It goes without saying."

"Then let us do our job. We'll be finished shortly. A cup of tea would be welcome."

Henry did as he was bidden. He was not used to being on the receiving end of another's orders, but was finding that, in the present political climate and when dealing with the Royal Ulster Constabulary, it was best to comply.

A few minutes later, Sergeant Hanson joined him in the kitchen. Lyle was nowhere to be seen. "Constable Lyle will continue searching the other rooms," she said, pulling out a chair at the table and settling herself. "You have no objection, Dr. Shevlin?"

"No . . . no, of course not." He set a mug of tea before her and took the chair opposite. At such proximity he could smell her scent: a light, flowery essence, not at all in keeping with her gruff personality. She removed her peaked cap—revealing an expertly cropped mop of glossy hair—and set it down on the table. Withdrew a notebook from her breast pocket. Every movement slowly executed. She'd performed this ritual many times.

"I'll be liaising with you from now on," she said, opening the notebook and taking out a pen. "I've been put in charge of your case. Now, tell me about Constance. I need to know as much as possible."

Henry shrugged. "Gosh, where do I start?"

"The day before she left, did you notice anything unusual in her demeanor?"

"No, not really."

"'Not really' would indicate to me that you *did* notice something."

She sounds like a trial lawyer at the bench, he thought. But giving evidence in court was, no doubt, part of her job.

"Just a bit pensive at breakfast. She hadn't slept too well, so I didn't read too much into it. When one is tired one's mood usually drops."

"She has sleep problems?"

"No, on the contrary, she's an excellent sleeper. Out like a light way before me, normally. Just on the odd occasion she'll have a restless night."

"The last time you spoke to her was over breakfast on the morning of Wednesday, the twenty-fifth of May?"

"That's correct." He noticed she was recording his answers in shorthand.

"What did you talk about?"

"Oh, this and that. She was working on some stage sets for . . . for *Arms and the Man*, I believe . . . in the studio in town. She was excited they were nearing completion."

"Which studio?"

"Mondrian's, on Kashmir Street. It's an art gallery as well . . ."

"How did you and Constance meet?"

"In hospital."

"She was a colleague?"

"No. A patient. She'd been admitted following the death of her mother . . . she'd taken an overdose."

Hanson stopped her shorthand and looked at him.

"Her . . . her mother had died very suddenly. She—I mean Connie—had been very close to her. She just couldn't cope with the loss. It was the first time she'd been confronted with death. Nothing had prepared her for it."

"How old was she?"

"Twenty-one. She'd dropped out of college. Had started her first job—"

"Which was . . . ?"

"Graphic design. Being creative, she wasn't cut out for the discipline of it. Hated the nine-to-five routine. Her mother had been a shoulder to cry on. Very unexpectedly, that prop had been taken away. It was all too much for her. She'd been left bereft."

"And you helped her through?"

"Yes. She credits me with having saved her from herself."

Hanson gave him a puzzled look.

"It's my job, Sergeant. To bring people to a better understanding of themselves—to save them, in a way. It's an expression I hear often in my line of work. Nothing more than that."

"When did your relationship begin? In the romantic sense, that is."

"We didn't start going out until after she was discharged from hospital, of course."

"How long?"

Irritated now. "Look, is all this necessary?"

"Yes. How long?"

"A few months, perhaps. I don't keep diaries. I don't record every detail of my private life. Sorry to disappoint you."

Hanson was unfazed. "And who contacted who first?"

"I called Connie. I was worried about her. I needed her to know that someone cared about her. She didn't have any support, really. Her sister, Betty, was married with young children, her college friends resented her for leaving, so she was more or less on her own. Our relationship grew from there."

"She was very vulnerable."

Hanson had looked up from her note taking for the second time. The unspoken implication "and you took advantage of her" quite plain in her bald, unblinking stare.

"Vulnerable? Yes, you could say that. That's why I felt very strongly she needed support."

"You felt she might attempt suicide again."

"Possibly."

"Has she ever attempted suicide since?"

"No."

"Is she on medication?"

"No."

"And you've been married for—"

"Nine years."

Hanson raised an eyebrow. "A whirlwind romance, then?"

"You could say that. We married within a year of meeting, yes."

"Constance is now thirty, correct?"

"Yes . . . Her birthday was just . . . just . . ." Henry had to fight the tears back, remembering their celebratory dinner at The Pheasant restaurant on Victoria Street. Could it now, in retrospect, have been their last celebration together? "Just . . . just three weeks ago."

"A milestone age, some would say. How did she feel about turning thirty?"

"Okay . . . I suppose. I mean, she didn't dwell on it, if that's what you mean. Not really."

"You have children, Dr. Shevlin?"

"No . . . no, we haven't."

"You didn't want them?"

"No, on the contrary . . . we wanted children, but Connie, she . . . she couldn't have children."

"She regretted that, obviously?"

"Yes, but had accepted that it was not to be."

Hanson laid down the pen, laced her fingers together.

"Where do you think your wife might be, Dr. Shevlin?"

"I don't honestly know. She's never done anything like this before. It's an absolute mystery to me."

"Wednesday evening, when she didn't return home, did you go out looking for her?"

"No. Why do you ask?"

"Would seem a natural thing to do in the circumstances." She took a sip of the tea but her eyes never left his face.

"I assumed she'd gone shopping. She often did on Thursday evenings. Only, for some reason I mistook the days. I waited until closing time, thinking she'd be back. When she didn't turn up I rang Betty. Look, I've been over all this with Constable Nelson. At the station. Is—"

"Does she work full time?"

"It depends. If there's a production on, she'll go in more often. If not, then she'll work on private commissions and the pace is more relaxed."

"By private commissions, you mean what exactly?"

"Oh, paintings, screen prints . . . for businesses, usually. Banks, public spaces . . . that kind of thing. She likes to work on large-scale projects." He pointed to a substantial triptych on the far wall, which showed a picnic scene in the woods. "That kind of scale."

Sergeant Hanson left her chair to take a closer look.

"She's very talented. Where is this?"

"Ravensdale, County Louth. We walked through it once and had a picnic. Connie took photographs. She's a recorder; she rarely leaves home without her camera."

Hanson turned from her inspection of the triptych and resumed her seat. "Did she take it on this occasion?"

"What?"

"Her camera."

"Probably."

"You haven't checked?"

"No. It never occurred to me. I checked for her passport and her handbag. The camera is small and she usually keeps it in her handbag. That's why I didn't feel it necessary to do a separate search for it."

"Hmm . . . Does she have a best friend?"

"No."

"No female friends?"

"Well, there's Geraldine, I suppose."

"You *suppose*?"

"Yes, from art-college days. They only meet three or four times a year."

"Did you call her? This Geraldine . . . er . . ."

"Reynolds. Geraldine Reynolds. No, I didn't call her."

"Why not?"

"Firstly, it would seem highly unlikely that Connie would take a bus a hundred miles to Sligo to visit Geraldine without telling me first. And secondly, I wouldn't dream of calling Geraldine, and so cause her unnecessary worry."

"Connie's answerable to you in everything she does, then?"

"No, not everything. Of course not. I find your line of questioning intrusive, Sergeant." Henry was really irritated now.

"Apart from her work at the studio, shopping, walking in Sir Thomas and Lady Dickson Park, visiting her sister, what other places might she be likely to frequent?"

"We go to restaurants, but always together. Can't imagine Connie wanting to eat out alone. She likes company."

"Your company?"

"Yes, I'm her husband. It's natural for a husband and wife to want to be together."

At that moment, Constable Lyle was heard coming down the stairs. He'd placed Connie's diary in a cellophane bag and was holding something else.

"Anything to report?" asked Hanson.

"Apart from the diary, just this." He handed her a bottle of pills.

Hanson read the label. "Indalpine? Can you explain these, Dr. Shevlin?"

"Yes, it's an antidepressant. What of it? I'm a psychiatrist; medications sometimes find their way home with me. It doesn't mean that either Connie or I are using them."

Sergeant Hanson set the bottle down in front of him.

"If that's the case, Dr. Shevlin, why is your wife's name on the label and why are they dated to within the last fortnight?"

Henry tried to hide his shock. He studied the small print on the label, noted that Boots, on Royal Avenue, had dispensed the medication ten days before. It was a central address, in the very heart of Belfast.

"To be honest, Sergeant, I have no explanation. I had no idea Connie was taking these. None whatsoever."

"Good work, Lyle," the sergeant said. She scribbled something at the back of her notebook and tore off the page. "My contact number, Dr. Shevlin." She handed it to him. "That's enough for now, I believe. But if you think of anything—anything at all—do not hesitate to call me. Honesty is always the best policy in affairs such as this. Always."

Henry showed them out, his mind in turmoil. Connie had secrets.

How could he not have known about the pills? How come he hadn't seen them?

How come she hadn't *told* him?

Chapter seven

A blue Austin Mini bumped down Oaktree Lane, just as Ruby had finished securing the final sheet to the line. It swerved into the yard, narrowly missing a hen, and puttered to a halt by the water pump.

Ruby concealed herself behind the washing line as Miss Ida Nettles extricated herself from the vehicle, an elaborate task because she wasn't used to the car, having just acquired it. Six months earlier, she'd accomplished the amazing feat of passing her driving test on the seventh attempt, setting a record and making of herself an absolute menace on the road. It was rumored that Mr. Reilly, her instructor, had bought himself a brand-new caravan for seaside breaks on the back of Ida's incompetence.

Ida, a former midwife, was never going to let retirement stall her. She needed to be out and about, a community activist of sorts, so had reinvented herself as an Avon-lady-cum-nurse who could do hair, makeup, manicures, pedicures, and provide any other kind of cure—whether medicinal or herbal—from the depths of her commodious doctor's bag. A bag she carried about clamped under her right arm like a bulging baby, fearing the straps too fragile for its many bottles of unguents.

Ruby berated herself for not remembering that Monday was "Ida day": her mother's toes got done on Mondays. Had her thoughts not been in such tumult from the weekend's events, she certainly would have remembered and made herself scarce. Because Ida was nothing more than a busybody who talked down to Ruby as if she were still seven years old, and carried stories from one house to the next, fattened with her own fictions, just for the hell of it. In another life she might well have been a tabloid hack.

From behind the shelter of the sheet, Ruby watched as Ida hauled the bag from the backseat of the car, slammed the door shut, turned, and gazed up at the sky. Then, shielding her eyes from the sun, looked directly across to the garden.

Ruby ducked behind the plum bush, but too late.

"Ruby, is that you?" Ida called out. "You can't hide from yer auntie Ida."

Damn!

"Oh . . . hello, Ida. Didn't see you there." She picked up the laundry basket and, with reluctance, went to greet her. "Just putting the wash out."

"I see that. Well, how's the mammy?"

"A bit poorly, but nothing too serious."

Ida was five feet one, with a frizz of tightly permed hair the color of churned butter. Her tiny face was never without makeup; eyebrows and lipstick crookedly applied, due to progressive myopia, which, for vanity's sake, she chose to ignore. Today she was in a frock of lapis blue, with eye shadow and sandals to match.

"Oh, that's terrible," she said, squinting up at Ruby. "And with what she's been through, with yer poor father dying like he did . . . so sudden and all. Is it any wonder she's poorly, but sure getting her toes done'll brighten her up a bit. And how's yourself, Ruby?" Without preamble, she loaded the doctor's bag into the laundry basket Ruby was holding. "Now, a big strong girl like you can carry that in for me."

"Busy, as usual, Ida, so I am," Ruby said, leading the way into the cool sanctuary of the house.

"Well, that's good. Takes your mind off your daddy. Now, put that down on the table there, like a good girl, till I get me biscuits."

Ruby had already plonked down the bag, having performed this ritual many times in the past. In seconds, Ida was diving into it.

"Now, where are they?" She'd flung out a tin of talcum powder, a jar of fish paste, a bottle of Yardley cologne, and a can of hairspray, before spotting the biscuits. "A fig roll for a cuppa tea. You put the kettle on there, Ruby, like a good girl, and I'll see to your poor mammy. She's in the bed, no doubt, and that's where she'll stay, for it's the best place to get the toes done."

"I'll bring up the tea in a minute," Ruby said—into empty space, for already Ida was gone, bag and all, up the stairs like a prairie province tornado, leaving behind a pong of scent in the air and a pack of Jacob's Fig Rolls on the table.

Soon, from overhead, came the sound of muffled greetings and a door closing. Then a thought struck Ruby. This would be the ideal time to go up to the attic and investigate Grandma Edna's case. The door to the mother's bedroom would be shut for the best part of an hour—the pedicure, four cups of tea, and a week of gossip having to be gotten through—therefore she would not be seen coming and going on the stairs.

Thinking ahead—the case would be locked, no doubt—she went out to her father's old toolbox in the shed and found a pair of sturdy pliers. She secreted them in her apron pocket.

A few minutes later, she bore the tea tray up the stairs. She was about to enter the bedroom, but halted when she heard the name "Jamie." She put her ear to the door. Her mother was speaking.

". . . and if she didn't put him out of the field . . . me promising it to him on the phone a couple of days before."

"Away with you, Martha! Put poor Jamie McCloone outta the field . . . and him so lonely now without his dog and all."

"Oh, Ida, you don't know the half of it. She ran out of the house like her backside was on fire, shouting at him."

"God, and what did Jamie do?"

"Well, I'm sure he was very shocked at her . . . but after a bit they shook hands . . . So he must have been all right about it . . . Then got on the tractor and left. I was so affronted. But you know, between you and me, Ida, I said nothing to her. I'm afraid of her betimes. What she might do—"

"God, d'you think she might attack you, Martha? 'Cos if that's the case I could have a word with Dr. Brewster, about gettin' her in."

Ruby's grip on the tray tightened. She knew that "gettin' her in" was code for having her committed to St. Ita's mental institution.

"Well, hopefully it'll not come to that. Don't know what's got into her since Vinny died . . . I'm afraid in my own house. And when May and June come home at the weekends, it's like the Divil himself gets—"

Ruby steeled herself. She pushed open the bedroom door, immediately killing the conversation. The room was shrouded in Ida's cigarette smoke. Both women looked her way, surprised faces confirming their guilt.

"I'm going upstairs to clean the windees," Ruby said, setting the tray down stiffly on a table beside Ida.

"God, isn't Ruby such a great help to you, Martha," Ida said, flicking her cigarette in the ornate trinket box she carried about with her as an ashtray. "Sure where would you be without her?"

"Oh, she does her best," the mother said, unable to meet Ruby's eye, "but she can be a bit of a handful at times, Ida."

"Well, you miss the farm work, don't you, Ruby? Must be hard to get used to women's work in the house." Ida lifted the teapot and poured. "But y'know, if you met a nice fella, a nice farming fella, you'd be made, now, wouldn't you?"

"Ruby's not interested in men. Not the marrying kind. Never has—"

"There's water in the kettle if youse want more tea," Ruby cut across her. "But you'll have to get it yourself. I've things to do."

She left the room, shutting the door sharply, snatches of that overheard conversation still fresh in her mind. "Put poor Jamie McCloone outta the field . . . and him so lonely now without his dog and all."

Well, that makes two of us, she thought. *He's lonely because he's on his own and I'm lonely because I'm not.*

Chapter eight

The attic was reached by a flight of stairs, which gave on to a rickety landing on the third floor. Ruby felt uneasy as she climbed up, not so much because of what she might find, but for her own safety. Would the worm-eaten flooring be able to sustain her extra weight? She could not remember the last time she'd been up there, but was sure it must have been about a decade before, when she was quite a few pounds lighter than she was now. Usually it was her father who visited the attic to store things.

The narrow door cried out as she pushed it open—as if protesting her intrusion—and she found herself in a hot, musty space, which smelled of mold and rancid apples. Long ago, her father used to make cider, and would store the fermentation buckets here in the cool darkness. Her eyes welled up when she spotted two of the big jars, one still unopened, yeast encrusting the sealed lid, sitting just inside the door. How long had it sat there? The cider he'd never got to drink.

When her eyes adjusted to the gloom, she saw that unearthing the case was not going to be such an easy task. Her father had been a hoarder, the opposite of her improvident mother—who was always wanting new things. There had been many arguments between the pair when Ruby was growing up. So, to keep the peace, their compromise had been the way station that was the attic.

The place was crammed: a steamer trunk belonging to Great-Aunt Agatha, which had crossed the Atlantic several times, a baby's pram filled with toys and stuffed animals, a cane chair and an old green rocker with a stand of corner shelves jammed on top. These items commanded the most space. Boxes in various stages of ruin proliferated—there must have been at least twenty—containing schoolbooks, magazines, vinyl records, and bundles of old newspapers. Scattered here and there were picture frames, lamps, vases, plastic flowers, coat hangers, and a large mirror that used to hang in the living room when Ruby was a child. Pocked now, with many black age spots, it was suitable only for the attic, where throwing back reflections was as redundant as the rest of the long-retired bric-a-brac.

She caught sight of a small red suitcase, faded to pink from sixteen summers under the skylight. It was the one she'd carried to Donegal for that ill-fated stint in the Queens Arms. Her only time away from home. Her only suitcase. She'd put it up there as soon as she'd returned home, not wanting any cringing reminders of Mr. Ryan and her failure as a waitress. Out of curiosity, she went over now, hunkered down, and snapped opened the hasps.

There was nothing in it apart from a hairgrip and a white metal badge with her name crookedly written in black marker. At the sight of the badge her heart sank. How unhappy she'd been back then! Thrust out into the big, cruel world—a lamb among wolves. She slammed the lid back down. Stood up and pushed the skylight free, needing air.

"THE CASE! YOU CAME HERE FOR THE CASE. LOOK BEHIND YOU!"

She jumped. The voice. It was the same one from her dream, but this time clearer and more insistent.

Ruby began to sweat; she wanted to flee the attic but instead found herself turning round, as instructed, and looking above the door.

There, perched on a shelf, was the object of her mission: an ancient, brown case studded with tarnished rivets.

Grasping the leather handle, she eased it down, shutting her eyes against a dust cloud of many vintages. The case, though small, was unusually heavy, and she could see why. It was made of wood with inlays of what looked like snakeskin, on top and along the sides. She found an empty place on the floor beneath the skylight and set it down.

On the front was the image her mother had so scorned: a line drawing of a naked woman with her arms raised, hands joined above her head. Ruby did not find the image offensive. If anything, it reminded her of a pair of closed scissors. On a nameplate underneath she could just about make out the word *Revelation*. Was it the name of the maker, or an indication of what she might find inside?

The case did not have two locks, as she'd expected, but one brass clasp in the middle, shaped like a half-moon and secured with a small padlock. Fortunately, it didn't look too strong. Two tugs with the pliers had it falling apart.

She slid the clasp free of its leather loop and raised the lid.

A cloth of blue velvet covered the contents, fastened at each corner with ribbons of the same shade, tied in neat bows. Ruby's fingers hovered over the first bow. She hesitated. Grandma Edna had died thirty-two years before. Those bows had been tied by her way back then. Suddenly, Ruby felt the weight of her trespass and sat back on her heels, closed her eyes, heart hammering with indecision.

"Don't be afraid. Look inside."

The voice again: but this time, soft, assuring. She began to breathe more slowly, and soon felt calmer.

Gently, she worked each bow loose, drew back the cover, and peered inside.

She was confronted with an odd sight: a tier of rich blue satin, within which were embedded four objects: a crystal ball, a flat gold disk engraved with a five-pointed star, a knife with a curved blade like that of the crescent moon, and a small silver cup with three chains attached.

Ruby ran her forefinger lightly over each object in turn, afraid to dislodge them. She knew what the crystal ball was for. In Donegal, a lady calling herself Madame Calinda used to do readings with one on the seafront. She'd heard her colleagues discuss how accurate her predictions were, but had been too afraid to venture into her tent. Life was horrible enough back then without hearing even more bad news.

There were tabs either side of the tier. Carefully, she lifted the tray of objects out and set it aside.

The second tier was just like the first, but instead of objects, it held two small books, placed either side of what looked like a length of silver cord wound tightly into a spiral shape. Curious, she pried it free, and was startled to find a very long belt unraveling across the floor. She gathered it up quickly, hoping the dust hadn't soiled it. It had three knots tied at either end. She attempted to roll it back into its original shape, but the effort was too much. She bundled it on top of the first tier and gave her attention to the other two items.

One, Ruby discovered, was not a book at all, but a pack of cards. The emblem on the front: an elaborate, monochrome drawing of what looked like a deer with the moon between its antlers; below it were the words *The Rider Tarot*.

Tentatively, she drew out the cards and shuffled through them, turning each one face upward as she went. She counted twenty-two in all. They were numbered 0 to 21 in what Ruby recognized as old Irish lettering. Each card bore a full-color illustration, and each came complete with a title. She read each one in turn, intrigued and frightened by their strangeness.

"Death" showed a skeleton in armor riding a horse.

"The Lovers." A naked boy and girl against a backdrop of what could have been the Garden of Eden. An angel hovering above them.

"The Devil." The same boy and girl, in chains in front of a throne. On the throne sat a huge, baleful entity. It had bat-like wings and horns growing from its head.

Ruby's hands shook as she quickly turned the card facedown, and returned it to the pack.

The second item was, indeed, a book: a dream dictionary. Remembering her lucid dream about seeing herself in the coffin, she turned the pages with trepidation, until she reached the entry under the heading "Death."

Death dreams signify a desire in you to end or escape a current situation, which is causing you unhappiness. They also denote that you are on the brink of great changes in your life.

She looked up from the page, stunned at the accuracy of that statement. She read on.

Dreaming of your own death often occurs when you are facing a major life-altering change. Something has died within you to make way for a new beginning.

There was the phrase she'd heard in her dream. The voice had said it twice. She repeated it now, aloud.

"A new beginning. A new beginning."

Ruby grew excited. Grandma Edna was talking to her. It was Edna's voice she was hearing. She was sure of it. That's why she'd been led to the secret case. That's why she'd had the dream. There was no need to be afraid.

She replaced the dream dictionary, and was about to restore all the items to their proper place and shut the case, when she noticed that this second tier had tabs either side, just like the first. Perhaps there was something underneath.

She lifted out the second tier. There *was* something. At the bottom, she saw a flat, rectangular object inside a black velvet bag. It had a drawstring of golden cord. Nervously, Ruby lifted it free. She untied the cord and drew out a book. But no ordinary book. This one was handmade. The spine was bound with string and reinforced with two lengths of branch cuttings. It was covered in thick black canvas.

She turned it over.

On the front, calligraphed in gold Celtic script, were the words:

THE BOOK OF LIGHT
Written by Edna Vivian Clare
1854–1952

The book fell from her hands.

Those dates!

Oh God, if Edna wrote the book, how did she know when she was going to die?

Suddenly, she felt sick. Nausea rose in her throat. The urge to flee the attic, strong again. Maybe her mother was right. Maybe she should simply burn the case and everything in it.

She tried to get off her knees, but the effort was too much. First, she needed to put everything back. With trembling hands she returned each item to its rightful place.

"Save it for me, Ruby. Save it for yourself."

She stopped. The voice had used her name. Now she knew for certain it was Grandma Edna. She started to weep.

"I'm afraid, Grandma!" she cried. "I'm afraid, so I am."

"There is no darkness but ignorance. You are protected."

"I am?"

She waited for an answer, but none came. She repeated the words out loud several times. "There is . . . no darkness but . . . but ignorance. I . . . am . . . I am protected."

Repeating the words made her feel calmer. A clearness of purpose overtook her. She knew what she had to do. She fastened the clasp, rose from her knees with ease. Through the skylight, she saw that Ida's car was still in the yard. Good. That meant the door to her mother's bedroom would still be closed.

She secured the skylight once more, carefully lifted the case, and left the attic.

She descended the two flights of stairs to the first-floor landing. Murmuring voices from her mother's room promised safe passage to her own bedroom. She tiptoed inside, crossed to the bed, and placed the case under it. A pelmet of pink valance made for the perfect hiding place.

She felt relieved as she exited the room. Relieved and exhilarated. She had done what her father would have wanted: protected Grandma Edna's legacy. Those ancient secrets in that black book were now hers to learn.

It was her duty to do so.

Ruby Vivian Clare's new beginning was about to begin.

Chapter nine

Hail, Holy Queen, Mother of Mercy, hail, our life, our sweetness and our hope. To thee do we cry, poor banished children of Eve; to thee do we send up our sighs, mourning and weeping in this valley of tears . . ."

Nine twenty-five p.m.: Ruby and her mother on their knees in the kitchen—exhorting God with a protracted rosary. Mrs. Clare's voice ringing out above Ruby's: more sonorous, more earnest sounding, as was the matriarch's right.

"Turn then, most gracious Advocate, thine eyes of mercy towards us, and after this our exile, show unto us the blessed fruit of thy womb, Jesus. O merciful, o loving, o sweet Virgin Mary! Pray for us. Pray for us. Pray for us. Amen."

In tandem they crossed themselves, kissed Christ's image on the crosses of their rosaries, returned the beads to purses, and rose. Ruby first, who then assisted her mother.

This duty of saying the rosary was strictly adhered to by Mrs. Clare. Even if she happened to be lying down of an evening and feeling poorly, she would make the effort to rouse herself at precisely 8:55 p.m. and come downstairs to kneel on the flagged floor for this devotional observance.

She balked at the idea of saying something as important as the rosary while lying down. One had to show reverence for Our Lady at least once during the day by kneeling to pray. It was a penance. Suffering the discomfort of painful knees on the unforgiving floor was appropriate, because Christ had suffered a lot more, had he not? Besides which, one gained a "plenary indulgence" for reciting it in the family home with other family members present. This added bonus meant time off for good behavior when one entered the purgatorial fires of the afterlife.

"How are you now?" Ruby asked when she'd got her mother upright. It had been an interesting day. She'd found and secreted Edna's case. And this deceit, carried out under her mother's nose while she gossiped with Ida, made Ruby feel more self-satisfied and willing to forgive and forget the fact that she'd slapped her. She was an old woman, after all, mourning a great loss.

"How am I? I'm as well as can be expected, Ruby." The mother sighed. "As well as can be expected in the circumstances."

Ruby helped her into an armchair by the stove and spread a rug over her knees.

"I'll get the cocoa ready, so I will. The kettle's already boiled."

The mother settled herself, feeling more reassured, having recited her prayers. It had been a good day. She'd enjoyed Ida's visit. After the weekend, Ida with her pedicure and chitchat had been a welcome distraction. She'd even allowed the Avon Lady to paint her toenails. Something her daughter June hadn't managed, despite all those years on the Rimmel counter. There was something, however, niggling at her, and she needed to know the answer from Ruby before retiring for the night.

"Did you burn that case like I told you?"

Ruby, in the pantry spooning the cocoa into mugs, was glad the query was being made at a safe distance. She was not a good liar.

"Yes," she said, a little too quickly, halting the spoon and looking up, only to see her guilt reflected in the window glass. "I . . . I did it today when Ida was doing your toes."

"Good. I thought I heard you coming and going on the stairs. I'm glad that's out of the house. I can rest easy now."

Ruby set the nightcap on a little table beside her mother's chair and withdrew to the recliner opposite. "I put an extra spoon of sugar in. But if you want more . . ."

"No, there's no need." Mrs. Clare took a tentative sip. "Where did you burn it?"

"Burn what?" Unnerved now, Ruby tried to buy time.

"The case."

"Oh, down—I mean in . . . in the wood . . . at Beldam."

Beldam.

She had the words out before she could stop herself. Beldam Lake was a no-go area, both in speech and thought. Not long after the grandfather's tragic death, five-year-old Declan, her father's younger brother, had wandered out onto the jetty, fallen in, and drowned. Forever a wound on the landscape of Oaktree Farm, it was fenced off with stout skeins of barbed wire, rusted now with age. Shut off decades ago, to shut out the pain of the family's unspeakable loss.

Martha Clare studied her cocoa, gripping the mug in cupped hands. "That's why she got into all that again . . . your grandmother. She lost her faith when the child died so soon after your grandfather."

Ruby shifted in the armchair, uneasy. The creaks of the old recliner pricking the silence in warning.

"What did she get into?" She'd seen the contents of the case and had an inkling of what her mother meant. But she needed to hear more.

"Trying to make contact with the dead. God had let her down, she said. So she turned to all that . . . all that mumbo jumbo . . . and made things worse. Far worse. Couldn't let it go. "

Ruby looked down at her cocoa. She didn't feel like drinking it. "But . . . but if it helped her, what was wrong with it?"

The mother's face darkened. "Who's saying it helped her?"

"I dunno . . . Daddy always said his mother was the best in the world. So she must'a been a good woman."

"You don't know the half of it. Your father was as mad as her when I met him. She had his head turned with all that nonsense. You can thank *me* for bringing some sort of sanity into this house. It was a godless place before I came about. Not a crucifix or a drop of holy water anywhere to be seen. See that prayer over there of Saint Michael? When I married your father and moved in here, I gave her that for her sixtieth birthday. I'll never forget the look on her face when she unwrapped it. She dropped it immediately as if she'd burned herself, and the glass broke. Then I knew for sure what *she was*."

The more Ruby listened, the more fearful she was becoming. "Maybe it was an accident?"

"Why are you sticking up for her? It was *no* accident. Archangel Michael, our protector against Satan. Oh no, she didn't want that in this house. But I stuck to my guns. I insisted that as long as I was living under this roof, I'd have religious pictures and a bit of Christianity about it. She didn't like that one bit. Started to stay more and more in her bedroom until she died. Your father never talked about that side of her to you. Oh no. In his book, she could do no wrong. But she did a *lot* of wrong, I can tell you that. We fought over that case when she went, your father and me. I wanted it burned there and then. But when her will was read, that settled it. She'd made a specific request that as long as Oaktree Farm was in the Clare name, the case should remain in the house and not be opened. Far be it from me to go against someone's dying wishes. So it was put in the attic, out of my sight."

Ruby felt relieved and anxious at the same time. She'd done the right thing by saving the case—but she had *opened* it.

"I'm glad you've burned it. As I say, I can rest easy now, knowing it's out of the way." Martha looked at the clock. "Time for bed. Tomorrow I have an appointment with Mr. Cosgrove, the solicitor. What time is it at? I forget."

Ruby got up and checked the calendar. "Half past nine."

"Good. You can make a shopping list in the morning."

After her mother retired, Ruby did the washing up, full of apprehension and forboding. What terrible fate would befall her now? Unwittingly, she'd gone against Edna's dying wishes. She dimly recollected a fairy tale she'd heard as a child. It concerned a box and a girl who'd opened it. Ruby couldn't remember her name but thought it was Greek. When the girl opened the box, she'd let loose all kinds of terrible things on the world.

Wicked things.

Before climbing the stairs to her own bedroom, she went to the framed prayer of St. Michael, which hung in a niche by the back door. She'd never taken much notice of it before. Like the other pictures that hung around the house, it had disappeared into the fabric of the wallpaper. But now that she'd learned of its origin, the picture took on a whole new significance. She lifted it from its nail, dusted it off, and held it up to the light.

> *St. Michael the Archangel defend us in battle.*
> *Be our protection against the wickedness*
> *and snares of the Devil.*

She looked up from the picture. "Grandma Edna wouldn't be consorting with the Devil," she whispered, half to herself. "Why would she be?" There was more, but Ruby didn't feel like reading it. She returned it to the nail on the wall and climbed the stairs to her room.

Once inside, she took the precaution of locking the door. Her mother's words had frightened her, but she knew her mother generally looked at everything in a negative light. She sat on the edge of the bed.

"THERE IS NO DARKNESS BUT IGNORANCE. YOU ARE PROTECTED."

The voice. The words had come to her just like they had in the attic when she'd felt afraid.

"I'm protected?" Ruby looked about her. "I'm protected," she said again, willing herself to believe it.

Quietly, she got down on her knees and retrieved the case from under the bed. She found *The Book of Light* and unsheathed it from the velvet pouch. Sat back on the pillows and opened it. There was a dedication on the first page, the writing rendered in what could only be Edna's hand.

Dana
The Great Mother Goddess. Beyond all other Gods of this World.
Queen of the Celts. Caretaker of the Faery Folk. Life-giver of Water.
Font of All Wisdom. Bearer of Knowledge. Bringer of Light.
Divine Ambassador to the Elemental Kings.
Bridge to the Underworld.
May she reign supreme.

The next page contained an illustration of a beautiful woman with flowing amber hair—not unlike Ruby's own—dressed in green and wearing a golden crown. She was standing in a forest, her left hand resting on the mane of a white mare. From her outstretched right hand streamed rivulets of sparkling water, which swirled about her feet, creating three spiral pools. Underneath the picture were written the words:

Dana. The Triple Goddess. Maiden, Mother and Crone.

Ruby studied the image, fascinated. The shapes around the Goddess's feet were familiar to her. They were Celtic in origin. She knew that much. As a little girl she used to do Irish dancing, and around the hem of her costume were embroidered motifs of a similar design.

Suddenly, a memory stretched itself and assumed shape. She saw herself racing home from school on her eager little legs, in that dress, proud as a princess. Her mother on her knees in the garden, repotting plants. "Mammy, Mammy, look what I won!"

Ruby's seven-year-old hand opening like a flower. In its heart: a shining silver coin. "Mr. Lagan, the dancing teacher, said I was the best in the class, Mammy."

The mother wiping the sweat from her forehead, her eyes studying the coin, serious. "Hmph! There mustn't have been much competition. Best to stick at your lessons. You'll make nothing of that." And she'd gone back to planting her flowers.

Ruby shut her eyes at the painful memory. Returned to the picture of Dana.

She was as beautiful as the statue of the Virgin Mary that sat on her windowsill. In fact, she could have been the Virgin Mary, but for the green dress. The image was comforting. No, there could be nothing bad in this book if was dedicated to such a beautiful lady.

She turned the page. Under the words "My Pledge" was written:

I, Edna Vivian Clare, do hereby solemnly
dedicate myself this day, May the First, 1940,
to her divine personage, the Goddess Dana.

May she bless me, and shower me with her eternal bounty,
and may she protect me from the snares and wickedness
of those who may plot against me.
I solemnly commit myself to her sacred work, and pledge
and promise to execute my duties for the good of all humankind.

She turned the page.

There was a painting of a lake surrounded by reeds with trees in the background. On the surface of the water stood a little boy, his image crudely cut out from a photograph. Ruby had never seen a photograph of little Declan, but knew it must be him. Underneath the image were the words:

Beldam Lake took my boy but set my spirit free.

On the reverse of this page were the following words:

O children of the Earth, adore the Goddess and God.
The moon and the sun. The shadow and the light.
Know that they have brought you to these writings
so that you may be the bearer of knowledge.
The bringer of Truth. The keeper of the flame.

There were charts in the book tracking the phases of the moon. Lists of herbs and stones, with directions on how they could be used in various lunar rituals. A beautifully colored illustration: "The Wheel of the Year. The Eight Sabbats."

Ruby gazed upon a circle taking up most of the page. It was divided into eight segments, with titles and dates, the topmost being "Yule–Mid-Winter (20–23 Dec.)." She ran her finger clockwise, stopping at each section. "Imbolc (2 Feb.)." "Ostra (9–22 March)." "Beltane (1 May)." "Midsummer—Litha (19–23 June)."

"Lughnasa (1 August)." "Mabon (21–24 Sept.)." "Samhain (1 Nov.)."

On a page headed "Signs of the Zodiac" there were hand-drawn symbols and dates.

It was followed by a poem. She found herself mouthing the words as her eyes traveled from line to line.

> *To work enchantment every time,*
> *Be sure the spell be spoke in rhyme.*
> *Cast the circle thrice about,*
> *To keep the baleful demons out.*
> *Bathe in waters pure and deep*
> *If weighty answers thou shouldst seek.*
> *Honour every living thing,*
> *And Sacred Dana joy will bring.*
> *Treat the globe with guileless heart,*
> *To exercise the scryer's art.*
> *Cingulum so unabased,*
> *Bind it three times 'bout the waist.*
> *Lay the cards, come rain or snow,*
> *And all our futures they shall show.*
> *Burn thy herbs in censer sweet,*
> *My new-born sickle for to greet.*
> *Place the disk upon the palm,*
> *And frenzy shall give way to calm.*
> *Raise the curv'd blade at the moon*
> *On the twenty-first of June.*
> *This rite shall make thy dreams come true,*
> *And wondrous powers shall thee accrue.*

She looked to the two tiers of objects beside her on the bed and sat up. Now she had a better understanding of what they were used for. The long, silver belt was called a cingulum, and you tied it around your waist. The pack of cards called *The Rider Tarot* was for looking into the future. The little silver dish was called a censer, and it was for burning herbs in. The silver disk with the five-pointed star made you feel calm. The knife with the curved blade was for saluting the moon.

This rite shall make your dreams come true,
And wondrous powers shall thee accrue.

"My dreams?" she whispered, excitement mounting. "This rite will make my dreams come true and wondrous powers I will accrue."

Ruby took her diary from the locker drawer, turned to a blank page at the back, and began to write. Three wishes. Wasn't that how it went, when you received power from "beyond"? You got three wishes. She knew what hers would be:

1. I want to see Daddy again.
2. I want to have lots of money.
3. I want to meet someone nice and be happy.

The silver disk with the five-pointed star suddenly glinted. Ruby took it as a sign. She placed it on her palm, fascinated. It was a beautiful object, and the more she stared at it, the more relaxed she became.

She felt her head growing light. Her eyelids droop. She tried to get up but her legs were like lead.

She yawned, fell back on the pillows, and before she knew it, was sound asleep.

Chapter ten

Five-past nine Friday morning, and Miss King, at her desk, poring over the patient list for the day, was alerted to the swishing sound of the revolving door and a man's voice raised in angst.

"Ah, Jezsis! What sort of a bloody thing is this?"

She looked up to see a shabbily dressed farmer type, pushing himself round in circles. Tut-tutting, she went to his aid and thrust a determined foot against one of the panels. But the man with his back to her, oblivious to her presence, responded by splaying his hands on the glass and pushing even harder.

"*Stop pushing!*" Miss King shouted.

He turned in red-faced shock and stared at her through the glass.

"Jezsis! Niver seen you there."

"Apparently not. Now stay where you are and *don't move!*"

Gingerly, she eased the panel toward her, and as if by magic, the visitor found himself in the foyer, face-to-face with the secretary.

"God, that's the damnedest thing!" he declared, relieved that she'd freed him from his glass prison. "What kinda dour is that?"

"It's a *revolving* door," Miss King explained, detecting an unpleasant whiff of alcohol coming off the farmer.

"Ah, I see."

"It admits more people at one time to this building as opposed to the traditional type. It is also relatively soundless and therefore less of a disruption to patients and staff alike. In winter it keeps the cold out while remaining open."

Miss King believed in answering every question a patient asked her as thoroughly and clearly as possible. She did this, knowing that it was within the gift of the cluttered mind of the depressive, and in this case that of the alcoholic, not to really listen to anything that was said.

"Aye, right . . . right ye be," the man said, not much convinced by the receptionist's little speech. He stood holding his arm, looking back warily at the door.

"You must be James McCloone." She went back behind her desk and checked her list.

"Aye, that's me. James Kevin Barry Michael. But I get Jamie for short."

The farmer removed his cap and crushed it between his hands, self-conscious, as Miss King gave him the once-over.

"That's quite a name."

"Aye, it's a long boy, right enuff. It was give timme by me aunt and uncle. But they're . . . they're dead now." He shifted from one foot to the other and consulted the floor. "Aye, dead a long time now."

"I'm sorry to hear that, Mr. McCloone. But, for the purposes of expediency, in the future I will refer to you as Mr. McCloone. That's if you don't mind?"

"Naw. That'll do me all right, Miss . . . ?"

"King." She pointed to the name badge on her left lapel. "Good. We like to know where we stand with all our patients at Rosewood."

Miss King referred to her list again.

"Aye, so, Mrs.—"

"Miss."

"Miss. Aye . . . aye so, Miss . . . Miss King," Jamie said to the crown of her gray bun.

"Now, Mr. McCloone, you're here to see Doctor . . . ?"

"Dr. Shelfin."

"*Shevlin*. Dr. Shevlin."

"Aye, him. A new boy. Dr. Brewster tolt me Dr. Baldy was away."

"*Balby*. That's correct. And Dr. Shevlin is indeed new to the practice. Now, do you have the appointment letter you received?"

"Should have it somewhere now."

Jamie reached into the inner pocket of his scruffy check jacket and produced a crumpled envelope. He set it down on the desk and smoothed it flat. Miss King observed the muddy paw prints of a small animal—possibly a mouse—patterned across it. She flinched.

"Would you be so kind as to open it, Mr. McCloone?"

"Aye, no bother," Jamie said, removing the page and handing it over.

"Your appointment is scheduled for ten o'clock." She checked her watch. "And it's just gone ten past nine. You're very early."

"Aw, well, y'see, I can explain that. I came that wee bit earlier 'cos it's the Fair Day in Tailorstown and I have a couple-a heifers tae sell, and they'll be coming up for auction at a quarter to ten. So I thought I'd get this wee appointment with the doctor over afore the auction, and kill two burds with the wan stone, as they say."

Miss Sharp understood Mr. McCloone's logic, but feared he did not quite grasp the importance of the clinic's rules with regard to punctuality and timekeeping. She felt an oft-rehearsed lecture coming on.

"Keeping to the correct appointment time is very important, Mr. McCloone. That is why we take the trouble to send you letters like this. Doctors are very busy people who see lots of patients in the course of a day. As a patient, you must come at the correct time. It is not for *you* to determine when *you* want to see Dr. Shevlin, but rather the other way round."

An embarrassed Jamie pulled on his earlobe, ran a hand over his carefully arranged comb-over. "Oh, I know what you're sayin' right enuff, Miss . . . Miss—"

"King!"

"Aye, Miss King. It . . . it won't happen again, so it won't. It's just that . . . just that Bertie Frogget—he's the auctioneer—couldn't fit me in no later, like."

"Yes, well, just so you know . . . for the future. In the scheme of things, doctors are rather more important people than livestock auctioneers." There was a pause, which Jamie filled by coughing and the secretary filled by recapping her fountain pen. "Now, as it happens, Dr. Shevlin arrived early today to catch up on some paper-work. So, just this once, I'll pop in and see if he'd be willing to see you now. There are no guarantees, mind."

"Oh, that would be grand, Miss King. Thank you very much."

———

By the time Jamie McCloone shuffled into the office, Dr. Henry Shevlin had already fully acquainted himself with the patient's medical history. He'd encapsulated the man's recent past in a series of bullet points penciled into his notebook:

- Occupation: farmer and part-time musician
- 1972: first major depressive episode when his adoptive "uncle" dies. James is 39
- Becomes alcohol dependent. Follows a course of antidepressants
- 1974: attempts suicide

- Relatively sober for past ten years. Has been taking Indalpine for three weeks
- Lives on his own on a small farm outside Tailorstown
- Reasons for return of depression and alcohol abuse: unknown

"I'm Dr. Shevlin," Henry said, getting up and extending a hand in greeting. "How are you, James?"

"Not so bad, Doctor. Dr. Brewster said I should come and see you, so he did." Jamie put his cap back on. Gazed about distracted. Then removed it again. "Don't know why he thought I should see you. 'Cos there's nothing much wrong with me."

"Well, he thought you might benefit from a little chat. Nothing to worry about. Please, take a seat."

The farmer backed himself into the chair. Misjudged the distance, and to Henry's astonishment, landed smack bang on the floor.

"What the blue blazes is . . . ?"

"Oh goodness, let me help you," Henry said, moving swiftly from behind his desk to help Jamie up. "Are you all right?" At close quarters, the smell of alcohol was explanation enough.

"Thanks, Doctor," Jamie said, dazed. "Don't know what happened tae me there."

Henry guided him into the chair. "I'll get you a glass of water."

"Aye . . . Aye, a glass of watter would be the thing. Sorry about that, Doctor."

"Oh, no need to apologize, James." Jamie's face was turning the color of a harvest moon. "Accidents happen to the best of us."

He watched as Jamie guzzled the water, making a noise like a hog in a barrel. Then, judging that his client was sufficiently recovered, he took his seat behind the desk again.

Jamie put the glass down on the desk and wiped his mouth. "Thanks for . . . thanks for seein' me early, Doctor, 'cos, as I was tellin' that lassie out there, I have a couple'a cows tae sell and they'll be—"

"That's fine, James. No problem at all. You're a cattle-farmer, then?"

"Aye."

"You enjoy the work? I'm sure it's hard."

"Och, it's all right. I love working with the animals, Doctor. Farm's not terrible big. Ten or so acres, so there isn't a lot tae be done . . ."

Henry had not met many farmer-types in his former practice in Belfast, but he got the impression he'd be meeting a lot more like Jamie in the days to come. Bachelors living on smallholdings in the rural community, suffering crippling loneliness, their emotional needs unmet, and filling the void with alcohol.

"Any other animals apart from cows?"

"Aye, as well as the cows I have a sow and four hens . . . and ten or so sheep on the mountain. But there's less work with them."

"Sounds like you're a busy man."

"Aye . . . I suppose . . ." Jamie sat with an elbow on each knee, directing most of his answers at the floor.

Henry cast about for something to ease the farmer's obvious discomfort. He glanced out the window and was confronted by a very unusual sight. Parked perilously close to his white Mercedes-Benz SL280 in the Reserved for Staff bay was a mud-spattered tractor. He got up to take a closer look. "I take it that's your tractor out there?"

Jamie roused himself. "Aye, that's her, all right."

"Looks like a very reliable machine. Have you had it long?"

Jamie brightened. "God, Doctor, that tractor's as oul' as me."

"My goodness! I take it, then, that it belonged to your uncle." Henry made a mental note to inquire about the "adoptive" uncle. But that would come later.

"Aye, that's Uncle Mick's Ford-Ferguson Model 9N. It was the first tractor in Ireland tae have a three-point hydraulic hitch and rubber tires, so it was."

"Really! How very interesting." Henry was glad he'd found an area of interest where Jamie could forget his blunder with the chair and lose himself for a while. "Pardon my ignorance, but what is a three-point hydraulic hitch?"

"Well, you see, it's so you can tow a plough or hay-shaker on the back of it. It goes at twenty horsepower, 'cos it has a three-cylinder engine."

The doctor took his seat again. He was happy to see that Jamie had lost his disconsolate look and was sitting more upright in the chair.

"How interesting! Wasn't it Henry Ford who said his only competition was the horse?"

"Aye, that was him, all right. Is that your white car, Doctor?"

"Yes, that's mine. Do you have a car yourself?"

"Naw, never bothered with them. The tractor does me all right, and me bicycle. Takes me into the town and home again. If I have tae go anywhere a bit farther, Paddy and Rose take me."

"Paddy and Rose are family, are they?"

"Naw, not family. They're good neighbors of mine, so they are. They take me tae Mass of a Sunday and the like."

Henry was glancing at his pencil-written notes. He read the first.

"I understand you're a part-time musician, James. What is it you play?"

He was regretting the words as soon as he'd uttered them. He recalled putting the same question to a Belfast patient several months before: Gavin Considine, a man in his late sixties with bushy gray sideburns and a paunch. Before Henry could stop him, Gavin had whipped a small harmonica from an inside pocket, put it to his lips, and launched into a medley of Larry Adler's greatest hits. The impromptu jazz performance had continued for a good ten minutes before Henry could—tactfully—put an end to it. He hoped that the harmonica was not Mr. James McCloone's choice of musical instrument.

He need not have worried. "I play the accordjin, Doctor," Jamie said proudly.

"Ah! A lovely instrument. There are two types, aren't there? A big one . . . What's this they call it? The piano accordion. And the . . ."

"Mine's a Hohner two-row button," Jamie said with even more pride. "They're wild hard boys tae play, so they are. The pianner accordjin is easier—though there's them that say it's harder, what with all that pushin' and pullin', and the shoulders would be cut off you by the end of an evening."

"Sounds fascinating. And are you in a band or what?"

"Nah, just meself, Doctor. I give them the odd tune in O'Shea's of a Sa'rday night, so I do." He looked at the floor in an endearingly modest manner. "There's them that would say I'm the best they've heard. Rose and Paddy and the like."

"I'm sure they're right." Henry smiled and glanced quickly at his bullet list. "Indalpine. Are they helping much?"

"Helping a bit, Doctor. Make me tired all the time."

"I know. They sometimes have that effect . . . When did you start drinking again?"

The good doctor had put the question in a light, almost casual tone of voice. Long, hard experience had taught him that it was the method that worked best. He'd schooled himself in taking his client by surprise. When the guard was down.

"The drinkin'?" Jamie looked up at the ceiling. "Must be the three weeks now. Naw, more than that. Must be the month. Aye, the month. When wee . . . when wee . . ."

He could not finish. Silence.

Henry broke it. "You see, your tiredness is down to the fact that antidepressants and alcohol don't mix, James. How much do you drink?"

Jamie shifted in the chair, uncomfortable. "Ah, well now . . . maybe a couple of half ones and a stout now and again."

"Half ones being whiskey, I take it?"

"Aye, a wee Johnny Powers . . . now and again."

"'Now and again' would be how many times a week? Once, twice, three times?"

"Oh . . . well, now . . . It's hard . . . hard to say right, Doctor, 'cos . . . 'cos I don't count them, like."

Henry suppressed a grin and scanned his notes again. "Hmm . . . I see you'd been off it for ten years. That's quite an achievement. Not many people are as strong-willed as you, you know." He pushed the notes aside and leaned across the desk. "So, James, together—you and me—over the next few weeks, we're going to talk about ways to get you back to your sober self. You can tell me anything and it will stay in this room."

"Aye . . . maybe. God, Doctor, is that the time?!" Jamie jumped up and pulled on his cap. "Me cows will be up in ten minutes. I've got tae go."

"Don't forget your appointment next week!" Henry called out to Jamie's back as he fled the room.

He went to the window and watched the farmer clamber up into the seat of his tractor. Winced at the swiftness with which he reversed the vehicle, narrowly missing the rear fender of the Mercedes convertible, and roared off.

A sharp tap had Henry turning round. Miss King stood in the doorway.

"I apologize for that, Dr. Shevlin. I should have warned you that often the care of one's livestock takes precedence over the care of one's mental health in these parts. I fear it's a hazard of the job."

"I have a lot to learn, Edith."

"Yes, a country practice must be quite a jolt after a hospital in Belfast. Not to worry. I'll keep you on the straight and narrow."

Henry smiled. He was in no doubt Miss King meant what she said.

"A cup of tea, perhaps? I'm sure you could use one."

"Splendid, Edith. Just splendid!"

Chapter eleven

Ruby, are you in there? Wake up this minute!"
Ruby woke with a start, her mother's voice clanging in her ears.
She sat up in the bed, shocked to see she was still fully clothed.
Around her lay the contents of Edna's case.

Reality dawned.

"Oh dear God!" She jumped up. "Aye, Mammy, I'm comin'.
I'm comin'. I must of slept in." She piled everything back in the case
and stuck it under the bed.

The door handle was being agitated vigorously. "Open this
door this minute!"

Ruby straightened the bedspread. Checked that nothing had
fallen. Ran a brush through her hair at the mirror. Took a deep
breath and pulled the door open.

"What in God's holy name's going on here? What time d'you
call this? Where's my breakfast?" Mrs. Clare stood in her night
attire, firing queries into the dartboard that was Ruby's heart.

"My-my alarm mustn't have . . . have went off. W-What . . . what
time is it?"

"A quarter to nine: that's what time it is, and I'm seeing the solicitor at half past. What's got into you? Why weren't you up at seven like you always are?"

"Don't know. Wasn't . . . wasn't able to get to sleep. I'll make your breakfast now."

"About time, too." The mother scanning the bedroom, keen for clues to this untypical transgression. "What's that on the floor?"

Ruby froze. Had she forgotten to lift something?

"Nothing. I need to clean up later. The room's a mess." She bundled her mother into the corridor and pulled the door shut. "I'll get us a cuppa tea."

She hastened down the stairs. "You get ready. I'll not be a minute."

———

Half an hour later, they were on the road, speeding toward Tailorstown. Ruby at the wheel of the old Ford Cortina, guilt and shame churning in her head like mixer gravel. What if she hadn't locked the door? What if her mother had seen the case?

"BUT YOU DID. AND SHE DIDN'T."

The voice!

She swerved across the road.

"What in God's name are you doing?"

"Sorry, Mammy, me hand slipped."

"YOU ARE PROTECTED."

"I am?"

"*I am what?* What's got into you? What are you saying?" Martha Clare, still high on the boil. Ruby's transgression setting the tone for a whole day of hectoring. She sat rigid in her Sunday best, mushroom dress and buff sandals, handbag clasped tightly in her lap.

"Sorry, Mammy."

"And why did you have your bedroom door locked? What's *that* about?"

"I THOUGHT I HEARD A NOISE DOWNSTAIRS."

"I thought . . . I thought I heard a noise downstairs."

"THAT'S WHY I WOKE UP AND COULDN'T GET BACK TO SLEEP."

"That's why I woke up and couldn't get back to sleep."

"SO I LOCKED THE DOOR, TO BE ON THE SAFE SIDE."

"So I locked the door, to be on the safe side."

"Could you not have gone down and looked, then?"

"I WAS AFRAID TO."

"I was afraid to."

"Oh, you were afraid to, were you? It was all right that *I* was lying asleep with my door wide open. You didn't have much thought for *me*, did you? Could have been murdered in my bed. But as long as *you* were safe, what did you care?"

"LOCK YOUR DOOR FROM NOW ON, THEN. WOULDN'T THAT BE THE SENSIBLE THING TO DO?"

"Lock your door from now on, then. Wouldn't that be the sensible thing to do?" Ruby had the words out before knowing it. Someone else was speaking through her—and she knew who it was.

Mrs. Clare turned in the seat, appalled.

"How dare you tell me what to do in my own home?!"

"IT'S MY HOME, TOO."

Ruby stared straight ahead. Her mouth clamped shut.

"GO ON, SAY IT. *SAY IT!* IT'S MY HOME, TOO."

"It's my home, too."

The mother slapped the dashboard hard.

"Stop this car this minute!"

Ruby kept her eyes steady on the road. She found her grip on the steering wheel relaxing. A calmness was descending, unknotting the tension, not only in her hands but in her stomach and head as well. It was a good feeling. She was free. Free to say what she felt. The words flowing from her like the purest water, pooling into sentences that were hers and hers alone.

"You want to get to Mr. Cosgrove's on time, don't you? You were in an awful hurry to leave the house. So, really, there is no time to stop."

"Right, that's it! You're not yourself. I'm going to ask Dr. Brewster to get you in. I've had enough of you. Causing all that upset for May and June at the weekend. Now *this*."

"What upset? May and June caused it by talking nonsense. And you finished it by hitting me. I did nothing wrong. So if anyone needs to 'go in,' as you say, it's perhaps all three of you." She looked across at her mother. "But most especially *you*."

The color had drained from Mrs. Clare's face. She was apoplectic with rage.

"Oh Jesus, what have I reared at all? Father Kelly will have to come and pray over you. 'Cos the Divil himself is standing in you to the neck."

Ruby ignored her. She slowed for the thirty-mile zone and cruised down the main street.

"Let me out of this car. Let me out this minute!" The mother frantic now, fumbling for the door catch.

"Well, you'll just have to wait until I stop," Ruby said.

She swung the vehicle left, reversed into a spot on the main square, and cut the engine.

Martha clambered out, her cane clattering to the ground. Ruby went to her aid.

"Don't you dare touch me! I'm warning you. You've done it this time."

"Done what?"

"You just wait till I get you home."

"Then what? Slap me again? I'm thirty-three, not thirteen."

"You'll not talk to me like that. By *Christ*—"

"How are you, Mrs. Clare?" A jaunty male voice.

They turned to see Father William Kelly, the local parish priest, raising a trilby off his shiny pate.

Martha's face burned with embarrassment. Had he heard her take the name of "the Lord Thy God" in vain? By heaven, Ruby would pay for that! She rallied to repair the damage with an ingratiating smile.

"Oh-oh, hello there, Father. And how . . . how are *you*, yourself?"

Father Kelly, a tall, thin man with weatherworn cheeks and a Greek nose, put a hand to his left ear—the one through which he funneled, filtered, and forgave all the sins of the parish—and stepped closer. "Can't complain, Mrs. Clare. Can't complain."

"That's good to hear, Father. I'm just on my way to see the solicitor, myself."

"Yes, indeed, Mrs. Clare. Hope that goes all right for you."

"Thank you, Father."

He turned his attention to Ruby, who was busying herself, locking the car. "And how are you, Ruby?"

"Fine, Father. Th—"

"Isn't she such a great help to you, Mrs. Clare?"

Ruby, ignored as usual. Her presence at her mother's side so constant as to render her invisible.

"Would you mind calling in with us, Father?" the mother said, shooting her daughter a fierce look. "Need to have a wee word with you about something."

"Not atall, Mrs. Clare. Any evening this week suit you?"

"That's good, Father. Oh, any evening that suits *you*. I'm always in the house."

"Good! Good!" He clapped his hands together and rubbed them vigorously as if about to warm them over a fire. "Well, if you'll excuse me, ladies, I must be on my way. Good day to you now."

When he'd taken off, Martha mounted the steps to Mr. Cosgrove's office without looking back.

"I'll do the shopping and come back for you in half an hour!" Ruby called out.

The mother turned, gave her a look that would kill a scorpion, before disappearing through the office doors.

Ruby sat back in the driver's seat. The strange calmness was ebbing away from her now. She felt faint. Her heart was beating like a cornered rabbit's. She gazed across at the cattle market. Friday was Fair Day, when farmers sold their cattle at auction. She had accompanied her father on many occasions and would sit in the car, just like now, watching as he chatted to his neighbors and finalized deals. She'd often begged to join him, but he'd insist it was no place for a woman.

She pictured him chatting to the auctioneer, Albert Frogget. Sharing a cigarette with him. Laughing heartily at one of his jokes. The other men milling about, slapping him good-heartedly on the back. He was popular with everyone. Then suddenly remembering his daughter and giving her the thumbs-up. A sign that he'd got a good price. At 12:30, the best part: fish and chips in the Cozy Corner Café.

Ruby sneaked a look at the café now, as if testing herself. But the steamed-up window with the gold lettering was just too much to bear. She fumbled in her pocket for a tissue and dabbed her eyes. Heard her father cracking jokes with the proprietor, Biddy Mulhern.

"Biddy, you're the best cook in Ulster. Better than Delia Smith, begod!"

"Och, away with you, Vinny!"

She'd never been inside the café since his death. How difficult it would be to step through those doors again! Sit down at the same table and face that empty chair. No, she could never do it.

Never.

She looked down at the shopping list. First stop: the post office, to collect her mother's pension. Then the supermarket, to get the sundry items, which rarely changed from week to week: flour, tea-bags, sugar . . .

A fat tear plopped down onto the paper, and all at once the words were running into each other, the milk into the butter, and the cocoa into the flour. Ruby swallowed down the pain. What if someone saw her like this? She kept her head down, dried her eyes and tried to compose herself.

"You are protected."

"No, I'm not! I've got no one. *No one.*"

Silence.

"Bring Daddy back, then. Please, bring Daddy back!" Ruby sobbing anew into her handkerchief.

"'Tis when the moon is at her peak / That weighty answers thou shouldst seek."

The poem. The poem in Grandma Edna's book.

"Raise the curv'd blade at the moon / On the twenty-first of June . . ."

"Why? What's the twenty-first of June?"

The voice more urgent-sounding now.

"This rite shall make thy dreams come true / And won-drous powers shall thee accrue."

"And you'll make my dreams . . . come true? You mean I'll . . . I'll see Daddy again? And I'll have . . . my own money? And . . . I'll meet someone—"

The sudden roaring of a tractor brought Ruby abruptly back to the present. There, tearing down Main Street, exhaust smoke pluming like gusts of demonic breath, was a man she thought she recognized.

He swerved the tractor into a space by the market stalls, spewing up gravel, and climbed down. It was only when he reset his cap and pulled on his right ear that she realized who it was: Jamie McCloone.

He disappeared into the crowd. Ruby's heart had lifted at the sight of him. She was hoping she'd see him again, and there he was. Maybe if she got the shopping over with quickly, she might run into him roundabout.

Inspired, she locked the car and made her way first to the post office, to collect the pension.

Doris Crink, on her knees behind the counter locating a fallen penny, was alerted by the ping of the doorbell.

"Hello, Ruby," she said, materializing like a crone in a folk tale, breathless from the search. "God, me knees are killing me, so they are."

Doris had been a fixture in the Tailorstown post office for more than two decades. Delicate, faded as a pressed flower, she complained of more ailments than would be present in a doctor's waiting room on a wet Monday.

"But it's to be expected with age, Ruby. A big, strong girl like you wouldn't know anything about that now."

Ruby smiled shyly. "My mother complains of her knees, too."

"What?"

Ruby leaned closer, taking in a lungful of rosewater scent. "I say: my mother complains of her knees, too, Doris."

Doris pulled a face and fiddled with an earpiece.

"Sorry, Ruby, had me hearing aid turned down 'cos of market day. The shouts and filthy language of them men out there would make a sailor blush. Now, who did you say had the knees?"

"Me mother, Doris."

"Och, aye, yer poor mother. But at least she's got her ears."

"That's true. Nothing wrong with her hearing." Ruby extracted the pension book from her handbag and laid it on the counter. These conversations with Doris usually followed the same pattern and could endure for ever.

She was anxious to get on.

"D'you know, between me ears and me knees I'm nearly kilt, so I—"

"You'll not friggin' do *me*, you squinty-eyed wee bastard!"

The raised voice reaching through the open window had Doris wincing and ducking, as though hit by a hammer.

"Oh dearie me!" She rushed over and looked out. "I *thought* it was poor Jamie's voice."

Ruby joined her, and, to her amazement, saw Jamie McCloone and the auctioneer, Albert Frogget, grappling with each other outside the market stalls. Jamie had Albert in a headlock, and both men were staggering round in circles like a couple of drunken crabs.

"Go on, Jamie, give him another belt!" someone shouted. But, at the command, the pair fell in a heap.

"Jamie who?" Ruby asked, feigning ignorance and wanting to learn more about the farmer.

"Jamie McCloone, God help him. It's that old drink that puts him like that. And he was doing so well, so he—"

Doris's comment was cut short by the wail of a police siren. Abruptly, an RUC Land Rover screeched to a halt, scattering the knot of spectators. Doris crossed herself.

"Oh dearie, dearie me," she said again. "The police."

The ladies watched as the passenger door shot open and resident police chief, the burly, red-faced Sergeant Ranfurley, stepped out, followed by a junior constable.

Ranfurley marched over to the fallen pair. He hauled Mr. Frogget to his feet with one hand and Jamie with the other. The sudden action had the farmer's cap falling off, revealing a rather unsightly comb-over. The crowd jeered.

"Did you forget tae put on yer toupee, Jamie?" someone shouted.

Ruby felt the shame that Jamie must have been feeling, as he scrambled to put the cap back on. She wanted to run over to the heckler, whom she recognized as the local bad boy, Chuck Sproule, and kick him hard on the shins.

Ranfurley barked something at his subordinate, who promptly handcuffed Jamie. Without ceremony, he was frogmarched to the Land Rover and pushed into the back.

The crowd booed and jeered as the vehicle roared off.

Doris turned away from the window, shaking her head sadly, and went back behind the counter.

"It's because of his dog, you see." She took a well-thumbed register from underneath the desk and opened it at the letter C.

"Did it die?"

Doris looked up at Ruby, a wistful look in her eyes, and nodded.

She stamped the pension book twice and pulled open a drawer.

"Here you go, Ruby: ten, twenty, thirty-five pounds, and . . ." She scooped some coins from the drawer. ". . . and fippence. He misses the wee dog something terrible. Nobody to keep him company no more. Men are no good on their own when they get to a sartain age. And poor Jamie, God bless him, well, he's not the marrying kind. A lonely soul."

The doorbell pinged again and Charlie Mutch—an animated toby jug on legs—blundered in, bringing the unwelcome odor of the cattle yard with him.

"Did you see that, Doris?"

"God, Charlie, what happened anyway?"

"Jamie was late, and Bertie Frogget went ahead and sold his heifer for less than what he wanted."

"God, I hope Sergeant Ranfurley doesn't put poor Jamie in jail."

"Och, I wouldn't think so. But you never know with that oul' Unionist bully."

Ruby excused herself and left them to it. "Not the marrying kind," Doris had said. It was a phrase she heard often.

———

She passed through the doors of Digney's supermarket and picked up a basket. Her mother had already decided that she, Ruby, was "not the marrying kind," either. But . . .

"LAY THE CARDS, COME RAIN OR SNOW / AND ALL OUR FUTURES THEY SHALL SHOW."

"The cards in the case? Of course! The answers to all my questions are in the case."

"Are you all right, Ruby?" a female voice broke in.

Ruby, standing in one of the aisles, staring at packets of washing powder, hadn't even noticed the shop assistant on her knees, stacking a shelf with bottles of bleach.

"Hello, Marian. Didn't see you there."

"It's the first sign of madness, you know," Marian said with an impish grin. She got up.

"What is?"

"Talking to yourself."

"Was I?"

"Well, if you weren't, maybe I was hearing things. Which wouldn't surprise me in this place . . . Looking for anything in particular?"

"Just the usual. Oh, there *is* something, Marian. Candles."

"Just farther along there." She pointed down the aisle. "Towards the end. Having an intimate supper for two then?"

"What?"

"Oh, don't mind me, Ruby . . . only kidding."

"Any green ones?"

"Sorry, only white and silver, I'm afraid. We only get colored ones in at Christmas."

Green—for life and nature—was the color of the Goddess. But Ruby had also learned the meaning of gold and silver in *The Book of Light*. The sun was God, the male aspect, symbolized by gold. The moon was the Goddess, the female aspect, symbolized by silver.

So silver would do just as well, then.

She reached for four and put them in the basket, an altar to Dana taking shape in her mind. Yes, she'd build an altar. She'd pray to the Goddess, for guidance. Edna had written instructions on how to build one and the voice would tell her what to do.

"How are you, Ruby?"

Ruby turned to see Ida Nettles peering into her basket. "Oh, Ida! Didn't see you there."

"Nice candles . . . Is your electric out or something?"

"No-no . . . it's not. I just . . . I just—"

"No, it wouldn't be, or you'd be buyin' just ordinary white ones." Ida regarded Ruby, tiny eyes a-glimmer, waiting for her to explain the purchase.

"It's really none of your business what I want the candles for, is it?"

"It's really none of your business what I want the candles for, is it?"

Ida's mouth fell open. She took a step back. Ruby loved the sudden surge of confidence the voice gave her.

Now it was time the nosy Mrs. Nettles explained *herself*. Ruby peered into Ida's basket. She spotted a pack of Colorsilk hair dye.

"Beeline Honey . . . nice color," she said mischievously. "And there was me thinking, Ida, that that lovely hair of yours was natural."

Ida reddened. "You're not yourself, Ruby Clare!" she spat, her little face contorting with rage. "I'm gonna be having a word with your mother, so I am. She said she thought you were going off."

With that she stormed off, leaving Ruby torn between dread of what might be coming—and satisfaction that she'd scored a small victory over the gossipy Mrs. Nettles.

Chapter twelve

S inclair Shevlin, onetime magistrate, now a spry septuagenarian, had opened his front door before Henry had a chance to ring the bell.

"The Mater just called," he said gravely. "A colleague of yours. Said his name was Batman."

Henry smiled to himself, despite his predicament.

"That would be Bill *Bach*man. He's covering for me. What did he want?"

"He said that somebody-or-other was refusing her medication. Why aren't you at work? You look terrible, by the way. Are you ill?"

"No. I'll explain in a minute." Henry followed his father into the open-plan kitchen, wondering how he was going to break the news about Connie. He always felt a little uneasy in his home. The elder Shevlin was a fastidious man; "hypervigilant" in psychobabble terms. He insisted his surroundings were as ordered and sterile as a forensic laboratory. Since his wife's death he'd gone through more cleaning ladies than the reclusive business magnate, Howard Hughes.

"He said you'd know what to do," Sinclair said over his shoulder, heading toward the sink. He lifted the kettle. "Cup of coffee?"

"Please. Do I need to call him?"

"No, he said he could handle it until you got back. He just wanted you to know that everything is under control." The elder Shevlin paused. "Oh yes, and he said that the manic session group was more challenging than he'd expected it to be. If that makes sense to you."

"It does. Thanks."

"What on earth's a manic session group?"

"Manic *depression* group. You misheard."

"Well, you know my opinion of all that tomfoolery. People talk about themselves far too much these days without *you* encouraging it. In my day, you put up, shut up, and got on with things. All that rummaging about in the past gets you nowhere."

"Where may I sit?" Henry knew that it was always better to ask. His father had issues regarding territory as well: certain chairs were for the senior Shevlin only.

"That one there," Sinclair said, pointing to a chair by the table.

Henry sighed and sat down, but said nothing. Yes, he'd heard his father's views on psychiatry often enough. Sinclair had taken it as a given that his son would follow him into the legal profession and was very disappointed when he didn't. But, sitting there exhausted and knowing how fond his father was of Connie, he was reluctant to break the bad news. For the present, he'd just give the old man the luxury of having his say unchallenged.

"Facts, facts, facts! That's what I care about, Henry. I've always dealt in facts. Tangibles." He handed him a mug of coffee. "What can be experienced by the five senses. Evidence: that's what I'm talking about. Where would we be without evidence? Eh? In the old days, I gave short shrift to any barrister who came to me with hearsay and innuendo. Was I right? Of course I was. But psychiatry? Hmph! Psychiatry isn't a science. Voodoo, that's all it is. Stuff you make up as you go along."

Henry sighed again. "If you say so, Father. But I'll have you know that the 'tomfoolery' I engage in is helping more people than you think. No, you're right. My therapy isn't a science in the strict sense, but the results are there, and we're pushing the boundaries all the time. We're finding out more and more about the human psyche." He pointed a finger. "And what are you judges and magistrates doing? All you do is punish people. You fine people or send them to jail. Fair enough, you're keeping the baddies off the streets, but we're the men who are trying to *improve* them, to make sure that they stay out of jail when they serve their sentences."

Henry sat back in the chair. "But enough of that. I didn't come here to cross swords with you. There's something I need to tell you."

"Oh . . . ?"

"It's . . . it's Connie. She's gone missing."

"Good Lord!" Sinclair set his mug down slowly and stared at him.

"She went for a walk on Wednesday and never returned. I—"

"You've informed the police?"

"Police? Yes, yes, of course. They've interviewed me twice. Suppose it's natural for them to assume that the husband's . . ."

"I'm sorry, Henry. I didn't know. Good God."

"I'm at my wits' end, if you must know. I've taken leave of absence from the hospital. That's why Bill Bachman's standing in for me."

Henry placed his briefcase on the table and undid the hasps. He drew out a sheaf of printed papers and placed one face upward. It showed a black-and-white photograph of an attractive lady with light-colored hair tied back. She was looking into the lens in the manner of a police mug shot. Large, bold letters above her head posed a question.

HAVE YOU SEEN THIS WOMAN?

Sinclair Shevlin read the rest of the message in grim silence. He returned the poster to the little pile.

"Good God," he said again.

"I've just been round all the libraries and post offices in Belfast. A couple of people at the hospital offered to put more up on lampposts in our area. Every little helps."

Sinclair got up and stood by the window, looking out. "I don't know what to say. Do you think she was unhappy? Did she give any indication that . . . ?"

"I'm still trying to get my head around it. That's strange language for a therapist to use, isn't it? But I can't understand any of it, Father. Why would she leave without saying a word? It's not as if we had a row or anything."

"No?"

"Oh, I know what you're thinking. And the police wanted to go down that road as well. But I assure you Connie and I were getting on very well."

Sinclair took his chair again. "Really?"

Henry abruptly stopped stirring his coffee. He was frowning. "What do you mean?"

"You know very well what I mean, son. It was obvious to me that you and Constance didn't see eye to eye on a great many matters. Your mother used to—"

"Leave Mother out of this!"

"How can I? You know very well she disapproved of Constance, right from the very start. She gave the two of you a year at most."

"Well, we know why that was, don't we, Father?"

The older man sighed. "We do. But please don't include me in it. Your mother had her views and I had mine. A girl's religion is of no interest to *me*. Never was."

"Mother was from the old school, of course. I can hear her now: 'I'm not sure I like the idea of a son of mine mixing with the other sort.' You'd have thought that Roman Catholics were the bubonic plague, the way she went on about them."

Sinclair patted Henry's shoulder. "I know, I know. It was a bit embarrassing right enough. But if I'm honest, Henry, I'm surprised you and Constance stayed together so long. Chalk and cheese. And I'm not talking about religion now. Polar opposites. Nothing in common, as far as I could see. You were too grounded for her."

"Rubbish! And stop talking about us in the past tense."

"Sorry, but wasn't it only last summer that she wanted to emigrate?"

Henry laughed shortly.

"Oh, that was nothing. Lots of people feel that way after a holiday abroad. There's even a technical term for it—in psychiatry-speak I mean. We call it post-travel depression."

"Oh dear. Why am I not surprised?" Sinclair shook his head slowly and sipped his coffee. He grimaced and reached for the sugar bowl. He ignored his son's frown of disapproval as he added two heaped spoonfuls to his mug. Both looked up instinctively at the sound of a low-flying helicopter. Business as usual in Northern Ireland, even here in Lisburn, the upscale, leafy suburb of Belfast.

"Did you phone her sister . . . What's her name?"

"Betty. First thing I did. Betty hadn't heard from her."

In clipped sentences, Henry related his actions of the previous days—and nights—leaving out nothing. The police questioning, in particular that of Sergeant Hanson, had focused his mind. It was helpful, too, he reasoned, to go over those details again and again. He was also of the opinion that, sooner or later, the verbalization of an obscure and minor detail would trigger a memory, one that lay long buried. Or generate a fresh insight, one that might solve the puzzle. Was this not what Henry put into practice in his therapy, the advice he gave to even his most difficult patients? He thought of the flowery words of one of his heroes, the Victorian philosopher

James Allen: "Every thought seed sown or allowed to fall into the mind, and to take root there, produces its own, blossoming sooner or later into act, and bearing its own fruitage of opportunity and circumstance."

It didn't work now, however. Henry sat back in his chair, a dark depression creeping over him.

Sinclair sensed it. "What about Greece?"

"What about it?"

"Well, I know I shouldn't be playing the shrink now—that's your job—but I was thinking that perhaps Constance remembered her happiest moments, and wanted to relive them. The pair of you were *so* very happy when you returned from that holiday in Crete. Constance never stopped singing the praises of the hotel. The Hype . . . Hypo . . ."

"The Hyperion."

"That's the one. You wouldn't think of giving them a call, would you? You never know."

"I've already checked. Did it as soon as I discovered her passport was missing. But, alas, no."

"Passport missing? Are you certain of that?"

"Well, it isn't in its usual place. And anyway, she didn't leave the country. The police have already checked airports and ferry crossings. At least, they claim they have."

"Oh dear."

"And her bank account. No withdrawals." Henry's face darkened. Sharing the raw facts of the situation with his father was making him conscious for the first time of how hopeless things looked.

He sat forward in his chair again and stared at Sinclair. A thought had struck him.

"What makes you think Connie wasn't happy? I never said she wasn't happy."

"You didn't need to, son. She told me herself. About a month ago."

"What?!"

"She came to see me. And not for the first time, either. Told me I was one of the few people she could confide in. Made me promise I wouldn't tell you. But—"

"She never told *me*." Hurt and angry.

"No. She knew you wouldn't understand. She said you were too wrapped up in your work. That was how she put it: 'Henry's far too wrapped up in his work.' She felt that other people's happiness meant more to you than hers. Strangers. Your patients." He pointed at an armchair. "She broke down over there. Sobbing her heart out. I didn't know *what* to do, son."

"You could have told me; that's what you could have done."

"No. Constance practically swore me to secrecy. I saw her glancing over at that old Bible of mine a couple of times. The one the court people gave me when I retired. I think she wanted me to swear on it. That's how desperate she was."

Henry was staring at the floor, his coffee barely touched.

"If you'd told me, maybe all this could have been avoided."

"Yes, son. I can see that now. But I was caught between the two of you. I advised her to see a therapist. Talk things over with a stranger. Isn't that what you yourself would advocate?"

"Did she . . . Was there someone else?"

"Absolutely not."

"How can you be so sure?"

"Well, to be honest, she was quite harsh on the subject of marriage. Ideal setup for the male, in her opinion. Women as chattels. You know, the usual feminist guff. Men cause wars, and make the world—"

"She never talked like that to *me*."

"Well, just goes to show you never really know anyone, Henry, no matter how long you've been around them."

Sinclair rose and went to a bookshelf. He extracted an envelope from between two books.

"She sent me this about a fortnight ago. Don't know if the words are her own or quoted from someone else."

Henry withdrew a card with an illustration of a single white lily on the front.

He read over the words on the back, written in Connie's ornate hand.

Oh how shallow life is! In spite of all the parties, the pills, those drunken diversions we lose ourselves to so the darkness won't close in. But it's always there, that darkness, hovering like a revenant at the edge of things.

I wish, so dearly wish, I could make myself anew, come to the world afresh, into a place as yet unscathed by all that's gone before. For the life we live has been imposed upon us from the womb.

We are snared in the myths of generations past. Netted like fish that struggle for a time then die. In this imperfect world, there is no truth, I fear, no matter what they say. That thread was cut, our suffering: the price we pay.

Hope you understand, Sinclair. Thank you for listening.

Love,
Connie

Henry burst into tears. The betrayal: just too much. The meaning behind the words, so beautifully crafted, hitting him with a cruel and terrible certainty.

He heard his father sit down in an armchair. Imagined his turmoil. Heard him rise again. Felt his hand on his shoulder, gentle, reassuring.

"Here, son." A box of tissues appeared beside him on the table.

Sinclair: the therapist now. Henry: the patient in need of solace.

"Now, Henry . . . son. They're just words. You shouldn't read so much into them."

Henry took a tissue and wiped his eyes.

"Sorry," he said. "It's just that . . . it's just that . . ."

"I'll get us a brandy."

"Thanks." He pushed the card back into the envelope.

Sinclair returned to the table and sat down. He handed Henry the drink and watched as he gulped it down. "It's just *what*, Henry? You were going to tell me something just then."

"I was going to say that those words sound like something Plath would write . . . Sylvia Plath, an American poet."

"So? That's good, isn't it? If they're not Connie's."

Henry shook his head.

"When I . . . when I first met her at the hospital, after her suicide attempt, she had a book . . . some sort of journal of Plath's writings. She made a gift of it to me when she left. It was only when I read through it that I realized how bleak and depressing the material was. Personal, confessional stuff. Too much introspection for a young, impressionable woman like Connie. I told her as much when we met again and started seeing each other. She promised me she wouldn't read it again."

"So . . . I don't really understand. What are you saying exactly?"

Henry was focused on the brandy glass. "When she turned thirty, Sylvia Plath committed suicide. And Connie . . . Connie is . . . Three weeks ago she . . ."

He didn't need to finish the sentence; Sinclair was well aware of Connie's age.

And the implication of what his son could not bring himself to say.

A helicopter passed overhead again, the rumble of rotor blades sending tremors through the house. Sinclair appeared at Henry's side again, the brandy bottle in his hand. No words passed between them as he replenished his son's glass. He sat down opposite.

"There's more, isn't there?"

Henry nodded. He took a sip of brandy before replying.

"She left a note on Wednesday."

"Yes, you told me. A short note, saying she was going for a stroll."

"But I didn't tell you how she ended the note, Father. The police have it now, of course. But I memorized it, word for word." Henry smiled without humor. "Easy enough. There were only eight words."

"Go on."

"She wrote: 'Going for a walk, darling. Love you. Always.'"

"Hmm."

"It's that final word: 'Always.' I didn't think too much of it at the time. God knows I had more on my mind. But when I left the police station that night it kept bothering me. Connie had never used it before. When I got home I checked. I'd kept all her love letters, you see. Even her Valentine cards. Had them in a drawer. I took them out and went through them carefully, just to make sure I hadn't misremembered."

"No 'always'?"

Henry shook his head. "Never. Not once."

"So you think she was trying to tell you something? With the note? You think the note was . . ."

"I think she was saying good-bye, Father . . . Saying good-bye for good."

Chapter thirteen

In the quiet of the night, in the safety of her bedroom, with her mother asleep and the day's chores done, Ruby laid the objects from the case about her on the bed, sat back on the pillows, and opened *The Book of Light*. It was a portal to another world. Within its pages lay the meaning of life itself. She was sure of it.

She looked forward to that time. That time between the hours of midnight and two, when it seemed the whole universe slept. Except for her, and Edna . . . and Dana.

Ruby read.

I am Dana. I am inspiration. I am wisdom. I am the creator of all things. I am older than time itself. I am god. I am goddess. I am the Divine Source of all you see. I am everywhere. I am in every living thing. I am goddess of the land you walk on. I am goddess of the air you breathe. I am goddess of the water that gives you life.

I am the Divine Feminine. I am the Triple Goddess. I am the Holy Trinity. I am the Maiden. I am the Mother. I am the Crone.

Ruby turned the page and was pulled up short by an image. It showed a circle colored in red, with half-moons flanking it—one black, one white. She clutched the book, staring, a terrible fear taking hold. In the mysterious dream, she'd been wearing a pendant just like it as she lay in the coffin.

Oh my God, I *am* gonna die!

Her thought was answered by "the voice." Gentle, soothing, but decisive.

"THERE IS NO DEATH. YOU ARE PROTECTED."

Feeling slightly calmer, she studied the caption.

Symbol of the Triple Goddess
White moon = waxing crescent = Maiden, goddess of birth
Red = full moon = Mother, goddess of love
Black = waning crescent = Crone, goddess of death

"YOU ARE BIRTH. YOU ARE LOVE. YOU ARE DEATH."

Ruby, growing afraid. There was that word again: "death."

"But . . . but I am not . . . d-d-death. I'm not . . . dead?"

"YOU ARE LIFE. YOU ARE SPIRIT."

"But . . . but, I'm not dead."

"YOU WILL DIE TO SELF. YOU WILL RISE AGAIN TO SPIRIT."

The urge to shut the book, bundle everything back in the case and burn it, like her mother ordered, was strong. She tried to get off the bed, but couldn't. She was paralyzed with fear.

"Oh God, help me!" Sobbing now. "Daddy, help me."

"YOU ARE SPIRIT. YOUR FATHER RESTS IN SPIRIT."

Hopeful. "Can . . . can I see him?" Ruby's heart lifted.

"WADE IN WATERS STILL AND DEEP."

"What waters? Where?"

"WHERE THE LITTLE BOY DOTH SLEEP."

"The lake? You mean . . . You mean Beldam Lake? Where . . . where . . . wee Declan . . ."

She waited for an answer, but none came.

"But . . . but Declan's not in the lake. Declan's a wee angel in . . . in heaven."

"THERE IS NO HEAVEN."

Ruby, weeping now, imploring. "There *is*. Declan's an angel in heaven and . . . and . . . and Daddy's there. I know they're there."

"THERE IS NO HEAVEN. HEAVEN IS WITHIN."

"I . . . I don't understand. You mean . . . you mean Daddy and . . . and wee Declan are in . . . ?" Ruby could not bring herself to say the word. But the answer came, regardless.

"THERE IS NO HELL. HELL IS WITHOUT."

She felt her limbs loosen.

"But . . . but where . . . Where are they? Is . . . Daddy still in purgatory? Is . . . is wee Declan in . . . in limbo?"

"THEY ARE IN SPIRIT."

"But how can I *see* them?"

"OPEN YOUR EYES. OPEN YOUR HEART."

"But me eyes *are* open." Ruby, not understanding, widened her eyes in the dimly lit room.

Silence.

She reached over to the bedside locker to fetch a tissue, and as she did so, several of the objects fell to the floor. She heaved herself off the bed and got down on her knees to retrieve them. To her dismay, she saw that the cingulum had unraveled. She was about to gather it up when:

"CINGULUM SO UNABASED / BIND IT THREE TIMES 'BOUT THE WAIST."

Whether for good or ill, she found herself moving toward the mirror. She put the belt on over her nightdress, and was pleased to see that, despite her bulk, it did encircle her three times.

That done, she bent down to pick up the Tarot pack.

"LAY THE CARDS, COME RAIN OR SNOW / AND ALL OUR FUTURES THEY SHALL SHOW."

The voice was guiding her; she must trust the voice. She sat down on the bed again and, hesitantly, began shuffling the deck. Five cards fell, facedown. Her future lay before her.

Ruby stopped, afraid. Should she look at them? What if they were bad? But then . . . they might be good. Her hand shook as she turned the first one over. "The Hanged Man, XII." The image was startling.

It showed a man in red tights and a blue shirt suspended upside down on a tree-shaped cross. His left leg was tucked under his right leg, which was tied to the top of the tree. A bright yellow sun was radiating from behind his head. Strange thing was: he didn't look as though he were in any pain. He looked calm and peaceful. Encouraged, Ruby leafed through *The Book of Light*, to the section headed "Tarot & Meanings."

Give careful thought to the decisions you make. You must be willing to adapt to new circumstances. You are in a period of transition.

Ruby dwelt on the meaning. Well, she *was* in a period of transition, with her father gone. And these *were* new circumstances. So the card was right.

Hopeful, she flipped the second one. "The Tower, XVI." Her newfound optimism faded. The black card showed a tower on fire, and a man and woman falling headlong into the darkness, pain etched in their faces. She didn't want to learn the meaning, but maybe, like "The Hanged Man," it wasn't as bad as it looked.

An unexpected event will lead to great conflict. There will be disruption to your life. If you can withstand the challenge, the future will be bright.

Conflict, disruption, challenge. The words leaped off the page in warning. They spoke of dark things to come. She did not want to read any further. There were three cards remaining. Should she turn them over? What if they told of more misfortune? How would she feel?

"THERE IS NO DARKNESS. YOU ARE PROTECTED."

Without hesitation, she reached out and flipped the third card over.

"The Fool, 0." She brightened at the sight of the carefree, colorful image. A young man with a stick over his shoulder and a bag tied at the end of it. A white dog was yapping at his heels. He looked happy, but . . . she noticed an odd thing: he seemed totally unaware that he was about to step off a cliff edge. And why, just like "The Hanged Man," did he look totally unconcerned? Perplexed, she read the meaning: "*A new beginning.*"

The words from her dream floated back to her. "*A new beginning, Ruby. A new beginning.*" She read on.

A door is opening into a new world, free from the constraints of the past. Seek out new people. New experiences. Follow your intuition, not reason.

The reassurance she gleaned from that card quickly vanished with the image on the next one, the one numbered "IX"; an old man with a long, gray beard, wearing a hooded cloak. "The Hermit" was standing on a mountaintop, holding a lighted lantern in one hand and a staff in the other. But, while the figure looked doom-laden, its meaning was far from bleak.

You will search within for answers. The insight you have gained is precious. Spiritual enlightenment is yours.

With a light heart, Ruby turned over the final card. "The Star, XVII" showed a naked woman kneeling by a lake. She was collecting water in one vessel and, from another, pouring it onto the earth. Above her head shone a brilliant yellow star.

Hope and healing are yours. You have chosen the right path. Cleanse in the waters of life and you will be awakened. Renewal and beauty are yours.

Ruby inspected the image of the woman more closely. There was something about it that appealed to her. Then she realized what it was. The woman's body was just like hers, heavy and solid. She could have been looking at her own naked self.

Cleanse in the waters of life and you will be awakened.

She thought about Beldam Lake. She was being guided toward Beldam Lake! All answers lay there. In *The Book of Light* she found the poem again. *Bathe in waters pure and deep / If weighty answers thou shouldst seek.*

"WHERE THE LITTLE BOY DOTH SLEEP."

She jumped, so loud was the voice.

"But when?"

No answer.

She looked back at the poem again.

Raise the curv'd blade at the moon / On the twenty-first of June / This rite shall make thy dreams come true / And wondrous powers shall thee accrue.

She took her diary from the bedside locker and found the date. June 21. It was only ten days away. She peered more closely, and for the first time noticed something she hadn't seen before.

By the entry date there was a small circle, one half black. She now realized what the symbol meant. In Edna's book there was a Phases of the Moon chart; a circle divided into eight segments with phases of the moon, from the new to the "balsamic" phase.

An excitement took hold of her. The little symbol in her diary meant that, on the 21st, the moon would be in its first quarter. She knew what she had to do.

Raise the curv'd blade at the moon / On the twenty-first of June.

In ten days' time she'd be doing just that.

This rite shall make thy dreams come true / And wondrous powers shall thee accrue.

"My dreams . . . come true?" Ruby didn't need to refer to her three wishes at the back of her diary. She knew them by heart.

"In ten days' time I'll be seeing Daddy again. I'll be getting lots of money, and I'll be meeting somebody nice. Can it be true?"

Silence.

Suddenly, from downstairs, the sound of breaking glass.

Ruby jumped.

"What was *that*?"

An intruder? There had been one in the past. A harmless old vagrant who'd robbed a block of cheese from the larder. Still, she needed to make sure.

She picked up a tire iron she kept by the bed, expressly for that purpose, and crept down the stairs.

All the windows below were intact. Had she imagined hearing something?

It was only when she was turning to mount the stairs again that her flashlight picked up the gleam of glass by the pantry door. She shone the light into the alcove.

The picture of Michael the Archangel was no longer in place.

It had fallen off the wall. The glass lay shattered on the floor.

Ruby looked with dismay at the mess. Well, she was too tired to clear it up now. It would just have to wait until morning. She found a brush, and swept the glass under the table.

As she mounted the stairs, she tried to console herself. Maybe . . . maybe she hadn't replaced the picture properly earlier on. Maybe the nail holding it had come loose. After all, it had been hanging there a long, long time.

But, try as Ruby might, those words of her mother's from that conversation earlier on, kept pushing into her head.

"See that prayer . . . Saint Michael . . . She dropped it immediately as if she'd burned herself, and the glass broke. Then I knew for sure what *she was.*"

Chapter fourteen

Sergeant Ranfurley, overweight, overwrought, and overtired from a fitful night, was enjoying a brief respite from the day's affairs with a mug of tea and a ham sandwich, when his assistant, Constable Johnston, knocked on his door.

"What is it?" he barked between mouthfuls, not a little annoyed at the interruption.

"Woman to see you, Sarge."

"Who is she, and what the blazes does she want?"

"Rose-Mick-somebody . . . here with her husband, Paddy. She won't tell me what it's about. Sez she wants to speak to *you*, Sarge."

Ranfurley sighed. "Show her in, then." He bolted down the remainder of the sandwich. Set the mug aside.

The woman's voice reached the room before she did.

"Com'on, Paddy. We can't keep the sergeant waitin', so we can't."

Presently, filling the room, was a middle-aged lady, face flushed to the hue of her pink frock. She dwarfed her husband, following behind like an aging schoolboy in a cap and check jacket.

"God, Sergeant Ranfurley, thanks for seein' me. Rose McFadden's me name." She came forward and offered a gloved hand. "And this here's my Paddy."

"Good day to you, Mrs. McFadden . . . Mr. McFadden. Take a seat there, won't ye. Now what can I do ye for?"

"Well, it's like this," Rose began. "Biddy at the café . . . You know, Biddy at the Cozy Corner. She'd be a cousin of—"

"I do indeed," Ranfurley cut in. "What's she done?"

"Oh, not Biddy, Sergeant! Well, what I was gonna say was, Biddy tolt me, when me and my Paddy were in having a bitta lunch today, 'cos on a Fair Day we usually have a bitta lunch . . ."

The sergeant sighed and switched off. He really hoped he wasn't gonna hear what Mrs. McFadden had for the "bitta lunch." But he didn't doubt it for one minute. Since coming to this rural outpost, he'd met her like quite often. It was living in the bog that obviously made them like that; as noisy as a pack of bloody monkeys with their asses on fire whenever they caught sight of a man in uniform. When he tuned back in, he was pleased to hear that she'd finally got to the point.

". . . well, what Biddy tolt me was that she seen you take poor Jamie McCloone away this morning, in hand-muffs, so she did."

"Yes, what of it?" Ranfurley shuffled some papers on his desk to give the impression he was a busy man, and so indicate to Mrs. McFadden that she needed to get the point, sharpish.

Rose clasped her face with both hands and turned to her husband. "God-savus, it's true, Paddy."

"Aye, looks like it's true right enuff," Paddy confirmed.

"God, and there was me thinking maybe Biddy might'a been seeing things, 'cos"—she turned her attention to Ranfurley once more—"'cos, you know, Sergeant, the eyes were never good . . . got the stigmata in both of them . . . runs in her father's side of the family, so it does, and a body—"

"Are yins next of kin, Mrs. McFadden?"

"Oh no, Sergeant. Biddy's just—"

"I *meant* James McCloone's next of kin."

"Oh no, Sergeant. Me and my Paddy are good friends of Jamie's and we're worried about him, so we are. His wee dog died of recent and he misses him something terrible, so he does. What we were wonderin' . . . ?"

Ranfurley glanced at his watch, resisting the urge to take it off, hold it up to his ear and shake it, just to give Mrs. McFadden the hint that his time was precious. He made a mental note to self that he wouldn't be detaining McCloone anytime again soon, if he was going to have to deal with this bloody, blethering nuisance of a woman every time.

"Well, what we were wonderin' was: where would he be now, Sergeant? He's not in jail, is he?"

"He's in a cell, cooling off. He was booked this morning for disorderly conduct in a public place. Does that help you out?"

"Oh God-savus! Jamie arrested for dis-ordin'ry behavior, Paddy. That's terrible, so it is. He's never done nothing wrong in his life before, the critter. Oh dearie me."

"He has a problem with alcohol, Mrs. McFadden, but you don't need *me* tae tell you that."

"I know that old drink's a problem, Sergeant. Truth be tolt, it's a problem for many a man in these parts, my Paddy included, betimes. Isn't that right, Paddy?"

"Och, Rose, I'm not *that* bad."

Ranfurley looked at the doubtless long-suffering Paddy with a newfound respect, and concluded that the ideal marriage would surely be one between a blind woman and a deaf man.

". . . now, Jamie's no alcoholic . . . a heavy drinker, but no alcoholic," Rose was saying.

"In my book there's no difference, Mrs. McFadden. Now, because I'm a decent man, I'm gonna release him, on the condition

125

that ye take him home with ye, out of my sight. And if I see him again brawling in public and wasting police time, I'll have him charged and before the courts quicker than you can say that pope of yours is a Catholic. "

"God, that's very good of you, Sergeant."

"Yooze can wait outside there, and I'll get Constable Johnson to release him. I take it yooze are in a car?"

"We are, indeed, Sergeant," Rose said, mightily relieved.

"Johnson!" he bawled.

Quick as a ferret, the constable was in the doorway.

"Yes, Sarge."

"Release McCloone, so these people can take him outta my sight."

"Yes, Sarge."

Ranfurley stood up to give the pair the hint that he'd more important things to be getting on with.

"Yooze can wait out there in the park," he said.

"We will indeed," Rose said. "And it was nice talkin' to you, Sergeant. Maybe we'll see you again, round about the town, like."

Not if I see you first, thought Ranfurley unkindly. *Not if I see you first.*

Chapter fifteen

Belfast, 1983

The persistent ringing of his doorbell startled Henry Shevlin and set his heart pounding. The police? Who else could it be at—he glanced at the hall clock—at eleven in the evening?

They have news, he thought. She's turned up. But, as his fingers reached for the door handle, another possibility occurred to him. A very grim possibility.

"Henry?"

It was a woman's voice. It was accompanied by a pounding on the door and a further urgent ringing of the bell.

As he undid the safety latches, he was expecting to see Sergeant Hanson. It was four days since she'd interviewed him and perhaps she had news. But she wouldn't call him by his first name, would she?

His visitor was a woman of about Connie's age: early thirties, Henry figured. In the unflattering porch light her face looked haggard and concerned. He held the door open and she entered nervously.

"I know you, don't I?" he said.

"Geraldine. Geraldine Reynolds."

Henry's heart lifted. "Of course! Geraldine from art college days. God, has . . . has Connie been in touch with you?"

She shook her head sadly. "Sorry to call so late, but I just had to come, when I heard."

He led her into the kitchen.

She was quite pretty when seen in the warm, more flattering light. Dark brown hair, long and crimped, framing a face of symmetrical, childlike features, but her skin, rough, patchy, spoke of an addiction of some sort.

Her style of clothing resembled Connie's: distinctive, colorful, what could be called "arty." A dark-leather bag with a *Ban the Bomb* insignia dangled from her left shoulder.

Henry tried to keep the atmosphere light. "I didn't recognize you for a minute. It's just that you look . . . er . . ."

"Older? It's called 'aging,' Henry. It happens to everyone. Even to men."

"What brings you to Belfast, then?"

"Well, believe or not, I'm giving a two-day workshop at the art college. That's when I saw the poster. Tell me it isn't true, Henry. Please tell me it isn't true."

He sighed. "Afraid it is, Geraldine."

"God, I'm still in shock . . . Poor, poor Connie."

"Can I get you something . . . coffee?"

She stood looking about the spacious kitchen. Henry could see she was admiring Connie's artistic contributions to the minimalist decor.

An artist admiring the work of another artist.

"I could use something stronger if you have it, Henry."

He glanced at her sharply. "I've only red wine and Scotch."

"A Scotch, please. I think I need one."

"We'll go into the front room."

He threw the switches in the big parlor and drew the shades. Geraldine sat down at the coffee table.

"You're still in Sligo, then?"

"Yes. I met a guy from the area. Long story, Henry. I won't bore you with it right this minute."

She took her whiskey. He was surprised to see her down it in one.

"Are you sure it's true?" He could hear the faint hope in her voice, the last-ditch bid for reassurance.

"Yes, but I haven't given up hope." He sat down opposite her.

"What did the police say?"

He told her about his two interviews, leaving out one or two of the intimate questions that Sergeant Hanson had been so keen on plying him with. Geraldine listened, nodding at brief intervals. He refilled her glass.

"It's not like Connie," she said, downing the second glass just as swiftly. "Not at all. She was always a bit . . . eh . . . wild, you might say, but all in good fun."

"Wild."

Geraldine blushed. "Did I say 'wild'? Well, maybe not wild, no. Not in *that* sense. I meant she was a real party girl—we all were, the three of us: Connie, Sheila, and me. But you knew that . . . She always said you'd rescued her from herself. And I think she meant it, too. But she was different in those days. She'd say the maddest things when she'd had a few."

"A few?"

Geraldine blushed.

"A few drinks . . . and the odd joint."

She saw his look of surprise.

"Oh, just cannabis, nothing major." Geraldine got up awkwardly, reached for her *Ban the Bomb* bag and draped it over her shoulder. "I'll go, Henry. I've a taxi waiting. Just needed to know if it was true. You've enough on your plate without me upsetting you."

"Tell me, please!" he said. "Tell me the truth now, Geraldine. I need to know. Was Connie using drugs when she'd visit you?"

There were tears in her eyes. "Well . . . no, no, not really."

"'Not really'? What's that supposed to mean?"

"Look, I've really said the wrong thing, haven't I? Don't read too much into it, Henry."

"What was she on? I have to know."

"Nothing. When she visited me just wine, I promise you."

"Are you sure?"

She nodded, but avoided his eye. "Look . . . at college, joints, whatever you want to call them. Cannabis, like I say. We drew the line at hard drugs, though. No heroin. Ever. We weren't addicts, nor was Connie. But that was a long time ago."

At the door, he watched her cab depart and wondered how truthful she'd been with him. He'd seen the way she'd knocked back the whiskey. No savoring or enjoyment there, and her skin had the appearance of a regular substance abuser.

His thoughts turned to the medication Constable Lyle had found on Connie's dressing table. He was wondering how much he actually knew about his wife. Her personal life, her habits, the secrets that she'd never confided to him.

He wondered if he'd ever really known her at all. He felt he'd been sharing his life with a stranger.

———

The following morning found him en route to Boots department store on Royal Avenue.

At the entrance to the store, he stood in line as customers waited to be frisked and have handbags checked by two security personnel at a table inside the door.

An old lady in hairnet and rollers was holding things up.

"Ye'll find nathin' in there!" she declaimed loudly.

"Just doing our job," the security woman said, rummaging through a capacious handbag. "You wouldn't like to be blown up in here, would you?"

"Do I look like an IRA mon, do I? In me hairnet and curlers, goin' about me bissness . . . Well, do I? Do I?"

The security man rolled his eyes and beckoned Henry forward.

He extended his arms, the drill now as instinctive as breathing.

There seemed to be only one assistant at the pharmaceuticals counter. She was young—he judged midtwenties—with short hair in the style favored by Princess Diana. She was making an entry in a sales register, her well-defined eyebrows knitted in a frown as her eyes switched repeatedly from the register to an arrangement of invoices close by. He sensed that she'd been aware of him as soon as he'd approached the counter but had chosen to ignore him—or make him wait.

Dysfunctional situational ethic, Henry thought idly. He waited another minute. Enough. He coughed loudly.

"One minute, sir." Gruff.

"I've already waited *five* minutes."

She continued writing. "Needs to be done, sir."

"You're here to serve customers, not to do paperwork in public."

This time she made no reply. He saw her smirk. He placed his palms squarely on the counter.

"Miss, are you going—"

"Dr. Shevlin?"

He turned at the sound of the voice. A young man in a white coat was approaching. Henry heard the assistant hurriedly finish whatever it was she was doing.

"Alfie! Didn't know you worked here."

The young man shook Henry's hand. "It's a living," he said with a smile. "What brings you here?"

"Oh, this and that." He tried to sound nonchalant. The blonde sales assistant, in the meantime, had assumed a customer-friendly professional air and was treating Henry to an ingratiating smile. The physician in him was convinced she might develop a temporomandibular joint disorder if she wasn't careful. "I'm trying to trace who it was who prescribed some pills for my wife. For Constance."

"I see. Well, I'm sure Miss Clare can help you there. Can't you, May?"

"I'm sure I can, Mr. Ross," the girl said fawningly. She turned to Henry. "What's the name, sir?"

"Shevlin," Mr. Ross said. "I'm sure the doctor's wife will be in our records."

The assistant was regarding Henry with a newfound respect. "Shouldn't be too difficult to find, Dr. Shevlin. We do it all alphabetically here."

She went to the rear of the enclosure and pulled open one of the filing cabinets. Even Henry was surprised by her efficiency, for in a matter of seconds she was back.

"Here we are, Dr. Shevlin." She handed him a prescription.

Henry studied the leaflet. He was mystified. Yes, it was from his prescription pad, stamped with the Mater Infirmorum Hospital address and made out in the name of Constance Shevlin: Indalpine, 10mg, May 5, 1983. He peered more closely at the signature. It looked like his.

But . . . there were several prescription pads at home. Was it possible that Connie had . . . ?

"I really don't understand," he said to Alfie. "I have no memory of signing this."

"Maybe your wife forged it, then." It was the bold May.

Henry stared at her, speechless.

Alfie cleared his throat, embarrassed. "Miss Clare, can you restock that shelf with Panadol over there? We're running low *again*, I see."

———

Back on Royal Avenue, Henry was sorely confounded. Nothing was making sense anymore. His final hope of tracing Connie's movements had been dashed. He had most definitely *not* prescribed those antidepressants.

He didn't even have the bottle of pills. The police were holding onto them. Yet he was certain of the date on which they'd been dispensed to Connie: May 5. The label had given him the address of the dispenser: Boots on Royal Avenue. There could be no mistake. His near-eidetic memory seldom played him false.

Connie was gone. That much was certain. Yet he felt that all remaining traces of her were being slowly and efficiently erased. As if she'd never existed.

The psychiatrist could have been forgiven for feeling he was going the way of his patients. *Am I*, he asked himself, *the crazy one?* But it was a moment of doubt he vowed he'd not be revisiting. No, Connie might be missing, but she was *not* dead. He was not going crazy. And he would find her. No matter what it took.

Chapter sixteen

"Oh my good God!"

Ruby, preparing breakfast, hadn't expected to hear her mother so early. She turned now from the stove, to see her standing, ashen-faced and staring at the spot where the picture of Michael the Archangel used to hang.

"Oh, that. It fell off the wall last night. I'll clean it up in a minute." She took two plates from the dresser and began setting the table. "It's scrambled eggs. I thought I'd do it for a change."

The mother didn't move, just stood there staring at the wall, as if paralyzed.

"Mammy, are you all right?"

"That's a sign!"

"What's a sign? Here, sit down. You might as well have breakfast, now that you're up."

Ruby took her by the arm. Martha allowed herself to be guided into a chair at the table.

"Look, I can explain that. Last night I took that prayer off the wall to have a wee read at it. I mustn't of put it back right and it fell. As I say, I'll clean it up in a minute, so I will."

The mother didn't seem to hear. She sat, hands in her lap, her eyes rooted on the alcove where the picture used to hang.

"You didn't burn that case, did you?"

Ruby paused before replying. "What case?"

"Don't you play the innocent with me."

Ruby avoided her eye, busied herself taking cutlery from a drawer.

"Where did you burn it?"

"I told you, Mammy. In the woods."

"You're lying! It's in that bedroom of yours. That's why you've started locking your door. You never did that before."

Ruby dished out the scrambled eggs. Returned the skillet to the stove, her mind in a fever. What if her mother demanded to see the bedroom? What if she looked under the bed? What if she found the case? What would Ruby do then?

She took her seat at the table again.

Martha pushed the plate away. She got up.

"Give me the key! I want to see what's in that bedroom this minute."

Ruby pressed her thumb and forefinger together. *The Book of Light* had told her that it was a means by which she could bring calm, and summon the Goddess's help. And she *really* needed Dana's help now, to get her out of this one.

"I TOLD YOU I BURNED THE CASE. NOW, IF YOU WANT, I CAN TAKE YOU DOWN TO THE WOODS AND SHOW YOU THE SPOT, RIGHT NOW."

Ruby hesitated. She looked up at her mother standing there with her hand out. She'd just have to trust the voice. There was no other way out of this.

"I told you I burned the case. Now, if you want, I can take you down to the woods and show you the spot, right now."

It was Martha's turn to hesitate. Ruby saw her quandary.

"BUT BE WARNED: I BURNED IT DEEP IN THE WOODS, SO THERE'LL BE LOTS OF BRIARS AND NETTLES TO GET THROUGH."

"But be warned: I burned it deep in the woods, so there'll be lots of briars and nettles to get through." Her confidence growing now, she added, just for good measure: "So maybe . . . maybe you should put your boots on."

Martha looked out the window, down the field toward Beldam. Ruby knew what she was thinking: mist clouds hanging low spoke of a damp trudge through the forest . . . a chill in the air at this early hour, even though it was a June morning . . . scratches and stings from those nettles and briars . . . the danger of falling on the slippery earth.

No, she wouldn't risk it.

"Do you want to go into town later?" Ruby, in her mind's eye, slipping another slide into the projector machine. A brighter image, a more tantalizing prospect. "You wanted to buy walking shoes . . . and you have that bill to pay in Harvey's."

Martha looked back at her. "You're . . . you're not yourself," she said.

"YOU MEAN I'M NOT THE PERSON YOU WANT ME TO BE. ISN'T THAT RIGHT?"

"You mean I'm not the person you want me to be. Isn't that right?"

"Oh my God, there it is! The way you're talking. That's not you. That picture is a sign. Edna Clare . . . your grandmother. She started to talk like that. Before . . . before . . ."

A shiver ran through Ruby. She set her fork down.

"Before? Before what?"

The mother made no reply. She went to where the picture lay and picked it up. "I'll get the glass replaced in this."

"Before what?" Ruby persisted.

Martha studied the picture but said nothing.

"See? You can't tell me, 'cos nothing happened. Edna died of a broken heart 'cos you didn't want her in this house when you married Daddy. And that picture fell 'cos I took it down to have a look at it, and the nail fell out."

Martha reached out and touched the nail. It was still firmly embedded in the wall. Hammered in there all those decades ago by Vinny, at her request. Oh, the wars that picture had caused between Edna and herself! And poor Vinny caught in the cross fire.

She placed it gently on the table. Turned back to Ruby.

"Harvey's, you say? Yes . . . yes, we'll go into town. I'll . . . I'll get dressed. A cup of tea . . . that's all I want, Ruby."

———

Each hour that passed was drawing Ruby closer to that great event: the enactment of the Goddess ritual at the summer solstice. There was much to prepare. In Harvey's, Purveyors of Ladies' and Gentlemen's Fashions, there was an important item she had to buy: a robe. She took the opportunity to have a look in the lingerie department while her mother was engaged with Mr. Harvey.

"You mean a nightdress?" said Mildred Crink, the shop assistant, flipping through a rail of night attire. Like her sister at the post office, Mildred had been serving behind the ladies' counter in Harvey's for the best part of thirty years. Such a position had bestowed upon her an encyclopedic knowledge of the vital statistics of every woman in the locality, and so provided some interesting gossip with Doris of an evening, if a purchase had been made that did not chime with a body's needs.

"*God, d'you know, Doris, that young one of Peggy Noone's has put on a whole lotta weight in just six months. Belly on her like a Cooney porker. Buyin' size sixteen knickers and a D-cup front-fastener, and her not long outta school. She wouldn't be pregnant, would she?*"

137

"*Well, that wouldn't surprise me, Mildred. Didn't her mother* have to *get married and her not long outta school uniform, either?*"

Ruby hesitated. She was taking a risk with her mother at such close quarters. So the transaction needed to be done as covertly and quickly as possible. She stole a glance up the shop. Mr. Harvey and Martha were still engrossed.

"No, not a nightdress, Mildred. More a . . . more a thing that goes *over* a nightdress."

Miss Crink ceased her flipping and looked over her spectacles. "You mean a bed jacket?"

"Aye, but . . . a bit longer than that. The thing that goes over it and ties at the front."

"A dressing gown, then? Well, we don't sell many of *them*." Mildred's brow creased with concern. She removed her glasses. "My goodness, you're not going into hospital, Ruby, are you? 'Cos that's usually the reason women in these parts buy the like of them. I hope you're not poorly, 'cos I thought you'd lost a bit."

"Oh no, nothing like that, Mildred. I just want it for—"

"Goin' away for a wee break. It's always nice to get away. Me and Doris always go to the Ocean Spray in Portaluce. Have you ever been?"

Ruby threw a fearful look in her mother's direction. "No, but I've heard it's a nice place. Would you have one in green?"

She'd settled on green, it being the color of the Goddess. Also, since she'd be attuning to Dana in her natural environment by immersing in Beldam Lake, it seemed the most appropriate choice.

". . . you know, you should take your mother away," Mildred was saying. "Do you both good to get away for a bit, after what you've come through. Green, you say?"

Finally, a garment was plucked from the rail and laid out on the counter. It was just what Ruby wanted: a beautiful oceanic green with velvet trim at collar and cuffs. "Now, that's the only green we have in your size. Lovely cotton-polyester mix, so it won't shrink in the wash. Do you want to slip behind the curtain there and give it a wee go?"

"No . . . no. That's lovely. Do you have one with a hood?"

"A hood?" Mildred looked perplexed. "Oh no, they don't come with hoods. Why would you want a hood on a nightgown? It's hardly gonna rain in the bedroom."

But Ruby was thinking back to what she'd read. "*A hooded robe is preferable, since it will shut off outside disturbances and control sensory input during ritual.*"

"What's going on here?"

Ruby froze at the sound of her mother's voice behind her.

"Och, how are you, Martha?" Mildred said. "Ruby was just sayin' that yins might go away for a day or two."

"That's news to me, Mildred. But then, Ruby doesn't tell me much." Mrs. Clare stared at the nightgown spread out on the counter, then at Ruby, her look a mixture of fear and accusation. "And what's *that* for?"

Ruby's face reddened. She struggled. It was time to invoke the Goddess. Curling the thumb and forefinger of her left hand into a representation of the crescent moon, she said, "At night, when I get up to go to the bathroom, I'm cold."

"How could you be cold in this weather? Anyway, who's going to be seeing you in the middle of the night?"

"That's neither here nor there. I like it. I want it, therefore I am buying it. I do not need your opinion or approval."

"That's neither here nor there. I like it. I want it, therefore I am buying it. I do not need your opinion or approval."

Ruby's delivery had been firm and confident. She drew herself up to her full height and smiled at Mildred, not really caring about her mother's reaction.

Mildred looked from mother to daughter, antennae quivering, mouth an O of astonishment. This was not the shy, quiet Ruby she knew. What would Doris have to say about this? There was an awkward pause that needed filling. Mildred found her voice at last.

"You're just right, Ruby. It's nice . . . it's nice to treat yourself now and again. I'll wrap it up."

Martha Clare stood rigid, lips clamped together, holding in the torrent of abuse that would be unleashed out of earshot of the shop assistant and Mr. Harvey. It was bad enough for her daughter to act like that at home; in public it was appalling. Being humiliated in front of Father Kelly, and now Mildred Crink, was a breach too far. It would *not* be happening again.

"I'll wait for you in the car," she said, before turning on her heel and marching outside.

"That'll be ten pounds and fifty pence," Mildred said, tearing off a sheet of tissue paper from a roll.

"Oh, just put it on Mammy's tab," Ruby said breezily.

"Are you sure?"

"Yes. Why would I not be sure? My mother spends a lot of money in this shop. Are you implying you won't get paid?"

"Yes. Why would I not be sure? My mother spends a lot of money in this shop. Are you implying you won't get paid?"

Now it was Mildred's turn to grow flustered.

"Oh no, I-I didn't mean that at all, Ruby . . . not for a minute."

Ruby signed the chit. The robe was expensive, but she didn't care. It was going to be used for a very good cause. It didn't have a hood, but no matter. She'd improvise, and make herself a garland of wild flowers, which would be a good alternative.

Satisfied, she left the shop.

Martha Clare erupted the minute her daughter had resumed the driver's seat.

"How *dare* you speak to me like that in front of people! There's something very wrong with you. You're not yourself. I want to see Father Kelly this minute. Take me to the parochial house."

"But I've more shopping to do."

"Doesn't matter." She slapped the dashboard hard. "You'll take me to the priest this minute or I'll . . ."

"Or you'll what?"

Ruby gunned the engine, reversed out of her parking space, and roared away.

———

Father Kelly was compiling the parish bulletin when he heard the sound of tires on gravel. He peered out the window, and was surprised to see Martha Clare and her daughter pull up in the driveway. Well, he had promised to drop in one evening. All the same, it must be rather urgent for them to have made a special trip to see him.

He went to the door. A visibly shaken Martha Clare stood on the doorstep.

"Hello, Father. I'm . . . I'm glad I got you in. Would you have a couple of minutes—"

"Of course, Martha, of course."

Over her shoulder, he saw that Ruby was still in the driver's seat. He thought it odd that she was not acknowledging him, but just sitting there, staring straight ahead.

"Isn't Ruby coming in, too?"

Martha gripped the priest's arm, suddenly fearful.

"No, Father. That's the problem; Ruby doesn't want to come in. I need to talk to you about her. It's very serious."

Father Kelly led the way into the sitting room.

"A cup of tea, perhaps? You look a bit pale, Martha."

Martha shook her head. "No, Father. Thank you all the same. Father, I . . ." She swayed slightly.

Father Kelly helped her into the armchair. "Now, now, sit down there for a wee minute and take your time. Nothing's ever as bad as it seems . . ."

"It's the case, Father. Ruby's got the *case* . . ."

The word had a profound impact. For a few seconds the priest did not speak. An image was looming at him out of the far past: the image of a young curate entering a darkened room in an old farmhouse, riven with fear and fright.

"Edna's . . . Edna's case . . . ?" he said at last. "Are you sure?"

She nodded. "I asked her to burn it, but . . . but I know she didn't." Martha looked about her, distracted, her eyes beseeching the holy pictures on the walls to lend her strength. "And now I think she's . . ." She couldn't bring herself to say the word.

"You think Ruby's what, Martha?"

"Po-po . . . possessed, Father!" Her face crumpled. "Oh dear God, Father!"

He tried to hide his consternation. Resolved to keep the atmosphere light.

"Oh now . . . what would give you that idea?"

"She *is,* Father. I'm convinced of it. She's not herself at all. She's driving very fast. Something she never did before. And . . . the things she comes out with . . . well, it's just not her. Sometimes . . . sometimes I'm afraid of her. Afraid, Father, in my own home."

"Well, now, this must be a difficult time for her. She's still grieving the loss of her poor father. People do and say strange things in the depths of grief. It's a hard time for both of you. You've come through a lot. Vincent is a great loss. Not only to you but the community as well."

Tears welled up in Martha's eyes. She groped in her sleeve for a hankie.

"Maybe I was too hard on her . . . taking her away from the farm like that. So sudden and all. But I couldn't see her doing all that work on her own. It's a man's job . . . and I needed her in the house with me. God knows, with my weak heart I'm afraid to be on my own, Father . . . and now . . . well, now I'm afraid to be with *her*."

"The Lord's always with us, Martha. Sure we're never on our own." He glanced through the window and saw that Ruby was still sitting in the same position, staring blankly through the windscreen. He wondered whether he should go out and have a word.

"And what has Ruby done now that would lead you to believe she might be . . . be possessed, as you say? Has she stopped saying her prayers?"

"Oh, we say the rosary every evening all right, Father, but . . ."

"That's grand."

"But her heart's not in it no more. I can tell. And I see her go down and stand by . . . by Beldam. And that's not good."

"The lake?"

Martha nodded. "There was never any luck with it . . . And last night—"

"Does she know what happened to her grandmother now?"

"No." Martha shook her head vehemently. "She'll never know that, Father. Not unless . . ."

"That's good. And last night, you were saying . . . What happened?"

"I got up to go to the bathroom and I . . . I thought I heard noises coming from her room. Like she was talking to someone. In the morning . . . well, it was in the morning that I saw it and I knew . . . I just *knew*."

"You just knew what, Martha?" Father Kelly was choosing his words carefully.

"The picture of Michael the Archangel smashed on the floor. That's when I knew. I would die, Father, if all that came back again. I just couldn't cope."

Father Kelly looked grave. "That's too bad," he said, gazing out the window again. Ruby still sat in that resolute pose. "I'll come over and do a blessing."

"When, Father?"

"Tomorrow evening, if it suits. The sooner the better, I think."

"That's good. D'you think . . . d'you think it'll be enough, Father?"

"Well, we can only do our best, Martha. The rest now . . ." He gazed out at Ruby again. This time she turned her head, looked at him, then quickly looked away. "Well, the rest, Martha . . . the rest is up to God."

Chapter seventeen

Belfast, 1983

Out of your vulnerabilities will come your strength," said the sage.

So which of the sages, thought Henry Shevlin, was that? Yes, he remembered: Sigmund Freud. The great Siggy, as his friends used to call him—though never to his face. Siggy, the founder of psychotherapy. Siggy, the man who gave us the notion of "hysteria," borrowed from that crazy French doctor who ran the lunatic asylum in Paris. It was, Henry mused, St. Ita's as seen by Dante: an Inferno housing 4,000 incurably mad women. *Hysteria . . . hysterectomy . . .* words derived from an ancient word for the womb. Did hysteria affect women only? Siggy was convinced it did. But Henry had seen his fair share of male sufferers, too.

He swung the white Mercedes convertible onto Finaghy Road—and slammed on the brakes immediately. Two heavily armed RUC officers were directing traffic past a fresh crater in the tarmac. It could have been made by anything, he thought, but most likely an explosive, given the political climate.

One of the policemen raised a hand. Henry wound down the window.

"Where you goin', sir?"

"Kashmir Road."

"Sorry, you'll have to take an alternative route. Through Broadway's the quickest, then the Falls and the Springfield Road."

He looked at the dashboard clock, didn't exactly relish the idea of driving through that part of town, a heartland of Republican sympathizers. But . . .

He turned left at the Broadway traffic circle as instructed, and was soon negotiating a maze of rough streets scarred with graffiti and gable murals commemorating various events in the Republican calendar. Not that murals and graffiti were alien to Belfast; they were part of the cityscape since the Troubles began. The Troubles: code for the bloody internecine feuding between Protestant and Catholic, Unionist and Republican, that had swept across Northern Ireland a decade before and which, sadly, showed no sign of abating.

There were several foot patrols of British Army personnel on duty. At the sight of them, Henry became unnerved. Foot patrols brought the ever-present threat of sniper fire. He tried to speed up but was forced to stop again for a red light.

Only then did he see it.

On a wall across from the junction was an enormous mural. It intrigued him because it was so unusual. Painted in black and white, it depicted three women "volunteers": one in uniform, and two brandishing firearms, all enclosed within a ♀ symbol. Three women fighters: a Muslim wearing a niqab, a black African, and the third one, the central figure, in the signature black beret of the IRA. There was a slogan daubed to the left of the image. It read:

SOLIDARITY BETWEEN WOMEN
IN ARMED STRUGGLE.

More hysteria, Henry thought. Is this what the—

The thought died abruptly. He was staring at the central figure: the Irishwoman in the paramilitary uniform and beret. She was gazing directly at him.

There could be no mistake: the woman's face bore a striking resemblance to that shown in the sheaf of posters that lay behind him on the rear seat of the car. The poster with the bold headline that asked, *Have you seen this woman?*

It was Connie. That was *Connie's* face painted on the brick wall.

He was stunned. His eyes were roving over the image. He was recognizing Connie's distinctive style of painting. He saw it in all her work. They'd once had a lighthearted discussion about it.

"Every artist paints herself," she'd said. "Or *him*self, if you want to be picky about it."

"Nonsense! Next you'll be telling me that the Mona Lisa is a self-portrait of Leonardo."

"How do you know it's not?"

"Oh, don't be daft! The very idea!"

"All right, let's stick with more recent stuff. You go along to any gallery with portraits—especially group portraits—and I guarantee you'll see that all the sitters resemble each other. That's because an artist doesn't paint what she sees in front of her. She paints what she sees in her head, and that's usually the face she sees every day in the mirror."

He recalled their weekend in Amsterdam in 1980. They'd visited the Rijksmuseum, and had stood in awe of Rembrandt's colossal canvas: *The Night Watch*. They'd annoyed the other visitors by laughing when Connie drew his attention to the almost familial resemblance between all the painted men. Henry had argued—somewhat weakly—that there'd been a lot of inbreeding in Holland in those days.

The loud blast of a car horn jolted him out of his daydream. The traffic light had turned green. He was holding up a line of cars.

Startled, he drove off. He needed to get to the gallery fast.

———

A knot of rough-looking youths stared sullenly at the shiny white convertible as he pulled up on Kashmir Street. Not to worry. He could keep an eye on the car through the Mondrian's big picture windows—windows, Connie had informed him, that were shattered more than once during the worst of Belfast's rioting. He saw a woman waving at him from behind the left window.

"Henry, good to see you," Maeve Hanratty said as she admitted him. Slim, she was dressed simply and wore little makeup. "Any news?"

"I was hoping you had some for me."

She was looking at the sheaf of posters in his hand. "You have more . . . ?"

"Yes. People are putting them up all over the place. It's very kind of them. I was hoping . . ."

"Of course. Let me—"

"I need to see what she was working on last," he said.

"Yes . . . yes, of course." Maeve led him through a door to the studio workshop.

The large, bright space was sparely furnished; there was a trestle table loaded with cans of paint and brushes, a swivel chair, and two stepladders supporting a broad plank. Several huge primed canvases leaned against one wall.

"There it is," Maeve said, pointing to a large canvas on the back wall. It was done predominantly in monochrome: a muddy brown on a cream background. The theme appeared to be one of violence—or, better said, armed female resistance to oppression.

Henry left the posters on a table and went closer to the image. But he didn't need to be too close; it was big enough to be viewed from a distance. It was large enough to fit on the gable wall of a house.

Nonplussed, he studied the figures rendered in brown. They dominated the foreground. They appeared to be women in combat uniform. Some held firearms; others were brandishing knives, axes, and what appeared to be tricolors. All looked furious and potentially homicidal. As a body, they were in hot pursuit of a band of fleeing males decked out in bowler hats and sashes. They were clearly members of the Protestant Loyal Orange Lodge.

"It's good, isn't it?" Maeve was saying.

"What production's this, for pity's sake?"

"Oh, it's not for a drama. It was commissioned a couple of months back by a private individual."

"A private individual? I don't understand."

"Yes, an American gentleman. Didn't Connie mention him? He'd been to the Lyric to see *A Touch of Class,* and was so taken with our sets he sought us out."

Henry, not for the first time in the past few days, found himself tongue-tied. But not for long. "When . . . when did she . . . when did Connie get involved in all of this?"

"Sorry, all of what?"

"This political stuff. I've just seen a mural on the Falls Road, which could only have been done by her."

"Oh, that. No, Connie didn't actually paint that. It, again, was a commission from Mr. Halligan. She painted the canvas to his specifications. She wasn't to know that it was going to be copied onto that wall."

"What?! Wasn't she annoyed when she heard about it?"

Maeve shrugged. "No, not really. She was quite flattered, actually . . . said it wasn't a bad imitation."

"God, I really can't believe what I'm hearing. Are you out of your minds? Why didn't you tell me?"

"Look, Henry, I really think you're blowing all this out of proportion. She didn't want to tell you because she knew what your reaction would be." Maeve sighed. "Besides which . . ."

Henry glared at her. "Besides which . . . *what*?"

"Well . . . he paid so well, there was just no question of turning him down. And always up-front. In that respect, it showed how much he trusted Connie to carry out the commission and do a good job."

"Who is this bloody man? I need his address and I need it *now*. The police have to be informed."

"The p-police?"

"Yes, the police!"

"Harris . . . Harris Halligan. And don't ask me where he lives. He never said. Nor did he leave us a telephone number. He could be back in the States now, for all I know."

"Didn't you ask him?"

"Yes . . . well, I did, but he . . . he just said he'd call us."

"My God, wasn't that evidence enough that you were dealing with someone not on the level?" He waved a hand at Connie's painting. "He commissions this provocative nonsense. He pays large sums of money . . . And just while we're on the subject, how much *did* he pay her?"

"One and a half thousand . . . give or take . . ."

"One and a half thousand *pounds*! Really! And how was it paid?" He held up a hand. "No, don't tell me . . . in cash, right?"

Maeve nodded. "Afraid so."

Henry was dumbfounded. The reason Connie's bank account hadn't been debited was staring him right there in the face. With fifteen hundred pounds she could disappear for quite some time.

Maeve sat down slowly on the swivel chair. "Look, Henry, I don't know how to say this, but . . . but he—I mean Halligan—he took Connie out to lunch a couple of times. But . . . I don't believe there was anything to it."

"Describe him for me, please. Or are you going to tell me your powers of vision have suddenly deserted you as well as your good sense?"

"Look, I know you're upset—"

"Damn right I'm upset! One minute I hear from my father that she was unhappy, and might—just might—be suicidal. Now you're telling me she's likely run off with a wealthy American with a fondness for IRA propaganda. Well, it's a pity you didn't think to tell me sooner, Maeve, before she disappeared off the face of the bloody earth."

With that, he took a Stanley knife from the cluttered table and advanced on the canvas. Before Maeve could intervene, he slashed it viciously a number of times.

"I think you should leave!"

"And I think you should tell me exactly what's going on. For, if you don't, I'll have this place closed down."

"You can't do that, Henry."

"Oh no? I own the lease on this building, or had you forgotten? Now, I want the truth. Was she having an affair?"

Maeve was distraught. She'd gone pale, frightened by Henry's unaccustomed show of temper. "Yes . . . no. I mean, I don't know, Henry. Honest. I was only here during the day. And what I'm saying is true. They went out for lunch twice."

"Where did they go?"

"Ah . . . hmm. I don't—"

"*Where did they go?*"

Maeve was backing away. "For God's sake, put that knife down! You're scaring me."

151

Henry looked down at his trembling hand, shocked to see he was still gripping the Stanley knife.

"Sorry," he said, realizing how menacing he must appear to poor Maeve. He set it back on the table. "Look, I just want the truth."

"The Europa . . . the Europa Hotel . . . I think."

"When?"

"The last time . . . about . . . about ten days ago."

———

He'd wasted no more time but had driven straight to the Europa. It was one of Belfast's best-known landmarks at that time; notorious for having earned the sobriquet "most bombed hotel in Europe."

He knew the query sounded daft as soon as it was out of his mouth.

The receptionist, a young woman, heavily made up with hair stretched painfully into a topknot, looked at him queerly.

"You're asking me if I saw a woman with blonde hair and a man with an American accent eat here ten days ago?"

"Yes, I know it's a long shot, but . . ."

"We don't keep a record of who eats in our restaurant, sir."

"His name's Halligan. Perhaps he paid with a credit card in that name. Could you—"

"Even if he did, that's confidential information. I wouldn't be at liberty to—"

"I know, but . . . Look . . ." He checked her nametag. "Look, Debbie, my wife's gone missing and I . . ."

At that news, and the sound of her name, Debbie's face softened and she dropped the official-speak.

"I'm sorry to hear that, sir. Was she . . . was she having an—"

"An affair? Probably. I need to . . . I just need . . ."

Debbie blinked sadly. Looked down at the register. Henry could see the impeccable line of her expertly applied false eyelashes. He thought of Connie and the many times she'd struggled to wear the blasted things, but could never get the hang of them. He almost wept at the memory.

"I could always check if they booked in," Debbie was saying.

"Sorry . . . I don't understand. Why would they . . . ?"

She blushed. "In lunch hour. Them that's having affairs, they often book in for . . ."

"Yes . . . yes, of course. I see." A trifle embarrassed at his naïveté. Or was it that he simply could not bring himself to think too far along those lines?

The receptionist flicked back several pages.

One half of Henry hoped she wouldn't find anything. The other half hoped she would. It would explain a lot.

"Yes, here they are."

His heart leaped and sank at the same time.

Debbie turned the register toward him and pointed.

There, scrawled in handwriting Henry didn't recognize, were the words:

Mr. and Mrs. Halligan, 13 Mountview Terrace, Belfast

Chapter eighteen

S he had the robe. She had the candles. Sunset on the evening of June 15 found Ruby in the woods that skirted Beldam Lake, hunting for herbs. Before her midsummer ritual, she needed to prepare an altar, to invoke Dana's special powers. She'd decided it was too risky to make one in the bedroom. Her mother had already demanded the key but she'd managed to thwart her on that occasion. No, it was much safer to build an altar right here in the woods. Was it not the Goddess's living room, after all?

She'd rarely ventured into the woods in her younger days. They were too shadowy and daunting for a child, their thickets of briars and obstructions of shoulder-high nettles killing any curiosity she might have had. But, since finding Edna's book, and learning of her beliefs, she was beginning to see that the great outdoors was where Dana flourished supreme.

She bloomed abundantly everywhere: in plants, flowers, grass, and trees. In the beasts, the birds, the rocks in the earth, the fish in the sea.

Dana, the source of fertility and endless wisdom, deserved the respect of every human being. She was the force that drove all existence.

There was nothing to be afraid of.

Ruby thought back with shame to that very different girl who worked alongside her father on the farm. The Ruby who so casually squashed insects underfoot. Who didn't think twice about switching an ashplant off a cow's rump to get it into a byre. The Ruby who swatted flies, and flushed spiders down drain holes. How cruel and thoughtless she had been! Slaughtering the Goddess's creatures without a moment's hesitation. From now on, she'd show respect for all living things, to make up for all those willful transgressions.

Ensure that thy actions are honourable, for all that thou doest shall return to thee threefold, good or bane.

The sinking sun was sending rods of golden light through the trees as Ruby trod the path. She was happy, alive to the Goddess. Heard her sing in the sweet birdsong, felt her breath on the wafting breeze, caught her laughter in the tinkling streams, felt her warmth in the sun's embrace.

Ruby's step was light. Her mind was clear. She was moving toward a great awakening. Words floated to her from the Tarot cards she'd read:

A door is opening into a new world, free from the constraints of the past . . . follow your inspiration, not reason.

How true. She was doing just that.

Hope and healing are yours. You have chosen the right path.

Yes, I'm on the right path. I've never felt so right about anything. And to think I might never have discovered this "new world" had I not opened the case and studied Edna's *Book of Light*.

In a bag she carried the objects for her altar: two candles, the censer and offering plate from the case, a piece of paper with her three wishes written on it, the names of the herbs she needed to collect, a length of purple cloth, and a knife with a curved blade. The white-handled sickle was one her father had used to prune hedges, but since it now was going to be used for a sacred purpose, it needed to be earthed with the positive energies of Dana.

She stopped under an oak tree and plucked one of its leaves. Took out the knife, rubbed it with the leaf and looked about her. She needed to lay it on the ground pointing south. The moss on the trees was her guide. Her father once told her that when you were looking directly at the moss you were facing south. She found a spot and set the sickle down. Through the trees she could see the rear of the house, but wasn't so bothered by this. When she left her mother, May had just telephoned. And Ruby knew such calls could last a good half hour, give or take. So, she reckoned she was safe enough.

She had a peek at the instructions.

Walk thrice around the knife in a clockwise direction, scattering oak leaves as you go. Pick up knife, point it skywards, and chant the following:

"Gracious Goddess, day and night I'm sheltered by your awesome might. Infuse this blade with all your power so it may choose the perfect flower."

Task completed, Ruby cast about for the flowers and herbs she needed to burn in offering. The list was long, but she need only concentrate on those that had associations with her three wishes.

She pointed the sickle at a clump of feverfew—it would protect her from evil spirits—and said, "Oh, little flower, I'm sorry I have to cut you. But you are for the Goddess, and my heart is true."

Some wild dandelion leaf was next. It would help increase her psychic powers so she could commune with her father.

Blackberry leaf: a powerful and important herb because it was special to the Goddess. Ruby approached the snarl of brambles with great reverence and awe, conscious that it was a favorite hiding place for Dana's children, the faerie folk. She intoned the little blessing in a low whisper, before gently cutting the leaf.

Some wild rose petals for love.

Love?

She'd never really understood what love was until her dear father died. Now she knew it was kindness and caring, everything her mother was not. Maybe if she wished hard enough, "someone nice," with qualities just like her father's, would enter her life.

Finally, some toothed leaves of vervain. It would attract wealth to her and make the action of the other herbs stronger when burned together in offering.

An old stump nearby would make the ideal altar.

Ruby knelt before it and set about assembling her paraphernalia. First, she spread out the purple cloth and put two silver candles on it, anchoring them in silver holders.

Between the candles she placed Edna's silver disk bearing the five-pointed star. She unfolded the paper containing her three wishes and read over them again.

1. I want to see Daddy again.
2. I want lots of money.
3. I want to meet someone nice and be happy.

Satisfied, she folded the paper into a neat square and set it on the silver disk. At the front, she put the censer dish of the herbs she'd cut to be burned in offering.

———

Back at Oaktree Farmhouse, Martha Clare replaced the phone, having finished her conversation with May. It being such a fine evening, her daughter had advised that she sit outside in the garden.

The air would do her good. She had a copy of *Ireland's Own* to read, and it would lift her spirits until Father Kelly's arrival at 7:00 p.m. She'd been very upset by Ruby's behavior, but Father Kelly had put her mind at ease. His blessing, with the help of God, would sort things out.

She settled herself in a lawn chair at the front, and turned to the recipes section of the magazine. There was a recipe for Nutty Apple Crumble, which Ida Nettles had drawn to her attention. Perhaps she'd get Ruby to make it for the girls at the weekend. June was especially fond of nuts. She perused the ingredients, noting that it was quite simple, apart from the addition of pear yogurt.

A recipe on the opposite page for Cottage Pie had Martha's eyes welling up. Cottage pie had been one of Vinny's favorites. She shut the magazine and gazed at an apple blossom at the bottom of the garden. Saw a youthful Vinny leaning on a shovel. Ruby, just a few months old, crawling about on the grass.

"There it is, dear. That apple tree will be there long after we're gone."

"Oh, Vinny, don't be so gloomy. Here, have some water. All that digging's thirsty work in this weather."

She saw him swoop down and gather up Ruby. "But Ruby here will see it. Won't you, sweetheart?"

Then a window being thrust open above them. A voice: sharp, demanding. "Vinny, can you come up here a minute?"

Vinny putting Ruby down immediately.

"You don't have to run to her every time like a puppy dog."

"She's my mother, Martha, and she's not well."

"I'm your wife, and there's not a thing wrong with her. She just wants attention."

"Now who's being gloomy? I'm sorry . . . have to see what she wants. I'll not be long."

Edna! For the last two years of her life, and the first two of their marriage, she'd tried to drive a wedge between them. She'd never expected her son to marry. That was the problem. With her husband and little Declan gone so early, she clung to Vinny for dear life. His marriage was a betrayal too far.

Against her will, Martha pushed further back in her memory, to the first time she'd met Vincent. Had his car not broken down all those years ago their paths might never have crossed. They'd boarded the same bus. He'd been on his way to collect his car from a garage in Killoran. She'd been on her way home from work. Thirty-three-year-old Martha sitting covertly weeping, wondering how she could have made such a terrible mistake. But the boyish young man in the gabardine coat had seen her distress.

They got off at the same stop.

"Miss, are you all right?"

She turned. There was genuine concern in his voice.

"Yes . . . yes. It's nothing . . . I'm fine. Think I'm catching a cold, that's all."

"Where do you live?"

She looked about her, only then realizing she'd got off the bus two stops too early.

They'd walked the short distance to the garage. He'd insisted on tea at Mooney's Hotel before dropping her home. How kind and thoughtful he'd been!

A raft for her to cling to.

"Anybody home?"

Martha jolted back to the present at the sound of Father Kelly's voice.

"Father, I was miles away there." She made to rise but the priest stayed her with a calming hand.

"Don't stir yourself, Martha." He took the other chair. "Sure isn't it a grand evening to be sitting out, altogether. And where's the lady herself?"

"She went down to the woods, Father. Picking blackberries to make some jam, she said."

"A bit early for blackberries, is it not?"

Martha's face took on a troubled look. "I know, Father, but that's what she said and I dare not confront her, in case . . ." She broke off, not wanting to think about the reality too much, and checked her watch. "I expected her home long before now. She's away an hour at least."

———

Ruby lighted the candles, kindled the herbs in the censer dish, and stood up. Spreading her arms wide, she intoned the invocation to the Goddess she had learned by heart.

"O Great Mother, Gracious Goddess, Crescent One of the Starry Skies, Flowered One of the Fertile Plain, Flowing One of the Ocean's Sighs, Blessed One of the Gentle Rain! Listen to the woes of your daughter. Shine your—"

"Ruby, are you there?"

A man's voice.

Startled, Ruby spun round. To her consternation, she saw Father Kelly in his long coat, pluntering over the field.

Had he seen her?

In a panic, she snuffed the candles out, stamped the burning herbs into the ground, and had everything out of sight and in the bag by the time he'd gained the clearing.

"Your mother . . . your mother said I'd find you here, Ruby. Hope you've got enough for a few pots?"

"Hello, Father . . . What?"

"The jam, so. You're pickin' the berries, I hear. What's that smell?"

"Oh, the blackberries. I-I didn't get so many . . . not many, Father. There's a . . . there's a blight on them this year."

"Is that so . . ." He sniffed the air. "Were you burning something?"

"No, Father."

He hunkered down, inspecting the spot where she'd flung the herbs, picked up a partially burned leaf.

"Hmm . . . I'm not so well up in my plants, Ruby, but I know this one. Vervain, I'd say."

"Is it?"

"Aye. Them pointed leaves . . . they say they were used to stanch the wounds of Christ."

He gazed in reverence at the leaves, made the sign of the cross, and looked pointedly at Ruby.

"I-I didn't know that, Father."

"Your mother's worried about you, Ruby . . . says you're not yourself."

Ruby put her thumb and forefinger together. She really needed the Goddess's help now. But on this occasion no voice came. She was on her own.

"She . . . she worries too much, Father. There's nothing wrong with me."

Father Kelly stood up again and looked about him. "God's good, aye. God's good, so . . ."

Ruby wanted to say, "You mean the Goddess," but that flash of confidence she was hoping for refused to come. Something was staying her tongue. She felt confused. Why couldn't she say what she believed?

Why was the Goddess not helping her?

She felt the weight of the bag on her shoulder. The bag containing her blessed things. It was because *he* had come along. He'd interrupted a sacred rite. It was *his* fault. This man in the black clothes and white collar.

". . . sure we'll go up to the house," Father Kelly was saying. "Say some prayers with your mother . . . just to put her mind at rest, so."

Ruby nodded and, against her will, found herself meekly following the priest out of the woods.

Chapter nineteen

Belfast, 1983

Henry Shevlin studied the houses on Mountview Terrace. A drab line of crumbling, brownstone dwellings that had seen better times. He didn't like the look of the place and felt uneasy. This was clearly Republican territory. Some houses had tricolors draped from upper-story windows. Other residents had chosen to mark their territory by painting the curbstones green, white, and orange. Several boys kicking a ball about stopped and eyed him sullenly. He double-checked the address that the hotel receptionist had written down for him. Yes, it tallied with the house he stood facing. A three-up, two-down, with a hall door crying out for a fresh coat of paint.

The doorbell wasn't working. He knocked twice and braced himself for an unpleasant encounter. After a lengthy wait, he heard several bolts being disengaged and the sound of a key turning. The door creaked open. An elderly little woman in a checked pinny stood blinking up at him. She was plainly nervous.

"He's not here," she said, glancing up and down the street.

"Mr. Halligan?"

"Aye. They said you'd be comin' round today. You'd better come in."

He was mystified. Clearly he'd been mistaken for another. Who that other could be was impossible to say.

But Henry Shevlin was no coward. The stakes were high: Connie was uppermost in his mind. This old woman and this dilapidated old house on the wrong side of town were his new and unexpected links to her possible whereabouts. If risks had to be taken, he was ready to take them.

The hallway smelled of mildew and the odors left by cheap cooking. The room the little lady led the way into was tiny, dim, and cluttered. He saw coverings of faded rose-print, photos from a bygone age, religious statues set about. Henry did his best not to stare too much. The tiny window frame rattled disagreeably as a British Army armored personnel carrier roared by out on the street.

"I didn't think they'd be sendin' a plainclothes detective," the little woman said. "Mr. Halligan must be very important."

Henry paused before replying.

That night, having dinner in his living room and replaying the events of the day, he thought again of the incredible stroke of good fortune that had caused his beeper to sound at that exact moment. With an instinct born of habit, he plucked the little instrument from his breast pocket and checked the readout.

Sure enough, it was Bill Bachman. He'd suspected as much. His locum therapist was requesting his help for the third time that day. Bill was a cautious young man; he seldom made a decision without the backup of a superior.

Henry nodded slowly and returned the pager to his pocket. He could see that the old lady was impressed.

"That was the station, Mrs. . . . . ?"

"O'Leary," she said at once. "Mrs. O'Leary. Would you be going to . . . eh . . . ?"

"I'll need to ask you a few questions, Mrs. O'Leary." He hoped to blazes she wouldn't demand to see ID but guessed she would not.

He could tell she was used to detectives nosing about the place. Nevertheless, he'd have to tread carefully. One slipup and she'd be onto him. "Impersonating an officer"—wasn't that what they called it in those American cop shows? "I must caution you, however."

"Yes, Inspector." She was more nervous now. "What is it you'd like to know now?"

"Halligan. He lodges with you, does he?"

"That's right, Inspector. He rents a room. But y'know, I hardly know if he's in or out. He comes and goes."

"When did you last see him?"

She thought hard. "A week ago . . . maybe two. It's hard to know 'cos he doesn't take meals here. He pays me a retainer, y'see. Oh, he pays very well . . . and him hardly ever sleepin' here."

"The last time you saw him, did he have a woman with him?"

"No . . . no. I don't think so."

It was an odd answer. "You don't *think* so?"

"Well, yeh see, women call here lookin' for him all the time. He's very popular with the ladies."

So Connie's not the only one. How could she be so gullible?

"And why would that be, Mrs. O'Leary?"

"Oh, he's very handsome, Inspector . . . eh . . . What did you say your name was?"

"McKenzie." The name had come almost instantly. He'd been thinking of an ex-colleague with that surname, who'd been popular with the ladies, too. "And . . ."

"And a real Yankee. Always dresses well. Ladies like that in a man, so they do."

Henry was aware of a little worm of jealousy wriggling its way into his psyche. He squashed it immediately. This was no time for such distractions. He sensed that he was closer to Connie than he'd been since the evening of her disappearance. It was vital that he kept a cool head. Mrs. O'Leary could turn out to be his greatest ally in the search. He had to play the hand she was dealing him—and play it well.

"How much are yins gonna pay me? It's just that it's dangerous for me and I'm takin' a risk, like."

What on earth was she talking about? He had to be extra cautious. "Don't know. You'll have to speak to the boss. I would like to see his bedroom, if I may."

Mrs. O'Leary hesitated.

"You've been most cooperative, and I appreciate it. A young woman may be in danger . . . and you can help her."

"Oh dear!" The landlady put a hand to her mouth. Henry was sorry he'd frightened her. But he really needed to see that room. "He's not a murderer? Mr. Halligan."

"No, he's not a murderer, but he may be playing with fire. These Yankees don't know how dangerous this city can be, that's all."

She got up and peered through the lace curtains, looking from right to left.

"By rights I should return with a search warrant but something tells me that a lady like yourself won't stand on ceremony, so I'll—"

"That's all right, Inspector." She went into the kitchen and returned moments later with a bunch of keys. "He usually keeps his door locked, but I'll let you in."

"That's very good of you."

She mounted the stairs ahead of him.

———

Henry stood staring at the spartan room. It contained a small four-poster bed with a threadbare eiderdown, a bedside locker, an ancient closet, and a dressing table.

"I'll leave you to get on."

"Thank you, Mrs. O'Leary. I'll lock up when I'm done."

He listened to her uncertain tread on the stairs, and waited until he heard the kitchen door shut with a light click. Reluctantly, he turned his attention back to the room.

Why was the wealthy American living in a dump like this? It just didn't add up. And what was Connie doing with him? He doubted he'd find the answer here.

The bed looked as though it had seldom been slept in. He checked the closet. Nothing. The drawers in the dressing table yielded nothing, either.

He was about to leave when he realized he hadn't checked the bedside locker.

A lonely biro rolled to the front of the drawer as he yanked it open. There was a torn sheet of notepaper, too.

Blank, alas.

He turned it over. There was something scribbled on it. Maybe nothing. But best to make sure. Any clue was better than leaving empty-handed.

He took the page to the window to have a closer look.

Thanks for everything, Harry.
Best of luck,
Holly

Harry was obviously Halligan.

But, Holly . . . ?

"*Well, you see, women call here lookin' for him all the time. He's very popular with the ladies.*"

Holly could be anyone. But that handwriting, that handwriting. There was something about it. The right-leaning slant, the disconnect between letters, which showed a sometimes impractical mind, the high-pressured hand. Those Rs always capitalized, even within words.

He took one of Connie's notes from his wallet, placed it under the writing.

Yes, it looked very like hers. The similarities were striking.

Could it be? Could this piece of paper be the first real link to her disappearance? He was uncertain.

What he was certain of, however, was that the elusive Mr. Halligan frequented this place. And that Connie had been seen in his company.

He could not but conclude that, strange though it seemed, this little house with its doddery old resident was trying to tell him something.

He put the note to Harry in his pocket and exited the room, the idea for his next step already taking shape.

Chapter twenty

Ruby was troubled. Father Kelly had upset her ritual and turned off the *voice* inside her—Dana's voice, or was it Edna's voice? That positive, decisive, powerful force she knew and respected so well, had been silenced by a man in a long black coat and clerical collar.

Why had it deserted her at that crucial moment?

Was it the fact he was a priest?

Was it because he'd invaded Dana's sacred space? Spoiled the sanctity of her ritual? Well, very, very soon Ruby would be enacting the real ritual: the midsummer ritual. And this time she'd make sure no one disturbed her.

Yes, she'd resolved that no one—not even Father Kelly—would stop her. At that special hour, under the light of a silvery moon, he'd be fast asleep, dead to the world in his shuttered house on the outskirts of Tailorstown.

Ruby in her bed, restless, was replaying what had happened when she'd followed the priest out of the woods. The confusion she'd felt. And the guilt she carried as she trudged in his wake, through the furze and the ferns, under a quickening sky, toward the farmhouse.

He strode ahead of her, as if anxious to put some distance between them.

Odd.

He'd always liked to talk.

She saw him glance in the direction of Beldam Lake, then raise his right hand and swiftly make the sign of the cross.

"Why did you do that, Father?"

He stopped and turned.

She'd had the question out before realizing how impertinent it sounded. You never asked a priest why he did things. Most especially holy things.

"I act on God's prompting, Ruby. And you must do likewise."

On their return to the house they'd said a decade of the rosary together, in the kitchen along with the mother. Then he'd taken some holy water from a bag and announced that he'd bless the bedrooms. Ruby's heart had skipped a beat. Edna's case? What if he looked under the bed?

She tried to stall him. "But why, Father?"

"What sort of question's that?" Martha, staring at her, incredulous. "Why wouldn't you want your room blessed?"

She saw her mother and Father Kelly swap looks. Closed, unreadable.

"Well . . . it's . . . it's just that . . . I didn't have time to tidy up my room this morning, and . . ."

"Father Kelly won't mind what state it's in. Isn't that right, Father?"

"Not a bit of it, Ruby. But, if it makes you feel better, you run on there—"

She was up and in the room almost before he'd finished the sentence. But where else to conceal the case? The wardrobe?

A voice behind her made her jump.

"Sure your room's grand, Ruby."

Father Kelly in the doorway, looking grim. "Now you go down and make your mother and me a nice cuppa tea." He draped a stole about his neck and smoothed it down. "And let me get on with God's good business."

Ruby squeezed her eyes tight now, recalling the pain of having to leave him in the room, alone.

Please, Dana, don't let him find the case and take my dreams away.

"The Father likes a strong cup," her mother said. "Put four spoons in the pot."

They sat at the kitchen table in silence.

Ruby had no stomach for the tea. She could hear him walking about in her bedroom. Could tell from the kitchen ceiling which portion he was in.

She looked up. Could barely keep herself in the chair.

"Why are you so worried? Is there something in that room you don't want the priest to see?"

"No, Mammy . . . it's just that . . ."

"It's just what?"

Thump.

A loud bang overhead had her racing up the stairs. She found Father Kelly on the landing. He looked pale. The door to her bedroom stood open, but nothing seemed disturbed.

"Are you all right, Father?"

"Yes," he said, but his grip on the banister was knuckle-white. "Now, where's that tea you promised me?"

Before leaving, he blessed her, making the sign of the cross on her forehead with holy water.

"Heavenly Father, protect Ruby from all harm, and keep evil spirits from taking their revenge on her in any way. Amen."

Evil spirits? Revenge? Why was he talking about evil spirits? She wasn't dabbling with evil. The Goddess Dana was good. But she could hardly tell him *that.*

"Is there anything you'd like to confess to me Ruby, now?" he said, resting a hand on her shoulder. "Anything at all that's troubling you?"

"No . . . no, Father."

"You'd better take them blackberries out of that bag, then. You wouldn't want them to stain it in this heat."

The bag! She'd left it on the draining board. Oh God, what if he asked to see inside it? The censer, the candles, the offering plate? Her three wishes. How would she explain those?

"I will so, Father."

"Looks like you picked quite a lot." He was looking through her, to the place where her secrets lay.

"I did . . . I'll just put them in the pantry. It's cooler in there."

"Good . . . good," he said, still studying her face. Ruby looked away. She was telling lies to a priest. A mortal sin. She wanted to weep.

"Say that prayer to Michael the Archangel every night before you sleep, now . . . just to be on the safe side." He pointed to the picture in the alcove. She saw that the glass had been replaced. She nodded.

Martha Clare saw him to the door.

They talked in hushed tones on the step. "Don't worry, Martha," Ruby heard him say. "The Devil is like a dog on a chain. He can only go so far as God permits."

Chapter twenty-one

Finbar Flannagan aka John Lennon sat in the waiting room of Rosewood Clinic with eyes closed, humming the melody of "Instant Karma" and, by turns, trying to touch his shoulders with the tips of his ears. He was listening for that telltale sign of a muscle popping in his neck. For if a muscle did tear, it would mean that the intergalactic superbeings who organized and maintained the New World Order had gained access, albeit fleetingly, to his subconscious processes, and in seconds would be decoding his thoughts, encrypting the information and using it against him when, later, they martyred him on a cross, not unlike the one they'd used for Christ, except this time the cross wouldn't be made of wood, but metal, and the tomb wouldn't be of stone but a capsule-pod of see-through plastic with reinforced clips that spewed sparks when touched by The Chosen Few. The snakes would say he deserved to die because he'd said the Beatles were bigger than Jesus. And he'd just have to die because none of the divvies round about would have the courage to stand up and say the truth that he, Finbar, was indeed the true Messiah, and his songs the true gospel according to John . . . and Yoko.

But so far, Finbar's neck muscle hadn't popped. If it did . . . if it did, then he'd have no option but to start screaming until his throat hurt, because that was the only way to disrupt their sensory input, dislodge them from his immediate force field, and to save himself from the agony of the cross.

Being so preoccupied with his hero, John Lennon, and the pernicious influence of that all-pervading New World Order, meant that the real Finbar Flannagan paid scant attention to the more mundane aspects of everyday life on his own little patch of boring earth just north of Tailorstown.

For example, at that point in time, he was under the impression he had an appointment to see Dr. Henry Shevlin. Miss King had already informed him in very clear and succinct language that he'd got his days mixed up. Had shown him Dr. Shevlin's appointment diary and her own patient list, just to prove the point, but Finbar was having none of it. Miss King was "one of them," in on the conspiracy of preventing him from living a normal life, by confusing him with dates and times totally out of step with his quest for peace and love and goodwill to all men, which was his life's mission here on Earth and the path he must follow.

> Let's go!
> All the world's talkin' 'bout movie stars,
> Racing cars, candy bars,
> And men from Mars, singers, wingers,
> Swingers, ringers, ring-ring, ding-ding,
> All we are singing is get down and dance,
> All we are singing is get down and dance.

From behind the rampart that was her desk, Edith King observed him.

She'd already asked him to leave, but Mr. Flannagan showed no sign of moving. She'd considered calling security, but since she was typing up an important report and wished to get it completed, she could not afford any unnecessary disruption.

She saw that his head was swaying from side to side now, in the manner of a carnival puppet. But he seemed happy enough in his own little world, so best to simply let him be. The report was coming on well, and she might even have it completed before the doctor's arrival.

She withdrew another page from the typewriter and laid it aside. Glanced out the window and saw a blue Austin Maxi pull into the Reserved for Staff parking bay. She tut-tutted to herself, wishing that patients would take the trouble to read the signs, so *clearly marked.* She checked her watch, eyed her list. James McCloone, it would seem. Once again, he was far too early.

She observed him bail out of the passenger side and hold the seat back to allow a lady to disembark from the rear.

Interesting, she thought.

So he'd come with backup on this occasion. His girlfriend? Hardly. She'd decided that Mr. McCloone was from that species of men who would remain resolutely unattached: generally unshaven, creased apparel, insouciant regard for protocol. His sister, perhaps? Well, maybe. Anyway—she inserted another page into the type-writer—she'd soon be finding out.

———

"God, this is a terrible grand place!" Rose proclaimed, emerging from the backseat of the car, fanning herself with Jamie's appointment letter, visibly awed at the sight of the modern glass-and-sand-stone structure that was Rosewood Clinic. "This isn't the mental hospital, is it?"

"No, Rose, it's a place you have to come tae first, afore you go tae St. Ita's. But I'm not goin' there."

Rose gripped Jamie's arm. "No, Jamie, you're not goin' there, 'cos there's nothing wrong with yer head, Jamie. That's why I decided to come with you tae see this Dr. Shelfin, so I can explain things. 'Cos you know what they say, two heads is better than three."

Rose, husband Paddy, and Jamie McCloone went back a long way, the couple really coming into Jamie's life when his beloved uncle died in 1973. At that time, they'd been a godsend, helping the grieving smallholder negotiate the rapids and whirlpools of the yawning chasm he'd been left to face. They were the shoulders that Jamie cried on. The people who broke his fall as he hurtled toward the abyss. Jamie knew his life would have little purpose without their friendship and good counsel. He trusted them completely, and Rose in particular. She was the only lady, apart from his beloved aunt Alice, whom he'd allowed himself to get close to in all the years of his troubled life.

———

Rose, a well-rounded lady of fifty-five, was a triumph of culinary prowess and domestic endeavor, with a heart the size of Cork, and a mission to set the world aright with the many skeins of homespun knowledge she'd garnered during thirty-three years of married bliss to husband Paddy. She believed a man's needs took precedence over her own, but at the same time, was shrewd enough to realize that men were no better than children when it came to the domestic side of things. God-blisses-an'-savus, if there were no women about, sure the world would be in a terrible state. For, from the minute they stumbled from the cradle on their tottery wee legs, sure wasn't it a woman's hand that reached out and stopped them before they fell a clatter?

No, in Rose McFadden's book, Eve hadn't tempted Adam with that notorious red apple in the Garden of Eden . . . or was it Gethsemane now? Can never mind right. No, not a bit of it! When she plucked the apple, sure wasn't she only using her head and getting the pair of them a bite to eat 'cos they were starving with the hunger? There'd maybe be none of us running about atall, atall, had she not had the sense to take a bit of action, 'cos men need a wee push from time to time to get things moving, so they do.

Such insights had endowed Rose with a powerhouse of wisdom in Jamie's eyes. She it was who'd encouraged him to answer an ad in the Lonely Hearts page of the *Mid-Ulster Vindicator* all those years ago. She it was who sat in the Royal Neptune Hotel with Paddy while he kept his date with one Lydia Devine. Rose had led Jamie into worlds he never thought possible. He trusted her advice completely. So, when she suggested accompanying him on his second visit to see Dr. Shevlin, he acquiesced without hesitation. After all, Rose could say things to the doctor that Jamie, maybe, couldn't say himself, or might forget all about completely.

―――――

"Now, Paddy, you go on to Biddy's café," Rose said. "To see about them talking teeth of yours. Me and Jamie might be an hour. Would that be right, Jamie?"

Jamie McCloone pulled on his ear, embarrassed at the trouble he was causing. "About that, Rose . . . God, I'm puttin' yins to a lot of bother."

"Not a bit of it," Rose said kindly.

"What are Paddy's talking teeth anyway, Rose?"

"Well, it's like this, Jamie: Paddy's got two sets of false teeth. A pair for talking with and a pair for eating with."

"And I took out the talking teeth when I was havin' a cuppa tea," Paddy explained.

Rose saw Jamie's confusion.

"Yes, Jamie, we were having a flaky knob and a cuppa tea in Biddy's. Have ye ever had one of Biddy's flaky knobs, Jamie?"

"Naw, just the fry, Rose."

"Well, next time you're in you should try one, 'cos she's very good at the flaky pastry, is Biddy. But that's beside the point. Paddy here took out the talking teeth to eat the knob, and that's when he lost them."

"Aye," Paddy said, picking up the complicated tale once more. "Had them in a hankie in me pocket and, begod, when I went tae pay Biddy, they must'a fell outta me pocket. Well, that's what I'm hopin' happened anyway, Jamie."

"That's why he has tae go to the Cozy Corner tae see if Biddy Mulhern's got the talking teeth," Rose added, belaboring further an already heavily embellished point. "'Cos maybe she saw them and has them behind the counter."

"So don't you worry about putting us out, Jamie," said Paddy, revving up the engine once more. "Sure anything tae help you on yer way. And it's a terrible thing you've come through in that police station. But sure this new doctor will see you right."

"Aw, now, it's very good of the two of you. Don't know what I'd do without ye."

Rose patted Jamie's arm. "Me and my Paddy will always be here for you, Jamie. Always mind that. Now let's see what this Dr. Shelfin has to say."

With that, they bade Paddy farewell and made their way across the car park, toward the space-age contraption that was the revolving door.

Rose halted.

"God, Jamie, what sorta thing's that?"

"I think she said it was an evolvin' boy or something like that, Rose . . . it goes round when we get into her. But if you go first, I'll push us, so I will."

Gingerly, Rose stepped into one of the glass chambers, Jamie into the one behind her, and off they went.

Miss King was alerted to a thumping sound and a man's voice loudly swearing. She looked up from the typewriter, to see a woman sprawled on all fours just inside the foyer and Jamie McCloone whirling round inside the door like a hamster on a wheel, unable to get himself stopped.

"Not again," she sighed, pushed back her chair, and went to assist the pair.

"Are you all right?" she said, bending over Rose. "*Stop pushing!*" she shouted at Jamie McCloone, whilst sticking her foot in the door so he could extricate himself.

"Jezsis, is there no other way in-tae this bloody place?" Jamie asked, retrieving his cap from the floor, comb-over undone. "But through that damned thing?"

"Are you Dr. Shelfin?" said an exasperated Rose, grabbing hold of Miss King's proffered arm. "Only I thought you were a man."

"What the feck are yins all doin'?!" Finbar Flannagan screamed. "I can't hear if I'm poppin' and they might be in me head already . . . so shut the feck up, ye pair'a culchies."

"I'll not have that language in here!" Miss King threatened, throwing Finbar a killer look. "Or I'll call security and have you removed."

She helped Rose into a chair.

"No, I'm not a man, as you can see, but Dr. *Shevlin* is, I can assure you. I'm Miss King, his secretary . . . and you are?"

"Oh God-blisses-an'-savus, Miss King, thank you very much. Rose McFadden's me name."

"Rose is a good friend of mine," Jamie explained, sitting down beside a much-winded Rose. "Are you all right, Rose?"

"The best, Jamie, the best. Don't you worry about *me*."

"You're too early again, Mr. McCloone. Your appointment letter, please?"

"Aye, I might be a wee bit early, Miss King, but I took a lift with Paddy and Rose—"

"That's the letter there, Miss King," said Rose, relinquishing her fan. "Yes, we gave Jamie a lift, for my Paddy lost his talking teeth in the Cozy Corner Café, and Jamie wanted me to come with him, so we could see Dr. Shelfin together, like."

For one unkind second Miss King thought that this McFadden woman might indeed be in line for a therapy session or two with Henry herself, given her propensity for incoherent rambling, but being the professional that she was, the secretary stayed her tongue and gave a little smile of understanding, before moving back behind her desk.

She ticked off Jamie's name in her appointment book and said, "Dr. Shevlin will be along shortly," before returning to her typing.

"I'm gettin' outta here!" Finbar Flannagan announced. He stood up and pointed at Rose. "'Cos you're one of *them*."

"God-blisses-an'-savus, one'a them what? What's he sayin' anyway, Jamie?"

"I don't have the divil of a notion, Rose."

"What's your name?" Rose asked kindly. "Doz your mammy know you're here?"

"Now what did I say? Go call it a day. Don't give me that mammy, mammy, mammy shit no more. Get outta my head! You hear what I said? Don't give me that mammy, mammy, mammy shit no more. 'Cos I found out. I found out, didn't I? I found out, eh, eh, eh?"

Having finished his spiel, Finbar spun on his heel and marched out the door, away from the intergalactic alien that was Rose McFadden.

"God, it's that old drink that makes a body talk like that. God help his mammy, Jamie, is all I can say."

"Aye, so," Jamie said.

Rose breathed a sigh of relief, reached for a *Woman's Realm* on the coffee table to calm herself. "There's maybe a couple of recipes a body could use."

Jamie, disconsolate and not a little nervous, gazed about the waiting room. His eyes fell on a desk calendar. He read the date.

He jumped up.

Rose shut the magazine. "God, Jamie, what is it?"

"Jezsis, the vet's comin' in ten minutes to vaccinate the cow. I forgot all about it."

"Are you sure, Jamie?"

"Aye, I'm sure. We better go, quick."

Chapter twenty-two

Belfast, 1983

The white Mercedes SL280 was hard to miss at the best of times. It stood out in broad daylight, and was even conspicuous at night. His father had shaken his head in disapproval when Henry visited the parental home shortly after buying it. Sinclair Shevlin disliked ostentation of any kind, or "drawing undue attention to oneself," as he phrased it.

"You're a psychiatrist, not a confounded nightclub owner," he said, inspecting the car. "A man's choice of vehicle should reflect his professional standing. An educated man impresses with his intelligence and not his wealth."

Henry thought about that as he sat behind the wheel of the stationary vehicle. He'd parked it close enough to 13 Mountview Terrace to observe the comings and goings, but far enough away so as not to draw "undue attention." He hoped that the one remaining streetlight—the vandals had smashed the rest—on the other side of Mrs. O'Leary's house was too far distant. The Mercedes was white, though, and its sporty lines caused it to stand out from the pack. But in poor light, the high headrest and low roof would, he believed, render him almost invisible to a casual passerby.

He looked at his wristwatch. It was approaching 10:00 p.m. Darkness had closed in over Belfast. He heard a church bell tolling somewhere in the distance. Its notes seemed to intensify the solitude of the deserted street.

And it *was* quiet. Much quieter than he'd expected for a Friday evening. Since he'd taken up his vigil two hours before, there'd been little traffic in either direction, and only a handful of pedestrians. Two small groups of teenagers: boys and girls alive with the lusts that summertime brings to the young, two elderly ladies walking small dogs, a drunk weaving slightly and steadying himself at each lamppost, and an RUC Land Rover, whose occupants gave the Mercedes no more than a cursory glance.

It was the third vigil. He'd visited the street on Wednesday, the day after his encounter with Mrs. O'Leary. He'd parked slightly nearer her home, and had maintained his surveillance for the best part of two hours.

Surveillance! Henry smiled grimly as he turned the word over in his head. But it *was* surveillance, he told himself. His activity—or, rather, lack of activity—went hand in glove with his impersonation of a police officer, the pretense that had convinced the elderly lady of his bona fides.

Now it was Friday, and Henry was seated in the parked car for the third night in a row. Three hours had passed, and like before, neither Halligan nor his mistress had shown.

Mistress. He reflected on that quaint, somewhat old-fashioned word. He associated it with the gentry, or the French political classes. Try as he might, he found it almost impossible to think of Connie in that light. She wasn't the "sort"; she was too independently minded to be somebody's mistress. And was it not the case that only married men had mistresses? Was Halligan a married man? Henry had no way of knowing. At that stage, it was all guesswork. He didn't even know—

He jumped. Without warning, the barrel of an automatic rifle had tapped his side window.

The soldiers had appeared from nowhere, or so it seemed. There were two of them. They stood on either side of the car. A third had moved into view just beyond the windscreen. He wore an officer's cap and uniform. With a lazy circling motion of an index finger, he was wordlessly ordering the window to be wound down.

"Good evening, sir," the officer said. The tone of voice was almost mocking, it seemed. "May I see your papers, please?" Henry reached for the glove compartment. "Slowly, please, sir."

He suddenly felt vulnerable. Not without reason. The British Army had already shot dead more than a hundred people in Northern Ireland, most of whom were unarmed civilians.

At the same time, he was confident that his background would count in his favor. He came from a long line of Protestants and belonged to the "Unionists," that section of the people who swore allegiance to the Queen and her armed forces. As he handed his driver's license to the officer, he told himself that a quick check would reveal where his loyalties lay. That he posed no threat to the soldiers.

"I'll have to ask you to step out of the car, sir."

Henry began to sweat. He hesitated.

"Please, sir. We have to do a quick search. Nothing to be concerned about."

The two soldiers—a private and a corporal—held their weapons nonchalantly as he opened the door and climbed out, but he knew that one false move would have them covering him again. He was shaking as the officer indicated that he should remain standing a little distance from the car.

Slinging their guns behind their backs, the soldiers went to work with practiced hand. The private switched on the car's interior lights; the corporal produced a flashlight and played it over the parts concealed in shadow.

"Nothing here, sir," he said.

The officer nodded at the boot of the car. The corporal opened it.

"Sir, I think you should see this."

The other soldier was keeping him covered with the fearsome weapon. The officer went to look. He returned to where Henry stood. In his hand were several boxes of pills.

"Yes, I'm a doctor. Medication is part of my job."

"And this?" The officer held up a transparent plastic pouch containing a small, flat cake of a brown-colored substance.

Henry was speechless. He made an effort to speak but could not. He knew what the substance was. He thought of Geraldine, Connie's friend from college days, and her comment about them enjoying the odd joint. Could this stuff be hers? Connie's?

He looked on in dismay as the officer opened the pouch and sniffed significantly. He nodded.

"Take him," he said to the corporal. "You," he told the private, "lock the car and give the keys to me."

———

"A *psychi*atrist?" Major Dunglass said, looking Henry in the eye with a stare that he swore had not wavered in ten minutes or more.

"Yes, a psychiatrist, a medical practitioner who deals with mental illness and emotional—"

"I know what a psychiatrist *is*, Dr. Shevlin," Dunglass said acidly. "My question is: What's a psychiatrist doing with a significant quantity of cannabis? And more to the point: What were you doing in your car, in that street, at that hour?"

"Nothing illegal, I assure you. And I resent being treated like a criminal. There was no need for your corporal to accompany me to the lavatory down the hall and watch my every move."

The major said nothing for a moment or two. Then he pushed his chair back with an abruptness that startled Henry, stood up, and went to a counter set against the wall. All the while, the two soldiers, still with automatic weapons loosely at the ready, stood at either side of the door, keeping watch. There was an RUC constable stationed opposite, keeping watch. A man in a business suit was observing the proceedings with interest, his face shaded by a fedora. He hadn't said a word since the interrogation began some minutes before. He was standing in one corner of the interview room, hands stuck casually in his pockets.

Major Dunglass returned to the table. He tossed the boxes of pills and the pouch of cannabis resin onto it.

"Amphetamines, Dr. Shevlin, and fifty grams of what our experts assure me is top-grade hashish. That constitutes an illegal substance, psychiatrist or not. Are you going to tell me what that quantity of drugs was doing in your car?"

"I was hoping *you* would tell *me*," Henry said coldly. He jerked a thumb at the corporal. "Or perhaps you should ask the young man who planted them there."

"That's a very serious accusation, Doctor. I hope you can back it up."

"My dear major, I'm a clinical psychiatrist with an impeccable police record. I haven't so much as a speeding ticket—or even a parking fine for that matter. You can check . . . if you haven't already done so." He narrowed his eyes. "The army, on the other hand, hasn't exactly got an enviable record in Northern Ireland. If you think—"

Henry flinched as the major brought his palm down hard on the table. He was livid. He expected a blow to the head at any moment. He was regretting his remark.

"I'm going to ask you directly, Doctor: Are you dealing drugs?"

"Don't be preposterous!"

"A straight answer, please: Are you or aren't you?"

"No. No, of course not."

"Then how do you explain the fact that you were observed on three successive evenings, seated in a stationary vehicle containing illegal drugs, within sight of premises used by a known terrorist and drug user?"

"What?!"

"You heard me, Doctor. And would you please address your answers to the tape recorder."

"I-I . . . Do you . . . do you mean Halligan?"

"To the tape machine, please."

Henry had gone pale. His voice was barely audible. The police officer came and moved the recorder closer.

"What's your relationship with Harris Halligan?"

"I don't know the man."

"I see. If that's the case, why were you keeping his lodgings under surveillance?"

"I wasn't."

"You were." He picked up a notebook and flipped a page. "On Wednesday evening, Thursday evening, and this evening." Dunglass leaner closer. "Furthermore, you paid a visit to Halligan's home on Tuesday afternoon at ten minutes past three, and left shortly before four. Do you deny that?"

How, thought Henry, could they have known all that? Mrs. O'Leary. That was the only answer. Or was it? Dimly, he recalled an army vehicle that had passed by out on the street when Mrs. O'Leary had admitted him. But the jeep had sped past without slowing. No, there had to be another explanation. He thought of the anonymous houses to either side of Mrs. O'Leary's, the houses opposite. Any of those dwellings could be harboring a watchful pair of eyes: eyes that kept tabs on visitors to Halligan's quarters. Yes, that had to be it. The owner of those eyes had alerted Major Dunglass to his presence.

"I'll not answer any more questions until I have legal representation," he said.

The major chuckled.

"Sorry to disappoint you, Doctor, but that's not how it works here. You're dealing with Her Majesty's Armed Forces now, not the civil authorities. Might I remind you that Northern Ireland is in a state of emergency at present, and that the Special Powers Act has been reinstated? I'm the law here, Dr. Shevlin, and I decide whether or not you need a solicitor." He leaned across the table again. "And my answer is 'no.'"

Henry realized he was in a very dangerous situation. He looked to the RUC constable for help, confirmation, clarification—anything. But the police officer dropped his gaze to the floor. No help there.

"Now, what was the purpose of your visit to the O'Leary house on Tuesday?"

"I was looking for my wife."

"Your wife."

"She's disappeared."

Dunglass switched off the tape recorder.

"Why didn't you say so sooner?"

"You didn't ask me."

At the major's prompting, Henry related the events surrounding Connie's disappearance. He was careful not to mention the Republican mural he'd seen on the Falls Road, or its "original": the canvas he'd attacked at the Mondrian.

"When did she disappear?"

"A week ago. On the twenty-fifth of May. I was led to believe that this Halligan person knew something about her whereabouts."

"Had she IRA involvement, Doctor?"

"No!"

"I don't believe you."

"Major . . ."

The voice was soft but heavy with authority. It was the man in the hat. He'd left the corner and had moved to stand next to Dunglass. Henry tensed again. He did not like the look of things.

"Please dismiss your men, Major," the stranger said. "And wait outside until further notice."

Dunglass, to Henry's bemusement, obeyed at once, but with bad grace. He made a curt gesture to the police constable, who at once went to the door. He rapped on it sharply and it was opened from outside by unseen hands. Without a backward glance, the four left the room.

"Now, Dr. Shevlin," the man said, coming out of the shadows. "We can dispense with all this." He laid a finger on the pouch of hashish and slid it to one side. He sat down in the major's chair and unbuttoned his jacket, pushed up the brim of his hat.

Eyes, colorless yet penetrating, met Henry's. A shiver ran through him. That glacial stare, the predatory presence. He hadn't met the real thing very often during his career but was in little doubt that the individual sitting opposite had the hallmarks of the psychopath.

"I want you to listen very carefully. If you value your freedom, and wish to avoid a serious criminal charge, you'll do exactly as I say. You stand accused of two offenses: being in possession of illegal narcotics, and impersonating a police officer. Do we understand one another?"

Henry could do no more than nod glumly. He'd guessed correctly: they'd spoken with Mrs. O'Leary, and she'd told them of his deception. His gaze fell on the other's jacket. Did he imagine a holstered weapon concealed by the fine tailoring? He thought he did.

"Your wife was foolish enough to involve herself with the IRA. This was—"

"That's a lie!"

"Be quiet, Doctor. I warn you: any more interruption and this meeting is over. I shall summon the duty sergeant and instruct him to charge you with possession of an illegal substance, plus the impersonation. You will stand trial and be sentenced to at least five years for those crimes, and will be struck off the medical register. In other words, Doctor, I will ruin you. I have it in my power to do so, and I will not hesitate if you continue to thwart this investigation. Nod if you understand."

Henry nodded again. His back was damp with perspiration. He thought he could smell his own fear. Nothing from his psychiatric training had prepared him for this.

"When you leave this room, Dr. Shevlin, you will forget everything I'm about to tell you. For your own good. I will not even tell you my name, because as far as you're concerned we never met, and this conversation never took place. Harris Halligan is one of our operatives, working undercover for British Intelligence. Unfortunately, your wife got involved with him. We do not know the details of her relationship with him, and to be honest, it's immaterial to me at present. The only reason I'm telling you this is that I don't want you jeopardizing the whole operation. If you want her to come out of this alive you must stop looking for her."

Henry was speechless. He knew enough to understand what it meant to be a British undercover agent, and the price an agent paid if unmasked. Such spies—for spies they were—ended up being tortured, executed, and buried in unmarked graves by the Provisional IRA. The thought of Connie being associated with such dangerous people was too horrible to contemplate.

"Have I made myself clear?" the man was saying.

Henry nodded dumbly.

"Good. You see, Doctor, if you go looking for your wife then you'll also be placing yourself in mortal danger. When the time is right we will contact you. So step back, and let us do our job."

"When the time is right? I don't understand. What do you mean, 'the time is right'?"

But the answer he gave was just as ambiguous.

"As I said, Doctor: If you want to see your wife again, *stop* looking."

Chapter twenty-three

Saturday afternoon found Ruby at the kitchen sink, scrubbing a saucepan. She hadn't slept well and was feeling anxious at the thought of the twins' arrival off the three o'clock bus.

The previous weekend, they'd gone to Manchester to see George Best playing at Old Trafford. Maybe they'd have his autograph, but she wasn't holding out much hope. They rarely gave her gifts, just stuff they didn't want themselves or had grown tired of. There was a drawer in her bedroom chock-full of half-used bottles of perfume, worn handbags, fake jewelry with bits missing . . . the works.

In the front room, Martha was having a chinwag with Ida Nettles. It was unusual for Ida to visit on a Saturday, but Ruby was in no doubt that her actions the previous evening, and Father Kelly's visit, had sent her mother to the phone with an invitation to her friend.

She rinsed the saucepan under the faucet and set it on the drainer, stood for a while staring out the window. It was a calm afternoon: the sun shining, Beldam Lake as smooth as glass, shimmering in the distance. The window was in need of cleaning, but Ruby didn't much care. She now had more important things to think about than cleaning windows and knitting tea cozies. She'd allowed the more mundane household chores to slide of late, but the mother hadn't seemed to notice. Or if she had, she didn't say anything. Ruby knew that her daughter's mental state was more of a concern to Martha these days. Why else had she summoned Father Kelly?

Thoughts of the priest stole into her mind. Every time they did, she pushed them out by envisioning the ritual she'd perform at the solstice, just four days away. It was now more important than ever that she stick to her plan. Because she was sure he was trying to break her connection with Dana. Snatches of Edna's writing came to her.

Be wary of one who would dominate you . . .
twist worship from you for their own gain and glory . . .

Yes, she knew his game.

But next Thursday night she'd be gaining access to a world that he, a mere priest, could not even begin to imagine.

Raise the curv'd blade at the moon
On the twenty-first of June
This rite shall make thy dreams come true,
And wondrous powers shall thee accrue.

The specter of May and June came hard on the heels of the priest. She'd learned so much in the two weeks since she'd last seen them; her inner life, enriched beyond measure by the secrets in *The Book of Light*. She was confident that she'd taken every measure possible to keep those secrets safe. The case was still under her bed. There it would stay. She'd thought about hiding it out in the shed, but felt it would be a betrayal of all that Edna and the Goddess stood for. Her grandmother's dying wish was that it remain in the farmhouse. That link she'd forged with Edna would not be broken. Not for the twins. Not for anyone. She'd simply lock the bedroom door against them.

A raven alighted in the back garden. Ruby blinked. It was a sign. When her father died in the field, a raven had landed beside his body. Now she knew what it meant. Her heart lifted. The raven was a symbol of the afterlife. It moved between the worlds of the living and the dead. And she, Ruby, would be moving between those worlds very, very soon.

"Wade in waters still and deep. Where the little boy doth sleep."

The voice was back! She was elated.

"Wade in waters still and deep. Where the little boy doth sleep. Yes, I will, I will, very soon."

"Are you all right, Ruby?"

She jumped and turned.

Ida Nettles was gazing up at her, small eyes glinting with presentiment.

"Yes . . . yes, Ida. I . . . I was miles away."

"Who were you talking to?"

Ida had never forgiven Ruby's jibe in the supermarket concerning her purchase of hair dye.

"No one. Is it more tea you want? I'll . . . I'll put the kettle back on."

Ruby made to move toward the stove, but Ida caught her arm.

"Where the little boy sleeps? What little boy were you talkin' about?"

"I . . . I don't know what . . . *you're* talking about."

"Oh, you know very well, young lady! Your poor mother's beside herself with worry about you. Now: what are you up to?"

"It is none of your business, you nosy, meddling busybody."

"It is none of your business, you nosy, meddling busybody."

Ida, aghast.

"Your mother is right. You're . . . you're not yourself, Ruby Clare."

"HOW WOULD *YOU* KNOW WHO I AM?"

"How would *you* know who I am?"

"Don't you talk to me like that! And don't you be going near that lake."

"Lake? Who said anything about the lake?"

"You were down in them woods and you weren't pickin' no blackberries neither. And you lied to the priest, God forgive you!"

Ruby had had enough. She didn't need the voice to prompt her; she knew what to do. She marched into the sitting room.

It was time to confront her mother.

"Come back, here!" Ida shouted. "Your mother needs peace."

"Right, Mammy, what's goin' on here? Why are you talkin' behind my back? If ye have anything to say, say it now to me face."

"I tried to stop her, Martha, but she wouldn't listen."

"You keep out of this, Ida Nettles. This is between me and Mammy."

Martha, seated in an armchair, put a hand to her heart. She looked frightened. "My goodness, what's got into you at all?"

"Nothing's got into me. I'm tired of being treated like a child. I'll say what I like, and if you don't like it, that's tough! All you do is complain about me to Father Kelly." She pointed at Ida. "And now *her*."

"You don't know what you're talking about, Ruby. You're . . . going the way of your grandmother. She—"

"You keep Grandma outta this! She was a good woman and you hated her 'cos she was in the way when you married Daddy. You wanted this house to yourself and . . ."

"SHE HAD TO GO TO HER BEDROOM AND LIVE LIKE A PRISONER, BECAUSE YOU HATED THE SIGHT OF HER."

". . . she had to go to her bedroom and live like a prisoner, because you hated the sight of her."

The color had drained from Martha's face. "How could . . . how could you know that? Dear God, you were only a baby. You . . ."

Ida stood behind Ruby, ears cocked for every last morsel of detail. There was enough mileage in this story to keep the whole village going for a week at least.

The mother began to weep.

"Now look what you've done." Ida pushed Ruby out of the way and went to comfort Martha.

"I've done nothing." Ruby rounded on her. "How dare you push me?!"

"What's all this?" Shrill voices in the doorway had them all turning to look.

May and June stood on the threshold, June carrying a large plaster angel under one arm.

At sight of them, Ruby sped up to her bedroom and slammed the door shut.

———

She settled on the bed and tried to calm herself. With those two home, all hell would break loose.

"There is no darkness but ignorance. You are protected."

"Yes, yes, I know . . . I know. There is no darkness but ignorance. I—"

A sharp rap at the door.

"Ruby, are you in there?" May's voice. Testy, impatient.

"Yes. What do *you* want?" Ruby pressed her thumb and forefinger together, hard. In the sure knowledge the Goddess would come through.

"I want to talk to you . . . for a minute."

"Why?"

"I'll let you know when you open the door."

Ruby heaved herself off the bed and turned the key in the lock.

May did not look well. There were dark circles under her eyes, and her face was chalk-white.

"Are you all right?"

"Of course I'm all right. Why wouldn't I be? You're the one that's not all right. Why are you upsetting Mummy again?"

"I WAS NOT UPSETTING ANYONE. I WAS MERELY POINTING OUT SOME FACTS."

Ruby took a deep breath and looked her sister straight in the eye. "I was not upsetting anyone. I was merely pointing out some facts."

May snorted, face twisting in a sneer. "'I was merely pointing out some facts,'" she imitated Ruby in a childish voice, shaking her head from side to side. "You wouldn't know a fact if it came up and bit you in your fat, ugly face."

"HOW DARE YOU SPEAK TO ME LIKE THAT, YOU WRETCHED WAIF."

"How dare you speak to me like that, you wretched waif."

"What did you say?" May in shock.

"I SAID HOW DARE YOU SPEAK TO ME LIKE THAT, YOU WRETCHED WAIF. YOU ARE BEHAVING LIKE A CHILD. NOW, GO BACK TO YOUR TOYS AND LEAVE ME ALONE."

"I *said* how dare you speak to me like that, you wretched waif. You are behaving like a child. Now, go back to your toys and leave me alone."

May began backing out of the room. "Oh God, you *have* gone mad. I know now what Mummy meant on the phone. She said you weren't yourself. And—"

Ruby shut the door quietly on May's stunned face. She turned the key in the lock.

The action had her sister hammering frantically. "You bitch! You mad bitch! You'll pay for this, Ruby Clare. You'll really, really pay for this. We're going to put you in the loony bin, where you bloody belong."

But Ruby had had her say.

My, did it feel good!

Chapter twenty-four

God-savus, Biddy, have you found the talking teeth yet?" Midafternoon, Rose, Paddy, and Jamie pulled out chairs at a Formica table in the Cozy Corner and settled themselves. At that slack hour there were no other customers, apart from itinerant scrap dealer, Barkin' Bob, in a corner, laboring over a gravy chip while humming a speeded-up version of "Amazing Grace."

"'Cos, you know," Rose continued, "from the time my Paddy was in with you last week, I thought maybe a body would of run across them, like."

Biddy Mulhern, for thirty-five years the proprietor of the greasy spoon that was the Cozy Corner, leaned over the counter, cradling her bosom in flour-coated arms, and said, "Well, you know, Rose and Paddy, you'll never believe it." She disappeared from view, and seconds later, a set of shiny pink dentures appeared on the trio's table.

"God-savus," said Rose, staring in disbelief. "Yer talking teeth, Paddy."

"Well, that's the damnedest thing." Paddy snatched them up. "Niver thought I'd see them again."

"Are you sure they're yours?" Jamie asked. "'Cos one pair-a dentures is very like the other."

"Oh, they're mine all right, Jamie . . . would recognize the wee blighters anywhere."

He pointed to the inside of a molar. "See that wee dot of red paint—"

"I put that there, Jamie," Rose chipped in, eager to have her say. "So he could tell the differs between the talking pair and the eating pair. But that's neither here or there. Who found them anyway, Biddy? And we'll have a cuppa tea and some of your flaky knobs. I was tellin' Jamie here how good they were."

"Good enough," said Biddy. "Well, you'll never guess who found them. Honest Thomas was the first to find them, and then Sergeant Ranfurley handed them in."

"Get away!"

At the mention of Ranfurley's name Jamie scowled.

"The sergeant came in here yesterday," continued Biddy. "Had them in a paper bag. Tolt me that Honest Thomas had found them sitting on Butcher Magee's windee-sill, and handed them into the station."

"But how did the sergeant know to give them to you, Biddy?" asked Paddy, perplexed.

"He said that since this was the only café in the town it was more than likely somebody had taken them out before having a bite to eat. And that *I* would very likely know who that body might be. They were his very words."

"God, he's a terrible smart man," said Rose.

"Oh, he's not a sergeant for nothin'," observed Paddy, attempting to put the teeth back in.

"Now, Paddy, where's yer manners?" Rose grappled the dentures from her husband. "I'll give them a wee warsh under the tap, 'cos you niver know how many pairs of hands have been on them, and you could end up with mumps in yer mouth, or worse." With that, Rose took herself off in the direction of the ladies.

Jamie felt moved to speak. "But, Paddy, if they're yer talkin' teeth, sure you don't need tae put then in now, 'cos you've got your eatin' teeth in already."

"Begod, ye know, you're right, Jamie. Never thought of that."

Biddy set a tray down on their table and off-loaded the tea and cakes. "Now, Jamie, flaky knobs for you and Rose . . . and some iced fingers for you, Paddy, 'cos the knobs might stick in yer dentures and we wouldn't want that."

"That Ranfurley's only an oul' bully," Jamie muttered, remembering how he was manhandled and handcuffed, and made to sit in a cell for the best part of four hours because auctioneer Bertie Frogget had pulled a fast one over the price of his heifer.

"I heard about that, Jamie." Biddy stood with the tray pressed to her chest. "But don't you know, he wouldn't arrest the like of Frogget, 'cos he's a big Prodizent with plenty of money . . ."

"Now you've said it, Biddy." Jamie laid into a flaky knob, grateful for Mrs. Mulhern's support and understanding.

". . . but wasn't it good that Rose and Paddy got you out? 'Cos, God knows, you maybe might'a been still sitting there, countin' the four walls."

"Oh, it was very good of Rose and Paddy . . . don't know what I'd do without them, Biddy."

Rose returned with one set of cleansed dentures.

"Now, Paddy, I'm putting these in me handbag. We wouldn't want yeh to lose them again."

"Good enough, Rose."

The door opened, bringing in the blare of a car horn and the sprightly Ida Nettles.

Biddy excused herself and went back behind the counter. She was eager to hear the latest gossip. Her friend rarely disappointed.

Ida plonked down her doctor's bag. "God, Biddy, you wouldn't believe what's happened since I seen you last."

At the table, Rose's ears pricked up.

Ida lowered her voice. "You know that daughter of Martha Clare's?"

"Ruby? Oh, I know Ruby surely. Her and her daddy used to come in here every Friday . . . but she's never been in since his death, God help her. Would maybe be too hard for the poor critter."

"Well," Ida said. "She's goin' crazy, so she is. Talkin' to herself, and poor Martha's beside herself with worry."

"What? Poor Martha doesn't need no bother, with Vinny not about no more."

"How is Martha?" asked Rose, unable to resist a conversation developing without her input. "Haven't seen her about in a long time."

Ida turned her attention to Rose. "Well, now, she's not so good, Rose, 'cos that daughter of hers . . . that Ruby one . . . is giving her a lot of bother, so she is."

"Oh, that's too bad," Rose said. "I wouldn't know Ruby that well."

"I know Ruby," Jamie announced suddenly, remembering the pleasant young woman he'd met in the field not so very long ago.

All eyes turned to Jamie. Rose's eyebrows shot up to her hairline. She thought she knew everything about Jamie's life, but how come he hadn't told her about Ruby Clare?

"That's right," Ida chipped in. "Martha was telling me that she put you out of the field you were wantin' to rent."

"God, Jamie, you didn't tell me that," said Rose.

"Och, I only met her for five minutes, Rose, and she didn't put me outta the field . . . She said her father died in the field and that's why she didn't want to rent it out."

"Well, that was a very good reason not to want to let it," Paddy added.

"Aye, I thought so, too," agreed Jamie.

"Anyway, she's going a bit crazy," Ida continued. "I wouldn't be surprised if she ended up in St. Ita's one of these days."

Jamie blanched at the very sound of St. Ita's. He knew what it meant and hoped Ruby would not have to go in there, either.

Rose, alert to the sadness in her friend's feelings, said, "God willing it won't come to that for poor Ruby. She must miss her daddy very badly. Vinny was a great man altogether."

Barkin' Bob stirred himself in the corner and prepared to take his leave. He came forward and left money on the counter.

"Good day tae you, Mrs. Mulhern," he said tipping the brim of a brand-new Stetson.

"Right you be, Bob," said Biddy. "See you again."

They all watched from the café window as Bob climbed into a shiny green van with the words *Bob's Wares* emblazoned in gold lettering on the side.

"God, Bob's lookin' terrible well these days," Paddy remarked. "He can sell stuff for nothin' and still make a profit. Don't how he doz it."

"Oh, bargains galore," enthused Rose. "I bought twelve toilet rolls, thirty-seven clothes pegs, two pairs of tights, and a hairnet off him yesterday, for only a fiver."

"Now, I heard that he was left a legacy by some relative in Amerikay," Ida said.

"Is that so?" Biddy put in. "Well, I heard he'd won the football pools. Now, what's this we were talkin' about before Bob?"

"Ruby Clare," Jamie declared, surprising them all.

Chapter twenty-five

The morning of June 20 dawned bright and clear. Ruby was delighted. The eve of the midsummer solstice, prelude to her great awakening, had arrived.

She was in the twins' bedroom, cleaning up. It was best to get all trivial tasks dealt with, so that the remainder of the day was hers alone, to relax and prepare.

She shut off the vacuum cleaner and got down on her knees to peer under May's bed. There was something lying in the far corner, which the vacuum brush could not reach. She stretched out a hand, retrieved an official-looking brown envelope, and sat on the bed to get her breath back.

May's name was scrawled on the front, along with a date: Saturday, June 9. Ruby grew excited. That was the Saturday the twins had gone to Manchester to see George Best play the "friendly" match at Old Trafford. This just might be his autograph. There'd been such bad feeling between the twins and herself the previous weekend that she didn't dare ask them for it.

The envelope had already been opened.

Ruby unfolded the sheet of paper. No, it certainly was not George's autograph.

The letterhead read: *Royal Infirmary, 12 Royston Road, Manchester*. But the words underneath, printed in heavy black type, had her staring in disbelief. *Abortion Aftercare Advice*.

Her hands began to shake. She looked up from the page. Now it all made sense. It was the reason they'd gone to Manchester. It was the reason she'd heard them arguing late at night just a fortnight before. It was the reason May looked so unwell at the weekend.

What would their mother say if she discovered what her favorite daughter had done? Ruby recalled a lecture Martha had given the twins, when at eighteen, they'd started going out to dances. "Now if any of the pair of you fall pregnant you might as well go down that field and walk into Beldam Lake, because this family will not endure the embarrassment of having a harlot for a daughter. Is that understood?"

Strange that the mother hadn't felt it necessary to give Ruby the same sort of lecture when she came of age. But in her heart Ruby knew why. Her eldest daughter was deemed too plain and graceless to be of interest to men. She was destined to remain at home, to be a toiler and caretaker, allowing for safe passage into old age at her parents' side. Getting dressed up to go out to dances would hardly figure in Ruby's life. Martha had already decided the route she would take when she failed to impress Mr. Ryan in the Queens Arms hotel. Donegal had been a test, a rite of passage to see if she could hack it in the world beyond the Oaktree doorstep. A test she'd failed miserably.

May and June were the daughters who would marry. Slim and pretty, they deserved to be courted; deserved the right to bridal gowns and the delight of children at their feet.

Yes, children.

Ruby glanced down at the letter again. Under the heading *What to Expect* were several typewritten paragraphs with subheadings: *Bleeding, Pain, Feelings of Guilt* . . . She didn't want to read any more. Was glad in a way that she'd been spared the world of men and dating, if that was the price one paid. May had her reasons for doing what she did. Now she, Ruby, by opening the letter, was also privy to the secret.

She stuffed the page back in the envelope, went immediately to her own bedroom, and placed the letter in a bottom drawer. She would finish the cleaning and prepare the more important business that lay ahead. She would not mention it to May, but if pushed, she might have to.

Back out on the landing she turned the key in her bedroom, but . . .

The sound of voices coming from below.

How could that be?

She'd left her mother alone in the sitting room reading a magazine. Martha hadn't mentioned anyone dropping by. No doubt it was Ida Nettles back for more gossip, the old busybody.

Ruby packed up the vacuum cleaner and went downstairs.

She barged into the sitting room—and was at once pulled up short. There, in the armchair opposite Martha, was May. An unexpected sight that left her sister speechless.

"May's not feeling well," the mother said. "She's taking the rest of the week off."

"What . . . what is it?" Ruby managed to say. May had never come home from work in the middle of the week before. Now here she was, just when she was about to enact her ritual. Feelings of resentment and sympathy began building. "Have you . . . have you been to see the doctor?"

May avoided her sister's eye. "No, it's just . . . it's a stomach bug. I'll be all right in a couple of days."

"You should go and lie down, May. Ruby, you've finished cleaning the room, haven't you?"

"Yes . . . yes. The bed's just been fresh made. I'll bring you up some tea . . . and a biscuit, if you like."

May picked up her vanity case. She swayed slightly, looked unsteady. "Just the tea. I can't eat anything."

"I'll ring Dr. Brewster for—"

"I'm *all right*, Mummy," she snapped. "I don't need a doctor."

"But what if it's more serious, May dear—"

"It's *not* serious. I just need to rest in bed a couple of days. Now stop fussing."

———

Minutes later, Ruby took the tray of tea upstairs.

She found May lying on top of the bedcover, palms pressed against her abdomen.

"Anything else I can get you, May?"

"No, thanks."

Ruby made to leave.

Then: "You didn't come across a letter belonging to me?"

"No . . . no, I didn't."

"Are you sure?"

The question forced Ruby to turn round. "Yes . . . I'm sure. Why? Was it important?"

May searched her face. The air between them tightened.

"It's a . . . a reference from . . . my boss," she said, her gaze sliding away to a statue of the Child of Prague. "I must have dropped it . . . at the weekend."

Ah, thought Ruby, might he be the father? Might he be the man that got her into this mess? The one she never ceased talking about. Suddenly, she felt very sorry for May.

"Mr. Ross?"

"Yes . . . him."

"Why, are you going to leave Boots?"

"Yes . . . that's why it's important I find the reference . . . don't want to give him the trouble of writing another one. Are you sure you didn't see it?" May's eyes were pleading.

Ruby felt bad, but she couldn't go back on her word; the lie would have to stand for now. "No . . . but I'll have a wee look round the house and outside. You could have dropped it coming up the lane."

"Thanks . . . thanks, Ruby. I think I'll try and sleep now."

Chapter twenty-six

She'd bathed in saltwater, to rid herself of negative energies. Made a pouch of herbs tied up with red wool to burn on the altar. Had assembled the objects of devotion in a carry bag. Now Ruby sat in her green robe on the bed, plaiting a garland of laurel leaves and ivy, laced with montbretia and buttercups, to wear on her head.

Twenty minutes to midnight. The time of celebration was here. Soon she'd be entering into the womb of the great Goddess Dana; would be purifying herself in the waters of Beldam and awakening to her new life. The veil between the worlds, at its thinnest now, would allow Dana's children, the faerie folk, to give her safe passage to the Afterworld, where her dear father waited. Ruby's heart lifted at the very thought. She was eager to be gone.

At that witching hour, the house was still. Martha and May sound asleep. She had to be very, very quiet, however. It was not her mother she was concerned about, but May. Her arrival home on this day of all days was a setback she'd never anticipated.

Task completed, she eased herself off the bed and went to the mirror, positioned the garland on her head. It fitted perfectly. Then stood gazing at her reflection, transfixed. In the half-light, with that crowning wreath of flowers, her amber hair falling loosely about her shoulders, and wearing that beautiful green robe, she could have been Dana herself. An overweight Dana, but Dana nonetheless.

This is how Grandma Edna must have looked, too.

Cingulum so unabased,
Bind it three times 'bout the waist

The cingulum! She'd forgotten to put it on.

Anxious now, she grabbed it from the case, opened the robe and bound it about her.

She retied the robe, careful not to glimpse her nakedness in the mirror.

Her girth made her refrain from too much inquiry. Her body: a foreign country. On the bureau lay the Tarot card, "The Star." She picked it up and studied it again. The naked woman in the picture was who she was. Yes: she, Ruby, was the star. Tonight she would shine.

Ten minutes to midnight. She hoisted the bag of altar things on her shoulder. Pushed her feet into carpet slippers. Took one last look around the room. Then quietly, very quietly, opened the door and peeped out into the corridor.

Silence reigned.

She was safe.

Noiselessly, she made her way down the stairs. Paused by the picture of Michael the Archangel.

Crossed herself.

Wondered briefly why she'd done that. Lifted a high stool. It would do duty as her altar.

She'd left the back door ajar in readiness. Now, as she moved toward it, it banged shut.

Ruby froze, her heart pounding.

She waited to hear a stirring from above. Prayed they hadn't heard. The grandfather clock in the hallway ticked down the seconds. It would not chime the midnight hour. She'd seen to that, too, and removed the gong.

"THERE IS NO DARKNESS BUT IGNORANCE. YOU ARE PROTECTED."

Ruby smiled. The house and its dwellers slept on.

She slipped out the door, stole down the field. The grass crackled underfoot. Above, the stars shone bright. Beldam gleamed like satin in the moonlight. Never had it looked so beautiful, so inviting.

At the jetty she set down the bag. Placed the stool on the grass and hurriedly assembled the altar. Shells and stones on the border, a silver candle, the censer dish with the pouch of herbs, and under it, her three wishes. Lastly she dipped a small dessert dish in the lake, emulating the naked lady in the tarot card, and put it beside the other offerings.

She struck a match, lit the candle, ignited the pouch of herbs, inhaled deeply their heady scent.

Cast the circle thrice about,
To keep the baleful demons out.

Ruby stepped out of the robe, self-conscious at her nudity. But who would see her here? Her allegiance was to Dana and Edna, and to that end she must carry out the ritual to the letter, if she wanted to see her father again and have her dreams come true.

She fetched the sickle, and holding it aloft, began dancing around the altar, intoning the chant she'd learned by heart.

Lady of the moon of the restless sea
And verdant earth,
Mother of all gods and of the Tuatha De Danann,

Great lady of the oceans,
Mistress of the fertile lands,
Grant me the wisdom to see thy presence here,
I call on you now to join me here,
In the waters of Beldam, that I may . . .

———

Back at Oaktree Farmhouse, May stirred in her bed. She woke up feeling nauseous. She rushed to the bathroom, and threw up into the toilet bowl.

Gripping the edge of the bath, she sat down awhile to recover. She wondered when the sickness would pass. At least the bleeding had stopped. A fortnight of illness was surely enough. But it was the price she must pay. The penance she had to suffer for her great sin.

She became aware of something strange under her bare feet. It felt like grit. Hardly, though; the bathroom was always spotless. Ruby was a diligent cleaner. She switched on the light to investigate.

There was a trail of white stuff on the floor. A drum of table salt sat by the bath.

Who was scattering salt in the bathroom, of all places? Ruby? Yes . . . would hardly be Mummy.

But why?

———

Down by the lake, Ruby was getting into the spirit of things: twirling and swirling round and round the altar under the solstice moon. Never before had she felt so happy, so free. Her eyes were closed, her face upturned. She was waiting for the call.

Suddenly, it came.

"Drink, my child."

Ruby stopped. She looked toward the lake. A swirl of mist descended. She blinked. Dana was there! She couldn't believe it. The Goddess was standing at the end of the jetty, tall and proud, with ivory skin and eyes the color of the sea. She wore a flowing robe of green and held a great silver dish from which all the waters of life were cascading. It was like the painting in *The Book of Light*. The Goddess raised a hand and beckoned.

Entranced, Ruby moved toward her. Behind her the lighted candle toppled.

It fell on the green robe.

The robe caught fire.

———

May switched off the bathroom light. Feeling uneasy, she went back onto the landing; glanced at Ruby's bedroom door. There was something on the floor. It looked like a playing card. She bent down, turned it over. But it was not a playing card. It showed a naked woman kneeling by a lake.

She tried Ruby's door.

To her surprise, it swung open.

"Ruby . . . are you there?"

But there was no one in the bed. It hadn't been slept in. Mystified, she looked down at the card again. A woman by water. Then it occurred to her.

Beldam.

She went to the window.

What on earth . . . ?! There was a fire burning by the lake.

May's heart sagged. She couldn't believe her eyes. Ruby, naked, holding aloft what appeared to be a sickle blade, was moving slowly down the jetty.

Jesus! She was going to drown herself.

"Mummy, Mummy, wake up, wake up!"

Martha Clare's startled eyes locked on her daughter. "What in heaven's—"

"Ruby's gonna do away with herself in Beldam! Quick, quick, get up!"

"Oh my dear God!"

Martha tried to get up, but the fright had sucked the energy from her. She fell back on the pillows.

"Run, May, run! Don't wait for me," she gasped. "I'll ring the doctor. Oh Jesus and His Blessed Mother. I knew this was coming . . . I knew it! I knew it."

May grabbed her nightgown, bounded down the stairs. No time for slippers. Her sister's life hung in the balance. Would she be in time to save her?

———

Ruby moved down the jetty, by turns elated and afraid. But as she drew closer, she saw that the beautiful woman was not Dana.

The beautiful lady was she herself. That was *Ruby's* face. Those were Ruby's eyes. She—ordinary, plain Ruby Clare—was the Goddess.

How could that be?

She halted.

Afraid.

"Afraid? How can you be afraid of yourself?"

The voice was everywhere. It came from the sky. Rose up from the water. Echoing through the woods and the hills beyond. A mirror reflecting. A hundred voices chorusing, over and over and over again.

"Afraid? How can you be afraid of yourself?"

The vision floated farther across the lake, borne upon a diaphanous cloud. Ruby had no choice but to follow. This chance would never come her way again. She *had* to follow.

The jetty descended into a series of steps beneath the water. She took the first one, then the next. Tentative. Hesitant. The water was warm, inviting. She thought of her three wishes. She thought of her father. The great prize was within reach.

Fear ebbed away.

Her tears ceased.

Soon she'd be *home.*

Down and down she went. Feet gracing the slippery treads. Limbs growing heavy. Sickle raised in salutation. Curved blade glinting in the moonlight.

The water of Beldam came up to meet her. Its graceful pull. Its powerful embrace, drawing her deeper and deeper, lulling her into the Afterworld. The world beyond. The one she'd soon glimpse, but from which she'd return, renewed, reborn, enlightened.

Ruby smiled as her chin caressed the surface of the lake.

"Ruby, Ruby, what the hell are you doing?"

A voice behind her. A woman's voice. But not Dana's. Not the voice from beyond.

Oh God!

All at once an arm was locking itself around her neck.

Ruby struggled. She kicked, tried to free herself, but someone was pulling her back.

She tried to scream, but the arm took her breath away.

It was useless.

Her body went limp. She ceased fighting, allowed herself to be dragged from the water, collapsed like a beached mermaid onto the jetty.

"Jesus, Ruby, are you all *right?*"

She opened her eyes. May's frightened face floated above hers.

"Wha-wha-s . . . what's . . . happen . . . ing?" She tried to speak but water, rank and bitter, churned up in her throat. She turned aside and retched.

"Oh, thank God you're all right."

Ruby attempted to sit upright. Only then did she become aware of her nakedness. She was appalled. She crossed her arms over her breasts and started to cry. Her whole body shaking, great shuddering sobs of deep despair.

May pulled off her nightgown and threw it about her sister's shoulders.

"Ruby, Ruby . . . Oh God, Ruby," she gasped. "You . . . you just tried *to kill yourself*!"

"No-o-o-o-o-o-o!" Ruby wailed, letting out a long, low, tear-jerking lament. The sound stretching away from her, slipping away from her, a wingspan flapping out of sight, everything, now, out of sight, out of reach, all her dreams gone: crumbling, fading, gone to dust in the catch of her prying sister's hand.

She howled, the howling despair of the soul that has just glimpsed the golden gates of paradise, only to be snatched back, cast down, down to the very depths of the netherworld.

Out of those depths she fought to find the voice that would let her sister know that she'd committed the most treacherous of acts—an act of the direst, deepest, darkest kind.

When she finally found that voice, it had all the force and fury of a dying soldier finally succumbing to the open arms of a Valkyrie.

"I was *not* trying to kill myself! I was only . . . tryin' to . . . to see Daddy . . . and you . . . you *s-t-o-p-p-e-d* me-e-e-e-e . . . I . . . *h-a-t-e* . . . y-o-u! O-o-h . . . G-o-d . . . I . . . *h-a-t-e* . . . y-o-u!"

Chapter twenty-seven

Henry had just gotten into bed when the phone rang. A distraught woman calling herself Mrs. Clare was pleading with him to come quick, because her daughter had just tried to drown herself and was in need of urgent attention.

Now, in the semidarkness, behind the wheel of his car, negotiating a series of country roads with no signposts, Henry hoped her garbled directions would take him to a set of wrought-iron gates with the nameplate *Oaktree Farmhouse*.

———

"Oh Holy Mary Mother of God!" Martha Clare stood shivering, rosary beads in hand, as May guided the half-naked, shuddering Ruby into the house. May's size 8 nightgown barely covered Ruby, and when the mother saw her daughter with hardly a stitch on, flecked with algae and dripping waterweeds, she very nearly fainted. May might well have been parading Satan himself before her.

Ruby could not meet her mother's eye. She wept and wept. The embarrassment she felt searing, scorching, burning into every part of her, taking her mind to the darkest of places imaginable. She saw her aunt in that tub chair in St. Ita's. That was the fate that awaited her. She was sure of it. Her mother had won. Better now to just flee the scene, race back down to Beldam and throw herself in. It's what they believed she was going to do anyway. At least the whole sorry episode would be over. She'd have no defending or explaining to do. No shame to endure. No guilt to carry for the rest of her days.

"What . . . *what* in under God was *she doing*?"

Mrs. Clare, not affording Ruby the dignity of a direct question, knew how to make her daughter suffer.

"She said she was trying to see Daddy," May said.

Then the mother exploded. "Get up them stairs and cover yourself up! You're an absolute disgrace to this family. I *knew* you were taking bad with your nerves, but God, I didn't know you were as bad as this. I've rung the doctor. God grant it, he'll get you into St. Ita's before the night's out."

"I'm not goin' nowhere!" Ruby bawled. She ran up the stairs. On the landing, she halted at the sound of a scream—her mother's.

"*Oh Jesus!*"

"What is it, Mummy? *What is it?*" May's frantic voice.

"The footprints . . . oh my God, the *footprints.*"

"What *about* them? They're Ruby's."

"*No-o-o-o-o,* you don't understand. *She's* back!"

Ruby understood none of it. She flew into the bedroom, slamming the door, locking it against them all. No doctor was going to put *her* in the loony bin. She'd kick. She'd scream. She'd fight. She'd rage against the moon.

She threw off May's nightgown, tried to wipe off the algae with a towel, but the rubbing action only made things worse, turning her skin green. She needed to get into the bath, but not now. She would not be leaving the locked room. She caught a glimpse of herself in the mirror and was shocked at the sight. With her green body and wet hair trailing leaves, she could have passed for the Incredible Hulk.

She pulled on her own nightdress and collapsed onto the bed, exhausted, and sobbed her heart out.

The desolation only matched by the pain she'd suffered seven months before as she crashed onto her knees by her dead father in the field; the scorching flame-hot pain of loss. Of knowing that in this cruel world you're on your own. That it was ever thus. That she wouldn't be seeing her father again. Not in this life. He was gone. He would not be coming back. That her dreams would not come true. That her three wishes had turned to ashes, quite literally, and vanished on the air. That the Goddess and Edna had abandoned her when she needed them most.

———

Henry pulled up in the yard of Oaktree Farmhouse. At the door he was met by a young woman whom he thought he recognized.

"I'm May Clare," she said sheepishly. "You must be . . ."

"Dr. Shevlin, yes."

She led the way into the kitchen, where an older woman came forward immediately, hand extended. "Oh, thank God you've come, Doctor! Ruby's in a bad way. I'm her mother."

Henry noted the hand, proffered first. This woman was clearly in charge. He glanced at the table. On it, a collection of bizarre items: shells, stones, a candle, two small dishes, a sickle, a length of blue material with holes burned through it, and a playing card lying facedown.

"It's what Ruby had at Beldam . . . the lake," Mrs. Clare explained. "They were on that stool, like it was an altar or something. God knows what she was at . . . calling up the Devil himself. She needs to be admitted tonight, Doctor . . . there's no other way of dealing with her . . . I'm not having her here . . . upsetting *me*. I know what she's like."

Mrs. Clare already had the situation well under control. Had diagnosed the daughter, was telling him what to do. The stress on the word "me" indicated a narcissist of the first order. No surprises there. The controller, the manipulator, and the narcissist were common bedfellows.

He studied the table, turned over the card.

"She was probably trying to imitate *her*," the sister said.

He turned, stared at her.

She smirked. "But Ruby's hardly a star."

It was then that Henry remembered. It was the smirk, the dismissive toss of the head. Of course! Boots the Chemist on Royal Avenue. He'd gone there to inquire about Connie's prescription after her disappearance last year.

This one was certainly her mother's daughter. The lack of empathy: striking.

He put the card back on the table.

"These things were private to Ruby. You shouldn't have them displayed like this."

"Hardly private, Doctor," said Mrs. Clare defiantly. "She was consorting with the Devil and there's the proof." She picked up the silver paten and thrust it at him. "That five-pointed star. It's an occult sign. She's just like her grandmother before her, God help her! May found *that* evil card outside her bedroom door. What more proof do you need?"

"Hmmm." Henry glanced briefly at the paten but did not take it from her. Clearly irked, Mrs. Clare tossed it back onto the table.

"I'll hold onto these things, if you don't mind," he said firmly. "It's best you don't mention finding them to Ruby. We wouldn't want to cause her any further upset, would we?"

He saw mother and daughter exchange glances. Looks that said: "Whose side is this doctor on?"

"Well, she's caused enough of that already," the mother muttered. "Enough *upset*."

"A carrier bag will do."

May produced a plastic bag and proceeded to fill it as the mother looked on, arms folded, mouth set in a grim line. Then: "When will the ambulance be here?"

"Ambulance?"

"Yes . . . to take her to St. Ita's."

May handed him the bag.

"Backseat of my car . . . if you wouldn't mind. It's open."

He turned back to Martha.

"Now, let's not rush things, Mrs. Clare. I know you've had a shock. I'll talk to Ruby now, if I may?"

———

Through her tears Ruby heard a gentle knock. She sat up abruptly.

A man's voice out in the corridor. "Ruby, are you in there? Can you let me in, please . . . I'm Henry . . . Henry Shevlin . . . the doctor."

"Go away! I don't need no doctor . . . I'm not goin' near no hospital."

"I'm not going to put you in hospital. But—"

"You're lying."

"I assure you, Ruby, I'm not lying. But, if you refuse to open the door I'll have no option but to call the police and have them break it down. In which case you will most definitely have to be admitted to hospital, for your own safety."

Ruby grew fretful, imagining the worst-case scenario.

"I don't want to have to do that, Ruby . . . and I know . . . I know you don't want that happening, either."

Something in the man's voice told her she'd better heed him. She got off the bed.

"I . . . I only want to talk to *you* . . . not . . . not my mother . . . or . . . or my sister."

"I promise, only me. Your mother and sister are downstairs."

Ruby opened the door, and knowing what an awful sight she must look, immediately turned her back. She again went to the bed and flopped down.

Henry, for his part, was greeted by a spectacularly odd sight. Ruby did indeed appear like someone who'd just tried to drown herself. Wet hair, blotchy green face; she was wearing a pink nightdress that came to her knees, showing equally green calves and feet.

He entered the room lit by two small bedside lamps. But he could see enough to form an impression of its occupant. The color scheme was pink. Cushions and frills everywhere he looked. There were stuffed toys lined up on an ottoman. Several dolls crowded the windowsill. It resembled the room of a little girl.

He found a chair with a large teddy bear on it and gestured. "Do you mind if I . . ."

"Sit where you like."

He positioned the chair in front of the door. Meeting a new patient in such a fragile state meant that precautions had to be taken. Ruby might well try to escape. But he'd cleared the first hurdle: she'd let him in.

"Now, Ruby . . . how are you?"

Ruby sat on the bed, her whole body turned away from him, arms folded. Body language screaming: "*No! Get out of here and leave me alone!*"

"All right," she said.

"Would you like to talk about it?"

She shook her head.

"In your own time . . . there's no—"

"She wants to put me in the loony bin. She's always wanted to put me in St. Ita's. Ever since I was seventeen . . . ever since I went to Donegal and had to come home 'cos . . . 'cos . . ."

"Your mother?"

"Yes, *her* . . . she's always hated me. Always."

"Why would that be?"

"I don't know. You better ask *her*. Since . . . since Daddy died she's hated me even more. She took everything off me . . . the farm and everything . . . Daddy and me did all the work and . . . and now I've . . . I've got nothin'. . . ."

"That's too bad," Henry said. Given what he'd seen of Mrs. Clare, he didn't doubt for one minute what Ruby was saying.

"So she's the one that needs to go in the loony bin and not me . . . so you should be down there talkin' to her and not me, 'cos . . . 'cos there's nothin' wrong with me."

"Hmmm . . . parents can be difficult, I know." He noticed a deck of cards on the bureau, picked them up. "Your mother and May say you tried to drown yourself. Is that true?"

Ruby twisted halfway round on the bed, kneading a hankie in her hands. She imagined how awful she must look to the doctor, and felt awkward and embarrassed. At the same time, she realized she needed to be very careful about what she told him. It was no time to talk about the case and the Goddess and the voices, even though all of that was true.

"No, I wasn't . . . I just . . . I just wanted to swim in the lake . . . to see . . . to see what it was like at night 'cos . . . 'cos it was . . . it was too warm in bed."

"Beautiful cards," Henry said. "Tarot, aren't they?"

Ruby was forced to turn fully toward him. Oh God! She'd forgotten to put them back in the case. A feeling of dread gripped her. How was she going to explain them?

"I . . . I don't know what they're called."

"I used to have a deck."

He saw her look of surprise.

"Oh, a long time ago . . . when I was a teenager," he lied. "Can't remember any of the meanings now."

"I know the meanings," Ruby said, proudly.

She moved an inch closer and watched him shuffle the cards. She thought him a very odd doctor. Why wasn't he telling her to get dressed? Why wasn't he filling out a form and asking her questions? Like her age, and if she was on medication, like Dr. Brewster used to, on the rare occasions she went to see him.

"Do you really?" he said. "All the meanings? I'm impressed . . ."

He saw the little compliment, all too briefly, light up Ruby's sad features.

"Right, I'm going to test you." He spread the cards facedown on the bed. "I'll pick one out and you tell me what it means."

He saw her hesitate, then nod.

"Good." Henry turned over a card. "Oh dear, Ruby, I'm afraid it's not good." He held it up. "It's the Death card."

"Oh, but that doesn't mean you're gonna die."

"Thank heavens for that."

"No, it means . . . it means that you're coming to the end of something . . . and you're gonna have a new beginning . . . and that things are gonna be better for you, so they are."

"I see. . . ."

"That maybe you've lost someone . . . and that . . . that part of your life's over and you . . . you have to move on, like."

For a couple of seconds Henry allowed himself to think of Connie. "That's very interesting," he said. "Did you ever pick that out, Ruby? That card?"

"I did, aye . . . and I knew it was right 'cos . . . 'cos I lost Daddy and . . ."

He heard her voice breaking. "Is that his photo?" There was a framed picture on the bedside locker. It showed a man leaning against a tractor, smiling broadly.

"Aye . . . that's him."

"You must miss him a lot?"

Ruby nodded. Dabbed her eyes with the hankie. "But I wasn't gonna drown meself."

"That's okay . . . I believe you, Ruby."

". . . and I'm not goin' into no hospital, 'cos . . . 'cos . . . there's nothin' wrong with me."

Henry took out his notebook. He scribbled down the clinic telephone number and address of Rosewood. "Now, tonight, if you need me, just call this number at any time. And don't worry about waking me up. I'm on call."

Ruby looked up, surprised. "You're . . . you're not gonna put me in St. Ita's?"

"No, not tonight, Ruby." In his bag he found a blister pack of sedatives and broke one off. "Take this. It will help you get a good night's sleep." He stood up. "Now, tomorrow at twelve p.m. I want to see you at the clinic in Killoran. I've written down the address. Does your sister drive?"

She nodded.

"Good. I'll ask her to take you."

"But I can drive meself."

"Best not to, having taken sleep medication." He moved to the door. "Now, get some rest. I'll see you tomorrow."

———

Henry shut the door of the bedroom on a much-relieved Ruby and headed downstairs.

To his surprise and at that ungodly hour, Mrs. Clare and her daughter had a visitor. A man was sitting with them at the kitchen table. A clergyman.

"This is Father Kelly," the mother explained.

The priest stood up. "How do you do, Doctor? William Kelly. You're new to these parts."

"Yes. Henry . . . Henry Shevlin."

"This is a terrible business with poor Ruby," Father Kelly said, shaking his head bleakly. "A terrible, terrible business indeed."

Henry said nothing.

"I asked him to come over in case we had trouble getting Ruby in the ambulance," Mrs. Clare put in. "She can be very awkward and abusive to me and May, but she wouldn't behave like that in front of the Father, you understand."

"Well, I'm sorry to say you've had a wasted journey, Father. Ruby is not going anywhere tonight."

"What?" The news had Mrs. Clare scraping back her chair. She rose.

"My daughter's just tried to kill herself and you're telling me she doesn't need the hospital? Well, I beg to differ, Doctor. I *know* my daughter better than you do . . . I *know* what she's capable of . . ."

She stood with hands splayed on the table, glaring at him. She made for a formidable foe. He immediately felt sorry for Ruby, and all she must have suffered down the years as a victim and target of this woman's wrath. He decided it best just to let the raging torrent run its course.

". . . *you* didn't see the state she was in when she came in here. May had to practically pull her out of that lake or she wouldn't be alive. She wouldn't even be sitting up in that room. What if she tries it again when you leave? What then? She's headstrong. You don't know what's she's like. She always gets her own way."

I doubt that, thought Henry, but said nothing, simply waited for her to finish.

"Do you want to have her death on your conscience?"

Henry didn't answer.

Mrs. Clare became exasperated. "Well, do you? *Do you?*"

Then: "Now, now, Martha . . ." It was the priest, patting her arm. "There's no need going and upsetting yourself. The doctor knows best."

The matriarch looked his way, lips pursed. The air thrummed in the fallout. Henry watched her struggle. But he could see where her allegiances lay. In Mrs. Clare's world, the clergyman—God's disciple—was the only man she would allow to overrule her.

"I see, Father . . . whatever you feel is best. Perhaps you could go up and have a word with her. She'll listen to *you*."

"That won't be necessary," Henry said. "I have given Ruby a sedative to help her sleep. She needs to rest undisturbed for the remainder of the night." He turned to May and produced a card. "She has an appointment with me at twelve tomorrow. Please drive her to the clinic, as she might be drowsy. Will you do that?"

May took the card. "Yes," she said, abashed.

"Thank you. Now: I'll be on my way. I think we all could use some sleep. Good night."

Chapter twenty-eight

"So James McCloone has finally kept an appointment?" Henry said. "No stray heifers or errant piglets needing his attention this morning, then?"

Ms. King allowed herself a little half smile. "I'm happy to report that he is indeed here in the flesh, Dr. Shevlin. There's just one small thing, though."

"Uh-oh!"

"He's brought a lady with him . . . a friend, Rose McFadden. And Mrs. McFadden is insisting, with Mr. McCloone's apparent blessing, that she comes in to have a word with you first."

"Really? Well, anything to make James feel more comfortable, Edie. Send her in."

"You don't feel it's a little unorthodox, Doctor . . . ?"

"Well, perhaps a little. But if she can help clarify things with regard to James's situation it can only be a good thing."

Ms. King withdrew, and seconds later, Mrs. McFadden in her Sunday best—crepe de chine frock in pixie pink and an elaborate hat to match—was filling the doorway.

"God, hello, Dr. Shelfin! I hope you don't mind me wanting to see you first." She came forward and shook Henry's hand with an enthusiasm he found disarming. "Rose McFadden's me name. Pleased to meet you, Doctor."

"And you—and you, Mrs. McFadden. Please take a seat."

"I will indeed. But just call me Rose, Doctor. None of that old missus or mister with me." She settled herself on the sofa but barely paused to draw breath. "I just thought I'd come to fill you in on a couple of wee things about Jamie. 'Cos he's not very good at the talkin', and maybe would be afeard to tell you things about himself that I could enlighten you about."

"That's no problem at all." Henry pulled up one of the arm-chairs. "Good of you to be so concerned for his welfare."

"Oh, Jamie and me go back a long way, Dr. Shelfin. Me and my Paddy would of befriended Jamie soon after Mick died, 'cos we were worried about him being on his own, so we were."

"Mick was his uncle?"

"Yes . . . Oh, Mick was the greatest man, Doctor! I remember me collecting for the Duntybutt Senior Citizens Ladies Friendship Club Luncheon, and Mick giving me five pound and three pence out of a tea caddy on the fireplace. The most money I got all day. He'd a heart bigger than the Rock of Cashel, truth be told. That's why him and Alice adopted Jamie when he was a wee one. Mick wanted tae give Jamie a better start in life from that old orphanage in Derry. And no better couple could he have landed with. God was surely smiling down on Jamie that day."

Henry consulted his notes. "That would be St. Agnes Little Sisters of Charity?"

"Yes, that one. Now Jamie was there till he was ten but he doesn't talk about it much . . . so me and my Paddy don't like till ask. 'Cos it kinda day-presses him. And that old day-pression isn't much good for a body, so it's not. But what I was gonna tell you, Doctor, was about a couple of wee things that happened Jamie in the past while that's causing him to be day-pressed, like. Well, they're not wee things . . . 'cos if they were wee things they wouldn't be day-pressin' him and he wouldn't have tae come here till see the likes of you, Doctor . . ."

Henry nodded. "Yes, indeed." He sensed that Mrs. McFadden's propensity for circumlocution had the distinct possibility of playing havoc with the morning's schedule. Wernicke's aphasia came to mind. He wondered idly whether she had possibly sustained a knock on the temporal lobe in infancy.

". . . and I know he'd be too embarrassed to tell you himself. That's why I thought I'd fill you in. Now you might think it's a wee bit cowardly of him not tae tell you himself, but better to be a coward for a minute than dead for the rest of your life, as they say. I—"

"Two things," Henry said. He really felt he needed to shepherd this conversation or he might be in the clinic well past midnight. "So, what's the first thing?"

"Yes, the first thing is: he's got a wee cut on his eyebrow, and I can explain that, Doctor."

"Oh . . . ?"

"Yes, he had a wee bit of a run-in with Bertie Frogget. Now you wouldn't know Bertie Frogget, being new to these parts. But he's the auctioneer. Would be a far-out relative of my Paddy's on his grandmother's side, twice removed. But that's neither here or there."

No, it isn't, Henry thought, unkindly.

". . . the thing is: he sold Jamie's heifer for a lower price than Jamie was expecting. Now, Bertie Frogget would be a fair enough man at the best of times, so I don't know what got into him that day. 'Cos, you know, he sold a pair of Belgian Blues for my Paddy last month and got him such a good price he was able to buy a kick-start lawn mower for himself and had enough left over for a Hotpoint twin-tub with automatic rinse for *me*. Not that I wanted the Hotpoint twin-tub with automatic rinse, mind you, Doctor, 'cos I've never minded warshing the clothes with me hands. Never been afeard of a bitta work, me. Sure haven't wommin been warshing clothes with their hands since Moses was runnin' about in short trousers? But you know, Doctor, now that I have it, I don't know how I managed without it. But isn't that the way of it? What you don't want you'll not miss, for when you haven't got it you'll not worry about it as me mother, God rest her soul, used to say . . ."

As a psychiatrist, Henry's great gift was his ability to listen and empathize. Now, sitting across from the voluble Rose, he felt that facility being sorely tested. He eyed the clock above her head. He needed to speed things along.

"So James had an altercation with—"

"Alter-*what*?"

"Sorry, a disagreement with Mr. Frogget *and*—"

"Oh, but that's not the end of it, Dr. Shelfin . . ."

Henry feared as much.

". . . you see, somebody rung Sergeant Ranfurley when Bertie and Jamie were scrappin' about on the Fair Hill. You wouldn't know Sergeant Ranfurley, Doctor, either, you being new to these parts. He's a big man with a square head and a red face on him. Been here a wee while now. Not that I would know him too well, thank God. 'Cos, as you well know, Doctor, no good ever came of a policeman having tae knock your door either day or night. But isn't that the way of it? No, the first time me and my Paddy spoke to Sergeant Ranfurley was last week when we went to the station to collect poor Jamie—"

"So James was arrested, then?"

"Well, yes and no, Doctor . . ."

Henry was sorry he'd spoken.

". . . 'cos I ast Sergeant Ranfurley the exact same question. Sez I, 'God, Sergeant, have you arrested poor Jamie, have you?' 'Not exactly, Mrs. McFadden,' sez he. 'Mr. McCloone is being detained at Her Majesty's pleasure for dis-ordin'ry conduct in a public place.'

Well, God, Doctor, the light nearly left me eyes. For it's only for its own good that a cat purrs in the middle of the night, and everything might be all right in the house till the cow jumps into the garden and interferes with your floribundas, as they say. For that would be the first time the like of that has ever happened to poor Jamie. And it was a terrible shock for him. 'Cos he's never been in a police cell in his life. But Sergeant Ranfurley was all right about it in the end. Me and my Paddy said we'd take him out—"

"That was good of you, Rose. And the second thing . . . ?"

Rose looked at Henry, mystified. "What second thing, Doctor?"

"You mentioned two things you wished to discuss with me concerning James. The first was James's alter—sorry, difference of opinion with Mr. Frogget and his subsequent arrest. And the second thing . . . ?"

"Oh yes, the second thing is that last month if Jamie's Shep didn't go and die on him."

"His dog?"

Rose nodded, sadly. "Oh, he was terrible close to Shep, Doctor. Mick got it for him when he was only a wee pup. And now that he's gone, Jamie misses him terrible badly, 'cos he was the last link to Mick and Alice—"

"I'm sorry to hear that. We can become very attached to our pets."

"Now, you might say he can always get another dog, Doctor, but it's not the same, is it? I had a wee cat called Ethel and she was the greatest wee thing . . . I called her Ethel on account of me mother. For if the wee thing didn't wander into the house the night of me mother's wake. So I took it as a sign that the wee pussy was me mother comin' back tae tell me she was all right on the other side, like, and—"

"Sorry to interrupt, Rose, but I really think it's time I saw James." He stood up.

"Oh, no bother atall, Dr. Shelfin. I'm sure Jamie's tired waiting out there anyway. I'll send him in to you." She got up and patted Henry's arm. "And you know, if there's anything else I can do to help Jamie out, just let me know. 'Cos he's a very good fella." Rose's voice dropped to a whisper. "But you know, between you and me, Doctor, all that Jamie needs is to meet a nice woman to keep him company."

Henry eyed the clock again, fearful that Rose might flood him with another tsunami of her long-winded opinions on how to sort out the farmer's love life. Yes, Wernicke's aphasia. He was now certain of what earlier had been a mere suspicion.

"It's the loneliness, you see. And men are not good on their own, if truth be told. They say they die sooner than married men, but you don't need me telling you that. You being a doctor and all. And would you be married yourself, Doctor?"

Henry smiled. "Yes, I am, Rose."

"Well, that doesn't surprise me, a well-lookin' fella like yourself. But you know, that's the thing about these wimmen: they all want a well-lookin' fella, and that's where poor Jamie falls down."

Henry put his hand on the door handle.

"Oh, and another wee thing before I go, Doctor. He's great at the accordjin, is Jamie."

"Yes, he told me."

"Does the greatest version of 'The Menstrual Boy.'"

Henry couldn't believe his ears. Then the penny dropped. "Oh, you mean 'The Minstrel Boy.'"

"Aye, that one, Doctor."

"Right. Thank you, Rose. I appreciate you filling me in."

Swiftly, he pulled open the door.

"Doctor Shelfin's ready for you now, Jamie!" Rose called out.

Jamie, head buried in the *Mid-Ulster Vindicator*, roused himself. "Right you be, Rose," he said, getting up.

"Now, I'm gonna sit out in that nice rose garden while I'm waitin' on you, Jamie. Too good'a day to be stuck inside."

"Aye, Rose. That'll do . . . see you in a wee minute."

Henry smiled, touched by the special bond the pair shared, and beckoned Jamie in.

Chapter twenty-nine

Ruby sat in the back of the speeding vehicle, heading toward Killoran. She was feeling dazed from the drama of the previous night and still sleepy from the sedative Dr. Shevlin had given her.

She'd been roused at 10:00 a.m. by May hammering on the door and trying the handle. But Ruby had made sure to lock it when the doctor departed, and again upon leaving the house. They would not be getting their hands on Edna's case.

Not ever!

Martha Clare sat stiffly in the passenger seat. May was at the wheel. Having just passed her driving test, she was being extra careful and driving at a steady 45 mph.

A taut silence hung in the car. Mother and sister had barely spoken to Ruby back at the house. Now Martha turned back to her.

"I'll be going in with you to talk to that doctor . . . just so you know. You needn't think for one minute you're going in by yourself, to tell him a pack of lies like you did last night . . . acting as though butter wouldn't melt in your mouth. Well, not this time you won't! You mark my words."

Ruby said nothing. Just stared out the window. She was mortally ashamed at what had happened and was inwardly cursing May.

If she hadn't been so damned nosy, none of this would have happened.

"Are you listening to me?"

Ruby kept her eyes fixed on the view beyond the glass, tried to concentrate on the landscape slipping past: the fields, the sheep, the herds of cows grazing lazily, the sweeping grace of the Slievegerrin Mountains. The terrain of her childhood. The terrain of her youth. Another world. A bygone world now, pulled so cruelly from her by the woman with the grim face and hectoring voice who sat in the passenger seat.

Ruby tried to ignore her now. Martha Clare could take everything from her, but not her memories. Her precious memories. She saw herself on the road, herding cattle from one field to another, her father positioned in the mouth of a gate. Motorists stopping for his kindly wave. Next minute, tramping the drilled fields with him, checking potatoes for blight. Felt the smooth firmness of the spade handle in her hands as she dug them out. Heard his voice reach across time. "A good crop, Ruby, a good crop. Aren't we blessed, now?"

A tear escaped Ruby's eye.

Martha unbuckled her seat belt, all the better to confront her daughter's impertinence.

"Now, you listen to me, young lady. You are not going to make a laughingstock of me. Your father and me did the best we could for you down the years, and this is *your* thanks. Trampling all over his memory, God rest him . . . dancing half-naked in the middle of the night round a bunch of stones on a stool, trying to drown yourself! Isn't it a blessing he's not here now to see how you've turned out? My God, I never thought it would come to this. Never in all my born days . . ."

"If Daddy was here it wouldn't have come to this," Ruby said under her breath. "Wouldn't have to put up with *you*."

"What was that?"

"I said I *wasn't* trying to drown meself."

"Oh, so walking into Beldam without a stitch on, in the middle of the night, isn't drowning yourself? What would have happened if May here hadn't had the presence of mind to look out the window? You wouldn't be in the back of this car now. You'd be at the bottom of Beldam. You have May to thank for saving your life."

Ruby looked at her mother's scowling face, and suddenly she was seventeen again, traveling with her father back from Donegal. Her mother's reproving eyes might be older now and more lined, the earrings more discreet, but the badgering message, the skirl of invective, was still the same. Ruby had let her down. Ruby had always let her down. It was as if the intervening years had never been. In her mother's eyes, Ruby was still seventeen. Her growth retarded. A life quashed, ignored, overruled, because Martha Clare willed it. She had written the script and forced her daughter to play the part.

Ruby started to sob; sob for the lost years, her dead father, the thwarted ritual and the fate that was surely hers; the prison of St. Ita's mental institution. She saw the wordless Aunt Marjorie in that tub chair. Faces, restless and resigned, behind locked doors. Kindly nurses in starched uniforms. She heard the jangle of keys and the clanging of tea trolleys. Worst of all, the grilled windows, high up and small, to keep the crazy people in and the daylight out.

"And you can stop that blubbering," her mother was saying. "You're not a child."

"*Then stop treating me like one,*" Ruby wailed, releasing herself from that awful reverie with an anger both sudden and brutal.

"How *dare* you—"

"Mummy, let it go. Don't go upsetting yourself. She's not worth it. We'll get her into St. Ita's today and then you can get some rest."

"*I'm not goin' into Ita's!*" Ruby roared. She thumped the back of May's seat out of sheer frustration, to drive the message home.

The car swerved onto the grass verge.

May screamed.

The mother, still unbelted and facing Ruby, was thrown backward. Her head hit the windscreen. She let out a long moan and fell off the seat.

"Oh God! Mummy!"

A horn blared.

A bridge came into view.

May, unused to driving, was losing control.

A truck loomed out of nowhere.

Ruby's instincts took over. She lurched over the driver's seat and grabbed the steering wheel.

"*Let go!*" she screamed at her sister.

May ducked down. Using all her might, Ruby managed to swing the car sharply, just grazing the side of the lorry.

She steered the vehicle off the road, crashed through a gate. Careered down a small incline. Bounced over rutted ground, before finally rattling to a halt in the middle of a field.

A dazed silence reigned inside the car. May, slumped over the steering wheel, was sobbing like a child. Ruby, collapsed on the backseat, was struggling to regain her breath. The mother was still moaning.

Then: "Jesus, Mummy, wake up, wake up!" May was leaning over Martha.

Martha's eyelids fluttered briefly.

"Jesus, Ruby, look what you've done! Mummy's dying . . . oh God . . . oh God!"

Ruby bailed out of the back. She felt her mother's pulse. It was weak, but not weak enough to merit concern.

"She's *not* dying."

"How the hell would *you* know anyway?"

"Oh, my head . . . my head," the mother moaned.

"See, she's able to speak. Look, help me get her into the back."

After a tussle, the sisters managed to get Martha into a sitting position on the backseat. She'd gone very pale. Saliva was dribbling down her chin; her hands felt clammy.

May got in beside her. "Mummy, Mummy, you're gonna be all right."

"I'll drive to the hospital," Ruby said.

But when she turned the key the engine would not respond.

"Oh God, what are we gonna do now?"

Ruby tried the ignition several more times. She sighed. It was useless.

May was frantic. Sobbing her heart out. "God, you are such an evil bitch! If you hadn't thumped my seat, none of this—"

"Shut up! If you'd kept your eyes on the road, none of this would've happened."

Ruby got out of the car and slammed the door.

"Where do you think you're going?"

"To get help. What do *you* think?"

———

Paddy McFadden's Austin Maxi rattled its away along the road out of Killoran. Beside him sat Jamie McCloone, and in the backseat sat Rose, getting side views of everything like a dog.

"He didn't keep you long, that Dr. Shelfin," she said. "And that was a good thing, 'cos I filled him in on a lot of things, Jamie, tae save you the bother."

"That was very good of you, Rose. I'm not much good at that oul' talkin' when it comes tae them doctors."

"I know what you're saying, Jamie. My father was something the same. But he always said a good laugh and a long snore will keep the doctor from your door. They were his very words. And you know, Jamie, he could snore like a buffalo in a tin mine . . . lived till he was ninety-nine and never darkened a doctor's door."

"God, he must of had great health altogether," Jamie enthused.

"Health? You never seen the like of it. He was driving his car, cutting his grass, drinking his stout and smoking his pipe a couple of hours from the grave, truth be—"

"God, there's a wommin on the road wavin' her arms," Paddy interjected.

Rose stuck her head between the men's shoulders.

"You're right, Paddy. She must'a broke down. Maybe you should speed up a wee bit."

At his wife's bidding, Paddy depressed the accelerator pedal and went from his usual 40 mph to an ungodly 45.

"Begod, I think that's Ruby Clare!" exclaimed Jamie as the car closed on the frantically waving figure.

"Is it, Jamie?" Rose put on her cateye spectacles and leaned farther into the front to get a closer look. "Well, she's a lovely, big, strong-lookin' lassie, so she is!"

Paddy brought the car to a halt and wound down the window.

"Thanks for stoppin'!" Ruby said, breathlessly. "We've had a wee bit of an accident. Mammy's hurt."

Rose bailed out immediately.

"God, that's terrible news. C'mon, Paddy and Jamie. You wouldn't be Ruby Clare, would you?"

"Aye."

"Rose McFadden's me name. God, that's a lovely cardigan, Ruby. Did you knit it yourself?"

"Thank you, Rose. Aye, I did . . . the car's down that field."
Ruby pointed. "We need to be quick." And with that, she galloped
off, not bothering to look at the two men.

Rose's Sunday shoes were not suited to the rough ground. She
nearly fell twice. Jamie and Paddy helped her up.

"Maybe you should wait in the car," Paddy said.

But a bit of rutted earth was not going to hinder Rose McFadden from being part of this great drama. Ruby had already impressed
her. The tumbling ginger hair, the modest blue dress cut on the bias
and that white hand-knit cardigan with them complicated stitches.
No, by Rose McFadden's lights, if this Ruby Clare could knit like
that she could maybe bake just as well, too: a gift for any man. And
she knew who that man was. He'd been sitting right there in front of
her in the passenger seat, beside husband Paddy. Rose's matchmaking skills, dormant for far too long, began firing into life.

"No, I'm all right," Rose assured the men. "You run on after
Ruby, Jamie. My Paddy and me'll be right behind you."

Jamie took off. He'd dressed in his Sunday best for the doctor
and his feet nearly left him as he slid down the incline. He could see
Ruby's car in the middle of the field. Ruby was already there, pulling open the rear door.

"God, she's a well-lookin' lassie!" Rose declared. "Isn't she,
Paddy?"

"Aye, a well-lookin' lassie right enough, Rose."

"And no engagement ring on her finger neither. 'Cos that
was the very first thing I looked for. And you see that cardigan
she's wearing? That's a double basket weave, slip-stitch honeycomb
rib, if I'm any judge. St. Anne the Astonishing couldn't manage a
stitch like that, and she tolt me she knit it herself, so she did. God,
wouldn't she be a great match for Jamie?"

"Would she not be a wee bit tall for Jamie maybe?"

"Och, Paddy, when did a couple of extra inches ever come between a man and a wommin?"

"Well . . . I s'ppose, aye . . . know what you're sayin' right enough, Rose."

———

Ruby arrived back at the car. To her complete surprise, she found her mother sitting upright, eyes wide open, taking tiny sips from a bottle of water held by May.

"Oh, thank God you're all right. I stopped some people out on the road. They're comin' now to help. They'll take you to the hospital."

Martha said nothing. Her hands were shaking. She didn't look at Ruby.

"She's not going to the hospital!" May snapped. "She says she doesn't need to."

"What?!"

"All right there?"

Ruby turned at the sound of a male voice. She was astonished to see a well-dressed man with a worried look peering at her. He looked familiar.

"Oh . . . I know you, don't I?"

The man shyly proffered a hand.

"Aye, I'm Jamie . . . Jamie Mc—"

"McCloone, yes, from the field . . . Jamie Barry . . ."

"Aye, James Kevin Barry Michael, but—"

"But you get Jamie for short."

"That's me," Jamie said. He tugged on his ear and adjusted his cap, self-conscious under Ruby's scrutiny.

"That was . . . that was a while ago now."

"Aye, three weeks and two . . . two and a half days ago, about," Jamie said.

Ruby smiled shyly. "I'm . . . I'm sorry I didn't give it to you . . . the field . . . I—"

The car door was thrust open, abruptly. "What on earth are *you* doing? We have to get going." May was looking out. "Oh, sorry," she said, on seeing Jamie.

"That's all right. Is your . . . is your mother all right, is she?"

"Cooee . . . cooee!"

Ruby and Jamie were alerted to the sound of a female voice. They saw Rose, hat askew, dress hitched about her knees, making the last perilous furlong toward them on husband Paddy's arm.

Ruby, embarrassed by May's outburst within earshot of Jamie, rushed to meet the pair.

"Mammy . . . Mammy says she doesn't need a hospital," she explained. She glanced back at the vehicle. Jamie McCloone was in conversation with May. "Maybe all she needs is a wee push to get her goin' again."

"What?" Rose mopped her brow with a lacy hankie. "Your mother needs a wee push to get her goin' again, Ruby?"

"No, the *car*, Rose, the *car*," Paddy exclaimed.

"Och, aye, the car. I'm with you, now, Ruby."

"Well, you haven't bogged the wheels," observed Paddy. "So me and Jamie'll give you a push no bother."

They moved toward the vehicle.

"I'll have a wee word with your mother first, just to make sure," Rose said. "'Tween God and his heavenly mother, hopefully she'll be all right. I was a nurse in me day, don't you know."

"That's very good of you, Rose." Ruby opened the passenger door and the former nurse settled herself. Ruby got into the driver's seat beside her.

Jamie and Paddy stood to one side, looking on. May remained in the back, holding her mother's hand.

"Hello, Martha!" Rose shouted. "Rose McFadden's me name . . . remember me, do you? I'd be Duttie tae me own name. A daughtur of the Longrod-Mickies of Ballymacrott Ridge on the mountain road."

Mrs. Clare opened her eyes briefly. "Oh . . . Rose . . ." she moaned.

"Now, Martha, you've just had a wee bit of a bump on the head . . . nothin' tae worry about. I'm just gonna check yer vitals."

"My . . . my what . . . Rose?"

"Yer vital signals, Martha," Rose clarified. She put a hand on Martha's forehead. "Now, you're not too hot and that's a good sign. So no fever tae worry about."

Next, she felt for a neck pulse, timing with her watch. "Now, Martha, you're tickin' at sixty tae the minute, and that would be normal for a woman your age who's hurted her head. So I think—"

"Look, she hit the back of her head quite hard," May said curtly. To May Clare's critical eye this McFadden woman was nothing but a country bumpkin who knew next to nothing. "She might have bleeding on the brain? She needs an X-ray and we're wasting valuable time here. I'm a pharmacist. I know about these things."

"You're *not* a pharmacist; you're a shop assistant," Ruby said acidly. "And Rose is an ex-nurse, so she knows more than you."

"And *you're* mentally ill," May shot back, jumping out of the car. "So keep your stupid opinions to yourself!"

Ruby was on her feet just as quickly. "I'm *not* mentally ill," she cried. "And—"

Just then, to everyone's astonishment, Martha Clare rose out of the car, like Lazarus from the tomb.

"*Now . . . stop . . . that . . . this . . . minute!*" she howled.

Everyone turned to stare.

"These people are here to help me and I'll *not* have a scene."

Ruby and May hung their heads.

Then, addressing Rose, Paddy, and Jamie, she said, "You'll have to excuse my daughter Ruby. She's mentally unstable. May and me were bringing her to the doctor because she needs to be admitted to St. Ita's. Last night she tried to drown herself, and just now she tried to kill us all in that car."

Ruby began sobbing. She splayed her hands, beseeching. "She's telling *lies.* It's . . . all lies."

She turned away from them all and ran off down the field.

Rose tut-tutted. "Paddy, Jamie," she said, taking control. "See if yins can get that car started. I'm gonna see tae poor Ruby."

"Och . . . there, there, there," Rose said, catching up to the weeping Ruby. "Don't upset yourself, daughtur dear." Rose put an arm about her and led her over to a low wall that bordered the field. "Now, we'll sit down on this wee wall till you get your breath back, and don't you worry about them."

She took a handkerchief from her handbag.

"Take that wee hankie and dry your eyes. Nothing's ever as bad as it seems. Your mother maybe didn't mean any of that. She's just upset after getting that wee knock on the back of the head. And your sister's just a bit shocked."

"They've always hated me, Rose . . . blamin' me for everything that goes wrong. When Daddy was alive he and me were so happy. He . . . he always took my side. And last night I wasn't trying tae drown meself. I was just going for a swim—"

"Yes, I believe you, Ruby. A lovely girl like you wouldn't be doing the like of that. And your father was the greatest man. Everybody liked him, so they did. It's understandable that you might be feeling a wee bit down with some of that old day-pression since he died. You must miss him terrible badly? How long's it been now?"

Ruby sniffled into the handkerchief. "Seven months . . . two weeks and . . . and four days."

"God, that's no length of time atall. Is it any wonder you're upset."

"And I wasn't trying to kill them in the car. Mammy was shouting at me, and May only got her test. She . . . she took her eyes off the road and lost control. I saved us all, 'cos I grabbed the wheel from her."

"I believe you, Ruby," Rose said. "Have no fear of that."

The sound of a car backfiring had them both looking up the field. They saw Paddy and Jamie giving the vehicle a push, with May at the wheel.

"Now, my Paddy and Jamie will have that car goin' in no time."

"That's good," Ruby said, feeling a little better. "I need to go to that clinic now. For . . . for if I don't, she'll get the doctor to sign me in tae St. Ita's, and I can't go in there."

Rose patted Ruby's arm.

"Now you listen to me, Ruby. I've just come from that Rosebud Clinic meself."

"You have?"

"Yes. D'you see Jamie there? He's a very good friend of me and my Paddy, and he suffers from that old day-pression, too."

Ruby looked at Rose, her sad eyes full of understanding. "God, does he, Rose?"

"He does indeed. His wee dog died a couple of months back and it's hit him something awful. Now, like yourself, Jamie doesn't like going near no doctor, so I went with him to explain things to Dr. Shelfin. And as long as you attend them appointments, that nice doctor will not be putting any of the pair of ye into that old hospital. 'Cos I could see he was a very understanding fella."

In the background, the car could be heard roaring into life.

"Look, Ruby! See, I told you my Paddy and Jamie would get her going."

After a few turns round the field, the car engine was ticking over nicely again.

"Now, Ruby," Rose said, always thinking ahead—and with her matchmaking hat firmly in place. "Before we go . . . do you have a wee phone number you could give me?"

"I do, Rose, aye."

Rose found a pen and took out her diary.

"It's two-eight-two-nine-four-five."

"That's great. I'll ring you the morra, just tae see you're all right."

"Thanks, Rose."

———

At the car, Ruby shook hands with Paddy and Jamie. "Thanks very much," she said. "I'm . . . I'm sorry about all that."

"No bother atall," said Paddy. "And there's nothin' tae be sorry about, Ruby. Sure there's not, Jamie?"

"Naw, nothin' . . . nothin' atall. Maybe . . ." Jamie stuck his hands in his pockets and scuffed the ground. "Maybe . . . maybe we'll see you about?"

"Aye . . . I hope so," Ruby said.

Rose smiled. "And I hope so, too," she said, giving Ruby's arm a squeeze. "Now, you go on there with yer mammy. God willing, everything will turn out all right."

"Hurry up!" It was the acerbic May. "We're late already."

Ruby got in the back and the car roared away across the field, turned out onto the road, and disappeared from view.

The spectacle might be over, but the real drama was about to begin.

Chapter thirty

G ood to see you, Ruby," Henry said, getting up from behind his desk. Ruby gave a diffident smile but said nothing. "And you, Mrs. Clare. Please . . . take a seat."

They took chairs opposite him. He thought the mother looked a bit off-color.

"Good afternoon, Doctor," she said. "I'm sorry we're late. We had a bit of an accident on the way."

"Oh?"

"Yes, my daughter, May . . . you met her last night. She was driving, and Ruby here thumped her on the back, making her lose control. She could have got us all killed."

"I *didn't* thump her on the back. I thumped the back of the seat 'cos you were shouting at me."

"Is it any wonder I was shouting at you?"

"Is this true, Ruby?"

Ruby shook her head. "May's only passed her test . . . she lost control of the car." She looked at her mother. "'Cos *she* was shouting at me so much. Only for me grabbing the steering wheel, we'd've crashed into—"

"And why d'you think I was shouting at you?"

"Just a minute, Mrs. Clare. You've given your version of events. Now I'd like to hear from Ruby."

"Why would you want to hear what she has to say? The fact that she's unstable is the reason we're here."

"Perhaps you should wait outside, Mrs. Clare."

"No, I certainly will not, Dr. Shevlin! You need to hear the truth, and you will only get the truth from me, her mother. You talked to her alone last night, and were no doubt fed a pack of lies. Now you will hear what *I* have to say."

Oh, that pesky need of hers to be at the helm! Henry imagined her in the front row of every public execution, knitting like a demon in the manner of the legendary Madame Defarge.

"You are not here to give me a list of what you consider to be Ruby's shortcomings, Mrs. Clare. I will hear what you have to say. After which, I would like you to wait outside while I speak with Ruby . . . alone. Can we agree on that?"

Mrs. Clare gripped her handbag more tightly. Ruby sat with head bowed, twisting her hands.

"First, Dr. Shevlin," the mother said, "you need to know about Ruby's grandmother, Edna . . . her father's mother. She was mentally unbalanced and that's who Ruby takes after. Not long after I married her son, she took her own life . . . walked into Beldam Lake, just as Ruby was trying to do last night. So it's in the Clare genes, I'm afraid."

"She wasn't trying to drown herself!" Ruby turned on the mother. "She was only trying to contact Arthur and wee Declan."

Mrs. Clare spread her hands in an imploring gesture. "D'you see what I mean, Doctor?" She glared at Ruby. "How on earth would you know what she was trying to do? You were only a baby, and still are by the sounds of you. Your grandmother was a *witch*!

And by 'contacting,' I suppose you mean talking to the dead, which just goes to prove my point that you're turning into *her*. Do you not realize how mad you sound, Ruby? Well, do you?"

Ruby understood she'd said too much.

"But *I* know," her mother went on. "Oh yes, I know all too well how mad you are. You did not burn her case like I ordered, did you? You kept it. You opened it, and now look at the mess you're in. And don't say I didn't warn you. You've brought all this on your-self . . . *this . . . this evil*."

Ruby started to weep.

"I think you've said enough, Mrs. Clare. Can you wait outside now, please?"

"Just so you know, Dr. Shevlin, this . . . this . . . godforsaken daughter of mine's been dabbling in black magic, like her grand-mother before her. It comes full circle, you know. God knows, she most likely needs an exorcism as well as the asylum. Father Kelly saw it immediately, when he came across her in the woods praying over a tree stump, her hands raised to the sky, talking some mumbo jumbo to God-knows-who. Her grandmother was at the same sort of non-sense before she took her own life. So now you know, Dr. Shevlin!"

Having finished her spiel, the mother got up.

Ruby clamped her hands over her ears.

"Stop it! Stop it!" she cried. "I just wish you would—"

"*Oooohhhhh*."

It was Martha. She staggered. Grabbed the chair.

Henry was on his feet, just in time to break her fall.

———

Martha could not have chosen a better setting to take her turn. The hospital was ten minutes away, and Henry had her checked and in the ambulance immediately.

Half an hour later, May and Ruby found themselves sitting outside the intensive care unit of St. Leonard's, weeping, and fearing to hear the worst. May wept for her mother; Ruby for the fact that she just might have caused her death.

She went back in her mind to that evening Martha had told her about Edna's case. If only she had done as she was told—taken it down to the woods there and then, and burned it—then, perhaps, none of this would have happened.

The swing doors to the unit opened and a nurse appeared, wearing a surgical mask. The siblings looked up, full of hope—and dread. But the nurse went to a man sitting farther up and whispered to him.

The man got up, his expression as grave as the leaden sky beyond the window, and accompanied her through the swing doors into the unit.

May discarded her sodden tissue in a bin. She rummaged in her handbag for a fresh one. "If Mummy dies, you're gonna have it on your conscience for the rest of your life. You know that, don't you?"

Ruby said nothing. She stared at the speckled terrazzo, the pattern blurring and clouding under yet another wash of tears. Yes, she would have her mother's death on her conscience. May was right about that. It would be the price she'd have to pay for "consorting with the Devil," as her mother put it.

She'd been right all along. Why had she been so foolish, thinking even for a minute that she could meet her father again through a set of silly cards? Have her dreams come true by burning a pouch of herbs in a silver dish?

It was all lies.

The cards.

The rhyme.

The voice.

The dream book.

And that other book: *The Book of Light*.

All lies. Wasn't that what the Devil was called: the Father of Lies?

Writing that book and believing in such things was simply Edna's way of coping with the unthinkable, the tragedy of not only losing her husband but her little boy *as well*.

Then the second tragedy: her only son meeting Martha and getting married. A stranger at the table, taking over Oaktree. Another loss, a betrayal too far.

Ruby intuited the terrible trajectory Edna's life must have taken, from the depths of despair in the farmhouse to the depths of oblivion in Beldam Lake, and understood all too clearly why she'd made that choice. There was nothing left to live for. Confined to the bedroom at the top of the stairs, a captive in her own home, there was no other way out.

This evening, Ruby knew what she had to do. She would go home, burn the case and everything in it. Only then could Grandma Edna finally rest in peace.

"You can go in now," a voice said.

Ruby looked up into the face of a nurse.

"But only one of you, and only for a few minutes."

"Oh God, has she come round?" May got up.

The nurse nodded. "Yes, but she's very weak. I'm Nurse Toner, by the way."

"I'll go," the twin said immediately, without consulting Ruby.

———

May found her mother at the far end of a room in one of six occupied beds, hooked up to a heart monitor, a drip attached to her left arm. She looked frail and small against the starched linens, appearing to have aged by years in the short time from her collapse at the clinic to her confinement in the bed.

Her eyes were shut, her mouth agape.

May went and stood by the bed, weeping silently. She gently squeezed the hand that lay on the bedclothes, but the gesture brought no response.

"Mummy . . . Mummy, can you hear me? It's May."

Martha's eyes opened briefly. Then, just as quickly, closed again. The seeming effort too much.

"You're going to be all right, Mummy. You . . . you just had a little fall, that's all."

"Hmmm . . ."

"Can you hear me?"

No response.

May leaned in closer. "Mummy, can you hear me? You're going to be all right."

But the mother just lay there, motionless. The only indication she was breathing: the barely perceptible rise and fall of the sheet across her chest.

All too soon, Nurse Toner indicated that the time was up.

"How is she?" Ruby said anxiously, at the sight of May and the nurse back in the corridor. "Can I go in now?"

"No, you *cannot*." May was back in character. "You've caused enough harm already. Do you want Mummy to get worse, do you?"

Nurse Toner stared at May. She turned to Ruby. "You must be . . . ?"

"Ruby . . ."

"Ruby, your mum is stable but weak. It's best that she just sleeps for now. I think you and your sister should go home and come back later this evening. The results of her X-rays will be through by then, and you can talk to the doctor."

"I'm not going anywhere," May announced in a challenging tone. "I don't want my mother to die alone. I want to be by her side."

"Hopefully your mother is not going to die," Nurse Toner said, with the resignation of someone who'd had to say the same thing many times in the past. "And I'm sorry, but visitors are not allowed in the intensive care unit. That is why it is referred to as an intensive care unit. We, the staff, must be allowed to care for the patients without interruptions from outsiders. Now, as I said, it is best you both go home. I will ring you immediately if there is any change."

"In that case, *I'll* wait here in the corridor. Ruby, you go home."

"As you wish," Nurse Toner said. "Now, if you'll excuse me, I've got work to do."

Chapter thirty-one

Jamie, there's plenty more where that came from," Rose said, spooning a generous portion of a stew-like mess onto the farmer's plate.

"Looks nice, Rose. What's it called?"

"That's corned beef coddle hash in pickled bread sauce with touch o' nutmeg, Jamie. Ida Nettles give me the recipe. Y'know Ida, don't you?"

"Aye. Sure I met her the other day in Biddy's. A wee low-set lady with yella hair?"

"That's Ida. Now, that's not her own hair color. I believe it's called 'Beeline Honey,' and I'll tell you how I know that. I was in the hair saloon one day getting me perm done and Julie, the wee stylist, sez to me, 'Rose,' she sez, 'you wouldn't like me to put a bitta Beeline Honey through them grays of yours? 'Cos I've some left over from Ida Nettles, and it's a pity to waste it, so it is.'" She returned the saucepan to the stove. "God, I wunder now if Ida knows about Martha's wee accident yet. I'll give her a ring when we're finished eating, 'cos maybe she could call round and see how she is. She does her toes on a Monday, don't you know."

Jamie was having a late lunch in the McFadden kitchen, a haven of cushioned plumpness and domestic delights. This was Rose's domain; examples of her handicrafts proliferated. Under Jamie's dinner plate there was a placemat appliqued with a tranche of Wessex Saddlebacks, the humble pig being Rose's favorite animal. And on the wall, what she referred to as her "farmyard college": a framed monstrosity showing three crocheted sows with powder-puff snouts, felt trotters sunk in Kellogg's All-Bran mud.

After the drama of the afternoon, the McFadden kitchen was a place of succor and much-needed sustenance, since it wasn't every day that Mrs. McFadden's services as an ex-nurse were called upon at the scene of an accident.

"God willing, Martha's all right," she said now, crossing herself and sitting down to her own loaded plate. "But, as I said to her, the pulse was beatin' at the sixty, maybe even the sixty-five, which would be normal for a wommin of her age."

"Och, she'll be all right," Paddy said, lifting the saltcellar and seasoning his food with such enthusiasm that his wife's plate got some as well. "That mother of hers—oul' Granny McRae—lived till she was nearly a hundred."

"Well, that's true," Rose agreed. "Now, Paddy, afore you start there, I hope them's your eatin' teeth you've got in yeh?"

"Oh, they are right enough," Paddy assured her.

"That's good. Now, more tea, Jamie?" Rose tipped the snout of the Royal Doulton teapot into the mouth of Jamie's mug, before he had time to answer. "Now Ruby: there's a great girl altogether. Misses her father something awful."

"What's that the mother was sayin' about her goin' into the mental hospital?" Jamie asked. "And her tryin' to drown herself and kill them all in the car? She wouldn't be doin' the like of that, would she?"

Rose set down her knife and fork and dabbed her lips with a napkin. "Now, I can explain that, Jamie." This was Rose's opportunity to defend poor Ruby and brighten the image so cruelly tarnished by the mother and sister.

Paddy read the signs. His wife was about to go about the delicate business of bringing Jamie and Ruby together. His input would not be required. He got up, plate in hand.

"Just gonna go in here tae listen tae a bitta news," he said, heading into the sitting room.

"Yes, you do that, Paddy. And watch you don't sit on me frosted frogs!" she shouted after him. She turned back to Jamie. "I'm makin' a couple of frogs for the Duntybutt Christmas Club Create and Care sale-of-work, Jamie. Would be afeard of Paddy sittin' on them, 'cos he broke his specs last week and is as blind as a rat without them. Between losin' his talkin' teeth and breakin' his glasses, I don't know what'll be next, God-blisses-an'-savus. Now, where was I?"

"You were gonna explain about Ruby havin' tae go into the mental hospital."

"Now, Jamie, Ruby's not going near no mental hospital. When I went down the field with her, I got her side of things. She tolt me she was only goin' for a swim in the lake and *they thought* she was gonna drown herself. And that May only passed her driving test, wasn't used to the driving, and nearly ran into a lorry 'cos she took her eyes off the road. Only for Ruby grabbing a-holt of the wheel, they might'a all been kilt. So Ruby saved them from crashing, so she did."

"God, there's two sides to every story, Rose," Jamie said, considering the rear of a Wessex Saddleback peeping out from underneath his dinner plate.

"There is indeed, Jamie. Now, what I was gonna say was that they were taking Ruby not tae the mental hospital but tae Rosebud Clinic, tae see that nice Dr. Shelfin that you meet every week."

"God, is that so?" Jamie was amazed.

"And who knows, poor Ruby is suffering from a wee bit of that old day-pression, 'cos she's only lost her father."

"Aye, her father. God, *I* know all about *that*, Rose." Jamie pushed aside his cleaned plate. "When Mick died it was the wildest thing. Sure I was thinkin' of endin' it all meself. So . . . so I know how Ruby feels."

"Oh, she was very close to her daddy, so she was. I used to see her on a Fair Day, waiting in the truck while he sold the cattle. A very big farm they have."

She saw Jamie's ears prick up.

"Have they now? How big . . . how big would it be?"

"Oaktree Farm? God, very big, Jamie. Wouldn't know the exact acreage all told . . . and Ruby's the eldest girl. She doesn't have no brothers. And them two twins—May and June—are both working in Belfast, so they wouldn't be interested in farmin' and the like."

Brring-brring. Rose's spiel was cut by the ringing telephone.

"I wonder who that could be. Excuse me, Jamie." She went into the hallway.

Jamie finished his mug of tea, mulling over what Rose had just said. He felt sorry for Ruby having lost her father so suddenly. But there was nothing he could do about that. Only the passage of time healed the hurt of losing a loved one. There was no other way through grief. He knew that only too well.

He checked the clock. It was coming up on three. Time to go home and feed Mabel, the sow.

He put his cap back on and got up.

"God, Jamie, that was Ida," Rose said, coming back into the kitchen. "She sez Martha's in the hospital in the intensive care. She took a turn when her and Ruby were with Dr. Shelfin."

"Och, that's too bad, Rose. Well, she's in the best place, I suppose."

"Just hope she doesn't die, Jamie, or poor Ruby will never forgive herself, the critter."

First her father and then her mother! Jamie saw nothing but sadness ahead of Ruby. He wished he could do something to help, but was at a loss. Maybe Rose could come up with something; she was good like that, was Rose.

Chapter thirty-two

Ruby returned to Oaktree Farmhouse, so deserted without her mother, so silent without her sister. She went directly to her bedroom, unlocked the door, and dragged the case out from under the bed.

She opened it for one last look. There were not many things in it now. The silver plate with the five-pointed star, the knife with the curved blade, and the little silver cup were missing. She'd used them during her solstice ritual so it was more than likely her mother had disposed of them.

Oh God!

Ruby suddenly had a terrible thought.

Was that why her mother had been struck down, because she'd destroyed the objects? Her mind went into overdrive. *What if I burn the case and something terrible happens to* me?

"I'm sorry, Edna!" she cried. "I have to do this. I understand why you turned to all this magic stuff, but it didn't help you in the end, it only made everything worse."

Behind her, the window banged shut.

Terrified, she turned.

The statue of the Virgin Mary that sat on the sill had toppled over. Was it another sign that something very bad was going to happen?

Oh dear God!

She grabbed her rosary beads from the bedside locker and started to pray. "O Lord . . . blessed Michael the Archangel, protect me. Give me . . . give me strength to burn this case and rid this house of all evil. Please, God, please!"

Hurriedly she gathered up the dream dictionary, the crystal ball, the stained cingulum, and the stack of remaining Tarot cards from the dressing table. She found *The Book of Light* under her pillow. But in her haste to bundle it into the case, it slipped from her grasp. A couple of loose leaves fell to the floor. They looked as if they were blank. But when she turned them over, she saw that one headed "Runes" was covered in drawings of strange letters, and the other was a poem, written in Edna's hand.

She began reading.

> *She came into the world last night,*
> *When you were full in Beltane.*
> *Our daughter of dark and light,*
> *The keeper of your flame.*
> *I heard her scream herself to life,*
> *Through the quiet rooms of Oaktree.*
> *And danced in my heart at the sound of her cries,*
> *For I knew you had made it be;*
> *You brought her to this world through tears,*
> *And stains of the darkest blood.*
> *But that misfortune had to be, so you*
> *Could give her whole to me.*
> *The first cub from the virgin womb,*
> *Who drew life's breath, was born too soon.*

And she will take my burdens on, and
Carry my wishes from beyond.
To you, the Goddess of this land,
Into the depths of Beldam.

It was signed *Edna Vivian Clare* and dated April 30, 1951.

The significance of that date had Ruby sobbing afresh. It was her birthday. Edna must have been writing about *her* birth.

"Anyone up there?"

A man's voice.

Footsteps on the stairs.

Before she could get off her knees, before she could push the case out of sight, Father Kelly was standing in the doorway.

"Ruby, I hoped I'd find you here. I've just come from the hospital."

Ruby shifted on her knees. "Father. Is Mammy . . . ?"

"God willing, she'll pull through."

"I was just—"

"There's no need to explain." He stared down at the case. "We'd need to destroy that now . . . you and me."

Ruby began crying again.

He held out his hand for the page. "May I?"

"Was she putting a curse on me, Father? She . . . she was writing about the night . . . the night I was born, wasn't she?"

Father Kelly read through the poem. He sat down on the bed.

"No, Ruby. No one has the power to do that. Your grandmother wasn't well. She'd suffered so much tragedy in her life she . . . she lost her way . . . stopped believing in God and"—he gestured at the case—"and turned to all that hocus-pocus. It was unfortunate you found it and opened it, but we can put an end to it all now."

Ruby dried her tears. "But did she . . . did she come back?"

"Come back?"

"After she died . . . it's just that Mammy said something odd when May brought me back from the lake last night. She said . . . she said something about footprints. I don't know what she meant."

He made no reply. Then: "Aye . . . we'll go down to the woods and burn this now, Ruby . . . that would be the best thing to do."

He picked up *The Book of Light*, replaced the poem, and put it on top of the other items. Ruby might have opened a Pandora's box, but the Spirit of Hope was still alive. He watched as she shut the lid, sliding the half-moon catch through its leather strap for the last time.

"I'll carry it," Father Kelly said. "Get some paraffin and a box of matches, there now."

———

The sun hung low as they walked the "afflicted" field. They passed the patch of memorial flowers and stopped briefly to say a prayer. They approached Beldam, a sheet of bronze in the gathering dusk, and turned toward the woods. The trees came up to meet them, dense and dark: a vanguard of susurrous shadows.

The priest led the way with the benighted case, picking his steps carefully on the forest floor. Ruby followed behind him with the kerosene can.

He stopped.

"We'll burn it here," he said. It was the tree stump Ruby had used as her first altar. The ritual he'd interrupted. "Yes, here would be a good place."

He set the case down.

"Will *you* burn it, Father?" Ruby said, holding out the can.

"No," he said. "That's *your* job."

CHRISTINA McKENNA

"But why?"

"It was what your mother wanted, Ruby . . . that you should burn it. I'll sprinkle the paraffin. You strike the match."

Ruby's hands were shaking as she struck the match. It flared into life . . . but just as quickly died. She tried again. But a sudden gust of wind took the flame. It happened several more times.

"It doesn't want to burn," Father Kelly said grimly. "But, by the power of God, we're stronger than *it*. You keep trying, Ruby. I will say a prayer." He spread his arms and gazed heavenward.

Ruby looked down at the spent matches. There were only two left in the box. It *had* to burn this time.

It *had* to.

She struck the match and held it to one corner of the case. But it was useless; it wouldn't light.

She began weeping again, desperate now. "I can't get rid of it, Father. I just *can't*."

"Have faith. Let me."

Father Kelly struck the final match. He threw it on the case lid, and immediately it burst into flames.

"How . . . how did you do that, Father?"

He didn't answer. Stood staring grimly at the blazing object.

"We'll go now, Ruby, so. It's done."

She did his bidding and followed him out of the forest—the smell of burning wood high on the air, her mind seething with images of the melting case. The secrets in *The Book of Light*, curling up, shriveling leaf by leaf, and fragmenting into ash, into nothingness.

Back at the house she made him tea.

"Your mother can rest easy now . . . yes, no more upset, Ruby."

"Will you tell me about the footprints, Father?"

"The footprints?"

"Yes, last night when May took me from the lake, Mammy screamed and said something about footprints. What . . . what did she mean?"

Father Kelly left down his mug.

He sighed.

"Well, Ruby, after your grandmother passed away there was some trouble in the house."

"Trouble . . . what kind of trouble?"

"She was not at her rest, you see. Your mother asked the parish priest for help . . . I was a young curate then . . . new to these parts, and he sent me . . . Aye . . . sent me to bless this place." He gazed up at the ceiling.

"But why? What was happening?"

"The footprints . . . they were there on the floor . . . wet footprints of bare feet every morning. After your grandmother drowned herself they began appearing. It was as if she was returning and . . . and roaming the house when your parents were asleep." Father Kelly shook his head, glanced over at the picture of St. Michael the Archangel in the alcove. "Oh, she needed a lot of prayers, Ruby, to find rest. And she received those prayers from Martha and your poor father. The only thing he wouldn't do was destroy that case. She'd made him promise, you see. Your father couldn't break that promise."

He drained the last of his tea, stood up, and put his hat back on. "But, it's over now . . . all over."

"But what if—"

"Just say your prayers, Ruby. Walk the straight path and no harm will come to you. Your grandmother took the wrong one. She paid with her life for that."

He took a bottle of holy water from his pocket, wet his thumb, and made the sign of the cross on her forehead several times.

Then, laying his hands on her head, he prayed: "Spirit of our God, Father, Son and Holy Spirit . . . of angels and archangels, St. Michael, St. Gabriel, and St. Raphael, descend upon Ruby. Banish from her all forces of evil. Destroy them, vanquish them. Banish from her all spells, black magic, malefice, ties . . . All diabolical infestations, oppressions, and possessions. Burn all these evils in hell, that they may never again touch her. In the name of God All Powerful, in the name of Jesus Christ our Savior, in the name of the Immaculate Virgin Mary, protect her always. Amen."

He made the sign of the cross and Ruby did the same.

"You'll be safe now, Ruby," he said. He looked at the clock. "Perhaps it's time you went back to the hospital. Your mother needs you there."

Chapter thirty-three

Martha Clare recovered sufficiently to leave intensive care, but unfortunately suffered a further setback: she had a stroke. She was discharged from hospital to be tended to at home. Paralyzed down one side, but still able to communicate, her speech slow, if a little slurred, meant that her daughter now became her full-time nurse and carer. Ruby did not resent this change, so suddenly foisted upon her. It was payback for all the trouble she'd visited on Oaktree, and her poor mother in particular. Being more confined to the house than ever before was her penance.

Ida Nettles proved a godsend in this regard. She agreed to look after Martha, so Ruby could continue her sessions at Rosewood Clinic and do the shopping once a week.

Today was one of those days. Ruby was seeing Dr. Shevlin for the first time since the accident.

She sat self-consciously in the consulting room, awaiting his arrival. She was nervous, not knowing what she was going to tell him. The last time she'd seen him was with her mother, who'd fainted, midsentence, right there beside her.

A lot had happened since that fateful day. Edna and the case were out of her life, but they weren't out of her thoughts. She could not sleep. She was having fitful nights and frightening dreams.

Added to that, a conversation she'd had with May and June at the weekend had really upset her. They'd only just sat down at the supper table, having spent an hour behind closed doors with Martha.

"You know, if Mummy dies, this place will have to go under the hammer," May had said, poking through her food and studiously avoiding Ruby's eye.

"Hammer? What hammer?"

"Well, this house and farm will be left between the three of us. June and I want no part of it. You've brought it on all on yourself. God knows what you've let loose here, with that stupid case and your crazy antics. Nothing but bad luck, no doubt—as if we didn't have enough."

"Yes, so that's why we want no part of it," June chimed in. "We'll be selling the lot. We'd like to buy a house in Belfast anyway, so the money from here will be very useful."

Suddenly, the worst-case scenario, one she'd never for a minute anticipated, was being laid before Ruby. She was devastated.

"You *can't* do that! You just *can't*. This . . . this is *my* home. And Daddy's land cannot be sold. Not *ever!*"

"Well, there's only one way around it, Ruby." May fixed her with a determined eye. "You'll just have to somehow raise the money and buy us out. And there's not much chance of that happening, because you don't have anything, do you?"

"Or," June said, taking up the baton, "or you get down on your knees, Ruby, and pray Mummy's health improves and she lives a very long, long time."

———

Dr. Shevlin opened the door of the consulting room, to find Ruby Clare in tears. She looked thinner than before, which wasn't so surprising, given what she'd been through of late.

He shut the door, gently. "Ruby . . . good to see you again."

"Hello, Doctor. I'm . . . I'm sorry I-I missed my appointment."

"That's all right. I understand. How is your mother, by the way?"

"She's at home now, Doctor. She had a stroke . . . but . . . but she's still able to talk."

Ruby started to sob again. Henry sat down. He pushed the tissue box across the coffee table. Just let her cry for a while more. Then: "In your own time, Ruby. There's . . . there's no rush."

Ruby balled the sodden tissue in her hand and withdrew another one. "When . . . when Mammy dies," she began. "When Mammy dies, I'm going to have nowhere to go . . . 'cos May and June say they're gonna be sellin' the house and farm 'cos of what I did. And . . . and I knew something terrible like this was gonna happen 'cos I burned the case . . . And now . . ."

"Ruby, do you know that ninety percent of what we worry about never actually happens?"

She shook her head.

"Now, first off: nobody knows when your mother's going to die, not even your sisters. She's still in her sixties, and many people can recover from strokes at her age."

"Can they?"

"Yes. Secondly: you can clear that other thing up by asking your mother how she's made her will."

"I can't ask her that, Doctor! She . . . she would only think that I was just wantin' her to die even more. I know what she's like."

"Her friend, the priest. Father what's-his-name?"

"Kelly."

"Father Kelly . . . You know, we psychiatrists and priests have quite a bit in common. We can help things along. You could ask Father Kelly to ask your mother. She wouldn't mind telling *him*."

"Maybe," Ruby said, brightening a little. "Father Kelly's very good. He . . . he helped me burn the case."

"Good. You burned it, then? How did that make you feel?"

"I was glad. But then . . . but then I kept thinking something bad's gonna happen. And now it *is* happening, 'cos they're gonna be selling Oaktree."

"And why do you think that something bad is going to happen?"

"'Cos Edna—that's my grandmother—she . . . she didn't want it burned. Now that it's burned, the house and land has to go, too."

"How do you know that's what your grandmother wanted?"

"She tolt me."

"So she was alive until recently?"

"No . . . she died when I was a baby. But . . . but when I found the case she started to talk to me."

"I see . . . So . . . if she died when you were small . . . how did you know the voice belonged to *her*?"

"I didn't, but it must of been her . . . or . . . or Dana." All at once, a look of terror came into Ruby's eyes. "Oh God, I shouldn't have tolt you about the voices. Now . . . now you'll put me in St. Ita's!"

"No, Ruby, I'm not going to put you in St. Ita's. Who's Dana?"

"She's-she's a goddess . . . an Irish goddess."

"Ah . . . the mother of the Tuatha de Danann."

Ruby amazed. "You know about them, Doctor?"

"The children of Danu? Yes, also known as the faerie folk."

"But, how did you know that, Doctor?"

"Oh, I read a lot and I studied Celtic mythology at school. Was it Dana you were celebrating at the lake that night?"

Ruby nodded and hung her head. "I thought . . . I thought I'd see her, but I only saw meself."

Ruby might be claiming that she heard voices, but Henry could see that she was no schizophrenic.

"Hmmm . . . And the voices you heard. Those voices, Ruby, they were yours, too."

"Aye, maybe." She kept her head bowed, too ashamed to meet the doctor's eye.

"Now, what I am going to do is help you to relax so that you can forget all about your grandmother and her case. All right?"

From listening to Ruby, and what he'd gleaned of her family circumstances to date, Henry drew the following conclusions.

She was a young woman who had suffered the loss of the two things in her life she held dear: her beloved father and the farm. The mother, while not the architect of that first tragedy, was certainly the author of the second one. Little wonder that Ruby went against her wishes by not burning the case. It was the only way she had of gaining some control in an otherwise dire situation. When Ruby opened it and found her grandmother's magical effects, her subconscious had set about creating the life she yearned for.

He thought back to the Tarot cards, the items from her ritual by the lake. Those objects she put her trust in because she couldn't face reality. It was safer to retreat into dreams and delusion. And, in that respect, the case had been of some benefit. It filled a need. Mysticism saved Ruby from suffering a dark depression. Something she was now in danger of falling into, since everything she'd put her faith in had been taken away.

Given how suggestible she'd shown herself to be, Henry concluded that a few sessions of hypnotherapy might prove to be the most beneficial approach in the first instance.

"Now, Ruby, we're going to try something called hypnosis to help you get rid of all these unhelpful thoughts."

"Are you . . . are you gonna put me to sleep, Doctor?"

"No, you'll hear my voice but you'll feel very relaxed, that's all. Afterwards, you'll remember all we talked about, but your worries and your thoughts about your grandmother—and the case and the voices you heard—I'm going to take them all away, so you won't be bothered by them anymore."

"Can you really do that?" Ruby asked in surprise.

"Yes. Trust me. The method I'm going to use is even more powerful than those Tarot cards you showed me. And more powerful than any of the objects you found in your grandmother's case. Okay?"

Ruby settled herself on the couch and, at Henry's instruction, closed her eyes.

"Now, I want you to imagine you're lying in a beautiful meadow . . . a beautiful meadow with the loveliest pink flowers. The sun is shining . . . the birds are singing. Everything is calm . . . calm and relaxed. You feel warm . . . and comfortable . . . and very relaxed." Henry slowed down his words to mirror Ruby's breathing. "You can smell the beautiful scent of the flowers. You can hear the birds singing . . . and feel the warmth of the sun on your face. Your body feels heavy . . . arms and legs heavy and comfortable and very relaxed . . . going deeper and deeper into this beautiful state . . ."

Very soon, with soothing repetition, Ruby had slipped into a trancelike state of measured, slow breathing.

"Now your body is floating, Ruby. Floating off the ground and above the meadow into the sky . . . and gently . . . very gently, you land on a cloud . . . the most beautiful, soft, white cloud. And the more you sink down into that cloud, the more relaxed you become. All the worries . . . and stress . . . they're all melting away . . . and now you are resting comfortably in a deep and peaceful state, lying on this soft, fluffy cloud . . . going deeper and deeper . . . relaxing deeper and deeper . . . until . . . I call you back. But for now . . . you will only hear my voice and accept those suggestions which will be of benefit to you, and which you are willing to accept.

"The past is over . . . the future is new and full of possibilities. You are happy and contented. Everything comes easily to you. Money . . . good friends . . . fine health . . . restful sleep. Every morning, you wake up full of joy, and this joy remains with you throughout every hour of the day, no matter how people treat you. No matter what happens. When others say bad things to you or treat you unkindly, you know they are just unhappy with themselves and their own lives. But that has nothing to do with you, Ruby, because you have the power within you to remain in this beautiful state of peace and joy. And no one—absolutely no one— can take this joy away from you, because they don't have the power to do that. You no longer give them the power to do that. For, anytime you feel threatened, you will bring your thumb and forefinger together to form the letter *O*, and this *O* will be a sign to your subconscious mind that you have the power . . . and you will use this power . . . this power that is always here within you, waiting to be used . . . waiting to help you."

Ruby's thumb and forefinger came together to form the *O* at Henry's prompting.

"This feeling . . . this beautiful feeling of peace and joy . . . is your natural state, Ruby. It was ever thus. Every night, you will go to bed contented, and fall immediately into a deep and restful sleep. Every morning, you will wake up renewed and refreshed, ready to face the day."

Ruby's features relaxed more, a smile forming.

"You will look back on this experience as the day your life changed, turning all the coming days into happy . . . fulfilling days. Turning all the nights into peaceful, restful nights. From this day forward, you will be able to act and think and feel like everything is possible . . . everything is possible.

"Now I am going to count from one to five, and at the count of five, Ruby, you will open your eyes and be wide awake, fully alert and completely refreshed."

Henry began slowly counting down. On the cue of five, Ruby opened her eyes. She smiled, looked down at her hand, and gasped.

"That's the sign of the Goddess," she said, eyes wide with wonder.

"Yes, it may well be, Ruby. It's the sign of creative power and now it's yours. Just make that sign anytime you feel stressed, and all the calm you felt during our session will return to you."

"It will?"

"Yes."

"So it's not bad . . . the sign?"

"No. Why do you think it might be bad?"

"My mother . . . she said that Grandma Edna was a witch."

"No, your grandmother was just trying to find peace after her loss. Just like you."

Henry helped Ruby to her feet. "How do you feel?"

"Nice . . . " Ruby said shyly. "Thank you . . . I've never felt like that before. Will I . . . will I be all right now?"

"You're going to be fine, Ruby, just fine. Come back and see me next week and we'll have another session just like that one."

He led her to the door.

"I . . . I won't have to—?"

"Go into St. Ita's? No . . . so long as you keep your appointments with me you'll be fine, Ruby . . . just fine."

Ruby smiled then hesitated. She looked at him strangely, as if seeing him for the first time.

"Yes . . . ?"

He sensed that she wanted to tell him something but was holding back.

"She's . . . she's all right."

"Sorry, I don't follow you, Ruby. Who's all right?"

"Your wife. You'll . . . you'll . . . be seeing her soon."

Henry felt a frisson of shock pass through him. How could she . . . ?

He shifted back a little in an attempt mask his confusion. "I-I don't . . . don't understand what you mean."

Ruby looked at the floor. "I'm sorry, Doctor, maybe I shouldn't have said that."

"No, no!" Henry tried to make light of it. "It's good to say what's on your mind . . . get things out in the open. Even if it doesn't make much sense."

He saw her redden. "It's just that the thought came into me head and . . . and I wanted . . . wanted to tell you, so you knew, like. Maybe I shouldn't of."

He patted her arm. "Don't worry, Ruby. See you next week."

Henry shut the door and leaned against it, breathing hard. How could she have known? This sheltered rural girl he'd met a few short days before.

How could she possibly have known about Connie's disappearance? He'd shared it with no one, not even Dr. Balby.

He crossed to the window and opened it to get some air. Tried to reassure himself. *I don't believe in extrasensory perception. Never have. Never will. There is only logic.*

Then it occurred to him.

Of course, the sister! Yes, there was the link. May: the twin who worked in Boots. She probably saw the poster.

But as he shut the window, doubt made his hand shake: an uncharacteristic phenomenon for the normally unflappable doctor.

Chapter thirty-four

In reception, Miss King was alerted to the sound of a car. She shifted her eyes from a line of typing concerning the value of placebos over antidepressant medication, and observed a blue Austin Maxi rattle its way into the parking area. Immediately, she recognized the McFadden couple bearing their friend James McCloone to his 12:30 p.m. appointment. She watched with a sense of weary sufferance as the vehicle once again nosed its way into one of the Reserved for Staff parking bays.

Alerted to the possibility of yet another calamitous entrance to the building via the revolving door, she got up and went immediately to stand guard. It was safer all round to make a preemptive strike.

———

Jamie McCloone debouched from the passenger seat first, followed by Rose, who hatched out of the back, like a large chick, clutching a bunch of flowers.

"Now, Jamie, you take them flowers and give them tae Ruby when you see her," she instructed.

"Aye," he said, self-consciously taking the bunch of swan-river daisies. "But, how d'you know she's gonna be here, Rose?"

"Oh, she's here all right, Jamie, for there's her car over there."

Jamie followed Rose's pointing finger. He recognized immediately the green jalopy he and Paddy had pushed out of the field. "God, so it is! There's nothin' wrong with your eyes, Rose."

Rose beamed. "Now I thought I'd bring the flowers just in case, Jamie, for there's nothing a lady likes more tae get from a man than a bunch of flowers . . . fresh picked they are from me garden this morning."

"Aye, so," Jamie said. "Look nice, right enough."

"They are indeed, Jamie . . . and I've put a wee bit of baby's breath and false goat's beard through them tae add a bit more color, like."

They made their way across the car park.

"God, there's Miss King at the door." Rose gave a little regal wave. "And thank heavens she's there, 'cos she'll help get us in through that contraption, so she will."

Miss King smiled and beckoned Rose forward through the glass. Rose obliged. Jamie took his cue, and stepped into the second chamber.

"Now, that wasn't so difficult?" the secretary said as the pair emerged, blinking with surprise, into the foyer.

"Thank you very much, Miss King," Rose said. "'Cos, you know, we were a wee bit nervous since the last time."

"You're very welcome . . . What beautiful flowers, James! Who's the lucky lady?"

"Aye, they're nice boys, right enough," Jamie said, reddening.

At that very moment, the restroom door opened and who should appear, glowing from her hypnosis session, but Ruby.

"There's the very lady now," Rose said.

"Aren't you the lucky lady, Ruby?" Miss King smiled, and withdrew behind her desk again.

Jamie thrust the bouquet at Ruby. "Hello, Ruby. These . . . these here are for you, so they are."

Ruby took the bunch of swan-river daisies, still warm from Jamie's tight grasp, and almost wept again. No one had given her flowers before. She didn't know what to say.

Rose came to the rescue. "Now, Jamie plucked them in my garden, 'cos he wanted tae give you a wee gift, Ruby."

Jamie, too, was lost for words. Rose gave him a discreet little nudge.

"Aye . . . aye, Ruby, thought . . . thought you would like them. They're called goat's breath with baby's beards."

"No, Ruby," Rose corrected. "Jamie got a wee bit mixed up. They're swan-river daisies with a wee bit of false goat's beard and some of that nice baby's breath through them." She gave Jamie another nudge.

"Aye, them, 'cos . . . 'cos it's terrible what you've come through with that accident . . . and yer mother bein' sick and all, Ruby."

Viewing the scene from behind her desk, Miss King felt her eyes welling up.

"Thank you . . . thank you very much," Ruby said finally. She gazed down at the beautiful trembling blooms. "They're lovely, Jamie. You . . . you must have a lovely garden, Rose?"

"Oh, I love the gardenin', Ruby. Like yourself, I'm sure."

The intercom sounded on Miss King's desk.

"But I'm not so good at it, Rose."

"How was . . . how was your meetin' with the doctor?" Jamie ventured.

"It was great, Jamie," Ruby said, putting her thumb and forefinger together as Henry had instructed. She suddenly felt flooded with happiness, and bestowed on Jamie a heartfelt smile. "It's your turn now, is it?"

"Aye, so." Jamie pulled on his ear and studied the floor.

"James, Dr. Shevlin will see you now." They all turned at the sound of Miss King's voice.

"That's you now, Jamie," Rose said, very pleased with the shape her matchmaking plans were taking thus far. "You go on in there and I'll wait on you. But first I'll leave Ruby out to her car."

"Aye, so . . ." Jamie touched his cap to Ruby. "Well . . . maybe . . . maybe see you about again, Ruby, so we will."

———

The ever-patient Paddy McFadden was enjoying a cigarette and a nose through the *Mid-Ulster Vindicator* when his wife emerged from the clinic with Ruby. He knew immediately what he had to do. Rose had schooled him in what to say. Just as she'd schooled Jamie in his lines concerning the presentation of the bouquet.

He watched them stroll over to Ruby's car. It was time he played his part. He stubbed out the cigarette and got out.

"Here's my Paddy," Rose said, at sight of him.

"Hello, Ruby, and how's the mammy?" Paddy removed his cap. "Hope she's . . . hope she's gettin' a bit better?"

"She's not too bad, Paddy, thank you."

"That's good."

"Now," Rose began, "I was just saying to Ruby that she should come out with us this Friday night, to hear Jamie play the accordjin in Slope's."

"Aye, that's a very good idea," Paddy agreed. "Jamie . . . Jamie would like that, so he would."

"I'd love to, but . . ." Ruby frowned and looked sad. "But . . . but I couldn't . . . I couldn't leave Mammy."

Rose had expected that reply and was ready for it. "Don't your sisters come from Belfast at the weekend, Ruby?"

"Aye . . . aye, they do, but . . . but I don't think they'd want me going out, like."

"Now, Ruby, that's where you're wrong. You're looking after your mammy all week, so you need a wee break from it. And a couple or so hours of a Friday night is not too much to ask, sure it's not, Paddy?"

"Nah, not a wild lot to ask atall, Ruby. Sure we'll collect you and leave you home again, so they've nothing to worry about."

Ruby thought of May and June and how cruel they'd been to her the previous weekend, talking about selling the farm when the mother died. Snatches from the hypnosis session came back to her. *You have the power, Ruby . . . you no longer give them the power . . . From this day forward you will be able to act and think and feel like everything is possible . . .*

". . . so what d'ye think, Ruby?" Rose was saying.

Ruby smiled, gripped the stems of the beautiful blooms more tightly. Thought of how kind Jamie had been in giving them to her. "Aye, I'd love to hear Jamie play."

"God, that's great, Ruby!" Rose clasped her hands together, barely able to contain her joy. "Isn't it, Paddy?"

"It's great, all right," Paddy said. "Me and Rose'll collect you at eight. Wouldn't that be right, Rose?"

"Eight would be great. You'll be ready for then, won't you, Ruby?"

"Aye . . . 'cos May and June come home at six. So they'll have time to have their supper first when I'm gettin' ready."

Paddy and Rose saw Ruby off.

A delighted Rose returned to the clinic, to await Jamie and impart the happy news.

Chapter thirty-five

Friday morning and Henry was running through his list of patients for the day. He was glad the weekend was in sight, and had planned on going to Lisburn to visit his father and check on the house.

He didn't often visit Hestia House, his Belfast home. After his move to Killoran, he would spend every weekend there, on the off chance that Connie might reappear. But as the weeks turned to months, and the light of hope dimmed, it was clear that each journey he made there was a futile one.

He'd employed Sinclair's housekeeper, the redoubtable Mrs. Malahide, to clean the place once a week and generally keep an eye on things. He'd also left a letter on the table, in an envelope with Connie's name on it, giving details of his new whereabouts and a declaration of his love.

He was dwelling on that letter now when Miss King put her head round the door.

"You'll be pleased to know that Finbar Flannagan is in the building, Dr. Shevlin."

"Really! He's actually got the date right? Wonders will ne'er cease."

"Yes." The secretary threw a covert look over her shoulder, came forward and lowered her voice. "I should warn you that you're in for a surprise. He hardly looks like the same person. John Lennon seems to have departed."

"Oh . . . Are you sure it is he?"

"Oh yes, but you will see for yourself. Shall I send him in?"

Henry grinned. "Please, Edie, please."

Henry was indeed surprised at the transformation. He hardly recognized Finbar. Gone was the beaded headband and long locks. He now wore his hair neatly shorn above the ears. The baggy clothes had been replaced with jeans and a cotton shirt. There were no love beads around his neck, and he no longer wore those signature Lennon spectacles. He still carried his roll-up tin of tobacco, though.

"Finbar, good to see you," Henry said. "How've you been?"

"Between worlds . . . aye, between worlds. That's why I've come to see you."

He sat down on the sofa.

The Liverpudlian accent had disappeared, too. So the metamorphosis seemed complete. The only question was: With John Lennon clearly gone, what persona was Finbar employing now to stop being himself and facing his own reality? Henry pulled up a chair.

"Go on, Finbar . . . in your own time."

"I joined the Screamers 'cos of Lennon, and I became Lennon 'cos he was a genius . . . and . . . and if I could be him . . . could be a genius, then I couldn't be just ordinary, boring Finbar Flannagan . . ."

"Hmm . . . you want to tell me about the Screamers?"

Finbar didn't answer. Instead he reached for the tin of roll-ups and started constructing a cigarette. His fingers trembled, but he kept his eyes rooted on the task, as if it were a mighty challenge he had to overcome in order to move to the next part of his story.

"They were all runnin' from something . . . just like . . . just like me . . ."

"Well, we all need to escape from things from time to time, Finbar."

"But I couldn't . . . couldn't escape, could I? Not from *him*."

"Your stepfather?"

He nodded. Lit the cigarette.

"You can't escape from your memories, Doctor. You can never out-run your bloody childhood, no matter how many pills you swallow, or how many needles you stick in your arms, or therapists you talk to. The struggle's always in the mind—that's what Lennon said. He said: 'We must bury our own monsters and stop condemning people. We are all Christ and we are all Hitler. We want Christ to win.'"

Henry was impressed. "I didn't realize he was such a philosopher."

"Aye . . . that's why I joined them: the Screamers. 'Cos if they were good enough for Lennon they were good enough for me. And I . . . I hated *him* for what he did to me . . . and . . . and I was angry."

He sucked greedily on the roll-up.

"Thought they would clear me head, 'cos you can't paint a pic-ture on dirty paper; you need a clean sheet. Lennon said that, too."

"And did it help . . . being with like-minded people and giving vent to repressed feelings in such a physical way?"

"Aye, they showed me how to cry. I'd never cried . . . not since I was a kid. That was a start . . . the crying. The screaming came easy after that. Then . . . then I met a woman . . . "

"On Innisfree?"

"Aye . . . Holly Blue. She told me she was—"

"Sorry, did you say 'Holly'?" At mention of the name, Henry saw himself reading a note in the dimly lit bedroom of a terraced house in Belfast many months before.

Thanks for everything, Harry.
Best of luck,
Holly

"Aye, Holly Blue she called herself. Nobody used their real name, see . . . too much stuff to hide. She told me she was on the run from the IRA."

All at once, Henry felt on edge. "I see . . ."

"Most of them were a bit weird, but she wasn't."

"So you started a relationship."

"Nah. She didn't want to . . . said she was married. But we had a lot in common, 'cos she was an artist and she liked poetry. We worked well together."

"As a team, you mean?"

"Aye . . . I'm a joiner . . . that's my trade. So I cut trees and made furniture . . . tables and chairs and stuff. We were self-sufficient . . . and she, Holly, she painted them. Not in the normal way . . . she put flowers on them."

A married woman, an artist who liked poetry, called herself Holly, and was on the run from the IRA. Could it . . . Could it be so? Well, he'd learned many strange things about his wife since her disappearance. He was intrigued. Just for a moment, he set his therapist's hat aside. Unethical, maybe, but . . .

"How old was Holly? Your age?"

"Thirty."

Henry's heart rate shifted up a gear.

"Unusual for a woman to tell a man her age," he quipped. "And especially that one . . . that milestone."

"She was different." Finbar reached for his tin of roll-ups again. "That's why I liked her. She wasn't run of the mill, as they say. But she had her demons like the rest of us. There was a lot she wouldn't say. In group sessions she'd just clam up. It pissed some of them off, 'cos we were there to rid ourselves of insecurities and be honest with each other." He grimaced. "Maybe the only thing any of us are sure of *is* our age."

"Will you be seeing her again?"

Finbar shook his head.

"She left. One day she was there, the next . . ." He blew on his bunched fingers, fanned them wide. "Gone, without a word to no one. As if the aliens had abducted her in the night."

He lit the roll-up.

Henry concentrated on the wavering flame of the lighter. He swore he could hear his own heart beating.

"One thing's for sure, though." Finbar drew on the cigarette, squinting at Henry through a plume of smoke. "Somebody was on her tail; that's for sure."

He had heard enough. It was time to move on.

"You're very perceptive, Finbar. Have you found a way to 'bury your own monsters and stop condemning,' like your hero said?"

"I'm trying . . . but it's hard. Without the drugs, it's hard."

"It is. But you've taken the first step. Not even a step—a huge leap forward."

"Aye . . . I suppose." He flicked ash into the little foil tray.

"Giving up the drugs is really giving up the stranglehold your stepfather's had over you all these years. Every time you took a shot of heroin, you were giving him power over you. Now, every time you resist that urge, that power gets weaker and weaker."

"It does?"

"Yes. You've dropped the disguise that kept you from owning up to the real you, Finbar. You identified with the childhood of Lennon because he was abandoned by his father and suffered an abusive childhood, just like you. But he overcame all of that—from what you're told me. He was a good example to follow. You see, we can go through life blaming our parents for our problems, or we can look back and see them for the deeply flawed, misguided individuals that they were . . . unwilling—or in most cases not even aware they had the choice—to live freely and authentically while they had the chance. A great many people go to their graves ignorant of this simple fact. But *you* won't. D'you know why?"

Finbar shook his head.

"Because you're willing to look for answers. You have enough insight to question things. You're creative. But most important of all, you've made the decision to stop abusing yourself. Whether for good or ill, our lives turn on the decisions we make, so we must be sure we make the right ones. And you've made the right one."

"But what if I relapse? What if the bad thoughts come back?"

"You won't relapse."

"Aye . . . but how do you know?"

"I'm going to let you into a secret, Finbar. Thoughts are not facts. They are mental events that come and go like the clouds in the sky. The trick is recognizing that, and choosing only to dwell on the good ones, the ones that empower you."

"You mean: don't pay attention to . . . to the negative ones . . . just . . . just ignore them altogether?"

"Exactly."

"More easily said than done, Doc."

"That's a belief. But beliefs are not set in stone. We can change them. You, and *only* you, can do that."

They talked some more. Finbar told of his plans. He had a friend in London—a craftsman who made bespoke furniture—who'd offered him a job in his workshop.

He got up. "I'm looking forward to going . . . getting out of here," he said, waving a hand.

"This room or Northern Ireland?"

They laughed. "Both, I suppose."

"We still have more work to do, Finbar."

"I know. Don't worry: I'll be keeping my appointments from now on . . . now that my mind is clearer."

"Good."

They shook hands and Finbar made to leave.

"Just one thing, Finbar, before you go. I wouldn't mind visiting your friends on Innisfree. Sound like an interesting lot of people. Could you tell me how to get there?"

"Aye, no bother. I'll draw a map for you. But if you have any problems, there's a guy called Max—Mad Max. He'll see you right."

"How will I find him?"

"Oh, don't worry, Max'll find *you*. Knows everyone who comes there. He's a regular in the pubs around Burtonport, so if you have any problems just go into one of them."

After Finbar left, Henry lifted the phone. No, he wouldn't be visiting Belfast or looking in on his father the next day. He called to mind the words of a sinister man in a dark suit and fedora.

"If you want to see your wife again, stop looking."

Well, he'd stopped looking for a whole year and they'd never contacted him. It was long enough to have waited.

Then, from nowhere, a voice he couldn't ignore: "Your wife. You'll . . . you'll . . . be seeing her soon." Ruby's voice.

His mind was made up. It was surely worth the risk.

Chapter thirty-six

The white Mercedes had covered the thirty-five miles from Killoran in well under an hour. If Henry Shevlin had been asked to describe the journey he'd have murmured vague words about "a more or less straight run to the border." He would perhaps recall encountering very little traffic upon entering Donegal, one of the most sparsely populated counties in the Republic of Ireland. When he reached the outskirts of the village of Burtonport, his mind was concentrated on the matter in hand. All else was immaterial.

Could this place hold the key? Could Connie—or Holly as she was calling herself—actually have visited this outpost? It was an exhilarating thought. A part of him found it hard to believe. Another part of him felt almost as though some mysterious force had drawn him here, had guided his path.

Nonsense of course. He was here because a patient who no longer thought of himself as a dead Beatle had discussed his encounter with an artist calling herself Holly Blue. The name had rung a bell, and had sent Henry to the public library in Killoran. Sure enough, there in *The Observer's Book of Butterflies* was a handsome illustration of the Holly Blue or *celastrina argiolus*. He recognized it right away. Only then, as he studied the illustration under a strong reading lamp, did he realize its significance. It bore a striking resemblance to the small tattoo on Connie's wrist.

"Holly . . . Holly Blue . . . The beetle meets the butterfly!" he'd exclaimed into the liturgical silence, a little too loudly, thereby earning himself a chilly look from the librarian and fellow readers.

There was a bar called The Islander a little way along the street. It didn't look too inviting but seemed a good place to start. He pulled over and parked the car.

There was nobody about, no sign of life. A sinister air prevailed. Gulls squawked high above. In the distance, the sound of a horn; a freightliner standing out to sea. From the road, the harbor was visible, and the ocean beyond. The day was overcast but he could make out the vague contours of an island not far from shore. Innisfree. It had to be. He looked at his watch. Two thirty. He straightened his tie, took a deep breath, and pushed open the door to the pub.

"Afternoon!" the bartender called out. He was doing what all bartenders seemed to do between serving customers: wiping the bar counter slowly with an insouciance born of boredom.

"Good afternoon," Henry said, giving his friendliest smile.

A good start, he thought. He scanned the room as he shut the door behind him. It resembled practically every other Irish pub he'd ever set foot in: gloomy, the daylight being repelled by several tiny windows of semitransparent glass. The ten or more tables dotted throughout were unoccupied, except for two men who sat in solitude, one reading a newspaper. They were barely discernible in the dim light. The air was shrouded in cigarette smoke, which seemed to emanate solely from an elderly man seated on a barstool at the end of the counter. He was staring sullenly at the newcomer, the stranger.

"A half pint of Guinness, please," Henry said. He remained standing; he liked to stretch his legs after a car journey.

He waited until the bartender had completed the order and was ringing up the cash register.

"I was wondering . . . What do you know about the people over beyond . . . over on Innisfree?"

A noteworthy silence. The elderly customer on the barstool grunted, and blew some more smoke in Henry's direction.

"Which people might that be, sir?" The barman passed along some coins. "Your change."

"Thank you. The Atlantis Foundation. But I believe you call them the Screamers in these parts."

The man eyed him with suspicion. "You wouldn't be another one o' them journalists, would you? 'Cos to be honest about it, we've had our fill of you lot."

"No, no, I'm not a journalist. I'm a doctor. I'm trying to trace one of my patients who went missing some months ago." He scanned the room, speaking loudly enough so they all could hear. "I believe she came here. A Belfast woman. Fair hair . . . in her early thirties. Attractive. Called herself Holly, but her real name is Constance."

More silence. The tribal instinct massing. Henry, the outsider—a threat.

Finally: "No, no one of that name, sir," the bartender said. "Can't help you, I'm afraid." He looked to the smoker for support. The smoker continued to smolder. "Not surprised she's a patient of yours. Cracked as paving stones, the lot of them."

"Are they still . . ." Henry began. "Are they still over there on the island?"

"Aye, they are. And that's the way we like it. Best place for them."

"They didn't make many friends in Burtonport, then?" He tasted the Guinness. Bitter. But refreshing.

"Friends? We couldn't wait to see the back of them. Bloody lunatics. Mad, as I say."

"Really? That bad?"

The man at the end of the bar counter began to cough loudly, while stubbing out his cigarette end. He was plainly in poor health. His eyes watered up and he mopped them with a soiled handkerchief. He'd got Henry's attention.

"Ah, they were worse than bad!" he announced in a hoarse, cracked voice. "They were possessed by evil, if you ask me. I used to live across the way from them when they moved in. Didn't mind at first, 'cos it was nice to see some fine-lookin' lassies comin' into town. Brightened the place up, so they did."

"That didn't last long, Mick, did it?" the bartender said. "The honeymoon, as I called it."

A long, painful cough. "Naw, that didn't last long. A week later and I see a couple of fellas out with cans o' paint. And aren't they paintin' them black magic signs on the front."

"Er, black . . . ?"

"Signs of the sody-ack," the bartender supplied helpfully.

"Zodiac, as in star signs?"

"Aye, them things. Painted them each side o' the door and a big 'Atlantis' on the lintel. Ruined the look of the place entirely, so it did. Then the screaming started."

"Aye, the screaming," said the old man. "They woke me up at four in the morning. Thought I was hearin' a whole flock o' banshees. Never heard the like of it. But that was just the start of it. Day and night from then on. Not a moment's peace with all that bawlin' an' screechin'. Didn't know what was goin' on in that place. Me, I swear it was that black magic, but nobody listens to me."

"Then we had the TV people and the journalists," the barman added. "They came from all parts: Dublin, London, you name it. Mind you, it was good for business. John McShay down the road got a holiday on the Costa Brava for himself and the wife outta them. But it messed the place up. We're quiet people, Doctor. We keep ourselves to ourselves, so we do. We couldn't be havin' that lot turnin' things upside down."

"I see . . ."

"We tried to have them shut down. I mean, we couldn't have all that dirty stuff goin' on, corruptin' our children, givin' the place a bad name."

"Dirty stuff?"

"Aye." The bartender leaned closer. "Orgies and the like. Women . . . with other women. Disgusting! Oh, maybe it was a good thing we didn't know half the stuff they were gettin' up to." He paused, seeming to remember something. "This patient o' yours, Doctor . . . the one who went missing. Was she . . . was she involved with that sort of thing? I'm just wundering."

Henry shook his head. "Shouldn't think so. All I know is that she was last seen on the island. But I thought somebody in Burton-port might have seen her, too. Spoken to her."

"And you say her name is Holly."

"Yes, Holly. Holly Blue, but her real name is Constance Shev-lin."

The bartender shrugged. He turned to the elderly smoker, who was busy lighting up another one. The smoker shook his head.

"What's the best way of getting over there? To Innisfree?"

The bartender consulted the clock behind him.

"You're in luck, Doctor. There's a boat leaving at four. Does a daily run. Bags of time."

Henry hesitated. He wasn't a good sailor, being one of those unfortunates who'd get seasick on a calm day on a duck pond. He was almost minded to forget the island. The thought of getting on a boat and heading out onto the ocean was unsettling. But he vowed to persevere. For Connie's sake. There was no going back now.

"Much obliged," he told the barman.

Outside, he took in a welcome lungful of sea air. He reached for his car keys.

"Doctor!"

He turned. An unkempt man had followed him out of the pub. Clearly he was one of the lone drinkers. Thirties, goatee beard, hair long and gathered in a ponytail, a Hawkwind T-shirt.

"You were asking about the Screamers." He was looking up and down the street. A solitary car was wending its way up from the harbor but otherwise Burtonport looked as deserted as it had been on Henry's arrival.

"I was," Henry said. "You wouldn't be one of them, would you?"

"Nah. I'm Max, by the way."

Max! Mad Max. It had to be. Henry recalled Finbar's last session. Yes, Max fitted the description. What had Finbar said? Something about Max hanging around in all the bars of Burtonport. He wondered how many there were.

"Right, Max," he said pleasantly. "So what can you tell me about them?"

The bearded man hesitated. He glanced back at the island. "I wouldn't go over there if I were you."

"You're not me."

"Aye, but they don't like *men*. Fruitcakes, maybe, but you're not one of them."

"You're a local?"

"I get around."

Henry wondered about the cryptic answer. "I know someone who knows you," he said.

"From Belfast?"

"I didn't say anything about Belfast."

"You did. Just now in the bar . . . said your patient's from there. Besides, you sound like a Belfast man to me."

He'd really been paying attention in the pub.

"But *posh* Belfast," he continued. "Not like a wee hard Prod from the Shankill. Who's this that knows me anyway?"

"Finbar Flannagan. A patient of mine."

"Finbar Flannagan? Mad Finbar?"

"That's what he calls *you*, Max. Mad Max."

A chuckle. "I don't mind. They all do. They're probably right, too. I am a bit of a loony. But I ask you: What would you prefer: a crazy guy who does no one any harm, or a stick-in-the-mud sane guy who never stops interfering in other people's business?"

"Point taken. How well do you know Finbar?"

"I might ask you the same thing."

"He's a patient of mine. I'm a psychiatrist."

"Fuck *me*. Then I'd stay well clear of the Screamers if I was you. They hate psychiatrists. Did you know that?"

"Well, I knew they didn't have a good opinion of us." He smiled. "But they're not alone in that, eh?" He looked at his watch. It was just after 3:15. "The barman said there's a boat leaving at four."

"Yep. You're determined to go, then?"

"It's my reason for coming here."

"Don't say I didn't warn you." Max pointed in the direction of the harbor. "You can park down there. Aurora's your woman. On Innisfree. A bit more approachable than the rest."

"Aurora. Nice name. Not her real name I suppose?"

"Not many of them use their real names, Doctor. I think they like it that way. All running away from something."

———

The clouds had lifted and the island was bathed in sunshine when the small boat put in alongside the little jetty on Innisfree. Henry waited for the two other passengers to disembark before stepping onto the rough stones.

The crossing had proved to be less challenging than he'd feared. The Atlantic was calm—at least when seen from this vantage point, in the lee of the island. He hadn't engaged anyone in conversation during the crossing, wishing to be alone with his thoughts. Again, he felt close to discovering something about Connie. Even closer now. As he stood on the quayside and looked up at the gentle slopes of the island falling away from him, he tried to imagine her here.

"What time can I expect you back?" he called out to the boatman.

The old-timer looked at the sky. The sun was still high. "About seven, mister," he said.

Henry had dropped the "doctor" bit as soon as he'd boarded the boat. He'd taken Max's advice and decided to say nothing about his profession. He'd no wish to antagonize people who might be able to help him find Connie. He'd also "dressed down" to a certain extent, shedding the jacket and necktie in an effort to blend in.

He watched idly as a cart drawn by a donkey made its way slowly down to the jetty. He heard the boat engine start up behind him. The cart stopped at the spot where the two passengers had placed their baggage, and an elderly man wearing a cloth cap alighted. He glanced in Henry's direction before helping stow the baggage in the cart. The chore completed, the two climbed in the back.

"Can I give you a lift?" the driver asked.

"No, thanks. I'll walk. Want to explore a bit."

"Fair enough."

"Where can I find the Screamers?"

All went quiet. Three pairs of eyes regarded him with hostility. He swore that even the donkey was glaring at him.

"What would you be wantin' *them* for?" asked one of the passengers. He was a man in his late twenties, slovenly dressed.

"Just curious," Henry answered, mustering his broadest smile.

"Up at the big house," the driver said. "Top of this road." He jerked the reins and the cart set off, back the way it had come.

Henry took his time as he watched it depart. He was trying to imagine how Connie must have felt, all those months before, when she was also seeing the island for the first time. Had she come alone? Or had she been accompanied by one of *them*? He thought of a poker-faced man in a hat, a man with colorless eyes and a predatory manner. How different their perspectives on the world were! The spy dealt in concealment and mystery; the psychiatrist's job was to coax secrets out into the open.

The little island seemed, at first, to be as deserted as Burton-port. The gulls were his sole companions, as they wheeled above the rocks and rough grass that overlooked the water.

Some distance away, close by a group of cottages, several figures were busy doing something in a field. Female—if their long clothing was anything to go by. They were engaged in work that involved a lot of stooping and collecting. Millet's *The Gleaners* came to mind. Another throwback to another time.

He made his way toward them.

At his approach, one of the women straightened and appeared to nudge a companion. They stared at the visitor.

In the background: a group of single-level dwellings white-washed and plain, relics of pre-Famine Ireland. Beyond them: a larger house with smaller buildings attached.

He saw now that the women were young. None seemed older than thirty. All had stopped their work and were regarding him with curiosity.

"Hello!" one of them called out, a tall lady with dark hair tied back.

There was a rough basket at her feet. It was half-filled with clay-soiled stones of many sizes.

"Hello, yourselves," he said. "I don't want to interrupt you or anything . . ."

"No bother. Have you just arrived?"

"Yes. Just over for an hour or two."

He glanced about him, taking in the beauty of the little island: the gentle slopes glowing with the purple heather that had given the place its name. He'd looked up the name in the original Irish. He was thorough that way; it paid a psychiatrist to be thorough. *Inis Fraoigh*: Heather Isle.

"I'm looking for Aurora."

"You'll find her over in the orchard," the tall lady said. She pointed.

"Much obliged." He hesitated. "Mind your backs with that work, won't you?"

The woman didn't return the smile. She looked sullen.

"Are you being condescending? I hope you're not being condescending. We don't like that here."

"Certainly not. I can see you ladies are well up to the job."

"Thank you. And we're not 'ladies,' by the way. We're women, *sir*."

"My mistake. In the orchard, you say?"

"Aye." And she bent once more to her task. The others followed suit.

Henry recalled something his father had said. "*Connie . . . well, to be honest, she was quite harsh on the subject of marriage. Ideal setup for the male, in her opinion. Women as chattels. You know: the usual feminist guff. Men cause wars and . . .*"

Was that why she'd come here? To be with her like-minded sisters? Ideal place from what he'd seen so far.

The orchard lay to the rear of the big house with the courtyard. There was a woman in a check shirt and jeans pushing a wheelbarrow filled with grass clippings.

She stopped on seeing him. Attractive, even without makeup. Blonde hair, not unlike . . .

"Aurora?"

"That's me."

"Max told me I'd find you here."

She tossed her head, making a swatting motion with her hand. "Damn flies. Max! Oh, him?"

"He sends his good wishes."

"Yes, he would. Do you have any cigarettes?"

"Sorry, don't smoke," Henry said, slightly abashed by her directness.

"Your accent is funny. Where are you from?"

"Belfast."

She was studying him. "We had somebody from Belfast stay with us last year. But you wouldn't know her."

"Her name wasn't Holly by any chance?"

"Who wants to know?"

"Henry . . . Henry Shevlin." He decided to take a gamble. "She's my wife."

"Oh . . ."

"Aurora!"

The call had come from the direction of the house. It was repeated.

"Coming!" the girl called back. She turned to Henry. "Have to go. What did you say your name was?"

"Henry. Wait. Did . . . did Holly ever mention me?"

She looked furtively about her. Then said in a low voice: "Meet me back here in an hour, okay? I can't talk now."

He watched her go toward the house, pushing the wheelbarrow. He looked at his watch: 5:15. He had enough time before the boatman returned at seven.

He set off to explore the island. It was exceptionally beautiful, made even more so by the sun in the western sky, causing the trees and rocks to stand out starkly. He noticed that there were few homes, and half seemed to be abandoned, the fields surrounding them long grown wild and unkempt. There was a certain wildness here that he found exhilarating. He guessed that it was the wildness that had attracted the Screamers.

He trekked across the untilled land beyond the homesteads, heading for the island's highest point. Having scaled it, he gazed out across the ocean. Burtonport was plainly visible beyond the sound, its harbor and buildings bathed now in the late-afternoon light. He wondered again about the strangeness of the whole place.

"Connie, Connie, Connie," he said aloud, confident that nobody might hear him, "what in the name of God brought you here? Why here? Why? *Why?*"

In that moment, he experienced a sense of utter desolation. He had never given up hope of one day being reunited with his beloved wife. He mentally ticked off on his fingers the number of avenues he'd ventured down.

One: he thought she'd committed suicide, perhaps because she'd been depressed at turning thirty and resorted to reading the morbid poetry of Sylvia Plath.

Two: he thought she'd run off with another man. That man had turned out to be a double agent, not a love rival.

Three: he'd feared that she'd met with an untimely end because she'd got involved in Republican politics.

Four: he thought she'd left the country immediately after her disappearance. The British secret agent had more or less intimated as much.

Five: Finbar Flannagan, a not too reliable source, had suggested that she'd been here on Innisfree.

Yet Finbar had been correct. A certain Mad Max had confirmed that. Now it looked as though a woman who called herself Aurora was about to corroborate Max's story.

He saw her again as he was halfway to the little orchard where they'd met. She was dressed in the same clothes but had pulled on a jacket. Her blonde hair was being tossed on the breeze from the ocean. With sadness, Henry saw that in the distance she bore a striking resemblance to Connie. His moment of greatest sadness—what a psychiatrist friend called the *Tiefpunkt*—had passed. He'd allowed the tears to flow. There'd been no witnesses apart from the wild creatures, and that was good.

"Walk with me," Aurora said.

"Where are we going?"

"A place Holly loved. The wildflowers are beautiful there."

It turned out to be a secluded cove some way up from where Henry had disembarked. The gentle water of the sound lapped at their feet as they sat on a rock overlooking the mainland. Behind them and on either side grew an abundance of heather, daisies, buttercups, violets, and many other blooms Henry could not identify. He could well believe that Connie would have felt in her element there. The wild child at home in the half-tamed wilderness.

"Holly used to take her sketchbook along," Aurora said. "She was never without it."

"I know," he said wistfully. "I can see why she liked it here." Then: "When . . . when did she come here? To the island, I mean."

"Last year. June, I believe."

He was stunned. June: immediately after she disappeared. She hadn't gone abroad. She was right *here*, in Ireland. If only he had known. But he'd no way of knowing. The powers that be had seen to that. Inwardly, he cursed them. Cursed their lack of pity, their lack of human feeling.

He turned his attention back to Aurora. He had some more questions she might be able to answer before the boat returned.

"Did you ever notice a small tattoo? Right here." He indicated the spot on his right wrist. "A butterfly . . . blue."

"No. But come to think of it, I rarely saw her in short sleeves. She complained about the cold, a lot. It's never too warm here, though. That breeze off the Atlantic . . . skin you sometimes."

That sounded like Connie, too, with her Raynaud's syndrome. There was one sure way of knowing, and Henry carried it next to his heart: in his wallet. He reached for the wallet, and drew out the little snapshot, the one he'd shown to the RUC constable on the night of Connie's disappearance.

"That's her," Aurora said at once. "That's Holly."

He sighed with relief. At last.

"I think she found peace here," she went on. "She never told me anything, mind you, but she was running away from something." She looked at him sidelong. "Would I be right?"

He nodded but said nothing.

"I hope it wasn't anything illegal. That wouldn't have been like her. She was really sweet. Everybody loved her. But you never know with people, do you?"

Henry felt a lump rise in his throat. He feigned a cough to banish it.

"Why do you want to find her?"

It was an odd question. "Why? I should think that's obvious."

"It's just that when we come here we're deprogrammed. The conventional concept of marriage goes right out the window. Women like us get to taste the freedom that you men take for granted for the very first time and it's exhilarating. We sleep with whomever we choose. We have children with whomever we choose. It's a complete role reversal."

"Did Connie . . . ?"

She glanced at him and giggled.

"Oh, you're such a *man*. Perhaps she did. That's why the men in Burtonport didn't like us and chased us over here. Claimed we were into black magic and witchcraft. Always a good old ruse to discredit women when they try to assert themselves, don't you think? Calling them witches . . . saying they're loopy."

"I see . . . Don't seem to be many men round here for you to sleep with, though."

She sniggered. "Yes, enlightened men are hard to find." She was teasing him. "But you'd be surprised . . . how docile and pliable they become when you lay down some ground rules."

He thought of Mad Max and Finbar Flannagan. Yes, they were certainly the type that Aurora would consider "pliable."

He checked himself.

"Did she . . . Holly . . . did she say where she was going?"

He didn't expect a straight answer, but the psychiatrist in him noted the impact of his query. The telltale psychomotor agitation: the shifting of the knees, heels digging deeper into the sand, the twisting of the stems of the daisies she'd plucked.

Aurora had him down as a stalker.

"No . . . but even if I did know, I wouldn't be telling you. She just disappeared one day without saying good-bye." She looked sidelong at him again. "Why are you so certain she wants to be found anyway?"

Why indeed? He'd never had the courage to ask himself that. Was he being selfish? Was Connie's involvement with Halligan and her flight to this place her way of showing him that?

"Why am I so certain Holly wants to be found?" he repeated. "I just *know* . . . know in my *heart*."

Aurora made no reply, letting the crash of the breakers and the shrieking of the gulls answer for her.

Then: "Your boat leaves soon?" She was gazing in the direction of the harbor. "Best not to miss it."

Before he knew it, she was on her feet and walking away from him.

"Thanks . . . thanks for talking!" he called after her.

She waved a hand but didn't look back.

He returned to the jetty and clambered aboard the boat, the sole passenger. A sadness, greater and deeper than anything he'd experienced before, fell about him like a funeral shroud.

That woebegone feeling Aurora had left him with. Oh, the cold, harsh loneliness of it all! The desertion.

Nowhere to go now, but home.

A ways out on the water he glanced back and saw a figure atop the rise, her loose blonde hair fluttering in the breeze.

Aurora. She raised a hand. He gave a cursory salute.

Atlantis, the Screamers, Innisfree—the island, now fast receding from him, was truly the realm of the lost. Women went there to lose themselves among the hills and the heather. In that wilderness they screamed away their despair and shared it with the cries of the gulls, the sighing of the winds and sea.

Connie had been there. That much he now knew for certain. She'd been lost there for a while on that island. Perhaps he shouldn't have gone. He'd left her in Belfast all those months ago, in a dimly lit room with a warning from an enigmatic man in a hat. "*Step back and let us do our job. If you want to see her again, stop looking.*"

He'd done precisely as instructed. Had ceased searching. Locked the memory of her away. The decision, finally copper-fastened with his move to Killoran and some kind of different life.

Then that tiny stumble, the quiver on the tightrope that was Finbar Flannagan. "Holly Blue . . . thirty . . . married . . . an artist . . . poetry . . . running away from something . . ."

How could he *not* find out? How could he *not* go looking for her?

Aurora's question, so painful to hear! "*Why are you so certain she wants to be found anyway?*"

He wasn't certain of anything anymore.

Perhaps it was simply best to close a door on the past and let its history be.

Chapter thirty-seven

Jamie pushed into Tailorstown on his well-worn bicycle—headlamp missing, seatpost crooked, button accordion strapped securely to the saddle. His big night at O'Shea's pub was upon him. He would be the support act for The Beardy Boys, providing a filler at the interval, when the bearded ones took a rest.

The farmer looked forward to those occasional nights Slope O'Shea invited him to play. Always enjoyed the feeling of happiness that the short time in the spotlight afforded him. Tonight, however, was going to be *extra* special: Ruby would be in the audience with Rose.

Rose didn't usually frequent pubs with Paddy, but she thought it would be nice for Ruby to get out for a night, after what she'd been through with her mother and all. Ruby was a nice girl, Jamie thought. She reminded him of his adoptive aunt Alice when she was younger. Maybe a wee bit fatter, but the same height, the same reddish color hair, the nice smile and manner. And she was easy to talk to as well.

Upon arrival at The Step Inside lounge on High Street, Jamie tethered the back wheel of the bike to the front one—an unnecessary precaution, since the bicycle should really have been on the junk pile and not the road—but old habits were hard to break, and Jamie had a fondness for the bicycle. It had carried not only himself between Duntybutt and Tailorstown countless times, but his Uncle Mick as well. He might have suffered the loss of his beloved Shep in recent weeks, but he still felt close to Mick when he sat on that bicycle, gripping the handlebars and working the pedals, riding back through history but forward through time, over the roads he knew so well.

"You'll be ridin' that bike long after I'm gone," Mick used to say, and Jamie knew he'd be keeping that promise for as long as he could.

———

"How do, Slope!" Jamie called out on entering the premises and taking his usual seat at the bar. The place was empty, but it was early yet. From out back he heard the sound of a beer barrel being rolled across tiles and minutes later Slope appeared: a tall, stooped man kicking the backside of sixty with a walleyed look that said, "It's not my fault that me ancestors decided to make a major detour from the evolutionary plan in the way back when."

"How you, Jamie?" Slope said, straightening up. "I did me bloody back in yesterday, liftin' one of these boys, so I'll be rollin' them from now on. Usual, is it?"

"Aye, a Guinness and a half'un, there." Jamie drummed his fingers on the counter and looked about him. "See a couple of your wee fairies are out up there."

"Are they, begod? Never noticed. With me stiff neck, don't look up there much."

Slope had sought atmosphere in his pub by braiding a high shelf behind the bar with a string of fairy lights. His thinking being that the festive atmosphere they imparted all year round would encourage his customers, especially when drunk, to lose the run of themselves, imagine it was Christmas, and so part with more money.

He set up the drink. "I need'a get a new set. Barkin' Bob maybe has them."

"Aye, Bob's your man," Jamie said.

"You've said it, Jamie. Begod, you wouldn't believe what I got off him the other day."

"Nah, what was that?"

"A Jonny Glow toilet finder." Slope puffed on a cigarette, enjoying the look of confusion puckering Jamie's features.

"What the divil's that?"

"I told you: a Jonny Glow toilet finder."

"Aye, I heard that bit, but what's it for?"

"What d'you think it's for? For findin' the toilet in the middle of the night."

"And how could you *not* find the toilet in your own house, in the middle of the night? It's not the size of the Vatican."

"Ah . . . but you see it might as well be the size of the Vatican, in the dark, at night, when you've had a skinful, and you can't find the light switch, let alone the bloody bathroom."

"Right, and where do you put this yoke? Round your neck?"

"Nah, round the seat of the toilet. It's green and it glows in the dark, so you know where to aim. Not that it would matter where *you* aimed, Jamie, havin' a whole backyard for your toilet."

Jamie took the insult on the chin. He was well used to Slope's jibes. But he was glad Slope had mentioned his lack of a WC. The council had just given him planning permission to build an extension to his farmhouse that very day, and he was able to bat back the good news, much to the crabby barman's chagrin.

At which point, Slope swiftly changed the subject, back to the itinerant salesman, Barkin' Bob.

"Lookin' very well these days, is Barkin' Bob. Business must be good, 'cos that's a new van and trailer he's got."

"Saw that, too," Jamie said. He offered the barman a fresh cigarette and lit one himself. "They say he came into a legacy from some oul' aunt in Amerikay."

"Well, *I* don't see much of it in here. Never buys a round . . . tight as a nun's friggin' knickers in this place, is Bob. Wish tae blazes some oul' aunt of mine would die and leave me a bit. Could get rid of this place—and the bloody wife, come to that."

"Where *is* Peggy? Haven't seen her about."

"Nah . . . her and young Mary are in the caravan in Portaluce for a week. And d'you know, since they left I think I've went deaf. Nobody yappin' at me night and day. I would divorce her only I'm Catholic, and anyway, a divorce would make her too happy. God, Jamie, I envy you not havin' a wommin about the place. Nivver get married, that's my advice to you."

"Aye, so . . ."

"'Cos y'know, I married for better or worse. She couldn't have done better and I couldn't have done worse."

It's the other way about, Slope, Jamie reflected, but didn't say, wanting to hold onto his accordion slot for this particular evening. He reminded himself that this Friday evening was destined to be a very special one.

"Ah, now," was all he said, considering the fairy lights once more. Out the window he saw the bearded ones' van pull up.

"See, the trouble with Peggy, Jamie," Slope continued, "is she can't take a bloody joke."

"She took *you*, didn't she?" Jamie shot back, the whiskey making him bold.

A thump at the door saved him from Slope's wrath.

The Beardy Boys had arrived.

Chapter thirty-eight

Ruby stood in front of the mirror in her bedroom, getting ready for her big night out with the McFaddens.

She was very excited because she hadn't been out for a very long time. Not since her school friend, Carmel, had gone to work in London all of eleven years ago. She used to accompany Carmel to the occasional dance in the Castle Ballroom, Dungiven. Looking back, Ruby didn't really miss those nights. Carmel, attractive and chatty, was rarely off the dance floor, leaving her to suffer the indignity of standing by the wall like a spare part. Often, she wished she could just disappear into it, especially when Elvis McGinty appeared, a bachelor with a clubfoot and bottle-thick glasses who, having been rejected by a succession of lovelies, would approach Ruby as a last resort. And Ruby, feeling sorry for him, would have no option but to accept, and allow herself to be steered about the floor, scattering the other dancers to the sidelines like frightened sheep.

This night, however, would be nothing like those awkward dances. She'd be in the company of Rose, a woman she liked very much. Rose had shown her nothing but warmth and kindness in the short space of time since they'd met. It's a pity Mammy couldn't be more like that, Ruby thought now, as she stood before the mirror.

Sadly, there had been little improvement with the mother since she'd been discharged from hospital. Ruby had just helped her eat supper, a complicated and painstaking affair that could take the best part of an hour to complete. The trembling spoon needed guidance, the cup of tea a challenge of spills and weary sighs.

Martha didn't say much. It was as if the effort of communicating, like the trial of eating, tired her unduly. She rallied, however, for the likes of Father Kelly, Dr. Brewster, and the twins when they showed up at weekends.

It being Friday, the twins were indeed in attendance. Downstairs, at that present moment, they were having their evening meal. Ruby had made sure to serve it promptly after they'd returned from their hour behind closed doors with Martha, the visit that had become part of their weekend routine.

Ruby had decided not to divulge her plans for the evening, fearful they might attempt to thwart her with some excuse about going out themselves. No, May and June would only find out when the McFadden car drew up in the yard.

Her good blue dress, the one she wore to Mass, was a bit loose, she now noticed. Not so surprising. With all the upset of the past weeks she hadn't felt like eating much.

Perhaps a belt would help . . .

She rummaged through the drawer full of castoffs the twins had given her, and found a lovely white one. It was leather with elasticated sides, and an attractive interlocking clasp in the shape of two swans' heads for the buckle. The diamanté eye of each swan was missing—hence the reason Ruby had received it—but the defect wasn't so noticeable.

She drew it about her waist and saw, to her delight, that it just about fitted her. Suddenly, the serviceable dress suitable only for the Sunday pew was transformed into something a bit more daring.

She wheeled in front of the mirror. It was just perfect, but the shoes were wrong. She dived into the closet. The bottom drawer served as another dumping ground for the twins' castoffs. The white high heels with the scuffed toes were ideal, but there wasn't any point in trying them. They were size 4 and Ruby's feet were 8. The sensible black flats that took her to Mass would have to do. But she'd make up for the inelegant footwear with a handbag. She rummaged some more and, to her delight, found a white one with a brass buckle. Incredibly, it didn't seem to show much wear and tear. She wondered why they'd thrown it away.

The bedside clock read 7:30 p.m. Not long to go.

She had unearthed a basket of cosmetics as well, full of rejects from June's Rimmel counter. Makeup was another one of those luxuries long forgotten, like those ballroom days. As she looked now at the basket of shadows, lipsticks, and pencils she felt a little daunted. What colors would be the best?

A dusting of face powder seemed the easiest to start with and, as she patted it over her red cheeks, She was delighted at the difference it made. The redness was gone. Some eye shadow next—blue seemed the safest. She chose a shade called Posh Peacock. Finally, a little bit of nail polish—Desert Rose, the one that had caused such ructions at the dinner table not so long ago—and the makeover was complete.

Ten minutes to eight. It was almost time.

She was nervous, having to run the gauntlet that was May and June before getting into the McFadden car. She made the sign of Power and Peace with her thumb and forefinger to calm herself, and went downstairs.

The twins were having an intense conversation in lowered tones when Ruby entered the kitchen, and so didn't see her at first.

"I'm going out," she announced.

Both looked her way.

"To O'Shea's pub . . . for the night."

"*What?*" May said, her tone incredulous.

"I'm going out now," Ruby repeated, trying to keep her voice even. "But I should be back by eleven."

"Well, I've got news for you: you're going nowhere. June and me are going out . . . to . . . to the Windsor later. Aren't we, June?"

June was caught off guard. "Oh . . . that's right. So we are."

Ruby knew it was a lie.

The welcome sound of the McFadden car reached into the kitchen. "Well, you'll just have to cancel that. There's my lift now."

She moved toward the door.

May, knowing she was defeated, lobbed another taunt. "Is that my handbag? I wondered where it'd got to. Give it here this minute!" She jumped up and stretched out her hand.

"You dumped it in the drawer in my room."

"Give it back to me *now*." May advanced on Ruby. "And you look like a clown in that makeup."

"You better give it back, Ruby," June warned. "We don't want a scene, and Mummy so ill."

A car horn sounded.

Ruby opened the door. She waved to Rose and Paddy.

"You'll get it back when I come home, May. Oh, and by the way, I found that *reference* you lost."

She saw her arrow hit its target.

Saw May's mouth fall open.

Shut the door sharply on her shocked face.

And smiled at the sight of her new friend, Rose, waving as she got out of the car.

Chapter thirty-nine

M-a-yyyyyy . . . M-a-yyyyyy . . ."
Martha's voice, quavering, barely audible, cried out from the darkened upstairs room. She lay in the bed, her mind a riot of images, horrific and all-consuming. They were showing her pictures she couldn't bear to look at. Pictures that were demanding she take action. She needed to unburden herself. The dark secret she'd carried for so long was clamoring to be heard before it was too late.

Down in the kitchen, the twins were smarting from Ruby's parting shot.

The reference.

Their initial indignation at her having the temerity to go out for the night without alerting them earlier, quickly being replaced by the realization of what she *knew.*

"But . . . but how do you know she *read* it?" June was saying.

"Oh, she read it all right, the fat bitch; have no fear of *that*." May put her head in her hands, tears of self-pity fighting the waves of anger flaring up at the sheer audacity of her sister. "Christ, how could I have been so stupid . . . carrying the damned thing home? But I didn't want flaming Mrs. Hipple coming across it. She snoops around our room when we're not there. *You know that*, don't you?"

"I'm not sure . . ."

"Oh, she does, the nosy so-and-so, you mark my words."

"Well, when we get our own house we'll not be bothered by that anymore." June, as ever, trying to appease. "Will we?"

May pushed back her chair.

"Tell you what I'm gonna do. Go through her bloody bedroom . . . turn every inch of it over."

"But she'll have it locked. She always locks it."

"I'll break the lock, then."

She raced upstairs, tried the door handle.

"M-a-yyyy . . . M-a-yyyy . . ."

"God, it's Mummy! June, come quick."

They dashed into their mother's room, to find Martha lying half in, half out of bed.

"Jesus, Mummy, what is it? Are you all right?"

They helped her back under the covers.

Martha gripped May's arm, her eyes fearful. "I . . . I . . . want . . ."

"Yes, Mummy, what is it?"

"F-Father Ke-elly . . . I need . . . Fa—"

"Father Kelly? What . . . *now?*"

Martha nodded before falling back on the pillows.

"God, Ruby, you're lookin' terrible well," Rose said. "Now that I can see you in the light, like. That wee belt with the ducks' heads is lovely, and where did you buy that nice white handbag?"

"Thank you. My sister got the handbag in Belfast." Ruby looked down at her feet. "But the black shoes don't match, Rose."

"Not a bit of it, Ruby. Sure nobody looks at a body's feet. And them flat sensible shoes are good for you. You'll not get no bunions or blisters like you'd get with them old high heels."

"That's a lovely dress you're wearing, too, Rose," Ruby said, feeling the need to return the compliment.

"God, do you think so, Ruby? I made it meself from a Butterrick pattern on me nineteen and fifty-seven Singer sewing machine passed down the maternal line, so I did."

"Youse go on there first," Paddy said over the roof of his car, before locking up the vehicle and preceding the ladies into O'Shea's establishment.

They entered a hot, seething mass of revelers, all eager fans of The Beardy Boys. Slope caught sight of the trio.

"Jamie's upstairs!" he called out. "He's kept a table for yins."

Rose, leading, spotted Jamie immediately at the back of the lounge. They negotiated their way through the mass of crowded tables.

"Who's that?" Ruby overheard a woman say.

"Martha Clare's daughtur," came the reply. "The one that tried tae kill herself . . . not too right in the head."

Ruby wheeled round and stared. What looked like a mother and daughter were gazing up at her. Abashed, they immediately dropped their gaze and turned away.

"How you, Ruby!" Jamie shouted, getting up.

"Hello, Jamie."

"Sit yourself down there."

"God, Jamie, it's a terrible big crowd," said Rose, hot and flustered, beige handbag clamped to her chest.

"Did you think it was gonna be this big?" Paddy added.

"Aye, The Beardy Boys pull them in, so they do."

After getting themselves settled and ordering drinks, Ruby felt a little more relaxed. She'd never been in a lounge bar before and was trying to absorb this new experience as she looked about her. Some faces she knew. She recognized Marian from the supermarket with a man who was plainly her husband. Marian caught her eye and waved. A young man was doing floor waiter, but she didn't know him.

Another familiar face caught her attention: a man in his thirties. He staggered slightly as he made his way across the room. Chuck Sproule. The last time she'd seen him he was shouting slurs at Jamie as he wrestled with Bertie Frogget on the Fair Hill. He sat down at the table occupied by the women who'd been gossiping about her. The beaky nose and stringy hair were unmistakable. It was obvious they were his mother and sister.

The drinks arrived: two Babychams for Rose and Ruby, two pints of Guinness for the men.

Up on the stage, The Beardy Boys—Des and Davey, twin brothers with matching beards and sweaters—launched into the first number of the evening, "Your Cheatin' Heart."

Jamie raised his glass. "A toast to Rose and Ruby!" he said.

"Aye, to Rose and Ruby!" Paddy repeated.

They clinked glasses, and Ruby took her very first sip of alcohol.

———

June met Father Kelly on the doorstop. He'd been about to retire when the call came through. Now, as she led him into the kitchen, he wondered aloud if the sisters had rung the doctor.

"No, Father. She said she didn't want the doctor . . . just you. She wants to make her confession. Will you have a cuppa tea first?"

He shook his head.

May came down the stairs, her face drawn and sad.

"How is she?" he asked.

May burst into tears. "Does this mean she's gonna die, Father? Wanting . . . wanting to make her confession?"

"No . . . no . . . your mother's a long way to go yet." He came forward and rested a hand on May's arm. "With God's help and our

315

prayers she'll make a good recovery, so. Now you and June have a cup of tea and I'll see to things."

Father Kelly climbed the stairs with his black bag of effects. On the landing, he halted outside the door to Ruby's room. Called to mind their last conversation over Edna's case before they took it to the woods for burning.

"*Was she putting a curse on me, Father?*"

"*No, Ruby. No one has the power to do that.*"

He'd forgotten to ask where Ruby was. Wondered if she was already asleep behind that closed door. He said a little prayer, and continued down the corridor to Martha's room.

———

"Now it's time Davey and me took a wee break and had some of that nice drink yins are all havin'!" a Beardy Boy announced.

A cheer went up.

"Thirsty work, this oul' singin'. But we won't see yins stuck for entertainment. For there's a man we're gonna introduce to ye now who, without a doubt, is the best accordjin player in these parts."

Another uproarious cheer went up.

"I'd nearly go as far as sayin' he's maybe not even the best player in these parts, but the best player in the whole of Ireland!"

An ear-splitting round of applause.

"Ladies and gentlemen, I give you, the one and only *Jamie McCloone.*"

Jamie squeezed a high-spirited chord from his accordion, to the roaring approval of the crowd.

"God, I didn't know Jamie was so well thought of," observed Rose. "Do you like that wee Babycham, Ruby?"

"It's very nice," Ruby said, smiling. Her cheeks were pink with joy and the effects of the drink. She'd never felt so happy. She loved the company of the McFaddens and Jamie. They were good people who treated her as an equal and didn't judge her. All the horrors of the past weeks were melting away. Perhaps this was the "new beginning" that the Tarot had predicted?

But at the same time, she didn't want to think about the case and its contents any more. That part of her life was over. With the help of Dr. Shevlin she'd be able to put it behind her for good. Her focus now was to make reparation for all the trouble she'd caused. Her duty was to care for her mother and bring her back to full health.

". . . this is a first for me, too," Rose was saying.

"Why? Do you not come out with Paddy at the weekends?"

"Well, I don't as a rule, Ruby . . . would prefer if there was another wommin with me. But sure now I've got you, we can come out and hear Jamie play more often."

"I'd love that, Rose! Can I buy you and Paddy another drink?"

Paddy waved the waiter down and another round was ordered.

Meanwhile, Jamie was playing the first of his three numbers: "The Boys from the County Armagh," a boisterous one to get things started.

Rose and Ruby clapped along as the audience beat time with their hands and feet, some singing out the lyrics, others letting out skirls of "Yip! Yip!" and "Hi-di-hi!"

———

Martha grabbed Father Kelly's hand before he had time to sit down. Entwined in her other hand, a rosary. There were tears in her eyes.

He was taken aback by the deterioration in her appearance. She seemed to have aged rapidly in just a week: the pallor more sickly, the face more skeletal, the lips displaying a blue tinge. And that doomful harbinger that he'd seen all too often at the sickbed: the mottled hands, blood pooling under the skin.

"Now . . . now, Martha. Everything is going to be all right." He pulled up a chair to the bed.

"Thank . . . you . . . Father . . . for com . . . coming. I need . . . I need . . . to tell you some . . . something before I go . . ."

Father Kelly draped his purple stole—the color of penance and healing—about his neck, crossed himself and leaned close.

"That's all right, Martha . . . I'll hear your confession now . . . if you want. Is that what you want?"

"Y-e-sss . . . Father."

———

Jamie finished the first number and moved into "Whiskey You're the Devil." He was in his element. There might have been over seventy in the room but for Jamie the only two people who mattered were Ruby and Rose—and Ruby most especially. He could see her through the mass of heads, smiling and clapping her hands, and her happiness was *his* happiness, her joy was *his* joy.

———

"Bless . . . me . . . Father . . . for . . . for I have sinned."

Father Kelly held Martha's frail hand. He peered intently at her, leaning in to catch the barely audible words.

"I'd . . . I m-i-s-s-e-d . . . the bus, you see. Had to walk . . . walk home . . . and took . . . took a shortcut through . . . through . . ."

"Yes, Martha. It's all right now. Take your time."

"The woods . . . then I . . . "

Father Kelly felt his hand being clasped more tightly.

"Then what happened, Martha?"

"A man. He . . . came . . . came from nowhere. Started walking behind me. To follow me . . . I started to walk more quickly, but I heard . . . heard him increase . . . increase his step as well. I ran . . . Oh dear God, how I ran!"

She shut her eyes tight, trying vainly to shut out the terrifying memory of what she had to tell.

"But I was wearing . . . wearing high heels . . . and the path, the path was rough and, and . . ."

She attempted to raise her head off the pillow. Looked at the priest, petrified.

"It's all right, Martha dear. There, there, now."

"I-I . . . fell, Father. Oh my God, I fell!" she cried, letting out a deep howl of despair. "He . . . he grabbed me. I tried, tried to fight him off . . . and I did. I hit him and pushed him . . . pushed him over . . . I got up . . . was . . . was just on my feet again. I ran for my life . . . when . . . when . . ."

She winced, eyes squeezed tight.

"But, there was a pot . . . hole. A pothole on the path and I . . . I tripped. Oh. God help me, I tripped." Her grip on the priest's hand tightened even more. "He . . . he grabbed me by the hair and . . . and dragged me into the . . . into . . . into the bracken . . ."

"It's all right now, Martha. It's all right."

She nodded and swallowed hard.

"Will you take some water?"

She shook her head, fixed her eyes on the ceiling, as if focusing there might give her the strength to utter the word—the terrible word—she could never bring herself to say, but which had to be said *now.*

"Then . . . then, he . . . he . . ."

Father Kelly saw her hand close tightly on the rosary. The pain on her face, explanation enough.

"You don't have to say any more, Martha. I know. I under—"

"*He* . . . *r-a-p-e-d* . . . me-e-e-e. He *raped* me, Father."

At last: the monstrous truth, which had torn at her heart for so very long, was let loose.

The shock of it reverberating in the small room.

Father Kelly, jolted, trying to come to terms with it. Trying to comprehend the violation she'd suffered and kept secret all the years. This frail, fast-declining woman he thought he knew so well.

He watched her, eyes shut tight, swallow down the shame.

What could he say? What words would bring her comfort? He strove to find the right ones.

"That . . ." he began. "That, Martha . . . that is not *your* sin . . . it is *his*."

She sighed, grateful.

"Did you . . . did you know this man?"

She shook her head. "I never saw him again." She opened her eyes and looked into his. "But there's . . ."

———

"Now," Jamie said, as the applause died. "I'd like to play a special—"

"Hi, do yins know that Jamie McCloone keeps his hair in a box under the bed?"

It was the foul-mouthed Chuck Sproule. The crowd laughed uproariously.

"Aye, that's where I put it when it started fallin' out," Jamie shouted to equal jocularity. Then: "I see, Chuck, that you're with your mammy tonight. Did she never tell you not to drink on an empty head?"

A deafening cheer went up.

Jamie's jeer had hit a nerve. Chuck's face turned to stone. He got up and staggered toward the stage.

"Oh God, he's gonna hit Jamie!" Rose called out. "Paddy, go and pull him back."

Paddy got up, but just as quickly was sitting down again. Several men in the audience were already upon the young rascal. They bundled him down the stairs, to loud whoops and hoots.

Mrs. Sproule and her daughter shot to their feet. They slammed down their drinks. A stunned silence fell.

"We're not stayin' in *this* dump!" the daughter declared.

"Aye, yins are nothin' but a pack of feckin' Fenians shites!" fumed the mother, adding a bit more color to the daughter's announcement.

"Booooo-o-o-o-o!" went the crowd as they stormed out.

"The apple doesn't fall far from the tree!" someone was heard to shout.

Ruby was glad to see the back of them. They were not nice people. She was very impressed at the way Jamie had handled the situation, and when the troop was safely out of sight, applauded with the others until her hands grew hot.

"As I was sayin'," Jamie continued, "I'd like to play a special number for two lovely wimmin there at the back: Ruby and Rose. It's their first time here tonight . . . so give them a big hand."

All heads turned in the ladies' direction, glasses held high.

"To Ruby and Rose!" they chorused.

The ladies and Paddy acknowledged the toast with raised glasses.

All at once, Jamie was launching into a rousing rendition of "The Star of the County Down."

The crowd sang along.

> From Bantry Bay up to Derry Quay,
> And from Galway to Dublin town,
> No maid I've seen like the sweet colleen
> That I met in the County Down.

Ruby sipped some more Babycham; tears rolled down her cheeks. Tears of the kind she'd never experienced before in her life—those of absolute joy.

———

"Forgive . . . me . . . Father . . . I had nothing . . . nothing . . . but . . . h-a-t-r-e-d in . . . my heart . . . for . . . R-u-b-y . . . from the be . . . beginning. How could . . . I love . . . her? She . . . she had . . . had come . . . from e-v-i-l . . ."

The lines of a poem came to the priest now, lines of writing inscribed on a page and signed *Edna Vivian Clare* on April 30, 1951.

> *You brought her to this world through tears,*
> *And stains of the darkest blood;*
> *But that misfortune had to be, so you*
> *Could give her whole to me.*

He saw Ruby's trembling hands passing the page to him; her tear-stained face. Heard her voice.

"*Was she putting a curse on me, Father? She was writing about the night I was born?*"

"We all come from God; none of us comes into this world through evil, Martha. Where there is life there is hope, and you and Vinny gave Ruby a good life. You did what you thought was for the best. You can't blame yourself."

"Before, before I go . . . She needs . . . she needs to know. But I can't tell . . ."

"I'll take care of Ruby, Martha. Don't worry about that."

She nodded, grateful.

"Vinny was a . . . a very special man. He . . . he loved Ruby as his own. He . . . never . . . blamed her. I-I never knew if he . . . if he *knew.* But his mother did. Edna . . . knew. And hated me . . . because she thought I'd . . . I'd used her son. And I did in a way . . . I met him on the bus after it happened. He was so kind . . . so very kind. It was as if . . . in the space of . . . of an hour I'd met the Devil and then . . . an angel. I told him I'd fallen down, which . . . which was the truth in a way. But I never told him what had happened. I told no one . . . not even my parents. They would have dis . . . disowned me. When I discovered I was . . . pregnant I had no one to turn to, so I-I clung . . . I clung to Vinny. It was Oaktree or Magdalenes. I deceived him. But if . . . if . . . he suspected that he never gave voice to it. He was a gentle . . . man. Such a gentleman."

The priest squeezed her hand tenderly. Martha gave a faint smile. Her eyes opened suddenly. She stared at the ceiling. Her other hand, holding the rosary, opened on the bedcover.

"Oh . . . the light, Father! The light . . . so . . . b-e-a-u-t-i-f-u-l . . . I . . . see . . . the gentle . . . tell . . . tell . . . Ruby . . . I'm . . . I'm . . . s-s-orry . . . so . . . v-e-r-y . . . sorry . . . for . . ."

Father Kelly gently freed her hand, laid it back on the covers with reverence. Her breathing was getting weaker and weaker.

Quietly, he left the room and went downstairs.

At the sound of his footfall, the twins turned their despairing faces toward him and got up.

"I'm sorry," he said, going to them and taking their hands. "You have to be strong now, girls. It's time . . . time to say good-bye."

———

Slope O'Shea took the call. He left his help to tend the bar and went directly upstairs.

Jamie, having finished his stint, had joined Ruby and Rose.

Paddy ordered another round.

"You play very well, Jamie," Ruby said, as Jamie took a seat beside her.

"Aye . . . thank you, Ruby. Been playin' that accordjin since I was ten, so I have."

"God, Jamie, that was lovely!" enthused Rose. "Never heard the like of it."

"Thank you, Rose." He sipped his pint. "It's very warm work." He caught Slope's eye. "Paddy, I think Slope wants a word with you."

Paddy got up. "Be back in a minute."

"Wonder what he wants," said Rose. "Hope there's nothing wrong."

Soon, Paddy returned to the table. He looked sad.

"We . . . we have to take you home, Ruby," he said. "I'm sorry. It's . . . it's your mother."

Chapter forty

There's a Mrs. Hanson to see you, Dr. Shevlin."

Edie hadn't bothered to knock. Or, if she had done, she'd been unusually quiet about it. He frowned. He'd been trying to concentrate on the notes he was making.

"Hanson? I don't recall seeing that name on our client list."

Edie shot a furtive glance out into the corridor and shut the door behind her. She came round his desk and stood beside him. She seemed uncharacteristically nervous. Something was up.

Then he remembered. He left his chair.

"Mrs. Hanson? A middle-aged lady? Short hair?"

"Yes, that's her. Nicely dressed. She has . . ."

Disconcerted, Henry stood staring at his secretary.

"Are you all right, Henry?"

His thoughts had returned to his home in Belfast, to a morning close on the heels of his wife's disappearance. He was reliving an unsettling—and highly intrusive—interview, conducted by a no-nonsense RUC sergeant who wore perfume that did not fit with her demeanor.

"Sorry, Edie. Please . . . please show her—"

"I was just going to say: she has a man with her."

"A man?"

"Yes . . ."

His mind raced. His heart sank.

"Is he . . . is he wearing a hat?"

"Yes. Shall I show them in?"

The nameless one. Who else would it be?

His presence alongside Hanson could only mean one of two things. One: Connie was safe and they could be at last reunited. Two . . . No, two didn't bear thinking about.

"Henry . . . Are you sure you're all right? You've gone a bit pale. I'll put the kettle on, shall I?"

He nodded gratefully. Hardly had Ms. King shut the door than she opened it again, admitting the two visitors.

Henry had sat down behind his desk, not only because he had, quite literally, gone weak at the knees, but also because he was obeying a cardinal rule of one-upmanship: he that is seated has a psychological advantage over he who is standing. Hence the age-old tradition of a king or emperor remaining enthroned while others are brought before him and made to stand.

As Edie had said, the sergeant was dressed in civilian clothes: a rather dull blue suit worn with a white blouse and a thin string of pearls. She carried a black clutch bag that matched her "sensible" shoes.

"Hello, Sergeant," Henry said carefully. "I didn't expect to see you here. Please, take a seat."

And the man? Yes, the sinister man was back. Not much changed from thirteen months before, in that dimly lit room of an army barracks. Except the hat was of a different color. He took it off. The reason for his wearing it evident now in his bald head, which made him look much older than before. The eyes, though! Those soulless eyes were unmistakable.

"I'm sorry that we had to come unannounced, Dr. Shevlin," Hanson said.

Her voice was somewhat kinder than he'd remembered it. That unnerved him. It was a well-known fact that police officers adopted a kindly tone when imparting sad news to . . . to . . . the next of kin. The phrase came unbidden, unwelcomed.

The next of kin.

"She's dead, isn't she?" Henry said. "Constance. That's why you're here."

Hanson exchanged a look with the man. He nodded slowly.

"Yes and no," she said. "It would depend on the course of action *you* choose to take, Doctor."

"I . . . I . . . don't understand. What . . . what are you saying?"

The door opened and Edie entered with a tray laden with tea things. All went quiet as she set them down before Henry and his visitors, and exited. He found himself wishing that Edie had brought something stronger.

But the man was pointing to the intercom on the desk in front of him.

"Would you mind switching that off, please, Doctor?"

The voice was precisely as Henry remembered it. It brooked no refusal. Henry did as he was bidden.

"Good," Hanson said. "What we're about to tell you must not go beyond this room, Doctor. Is that understood?"

"Yes. Yes, of course."

"This is Mr. Webb. He's a member of the Intelligence Service."

"You mean MI5."

"Yes. He's been working closely with the authorities in Belfast these past couple of years. I should tell you that myself and Constable Lyle have been liaising with Mr. Webb and his colleagues. You might say it's a joint effort. Counterterrorism. I'm sure you're familiar with the term."

Henry nodded, studying the man as he sipped his tea. MI5. Her Majesty's Secret Service. A real-life James Bond. But he knew that there was nothing glamorous about MI5. Not in Northern Ireland at any rate. He read the papers; he followed the news. The "dogs in the street" knew that MI5 had infiltrated the terror gangs of Ulster. To be sure, their efforts had brought several dangerous killers to justice, yet theirs was a murky world of vicious double crosses. A world wherein it was often hard to tell who the good guys were.

Webb set his teacup down and mopped his lips with a handkerchief. He fixed Henry with a steady look.

"Your wife—Constance—had got herself mixed up with some very dangerous people, Doctor," he began. "I explained some of this last year. Let me recap. One of our American associates, Harris Halligan, was passing on valuable information concerning the movements of the Irish Republican Army. Constance was unaware of Mr. Halligan's true identity and motives. While in his company she witnessed a murder."

"Oh my God!"

"It was plain bad luck that your wife got mixed up with Halligan when she did. It appears that he liked her paintings and saw them as another way to curry favor with the Republicans. But, alas, he overplayed his hand. We had to get him out very quickly to a place of safety. And as a consequence, Constance, too. Their lives were at risk. Anyone associated with her was also in grave danger."

Henry could barely take it all in.

"So that was why you planted those drugs in my car."

"Quite so. You understand now that we could not have you pursuing your search for Constance. There was the clear risk that you'd be putting at least three lives in danger: Halligan's, your wife's, and your own. Do you understand?"

"Yes, I understand, Mr. Webb, I think."

"We planted the drugs in your car in order to threaten you with imprisonment. You were what we call a loose cannon, Dr. Shevlin.

You could have gone off at any moment, and blown a hole right through our operation."

Henry grimaced at the man's choice of language. He was in little doubt that the cannon metaphor was one in frequent use in the London offices of MI5.

"Am I to take it then that I'm no longer a risk to your, er, operation?" Henry asked cautiously. "That Connie is safe."

"The operation has been terminated, yes . . ."

Terminated. He groaned inwardly. Despite himself, despite his medical training and his years of applying that training, he was quickly developing a healthy contempt for the man sitting opposite. He was seeing Webb for what he was: an individual engaged in an unnatural business. Spying. Working behind the scenes, flouting the laws of the land on a whim. In Webb's twilight world operations were "terminated." But so, too, were human beings. When they posed a threat, or when they'd outlived their usefulness.

". . . the risk factor for you, however, remains."

"Is Constance *alive*?" He was looking at Hanson.

"Yes. She is."

Oh, the relief of hearing that! He put his head in his hands, took a deep breath, summoning the courage to ask the next vital question.

"Where is she? Where *was* she?"

"For the first three months, on Innisfree, until her cover was blown."

"Wha—"

Hanson looked at Webb.

"We had to move her around several safe houses after that."

"Safe houses? Safe houses *where*, exactly?"

"We're not at liberty to say, for the simple reason that they would no longer *be* safe houses, Doctor. That is classified information."

"Oh yes, that old chestnut. When a question doesn't SUIT YOU, it's suddenly classified information. Where is she *now?*"

They didn't answer him.

"WHERE IS SHE NOW?"

"Keep calm, Doctor." It was Webb.

"No, I bloody-well *won't* keep calm! This is my wife we're talking about, not some statistic in some dreadful operation of yours. So tell me where she is."

"If I tell you that, Doctor," the man said evenly, "your life will no longer be the same. Everything you hold dear will be gone. You will have left it behind—as Constance had to."

"I don't know what you mean. I—"

"When you visited Innisfree—"

"Oh, so that's what's brought you here? How did you know I went there? Were you following me?"

"No, Doctor. You weren't followed. But one of our operatives in the area informed us of your movements."

Henry shut his eyes and raised a hand to his brow. A name came unbidden.

Max. Mad Max, the latter-day hippie, the Screamer.

It had to be. He thought back. Max was the last person he'd have suspected of being an agent for Her Majesty's Government. The clothing, the drinking, the alternate lifestyle.

And that cryptic answer to his question:

"*Are you local?*"

"*I get around.*"

But wasn't that how the operatives worked? They blended in. No one would suspect them.

"Mad Max," he said, eyes open again. "You people have no morals."

"When it comes to saving lives, morals take second place," said Webb.

"Tell me what I have to do. Tell me how I can get to Connie."

"Go back home," Hanson said. "Leave here as quickly as possible. We'll alert the health service, have them send a replacement. Go home, Doctor. Say good-bye to your father, your friends, and colleagues. Tell them you're going abroad." She smiled. "And that won't be a lie."

"You will hear from us in two weeks' time," said Webb. "When you do, we'll escort you to your wife's location. You and she will be reunited. You and she will also share this: you will be exiles. You will no longer be Dr. Henry Shevlin. You will, like your wife, be given a new identity. That is the choice you must make. You will be in witness protection for the rest of your lives."

"Think it over, Doctor," Hanson said, getting up. "It's a big decision to make."

"I've already made it," Henry said without hesitation.

She smiled. "I guessed you would say that. I'm glad."

Chapter forty-one

The heavens opened on the morning of Martha Clare's funeral; a fitting metaphor for Ruby's grief. The daughters could never have guessed that their mother would follow so quickly in their father's wake. A wound beginning to heal over, torn open again like the grave in the cemetery itself. Father Kelly conducted the Requiem Mass.

Ruby stood at the graveside, supported by Rose and Jamie, experiencing the raw closure of another parent's life. The heaped wet soil waiting to refill its weight under the granite headstone. The rain battering the lid of the descending coffin, the priest hastening through the prayers for the dead with the gathered mourners, brought back recent memories she could hardly bear to face.

Several nights after the funeral, her mother invaded her dreams. Always the same image: her face imploring, her arms spread wide for the hugs Ruby never received in life.

And Ruby would see herself as a little girl, running through the fields toward the gift of that embrace. But, at the point of blissful union, at the moment their fingers touched, the vision would retreat—like the vision of herself she'd seen over Beldam—and move farther and farther away. Ruby would run faster and faster, her feet flying over the grass, arms outstretched, but it was useless. She could never catch up. As in life, her mother was forever out of reach. And the cries she heard as she collapsed on the grass were the cries of a love long lost, that never was and never now would be.

She'd awaken, breathless, and weeping into the aftermath of those dreams to the loneliness of Oaktree, where the only sound was her heartbeat and the darkness stood like heat.

The daylight hours brought fresh assaults with all the power that being changed can bring. She was intensely aware of herself as a lone figure in an isolated space. The house that was Martha's domain, shaped to how she'd lived, mocked her. There was no one now to please. No setting tables or trays for two. No climbing stairs with gifts or news. The room: lifeless. The bed: empty. Plants wilting on the windowsill. She missed the edge of that sharpened voice razoring the quiet; the voice, which in her final days had faded to a rasping sigh.

Father Kelly visited in the subsequent days. She told him about the dreams.

"It's because I didn't get to say good-bye, isn't it, Father? I was out enjoying meself when . . . when I should have been here at her side."

They sat at the kitchen table, the tea going cold between them. The twins already back at work, because the pain of being in Oaktree without Mummy could not be lightly borne.

"Now, Ruby, you can't blame yourself. None of us had any idea God was going to take your mother home . . . so soon."

"Did she say anything, Father? Anything about me . . . before . . . before she . . . ?"

"Yes, Ruby. She said she was sorry . . . sorry that she hadn't been the best mother to you."

Ruby broke down. "She did?"

"Yes . . . she wished things could have been different between you. That she was so hard on you. She regretted that. Yes . . . she regretted that, Ruby, very much."

How could he tell her what *he knew?* The secret he'd taken ownership of was his, and his alone, to carry.

He patted Ruby's hand, shifted in the chair, the one Martha used to occupy.

"I'll always be here for you, Ruby. Have no fear of that. Sure I'm only down the road. You can depend on that. Any time you feel like talking, just give me a call."

"Thanks, Father." Ruby blotted her eyes.

He stood up. Put on his hat. Gazed out the window at the patch of flowers where Vinny fell.

"She's at peace with your daddy now, so. Aye . . . at peace."

———

In the afternoon, Ruby made the first journey of several into Tailorstown. A journey of despair, and longing for what might have been had she not opened the case, not gone down to the lake, not gone out with the McFaddens and Jamie. Would her mother still be here? Sitting on the faded cushion in the passenger's seat, maybe giving out about something, but *there,* nonetheless, beside her. In the flesh.

She felt an immense ache in her heart. The courage she'd mustered from Father Kelly's visit deserting her, thawing into a river of tears as she entered the town's main street and parked in the same spot, opposite the sale yard. She recalled the last time she'd taken her mother to town.

Saw her clamber out of the vehicle, cane clattering to the ground.

"Don't you dare touch me . . . You've done it this time."

"Done what?"

"You just wait till I get you home."

She'd been visiting the solicitor, Mr. Cosgrove, that day. The thought of the lawyer brought on another wave of grief. The twins and she would be meeting him tomorrow for the reading of the will.

She'd no longer be able to live at Oaktree. The house and farm would be sold. Where would she go? What would she do? She could never have believed that the deaths of both parents would cause even greater upheaval in her life, their parting separating her from all she held dear.

Images of Beldam reared up at her. Maybe it was the answer. Just walk in. Let the waters claim her, as they had Edna. She now understood what grief was, and why her grandmother had done what she did. She'd lost her husband and then her child within the same short time period as she, Ruby, had lost her parents. And then, upon the marriage of her only son, she'd lost her home as well. Been driven up above to the bedroom at the top of the stairs. The one Ruby now occupied. No, Edna was never crazy, as Martha had claimed. She was heartbroken, mourning a loss that was unbearable, that she knew she'd never fathom or get the measure of. What was left to her in the hollow afternoons? Nothing but the seasons turning beyond the window and the field where her husband died; and in the brooding darkness of night, the alluring gleam of Beldam under a starlit sky.

Ruby rested her head on the steering wheel, sobbing uncontrollably, paralyzed by fears of a future only the gods could know. The shopping list in her pocket, the errands she had to run—her reasons for making this trip—becoming the most trivial things in her world.

She had no idea how long she'd sat like that, but a gentle tapping on the window brought her back to reality. She looked up—to see Jamie McCloone's concerned face through the glass. She wound down the window.

"Are you all right, Ruby?"

"Yes . . . yes, Jamie. I was just . . ."

She burst into tears again.

Jamie shifted from foot to foot, adjusted his cap, uncomfortable. "I'm goin' . . . I'm goin' . . . into Biddy's for a cuppa tea. Maybe you'd—"

"Don't know . . . don't . . ." Her voice faltered. "Don't want anybody tae see me like this."

"It's . . . it's better . . . better, Ruby, to talk tae somebody." He looked over at the café. "Sure there's nobody in it at this time of day."

She knew he was right. The only one she'd talked to in recent days was Father Kelly. She needed to unburden herself. Her mind made up, she fetched her handbag and left the car.

Inside the café, Ruby was relieved to see that the only other customer was Barkin' Bob, seated in the corner. Bob was a good man because he wasn't a gossip and didn't have much time for conversation.

"We'll take this nice table at the windee," Jamie said, pulling out a chair.

Ruby halted. He could not have known it, but the table Jamie selected was the one she and her father used to share.

She dissolved again into tears.

"It's all right, Ruby," Jamie said gently. He rested a reassuring hand on her arm. "You sit down and I'll go up and get us a drop of tea and a bun. You'll be all right in a wee minute, so you will."

Ruby had no option but to sit down.

In a couple of moments, Jamie was back. He sat down—in her father's chair.

"Biddy'll be down in a minute," he said.

Ruby composed herself. Dried her eyes.

"Thanks, Jamie . . . it's just that . . . just that . . ." But she was unable to verbalize how she felt.

Jamie lifted the saltcellar and began toying with it. "Aye . . . it's . . . it's terrible hard when . . . when . . . somebody goes sudden. I know . . . know what you're goin' through. When Uncle Mick passed away . . . I wanted . . . wanted tae die, too."

"Did you?"

"Aye, so. But there . . . there wasn't much point in doin' that."

"Why not?"

"'Cos it wouldn't of brought Mick back, and I couldn't let Rose and Paddy down." He replaced the saltcellar, gazed out the window. "Aye . . . and I couldn't leave Shep on his own . . . 'cos Mick had give him tae me when he was only a pup—"

"Your dog?"

"Aye." Jamie averted his eyes.

"You must miss him now, Jamie? Rose tolt me he'd passed away."

"Oh . . . something terrible. Mornin's be the worst, 'cos . . . 'cos he used tae wake me up . . . jump on the bed . . . and lick me face." Jamie smiled at the memory. "God, he was the greatest wee dog."

"I'd always wanted a dog, but Mammy never liked them . . . said they were smelly."

"You could get one now."

Ruby fought back the tears again, wondering if she should share with Jamie her fate with regard to Oaktree.

"Would be good company for you now, so it would."

"Aye, maybe."

Biddy soon arrived with a tray. She off-loaded the cakes, and a pot of tea the size of an urn.

"Now, Ruby . . . a good cuppa tea will give you a bit of strength. Won't it, Jamie?"

"It will indeed, Biddy. A bitta whiskey in it, too, would be even better," he quipped. Ruby smiled.

"Och, away with you, Jamie," Biddy said. She leaned closer and whispered. "Well, d'ye know, if you have a word with Bob up there, I'm sure he could get yins a drop from that van of his out there. He's got everything, don't ye know."

They all looked Bob's way, but the traveling "salesman" was too occupied with his food to notice.

Another customer entered and Biddy excused herself.

Ruby tried not to weep by concentrating on Jamie's words. It was hard to be sitting across from him. He was in her father's chair. Taking up the space her daddy used to fill, in a place she never thought she'd have the heart to enter again. But here she was in the café for the first time since her daddy's death. And it wasn't so bad after all. Because Jamie was there.

"Do you do a bitta farmin' yourself, Ruby?" he was saying.

"I did . . . but when . . . when Daddy died, Mammy set the land."

"Aye. Suppose you miss it, right enough? But sure you . . . you could always start it up again."

Ruby nodded. How could she tell him that by this time tomorrow the will would be read and Oaktree Farm would no longer be hers? She tried not to think about it, focused all her attention on Jamie: noted the creased collar of his shirt that she could iron, a tear in his sleeve that she could mend.

"What's *your* farm like, Jamie?"

"Oh, it's not terrible big . . . just ten or so acres. Doz me all right. I would say yours would be a bit bigger than that."

"Aye . . . a wee bit . . ."

"Now how's that tea? Will I get yins a fresh pot?" Biddy had appeared at the table. "And that's a lovely sight: an empty plate."

"That would be nice, Biddy," Ruby agreed.

"And more of them buns, too!" Jamie called after her.

They talked some more. The conversation easy, words slipping between them like precious coins.

And the more Ruby listened to Jamie, the calmer she became. She drew strength from his unaffected ways. He was easygoing and kind, but also brave. Brave because he could play his accordion in front of all those people. Kind because he'd seen her distress and invited her for tea.

She thought back to that first meeting in the field all those weeks before. And how her father's passing and her mother's greed—"it's my land and we need the money"—had brought their little worlds together.

Now that frail coincidence, and all it held—stood ready to be loosed.

Chapter forty-two

They'd given him fourteen days to sort things out: Hanson and Webb. Except they hadn't put it quite like that. They'd used that formulaic phrase "to put your affairs in order." An expression usually delivered by doctors in sterile rooms to people facing the bleakest future.

Just fourteen days to "die." For, in a way, he was dying—dying to his old way of life.

In the preceding days, he'd set about dismantling all that he held dear. He'd put the house on the market. Informed Maeve at the gallery that he'd be relinquishing his part in the business. Had visited Betty, Connie's sister, to say he'd been offered a position overseas.

"You'd better tell me *where* exactly," Betty had said. "In case . . . in case Connie turns up."

"Sorry, Betty." He'd hugged her. "When I get settled I'll write to you. Promise." Those parting words leaving her puzzled on the doorstep.

The hardest farewell he'd leave to the end: his father.

Now Henry stood in the home he'd shared with Connie for more than a decade, taking one last look around. She'd been drawn to it by the gardens, and the picture-perfect windows, where daylight thronged the glass; ideal for her work. It was their first home together, their first joyous shot at all things new.

Yes, they'd had many happy times in Hestia House. She'd insisted on calling it that, after the Greek goddess of hearth and home. There was a time not so long ago when he believed this home would be theirs for good. But oh, how very quickly things had changed! It was an end he'd never seen coming.

And very soon now, another house in a far-off land. With that thought, the image of his dear father came quick in his mind, and the reality of what lay before him hit him like a tidal wave.

He could not allow himself to weep.

He wandered into the living room. On the table his letter, in the same spot where he'd left it all those months ago. He smiled at the memory. Was about to bin it, but changed his mind. He'd keep it and give it to Connie. The letter she'd now finally get to read.

The thought of seeing her again made him leap with joy.

He raced upstairs. Hauled down their suitcases from the attic space. He'd pack one with Connie's clothes and effects. She'd like that: having something back of their old life together.

———

A couple of hours later, he pulled up outside his father's place in Lisburn.

The time had come to say his last good-bye.

He found Sinclair having tea with his housekeeper, Mrs. Malahide.

"You haven't met Matilda, Henry, have you?" Sinclair getting up, smiling, happy.

"No . . . no, we haven't met," Henry said. "Thanks for taking care of the house."

A tall woman rose to greet him. Henry was surprised. He'd expected his father's "help" to be the quintessential Belfast cleaner type: hair-rollers, housecoat, cigarette permanently in hand.

Matilda was anything but. Tall, with grayish hair worn in the inverted teacup style favored by Her Majesty, she cut a striking figure in a navy-blue dress and sensible brogues.

"Do call me Tilda. I knew Dymphna would do a good job," she said in the voice of an adroit headmistress. "Very dependable girl."

Sinclair saw Henry's confusion.

"Tilda runs the cleaning business, Henry. Sweeping Beauties. Wonderful name, don't you think?"

Henry grinned. "Well, your sweeping beauty did a very thorough job."

"Glad to hear it, Henry." She plucked her bag from the sofa. "Now I really must be off. You two have lots more interesting things to discuss, I'm sure."

Sinclair saw her out.

"Would you like to eat here this evening or shall we go out?" Henry overheard his father say through the partially opened window.

"Let's go out," Tilda said. "Treat ourselves for a change. He's very handsome, your son."

"Takes after me."

They chuckled.

Henry was surprised. His father wasn't the easiest man to get along with. The judge's wig and gown hard to shrug off. But he was glad—glad that he would not be on his own.

He heard Tilda's car take off. Sinclair reappeared.

"Didn't expect you, Henry. You didn't say." He made a beeline for the kettle. "Shouldn't you be at work? No word of Connie, I suppose? Cup of coffee?"

Henry braced himself. "A brandy would be better."

Sinclair turned, kettle in hand, eyebrows raised. He checked the clock. "Really . . . at this hour of the day? I hope you're not turning into one of your patients."

But already Henry was by the drinks cabinet.

A pause.

A tightened brake of fear.

His hands trembling with the glasses.

"There's something wrong, son. Isn't there?"

Henry kept his back turned, willed himself to be strong.

Then: "I have to go away, Dad."

Not the customary "Father" but "Dad."

He took the drinks to the table.

Sinclair sat down slowly, his eyes never leaving Henry's face. "Away . . . where?"

"I can't say."

"I-I don't understand." Fear already in his voice. "What have you done, son?"

"I've done nothing. But this . . . this is the price I have to pay."

He gulped the brandy down to keep the tears in check. There was no easy way to . . .

"This concerns Connie, doesn't it?" Sinclair stared at the glass.

Henry knew what he was thinking. She'd been trouble from the start. Flighty, a blithe spirit. The live-for-the-moment type who'd often stood before Sinclair in the dock. Act first, think later, and to hell with the consequences. And he was right on all those counts, as the past year had proven. It was Connie's actions that had brought them to this pass.

"Is she . . . is she alive?"

Henry gave an imperceptible nod. His eyes filled with tears.

"But that's . . . that's . . . good. Isn't it?"

The hesitation.

The falling timbre on those last two words.

"She . . . she got mixed up with an undercover agent who'd infiltrated the IRA. She witnessed a murder. His cover was blown and they . . . MI5 . . . they had to get her out . . . out of harm's way."

There, he'd said it.

Silence.

The air charged with a damage done.

He sensed his father coming to terms with what he could not bring himself to say. He could not look his way and face the dawning realization in the eyes. The look that said: "You're leaving me for good."

"She's in . . . she . . . Connie's in . . ." The normally lucid and self-assured Sinclair stumbling over the words. "She's in Witness Protection, isn't she? I . . . I understand now. Yes, I understand."

He placed his hand on Henry's. The hand that should have been comforting, reassuring, only magnifying the sense of utter betrayal Henry felt. A touch, speaking its own language in the ruinous silence; a touch that said: "Son, you will not be here to hold me when I depart this life. This hand, the hand that took yours through those first uncertain steps of boyhood, will not be here to guide me 'into that good night.'"

Henry couldn't bear it. He stood up. A damburst of tears pent up and held in check for months, falling now like rain.

"It's all right, son. You have to do what you have to do."

With all the courage he could muster, Henry turned to face him. There were tears in the old man's eyes. He held out his arms.

"A handshake from the heart, son. Come here."

Through the open window, the menacing drone of a helicopter high up in the sky. Children at play: "That's *my* ball, give it back." A car door slamming and a woman's voice: "I *told* you. Don't play in the road." The world beyond amplified, and the woman, the child, never knowing that their lives contained this moment. This precious moment—of a loss that only love could rescue—for ever carried forward by a father and a son.

"I'm sorry . . . so . . . so very, very sorry it has to be this way," Henry said, finally allowing himself to be freed from his father's embrace.

"There, there, son. You'll be seeing . . . seeing Connie again. That's all . . . all that matters. And you never know: there may be peace here soon, and you'll both be able to come back."

"Maybe, Dad . . . stranger things have happened."

The feeble riposte because there was nothing more to say.

"I'll be fine . . . Tilda . . . she makes a very good lasagna, you know." The comment brought a weak smile. Sinclair lifted his glass from the table.

"Here's to Connie," he said, smiling bravely. "And . . . and your new life."

They poured more drinks, sat in the easy chairs. Conversation less difficult as the fine brandy took hold.

Finally, after an hour, Sinclair got up, went and stood by the window.

"You'd best get going, son."

"I know."

Henry turning to go, blinded again by grief.

He got back into the car. Looked to the window where his father stood.

Sinclair raised his glass.

Henry raised his hand.

And that was how they parted.

Each holding fast their courage into that great unknown.

Chapter forty-three

The dreaded afternoon had arrived. The reading of Martha Clare's Last Will and Testament was inching closer and closer. In an hour's time Ruby would know her fate. She'd steeled herself for what lay ahead by recalling the words of Dr. Shevlin: "*The past is over . . . the future is new and full of possibilities.*"

Now, sitting in the kitchen of Oaktree, she tried to reassure herself that everything would be all right.

The previous afternoon, she'd had tea with Jamie in the Cozy Corner Café. That meeting had helped her a lot. She realized that she *could go* to places she and her father had visited without dissolving into tears. That she was no longer alone. Jamie would be there to help her through. He was her friend now. And she also knew that the support of Rose and Paddy was a given.

She sat at the table, gazing out the window: a surprise of tiny sparrows on the clothesline, a gentle breeze teasing the alder leaves. And beyond: the patch of flowers she'd planted in the field where her father fell.

"Please, Daddy, don't . . . don't let them take Oaktree away."

She'd said it aloud to give weight to the words—her voice hollow-sounding in the empty house.

She got up, suddenly galvanized. Looked about the kitchen.

This was *home*. No matter what the future might hold, she'd always remember it as such. The place that had shaped her, borne witness to her hopes and dreams, the sorrow and pain down all the years of growing from child to girl to woman; an adult woman now. Yes, surely an adult finally, with the mother gone.

Slowly she climbed the stairs.

In the twins' room she checked that their beds were nicely made, plumped the pillows again. They'd bought a car between them, so were driving up from Belfast and meeting her at the solicitor's office for the reading.

Planning ahead, she'd done all she could well in advance to keep the peace. Had made a nice pot of spaghetti bolognese. Pasta was never a favorite with Martha, but Ruby had heard the twins enthusing about having the dish in a restaurant once, and thought she'd surprise them. It would be their first time at the supper table since their mother's death.

May's parting shot had been less than kind, though. In the aftermath of the funeral, she'd interrupted Ruby's grieving to shout at her for being "out drinking and partying" the night their mother died. But Ruby had expected as much. She knew she'd been cruel to May in telling her she'd found the *reference*. The barb expertly aimed to let her sister know she'd read it. Looking back on the incident, she realized she probably shouldn't have done that.

The reference. It was still in a drawer in her bedroom. No longer a secret. Martha's death had shut the door on the shock and shame that only its discovery by the mother could bring. A daughter pregnant out of wedlock was the gravest sin a girl could commit.

Poor May had been faced with a terrible choice.

In her mother's bedroom, Ruby wondered why Martha had been so harsh in that regard. Thanked her lucky stars that she—Ruby—had not been born out of wedlock, that she'd stayed at home and so evaded the dangers of the wider world. She felt a pang of sorrow for all the orphaned children being brought up by religious orders because of family shame.

She opened Martha's closets, gazed on the serried ranks of frocks and jackets that would never again be worn. What would be done with them? Perhaps the twins would take care of that side of things. Ruby didn't feel she had the right to make such a decision. They had been closer to their mother. That had always been the case.

The phone rang. She rushed downstairs.

"God, how are you, Ruby?"

"Och, Rose . . . hello. . . ."

Rose, in full matchmaking mode, was determined to build on the great progress she'd made so far.

"Glad I got you in, 'cos Jamie was telling me yins had a great chat in Biddy's, so he did. I was terrible pleased to hear that . . . 'cos he's a lovely fella, is Jamie, and he's on his own like yourself."

Ruby didn't know what to say.

"Aye . . . he's . . . we . . . we had a nice chat, Rose."

"God, that's great to hear. Now me and my Paddy were gonna drop by this afternoon with a cake I baked for you."

"Thanks, Rose, that would be nice. But I have to go now. To . . . to Mr. Cosgrove's, to hear Mammy's will and . . ."

She broke off, wondering whether she should confide her true fears to her new friend.

"Well, that's very important, Ruby. I understand completely. There's always tomorrow. Hope everything goes all right, and I'm sure it will, 'cos your mammy struck me as a fair-minded woman, so she did."

Rose's assessment was wide of the mark. How could she have any idea what Martha was *really* like? The comment had Ruby blurting out what was bothering her.

"I . . . I don't know, Rose. May and June say they want to sell everything . . . to buy a house in Belfast."

She broke down.

"Och, Ruby, dearie me . . ."

"So, maybe . . . maybe after today . . . I-I won't have a home no more."

"Now, Ruby, that's hardly gonna happen. And even if it did, sure me and my Paddy have a big house here with three bedrooms and nobody to fill them. God-blisses-an'-savus, sometimes I wonder why we built such a big house atall. So you'll never be stuck, Ruby. You're only thinking the worst 'cos you've come through so much this last while, losing your daddy and mammy so close. So it's very understandable that you might be feeling a wee bit down."

"Aye . . . maybe. . . ."

"So you go on into Mr. Cosgrove now. For, as they say, you'll never plough a field by turning it over in your mind. What time did you say your wee appointment was at?"

Ruby checked her watch. The time was fast approaching.

"In half an hour, Rose."

"Oh, you better get going then. But I'll tell you what, Ruby: me and my Paddy are going into Tailorstown now to do a bitta shopping, and when we're done we'll wait for you in Biddy's. For I'm sure you'd need a cuppa tea after a meeting like that. Is that all right?"

Ruby dried her eyes, feeling a bit more heartened. "Aye, Rose. Thanks . . . thanks very much."

———

Mr. Cosgrove, a cynical toad in a pin-stripe suit and silk cravat, had been in the legal profession for far too long. He enjoyed his job, but the reading of wills could be a tricky business. All sorts of family skirmishes had broken out in his office down the years. For the most part, verbal harangues of the sort that would make Lucifer himself bridle. But there were those rather more unsettling occasions when Sergeant Ranfurley's aid had to be sought. And that was unfortunate. Had there been a contest for brainlessness then the McGinty brothers would surely have claimed first prize. On learning their old man had drunk their four fields *plus* the hovel that was home, they not only laid into each other but Mr. Cosgrove, too.

He shook his head at the memory, as if trying to dislodge the ugly image of Jeremiah McGinty referring to him as the intimate part of a woman's anatomy, while trying to throttle him over the desk.

He dunked another digestive in his afternoon cuppa and checked his list.

Next, the Clare sisters.

"Hmmm . . . might be tricky, that one."

As if on cue, the buzzer sounded.

"The Clares are here," his secretary announced.

"Right-o, Janet. Give me a minute, will you?"

He slid a box of tissues to the front of the desk—tears, an ever-present risk with the ladies—and repositioned a carafe of water, likewise always a feature, in case of fainting spells. There was a bottle of Bushmills whiskey in a cupboard, too, but that was rarely availed of. Not unless a solitary individual suddenly found himself—or, indeed, herself—the inheritor of some squirreled-away fortune that an ancient relative had never before disclosed.

Finally, he checked his zipper—always a good idea when dealing with the public—and pressed the intercom button.

"Send them in, Janet, please."

"Ladies . . . Ruby, May, and June, I believe." He got up, smoothed down his tie, and offered his hand. "How are you? Please take a seat there now."

He knew Ruby, of course. Had seen her regularly in town with the mother. The twins, though, were a surprise. They looked nothing like their older sister: thin as whippets with Martha Clare's delicate bone structure.

"Tragic business . . . the loss of your mother." He made the obligatory tutting noises reserved for such occasions. "My condolences to you."

The ladies murmured their thanks.

"Well, I expect you'll want to get this over as quickly as possible," he said, sitting down again.

Janet had left the door ajar. Another one of those little post-McGinty precautions, which had proved most useful in the past. The secretary would be an on-hand witness to the outbreak of any unpleasantness.

He snapped his fingers and called out, "Janet, have you got the Clare file there?"

Mr. Cosgrove enjoyed using the finger-snapping gesture when he had clients in the room. He'd seen a lawyer in an episode of *Kojak* use it once, and loved the air of busied authority the signal conveyed.

"Will that be all, sir?" Janet asked, placing the file in front of him.

"Thank you, Janet, yes. That's all for now."

He put on his spectacles, riffled through the file.

"Will this take long?"

He looked up. "Pardon me? Which one of you? May or June—?"

"May."

Impertinent *and* impatient. Not a good combination. He studied her over the glasses.

"No, as a matter of fact, it won't take long. Your mother's will is quite a simple one, because your father saw to all the details in the first instance."

May looked at June, who shrugged, and then looked at Ruby. Ruby made the Sign of Calm in her pocket. She'd learn about her future within the next few minutes. Rose's kind words came back to her: "Three bedrooms here and nobody to fill them . . . so you'll never be stuck . . ."

"I don't understand," May was saying. "What's Daddy's will got to do with Mummy? He left everything *to* Mummy."

"Indeed he did." Now came the difficult part. Mr. Cosgrove eyed the slightly opened door. "Shall we proceed?"

He focused again on the page, cleared his throat.

"'This is the Last Will and Testament of me, Martha Florence Clare, of Oaktree Farm, Five Lakeside Road, Tailorstown. To the role of Executor and Trustee of this, my Last Will and Testament, I hereby appoint my eldest daughter, Ruby Vivian Clare, to dispose of my estate as laid out by my husband, Vincent Alfred Clare, on the twentieth of September, nineteen seventy-six.'"

The twins exchanged worried looks.

"'. . . and in the event that the aforesaid should die in my lifetime, I appoint my daughter, May Bernadette Clare, to act in her absence hereof.'"

May's ears pricked up.

Mr. Cosgrove gave a little cough.

The show was about to begin.

"'To my daughters, I leave the following legacies.

"'One: To my daughter, May Bernadette Clare, I give, devise, and bequeath absolutely the sum of one thousand and five hundred pounds, to dispose of as she sees fit. Also my wedding ring and gold watch as to same.

"'Two: To my daughter, June Elizabeth Clare, I give, devise, and bequeath absolutely the sum of one thousand and five hundred pounds, to dispose of as she sees fit. Also my engagement ring and seeded pearl necklace as to same.'"

Mr. Cosgrove eyed the ladies. He braced himself for the onslaught.

"'Three: To my daughter, Ruby Vivian Clare, I give, devise and bequeath absolutely, all the rest of my estate, to—'"

"*What?!*" May shot to her feet. The solicitor blinked rapidly. So swift was her action that he was reminded of a False Water Cobra suddenly poked, he'd once seen in an Attenborough nature program.

Ruby was stunned. Hadn't even registered her sister's bolt out of the chair. She put a hand to her mouth. Had she heard him correctly? It couldn't be true, could it?

"That *can't* be right. It just *can't be.*" May slapped the desk, hard.

Mr. Cosgrove shut his eyes briefly. He felt an attack of his dyspepsia coming on. Knew exactly the play of emotions the aggrieved party would now demonstrate. First the shock, then the anger, and finally the tears, coming in at third position. Always in that order. People rarely surprised him.

He shifted in the chair. It was time to engage the ploy of his old headmaster: stand straight, hold position, speak slowly, and if need be, raise the volume, to get the point across.

He got to his feet. "I would appreciate it if you *sat down,* Miss Clare. I have not completed the reading yet."

"No, I will *not* sit down."

May lunged for the page. But Mr. Cosgrove's reflexes were quick—the scuffle with Jeremiah McGinty had taught him a thing or two. He kept a tight grip on the will, throwing his right arm aloft, holding it well out of harm's way.

"You're in on it with *her.*" May swung round, stabbing a finger at Ruby. "Mummy would *never* do this to us. *Never!* Isn't that right, June? Well, isn't it?"

June burst into tears.

"I can assure you I am not *in* on anything, as you put it," Mr. Cosgrove said evenly. "Now, *please* sit down."

Ruby felt moved to speak. "May . . . May, it's all right, I'll—"

"Oh, you keep out of this, you scheming bitch! Sitting there like butter wouldn't melt. You planned all this, didn't you? Made Mummy change her will to suit *you* . . . when we were away in Belfast and her . . . and her not well!"

"Ladies, *please!*" The time had come to use the magic word. "Now, if you do not sit down, Miss Clare, I'll have no option but to call *security.*"

There was no security. But the word was enough. That was another little stratagem he'd picked up from *Kojak.*

May scowled at him. She was what his mother would have termed "a brazen hussy." But he stood his ground and glared back at her in an equally assertive manner. These young women could be a handful. And so very tedious, having to go through the theatrics with the injured party time after time. But not to worry: the tactics he deployed usually resolved things pretty quickly.

Much to his relief, he saw the angry twin do his bidding. Slowly, and with a show of pained reluctance, she took her seat again.

"Thank you," he said, returning to his chair. He slipped his spectacles back on.

Ruby's heart was beating like a drum. What would the result of all this be? She glanced at her sisters. May's face was grim and angry; June's, wet with tears.

"Now, where was I? Yes . . . here we are . . . 'To my daughter, Ruby Vivian Clare, I give, devise, and bequeath all the rest of my estate, as my husband, Vincent Alfred Clare, desired thereof. The dwelling known as Oaktree Farmhouse, its contents, and the lands on which it stands, sixty-three acres and three quarters in total, entirely and absolutely in perpetuity.'"

"Perpee—what . . . ?" June asked through her tears.

"Perpetuity. It means that Ruby has ownership for life. Only on her demise will it pass to you, and only on the assumption that she *wants* to pass it to you. If, for example, she decides to marry, and has issue, then that would most likely present a very different set of circumstances."

May sniffed with derision. "Not much chance of that," she muttered, whipping another tissue out of Mr. Cosgrove's box.

"Of course she is also free," continued Mr. Cosgrove, "to leave it to a charity of her choice, or indeed the Church." He shifted his eyes back to the will. "And just on that subject, the Church, there are a couple of other small bequests. If you'll allow me?"

Ruby sank back in the chair. Oh, the joy of hearing it all explained in plain terms! Her father had stood by her in the end. Tears fell, tears of sadness mingled with joy.

The twins now refused to acknowledge the solicitor. They sat with heads drooped, eyes cast down.

"'To Father William Kelly, parish priest of St. Timothy's parish, Tailorstown, I give, devise, and bequeath the sum of four hundred pounds absolutely, to be used in his ecclesiastic ministry in whatsoever way he sees fit. Also, the sum of fifty-five pounds for Masses to be said for the eternal repose of my soul. And the souls of all the faithful departed, especially that of my dear husband, Vincent Alfred, and his little brother, Declan Gerard.'"

Ruby noted the absence of Grandma Edna's name. No forgiveness for poor Edna . . .

"I should inform you that Mrs. Ida Nettles sends her apologies that she couldn't be with us today," Mr. Cosgrove announced. "However, that fact should not detain us."

He coughed politely and returned to the reading.

"'Finally, I leave, devise, and bequeath the sum of one hundred pounds absolutely to my friend, Ida Mavis Nettles, for all the good times. Also my Tara brooch and'"—Mr. Cosgrove hesitated—"'and matching . . . clip-on earrings with the green glass studs . . . which she so admired.'"

He regretted the mention of green glass studs at the close of his summation. It was an unworthy, trivial note to end on, but you never knew with people. Perhaps the trinkets in question were of immense sentimental value to the deceased.

Anyway, it was done. And not a broken bone, blackened eye, or fainting fit to deal with.

He handed out three copies of said will. Then got the weeping sisters to sign the appropriate documents, before releasing their checks.

———

The twins marched out the door ahead of Ruby, ignoring Mr. Cosgrove's cheery good-bye. Ruby followed behind, elated, but not knowing what to say. They crossed the street without looking back, heading in the direction of the car park.

Ruby was forced to run after them.

"May! June!" she called out, catching up with them.

"Will I see yins . . . see yins at the house? It's just that I'm meeting somebody in the café for half an hour. I made some spaghetti bolognese for supper."

"How *dare* you speak to us after what you've done!" spat June, feeling the need to continue what May had started back at the office.

"But . . . but I didn't do anything!" Ruby cried.

"Like hell you didn't."

May unlocked the car door.

"Don't waste your breath, June. She's mental, always bloody has been. Well, let me tell you something, Ruby Clare: you can have the house, the frigging land, and all the bad luck that goes with them. You killed Mummy with your antics. Pity I didn't let you kill *yourself* that night in Beldam. None of this would be happening now. Mummy would still be alive and there'd be peace. I *saved* you and this is all the thanks I get."

"*I didn't kill Mammy. Her heart was never good.*"

"You *killed* her! You've got that on your conscience. Now get out of my way."

Ruby stopped to draw breath. She met May's dangerous gaze. Dr. Shevlin's words came to her: "*And no one—absolutely no one—can take your peace away from you, because they don't have the power to do that. You no longer give them the power to do that.*"

Well, May had taken quite enough away from her down the years. But not anymore. It was time to square the circle.

"And *you* killed a baby. You've got that on *your* conscience."

The words, once freed that could never be taken back. "I could easily have told Mammy what *you* did. But I didn't. So, *I* saved *you.*"

"Coo-eee . . . Ru-u-uby." The sound of Rose McFadden's cheery voice.

Had she heard them?

May, knocked sideways, staring. June helpless in the passenger's seat. Ruby so relieved at the appearance of her friend.

"I was just over in the café there and saw yins through the windee. I'm sure yins are all glad that old meetin's over. What about a nice cuppa tea?"

"Aye . . . Rose." Ruby moved away from the car.

She heard May get in and slam the door.

"Everything all right? Are your sisters not coming, too?"

Ruby shook her head.

Rose's question was answered by the vehicle roaring off.

Chapter forty-four

Tuesday morning, August 28, found Henry at the wheel of his car, speeding along the Killoran road on his final trip to Rosewood.

Two weeks before, he'd been ordered to leave by Hanson and Webb, so that he could "put his affairs in order."

Now those affairs had been seen to.

It hadn't taken long, he reflected, to leave a life behind, when you had to. To dismantle all the certainties, kick away the props, shred the documents that linked you to a name—birth, marriage, and degree certificates, check books, bank statements—and the love letters you once held dear.

All that was left now of Dr. Henry Shevlin sat on the backseat of the car in a suitcase: his clothes and a book, *In His Own Write* by John Lennon. A parting gift from Finbar.

He pulled up at the clinic, picked up a bouquet of white lilies from the passenger seat, and left the car.

Edie was already at the door to greet him.

"Henry, how very good to see you! I didn't expect you at all."

"For you, Edie." He handed her the flowers. "Couldn't leave without saying good-bye."

"Oh, goodness me, they're beautiful!" She blushed. "How very kind. It's not often I get flowers." She sniffed them deeply, savoring the scent.

"How are things?" Henry asked, looking about the empty waiting room. "No one here?"

"No. Dr. Balby rearranged his schedule, and your locum, Dr. Lewis, has just been called out on an emergency."

"Nothing too serious, I hope."

Edie shook her head wearily. "Oh, the Sproule family. I don't believe they figured on your radar, which was very fortunate for you. The eldest boy, Chuck, has a tendency to go off from time to time . . . alcohol, you understand. In the early hours he climbed onto the roof of a house in town, singing 'Wrap the Green Flag Round Me, Boys' at the top of his voice."

The secretary saw Henry's puzzlement.

"It's a rebel song, I fear, and the roof belongs to Mr. Wilson-Paisley . . . a Protestant gentleman and chairman of the county council, who did not appreciate being woken up by such a racket *and* such a provocative song."

"I can imagine. Isn't it a job for the police?"

"Yes. But apparently Chuck threatened to jump off the roof if the police dared arrest him, so Sergeant Ranfurley rang us for assistance. Hopefully Dr. Lewis can coax him down."

"I see . . ."

"It's a pity you're missing Dr. Balby . . . but we didn't know you were coming, you see."

"Yes . . . sorry about that. Give Sylvester my best wishes, won't you?" Henry checked his watch, moved to the door. "Well, I'd best get going."

Edie deposited the blooms on her desk. "I'll just walk you to the car," she said.

They exited through the revolving door into the morning sunlight.

"Oh, meant to ask . . . how is James McCloone? Still attending his sessions?"

"Well, to tell you the truth, he turned up once, and when he discovered you weren't here, he took off again."

"Really!"

Edie gave a mischievous little smile. "And the following day, Ruby Clare did the same. Shows you how much you were appreciated. But to tell you the truth, Henry, I do believe he and she are an item, as they say."

Henry grinned. Poor put-upon Ruby and the lonely farmer? A match made in heaven surely.

"That's delightful news!" he said. "So Rosewood Clinic is now doubling as a dating agency."

"Yes, Henry, see what you started. But, between you and me"—she threw a look back at the clinic—"isn't it the loneliness that drives most of them through those doors?"

"Yes . . . more or less, Edie. More or less."

"So perhaps now that they've found each other, there'll be no need to visit Rosewood at all." She smiled broadly. "I love a happy ending, don't you?"

He didn't answer. Just grinned. "Thank you . . . thank you for everything, Edie. It was a pleasure to work alongside you."

He hugged her warmly.

"The feeling is entirely mutual." There was the glint of a tear in Edie's eye. "We'll miss you . . . You were a breath of fresh air . . . made us all feel special."

He squeezed her arm gently. Got back in the car.

"Oh, you haven't told me where you're going."

"Abroad . . . somewhere . . . Things aren't finalized yet." Which was the truth.

"You're a dark horse, Henry. Send us a postcard, won't you?"

"I will." But, as he said the words, he knew that he could never honor her simple request.

He pulled out through the clinic gates, saw her in the rearview mirror, and raised a hand.

She fell from sight.

Another ending.

Another good-bye.

His last on Northern Irish soil.

Chapter forty-five

The parting with May and June had been less than harmonious, and Ruby was glad Rose had been there, a shoulder to lean on. Lean on, but not cry on.

She'd done enough of that.

Again something Dr. Shevlin had said came back to her now, as she sat in the car in Tailorstown, running through her shopping list. *"The hard times, Ruby, make us realize we are stronger and more capable than we thought."*

Only now in retrospect did she understand what he'd meant.

Yes, she *was* stronger. There was no doubt about that. She'd survived the worst. Her father's death, then her mother's. Oaktree would not be sold. The farm was hers. *Really hers,* to pick up again where he'd left off.

She'd won the right to fully take her place.

A winner, not a loser.

A survivor; helpless victim no more.

The yelping of dogs pulled her out of her reverie. Barkin' Bob, the peddler, was drawing up alongside her. She saw that the source of the commotion was a trailer full of little puppies hitched behind his van.

She got out to take a closer look.

Bob climbed out. "How ya, missus," he said, raising his hat in greeting, and launching immediately into his sales pitch. "Would yeh loike tae bouy one'a them wee puppies? Wan pound and fifty, and cheap at twoice the proice."

Ruby hesitated. She didn't really know what to do. Then she thought of someone. It would be the perfect gift.

Bob waited.

"I would," she assured him. "But I don't know . . . don't know how I'd get it home, Bob."

"I've a box with a hole in it, missus." He gestured at the Cortina. "Just sit it there in the back."

Ruby grew excited. Should she?

She'd never conducted a transaction of this nature before. Everything she'd bought in the past had to be first approved by her mother. And this purchase she would definitely *dis*approve of. "*Smelly things, dogs. Do not want them about the place.*"

Ruby dipped into her handbag for the money.

Bob smiled, eyes twinkling in his weathered face. "Any wan in partickler, missus?"

There were four in the trailer. Ruby pointed to a little black-and-white bundle with a white star on its forehead. It was the least lively, and lying half-asleep.

"That wee one *there* . . . I think is nice."

Bob gathered up the puppy and placed it gently in Ruby's arms. "Hould her there a minute till I get the box for yeh now."

He leaned into the van and quickly reemerged, a Smoky Bacon Crisp box in one hand, a length of twine in the other. Ruby eased the puppy into it. Passed the money over and the deal was done.

Chapter forty-six

Henry parked his car in Lane H, Bay 22, at Belfast International Airport, leaving the keys in the ignition, as instructed.

He loaded his luggage onto a trolley and made his way to the check-in area. It was late afternoon and he was happy to see that the lines were not so long.

He went directly to the information station. There was a young man behind the desk. He checked his nametag. *Gerry.* He was attending to a large lady in a brightly colored dress, her hair built up into an elaborate pyramid of plaits.

"But this is pre*pos*terous," the woman was saying. She spoke with a cultured English accent. "I'll have you know I am Mimi in *La Bohème* at the Grand Opera House tonight, and I simply *must* have my gowns, young man. How could you possibly have lost my bag between London and here? We're not in Outer Mongolia, you know. But you people in Belfast might as well be, I suppose."

"I'm sorry, madam, but we're doing everything we can."

"Well, your *everything* is not enough. The show . . . that is, *my* show, *must* go on, you understand. I simply *must* have those gowns."

Henry caught Gerry's eye.

Gerry nodded and lifted the phone.

"Why are you attending to *him* when you are still attending to *me*?" She gave Henry the once-over from her haughty perch. "Can't you see I was here before you?"

"I'm in rather a hurry, madam; I do apologize," Henry said. "My plane is leaving in twenty minutes. Good luck with Mimi."

———

Gerry escorted Henry to a door marked Private, knocked politely, nodded, and set off back to his station.

Henry pushed the door open. He found Hanson and Webb seated at a desk in a brightly lit office.

"You made it, Henry," Hanson said, getting up. "Good to see you. This can't be easy for you."

"No," he said flatly.

Webb eyeballed him, and Henry met him with an equally glacial stare.

"Please . . . sit, Dr. Shevlin," he said. "Except you're no longer Dr. Henry Shevlin now."

He slid a passport across the desk. "Pleased to meet you, Kenneth Marcus Lawson."

Henry refused to inspect the passport. "May I be allowed to know where I'm going, please? And how do I know this isn't another one of your games?"

"We don't play games . . . Mr. Lawson."

It was Hanson, back in her official role. He saw her sitting at the kitchen table in Hestia House over a year before, giving him a grilling. How could he have known back then that it would all end like this?

"No, we certainly don't," Webb added grimly. "You are still in danger until you alight from that plane at your destination. We're not out of the woods yet, you know. We are doing everything to aid your safe passage out of here." He leaned back in the chair. "Isn't it a pity now that you didn't know your wife a bit better? Then none of this would have been necessary."

Henry lost his composure. The pent-up anger. He could contain it no longer. He glanced about the room, noted the tiny surveillance cameras spaced at intervals in the ceiling. He'd no doubt that this office was under constant scrutiny by the authorities. He didn't care.

"How dare you?! My wife is an innocent bystander in all this! She got caught up in something murky. Something that *you* people set in train."

Webb's response was to slide a large envelope across the desk.

Hanson spoke again. "You may open that after takeoff. And I *mean* after takeoff. It contains important papers, birth and marriage certificates, details of your new identity." She attempted a smile. To calm him, no doubt. There was a lot riding on Henry keeping calm.

"We will escort you to the plane. You will sit in row twenty-seven, seat A. You will talk to no one, *absolutely no one*. Not even during the flight. Is that understood?"

Henry nodded.

They all stood up.

It was time to go.

———

The plane climbed into the evening sky above Belfast, a setting sun making of the landscape a golden quilt of patchwork. Henry looked out one last time, allowing himself a pang of regret for all that was now lost: his identity, his career, his colleagues, his patients. But most of all: his father, his poor, dear father.

Oh, the irony! Terminating one life to gain another.

But his darling Connie was worth it.

Soon he'd be seeing *her* again.

And his father would be all right. He would have Matilda, the love of a good woman—a love perhaps more precious to a man than that of a father for a son.

Henry consoled himself with that.

He tore open the envelope.

It contained the items his handlers had listed, together with a smaller envelope. On the front: *FOR MY LOVE*, written in Connie's distinctive hand.

Inside: a photograph. Connie and he on the balcony of the Hyperion Hotel in Crete. She must have taken the snapshot with her when she left their home in Belfast. He recalled the kindly waiter who'd taken it and—just moments afterward—their little contretemps.

"*Only trees stay in one place all their lives, Henry. And we're not trees.*"

Well, now their uprooting was complete. Not in the way Connie had envisaged, perhaps, but they'd make the most of it. Change is growth. Isn't that what he told his patients sometimes?

But where was he headed? There was no clue in the envelope and he'd been given strict instructions to talk to no one. He'd only his intuition to guide him. Through the porthole he could make out the Irish Sea. But that gave no clue; most flights out of Belfast followed the contours of that stretch of water. Who knew but he might be bound for some distant continent, to change planes in London.

The snapshot. Was that the hint? Greece?

"Is this seat free?" He looked up to see a stewardess. Beside her a woman, dark hair in bubble curls, thick glasses, baggy clothes.

He nodded. Quickly stuffed the papers back in the envelope, as the stranger sat down.

Henry really would have preferred if the woman had chosen another seat. He could no longer peruse the contents of the envelope with her in such close proximity.

She sat with her hands in her lap, not moving, her head bowed. Perhaps she'd connected from a long-haul flight and simply wanted to sleep. Well, that was all right with him.

He pulled his table down and found John Lennon's *In His Own Write*. The writings of the former Beatle might prove a worthwhile distraction.

But when he flipped idly through the slim volume, he saw it was full of unorthodox drawings, crazy cartoons, with not much reading to speak of.

The inflight magazine it would have to be. It fell open at a feature: "Things to do in Istanbul." Attracted by the beautiful photos, he began to read.

> *Istanbul, an ancient and magnificent city, bridging the continents of Asia and Europe, is a destination as no other. Its rich history, stretching back thousands of years, is a heady mix of many civilizations and cultures.*

Henry was aware of the woman beside him bending down to her handbag. She freed the table in front of her.

> *You may begin your Istanbul tour in the Grand Bazaar, which will enchant you with its glittering treasures and curious delights, while a sense of peace and quietude will envelop you as you enter glorious Hagia Sophia, close by.*

The woman passenger had taken out a pen and was writing something.

A tour of the pearls of the Bosphorus, Ortakoy, Bestiktas, and Kabatas will let you enjoy the splendid views along the deep blue coast. With the Black Sea in the north, the Marmara Sea in the south and the Istanbul Strait running in all its glory through the middle of the city, you will experience the distinctive combination of Mediterranean and Black Sea—

Henry gave a start as the seat in front of him was jerked back. God knows how long he was going to be on the aircraft. He would much prefer to have the little space that had been allotted to him for himself.

"The rudeness of some people," he muttered under his breath, shut the magazine, and got up.

He leaned forward to speak with the offender.

"Excuse me. D'you mind?"

A gangly teenager looked into his face.

"Do I mind wha . . . ?" he said with apparent innocence.

"You have just pushed your seat back into my space. It is cramped enough here. Now I would ask you kindly to return it to the upright position."

"Och, you! Keep yer hair on, mister." He spoke with a thick Scottish accent, but refused to budge.

"Please . . . I'd much appreciate it."

Finally, with a show of reluctance, the teenager relented. The seat was jerked upright again.

Henry sat down.

He returned to his magazine.

Strange!

He saw now what looked like a folded sheet of paper wedged between its pages.

He glanced at the woman, but she didn't look his way. He saw the notebook and pen in front of her. Perhaps she was dumb: a mute who needed him to ask the stewardess for something.

He opened it.

Henry, it's me, Connie. I'm sorry for everything. We cannot speak until we land. I love you so much.

"What on earth . . . ?"

He turned. Stared at the woman. Stared in disbelief.

"*Conn—*"

She put a finger to her lips, but kept looking straight ahead.

Could it be *her?* The hair was different, the face more gaunt. But that profile . . . that beautiful profile . . .

"What—"

He felt a hand go into his.

A tear escaped from under her glasses and rolled down her cheek. Under cover of the table, the grip on his hand grew tighter.

There was only one way to know for certain.

He eased back the right cuff of her sweater.

And there it was.

The butterfly. Holly Blue.

His butterfly.

It *was* Connie—his beloved Connie—at last.

He turned to her again, tears in his eyes.

The urge to hold her, strong.

"Tea? Coffee?" a stewardess asked.

They looked up, shook their heads as one.

The stewardess passed on, the drinks trolley trundling farther up the aisle.

But still he could not believe his eyes. He leaned closer and whispered. "Connie . . . Connie, darling, is it really you?"

She lowered the pebble-thick glasses. Those blue eyes misted up with tears, unmistakable. "I love you," she mouthed.

And clasped his hand more tightly.

That touch: the fleeting language for the words they could not speak.

That was how they traveled, all the way to Greece.

Chapter forty-seven

Paddy and Rose had to be enlisted to help Ruby with the delivery of her gift. She had no idea where Jamie lived.

"But I don't want Jamie to know it came from *me*," she said to Rose on the phone.

"That's no bother atall, Ruby. God, Jamie'll be delighted with that. I'd love to be there to see his face, 'cos he's been very lonely without Shep, so he has. I'll get my Paddy to do that surely."

"But it has to be a surprise, Rose. Could Paddy slip in and just leave it on the doorstep?"

"Aye, he'll go in round the back. That way, Jamie won't see him. His sitting room's at the front anyway."

———

Paddy McFadden played his part to the letter. He saw Jamie on his tractor in one of his fields, and let the little puppy in his front door. It would be warmer for the wee critter to be near the hearth fire than sitting out on the cold doorstep in a box.

An hour later, Jamie was on the phone to Rose.

"God, Rose, it's the loveliest wee thing, and divil do I know where it came outta."

"That's the best I ever heard, Jamie. And where did you say you found it again?" She held out the phone so Paddy could also join in the excitement.

". . . curled up in me bed no less, and me sittin' down to take me boots off. Could'a set on the wee thing."

"Heaven's above, that's the best I ever heard! And you only after losin' Shep. It's a merickle, so it is."

"A miracle is right, Rose."

"You know who I was talking to today, and who was asking about you, Jamie?"

"Naw, Rose, who was that?"

"Ruby, no less."

"Oh, Ruby . . . and how is she?"

"Well, you know, Jamie, you'll be able to find that out for yourself, for she ast me to ask you would you go over to Oaktree for a cuppa tea this evening."

It was a little white lie. But a little white lie in the service of romance was no bad thing in Rose's world.

"She didn't!"

"She did indeed, Jamie. Now, me and my Paddy will drop you off, 'cos we're going in to do the flowers for the church, so we are."

Jamie hesitated. He'd have to change out of his farm clothes.

Rose read his mind. "And don't bother changin', Jamie. Sure Ruby's a farmer, too, so she won't notice."

———

Ruby walked the green field, past the memorial patch of flowers under a sky of windblown clouds, down again to Beldam.

She was happy. Oh, so very happy!

The evening sun was putting an edge to things. Birdcalls bright in the air. The world alive with possibilities.

She stopped near the jetty and gazed about. Saw the spot where she'd placed the stool. Smiled at the thought of her naked self, dancing under the moonlight in the name of the Goddess Dana.

The Goddess and *The Book of Light* had given her one valuable insight: a renewed appreciation of the natural world and the energy—the life force—that drives and runs it all. She thought of the many little winged creatures busy in the wood, the soil, the grass. Felt bad now that she might be crushing some, and looked down at her feet.

It was then that she spotted it. A piece of pink paper wedged in a slat of the jetty. She bent down and picked it up.

Her three wishes, charred a bit at one end. She read.

"'I want to see . . .'" The word *Daddy* was gone. "Daddy," she said aloud. "Yes, Daddy . . . and no, I didn't see you, but I will in the next life."

The second wish: "'I want to have lots of money.' With Oaktree now in my name I *do* have lots of money."

Third wish . . .

The sound of a car, slowing for the gate, distracted her.

It couldn't be May and June. She wasn't expecting to see them anytime soon. The twins could hold a grudge in "perpetuity": an important new word Ruby had learned from the solicitor, Mr. Cosgrove, and now knew the meaning of. They'd come eventually, though. Their mother's jewelry bequest had to be collected.

She started back up the field. Looked down at the piece of paper again. Third wish: "'I want to meet someone nice and be happy.'"

Footsteps in the lane.

She turned. Incredible. For *there* was her third wish: Jamie McCloone, a bunch of flowers in one hand, a small bundle in the hook of his arm, making his way toward her.

"Hello, there . . . Ruby," he said.

"Jamie . . . my goodness . . . I'm so glad to see you . . . didn't expect you at all."

"You didn't?" Jamie frowned. "Rose . . . Rose said you wanted me over for a drop of tea."

Ruby smiled. She just *knew* Rose had to be involved.

"That's right . . . now I remember. I forgot . . . yesterday with the readin' of the will and all . . ."

"Aye . . . a lot on your mind, Ruby, this past while . . . I know."

Out on the road, Rose McFadden, hunkered down behind the hedge, was giving her husband a running commentary on proceedings.

"God, he's giving her the wee bunch of flowers now, Paddy . . ."

"Aye, so," said the ever-patient Paddy through the rolled down window of the driver's seat.

"Now I hope he minds the right name for them flowers this time," Rose said.

———

"There's some . . . some . . . of them flowers for you, Ruby. They're called . . ." Jamie inspected his toecaps, trying to remember the name. "Begod now, what are they called? Aye, I mind now: swan's babies breath and—"

"They're lovely, Jamie. Swan-river daisies with false—"

"False goat's beards and baby's breath," they chorused together, and laughed.

"Is that a wee dog you've got there?"

Jamie, his mind so taken up with the presentation of the bouquet and getting the names correct, had forgotten about the sleeping furry miracle he was carrying.

"God, Ruby, that's my wee miracle. I found her curled up in me bed only a couple of hours ago."

He off-loaded it into Ruby's arms while he held the bouquet.

"Ah . . . what a lovely wee thing! What do you call it?"

The puppy opened its little eyes and yawned widely in Ruby's face.

———

"Paddy, Paddy! Jamie is putting the wee pup in Ruby's arms now."

"Hope . . . hope it doesn't wet on her, Rose. Them wee pups have to be toilet trained, you know."

"Och, away with you, Paddy . . ."

———

"Haven't thought of a name," Jamie was saying. He looked at the sky. "God must'a sent her down from heaven."

Or the Goddess, thought Ruby briefly, but didn't say.

Jamie shifted from foot to foot. "Sorry . . . sorry I'm not better dressed. Didn't have much time tae change."

"You . . . you look grand, Jamie . . . just grand, so you do. And it's . . . really good to see you, so it is."

"Aye . . . Rose and Paddy dropped me off there. They're goin' to St. Timothy's to do the flowers for the morrow's Mass." He studied the patch of flowers. "That's where your father . . ."

"Aye . . . but he's in a better place now," Ruby said. "Mammy, too."

"Aye, so . . . that's the way it goes." The farmer gazed about him. "Big place you've got here, Ruby. How many acres would she be?"

"Sixty-three and three-quarters . . . about."

"Very big right enough. Suppose . . . suppose you'll want to be startin' things up again, now that you're . . ."

"I'd love to. Maybe you could help me . . . couldn't manage it on me own."

"I'd love to help you, Ruby, surely."

"Come on to the house . . . sure we'll talk about it over a cuppa tea."

Jamie pulled on his ear, righted his cap. The puppy in Ruby's arms yawned again. She gazed across at Beldam.

"I know what we'll call this wee thing, Jamie," she said.

"You do?"

"Aye . . . Dana. We'll call her Dana."

"Dana . . . oh, you mean like that actor? What's he called . . . Dana, Dana Andrews."

"Aye, but this Dana was a goddess. She . . . she was the Mother of the Little People."

"The fairies? God, I never knowed that. Niver seen a fairy meself, but me Uncle Mick now, he said he did."

They turned to go. Unseen by Jamie, Ruby looked over her shoulder and gave Rose a covert wave.

Rose popped her head above the hedge, and waved back excitedly, before getting back in the car.

Paddy reengaged the engine.

"God, Paddy, it's all gonna work out. And you'll have to get yourself a new suit with Mr. Harvey, so you will."

"A new suit? Why's that?"

"Och, Paddy, for Jamie and Ruby's wedding! What else would it be for?"

"Not a wee bit soon to be talkin' about a waddin', Rose?"

"They'll be married within the year. Now, I'm no fortune-teller, like that Madame Calinda . . . but I can see that for sure."

Rose sighed blissfully. "And to think, Paddy, if Ruby's father hadn't of died, Jamie and Ruby might never have met. Funny how things work out, isn't it?"

"Aye, funny enough all right, Rose."

———

They strolled across the field.

Ruby with the puppy. Jamie with the flowers.

So much for them to talk about.

So much for them to share.

Dana gave a little bark.

A wondrous silence fell.

As they walked toward the farmhouse.

And a future that was theirs.

Author's notes

As many as 3,000 people are in witness protection programs in the United Kingdom and Ireland at the present time.

For decades, witnesses threatened during the "Troubles" in Northern Ireland were given sanctuary overseas. They can literally never go home again.

The Atlantis Foundation was begun in London in 1974. Its practices included primal therapy, introduced by psychotherapist Arthur Janov. When Atlantis moved to Burtonport, a village on the coast of Donegal, the local people dubbed the group "the Screamers." Finding themselves no longer welcome, the commune soon relocated to the nearby island of Innisfree, and thence to Colombia, where a small group of devotees still exists.

Acknowledgments

I wrote *The Godforsaken Daughter* in the course of a year, in three locations: starting in a lovely town in central Mexico, touching down briefly in Lucca, Italy, before finally coming to rest in my beloved Newry, Northern Ireland.

I am truly grateful for the encouragement and support I received from Terry Goodman, senior editor at Amazon Publishing. He gave me such a wonderful reception of the first few chapters that I felt compelled to continue the journey I'd started with my hesitant heroine, Ruby Clare.

To Terry's successor, Tara Parsons, for picking up the book in the final stages and helping me to cover the final furlong.

To Steven Roman and Toisan Craigg for their eagle-eyed copyediting and proofreading.

Finally, David M. Kiely, the Renaissance man, who not only is my husband but a walking compendium of wide-ranging talents: author, cover designer, first-look editor, researcher—as well as a living dictionary, thesaurus, and encyclopedia, all rolled into one. His guidance and advice continue to be invaluable to me.

Bibliography

Cunningham, Scott. *Wicca: A Guide for the Solitary Practitioner.* Woodbury, Michigan: Llewellyn Publications, 2004.

Forward, Susan, and Craig Buck. *Toxic Parents: Overcoming Their Hurtful Legacy and Reclaiming Your Life.* New York: Bantam Books, 1989.

Kabat-Zinn, Jon. *Wherever You Go, There You Are: Mindful Meditation for Everyday Life.* New York: Hyperion, 1994.

Lennon, John. *In His Own Write.* New York: Simon and Schuster, 1964.

———. *A Spaniard in the Works.* New York: Simon and Schuster, 1965.

Morrigan, Danu. *You're Not Crazy—It's Your Mother: Understanding and Healing for Daughters of Narcissistic Mothers.* London: Darton, Longman and Todd, 2012.

Ono, Yoko. *Grapefruit: A Book of Instruction and Drawings.* New York: Simon and Schuster, 1970.

Phoenix, Storm. "Danu: The Great Goddess of the Tuatha De Danann." The Goddess Tree. November 2010. Accessed December 8, 2014. http://thegoddesstree.com/GoddessGallery/Danu.html.

Plath, Sylvia. *The Journals of Sylvia Plath.* New York: Anchor Books, 2000.

Soraya. *Spells & Psychic Powers.* New Lanark, Scotland: Geddes & Grosset, 2001.

Tillery, Gary. *The Cynical Idealist: A Spiritual Biography of John Lennon.* Wheaton, Illinois: Quest Books, 2009.

About the author

Photo © Michael McKenna

Christina McKenna grew up on a farm near the village of Draperstown in Northern Ireland. She attended the Belfast College of Art where she obtained an honors degree in Fine Art and studied postgraduate English at the University of Ulster. In 1986 she left Northern Ireland to teach abroad. She has lived, worked, and painted pictures in Spain, Turkey, Italy, Ecuador, and Mexico. *The Godforsaken Daughter* is the third novel in the Tailorstown series.